RUMORS

BOOKS BY ANNA GODBERSEN

The Luxe

Rumors

Envy

Splendor

Bright Young Things

Beautiful Days

The Lucky Ones

When We Caught Fire

A LUXE NOVEL

RUMORS

ANNA GODBERSEN

HARPER TEEN
An Imprint of HarperCollinsPublishers

alloy**entertainment**

Produced by Alloy Entertainment
151 West 26th Street, New York, NY 10001

Library of Congress Cataloging-in-Publication Data
Godbersen, Anna.
    Rumors : a luxe novel / Godbersen, Anna.— 1st ed.
      p.   cm.
    Summary: As rumors continue about the untimely demise of Elizabeth Holland, an
outwardly stricken Penelope Hayes determines to use any means necessary to claim her
friend's pre-eminent place in 1899 Manhattan society and to get and keep the attentions
of Elizabeth's former fiancé, the wealthy Henry Schoonmaker.
    ISBN 978-0-06-285217-5
    [1. Conduct of life—Fiction.   2. Secrets—Fiction.   3. Social classes—Fiction.
4. Wealth—Fiction.   5. Love—Fiction.   6. New York (N.Y.)—History—1898–1951—
Fiction.]   I. Title.
PZ7.G53887 Ru   2008   2008274489
[Fic]—dc22   CIP
                                                                                   AC

Design by Andrea C. Uva
❖
Revised paperback edition, 2018
18 19 20 21 22   PC/LSCH   10 9 8 7 6 5 4 3 2 1

For Jake and Nick

Prologue

I have just been invited to a most secretive, but assuredly most elaborate, celebration in Tuxedo Park sponsored by one of Manhattan's finest families. I have been sworn to secrecy for the time being, but I promise my loyal readers that I will report all when the week is over and the general word is out. . . .

—FROM THE "GAMESOME GALLANT" COLUMN IN THE
NEW YORK IMPERIAL, SUNDAY, DECEMBER 31, 1899

*I*T HAS BECOME ALMOST REGULAR FOR THE LOWER classes of New York to catch glimpses of our native aristocracy in her city streets, tripping in for breakfast at Sherry's after one of their epic parties, or perhaps racing sleighs in the Central Park, that great democratic meeting place. But here in the country it is different. Here the rich do not have to suffer the indignity of being spied upon by a thousand eyes. Here in the snowy hills forty miles northwest of Manhattan, whatever business deal, whatever hustle, whatever random act of violence is being done back in the city, cannot touch them. For they and they alone are allowed in.

In those final, frigid days of the year 1899, the beau monde had escaped the city quietly, in small groups, according to the instructions of their hosts. By the eve of the New Year the last of them had arrived by special train to Tuxedo Park, disembarking at the private club's private station. There had been special trains all afternoon: one bearing orchids, another caviar and game, another cases of Ruinart champagne. And

now came Schermerhorns and Schuylers, Vanderbilts and Joneses. They were greeted by coaches newly painted in the Tuxedo colors of green and gold and decorated with commemorative silver bells from Tiffany & Co., and whisked across the freshly fallen snow to the ballroom where the wedding would take place.

Those who had their own self-consciously rustic residences there—one of those shingled cottages, say, with touches of moss and lichen—went off to freshen up. The ladies had brought their historic jewels, diamond-tipped aigrettes for their hair, silk gloves. They had packed their newest and best dresses, although there were several despairing of being seen in gowns they had already been described as wearing over the course of what had been a rather unhappy season. The city's most charmed socialite, Miss Elizabeth Holland, had met with a watery end right in the middle of it, and nobody had felt comfortable acting joyful since. The best people had been sitting around waiting for January, when they might finally escape for cruises in the Mediterranean and other points east. Now, so near New Year's, with a blessed but unexpected fete on the horizon, the mood seemed likely to pick up again. One or two of the women mentioned, in low tones, as they dabbed perfume behind their ears, that the bride was reported to be wearing her mother's dress in the ceremony, which would add a touch of humility to the proceedings. But then, that was a sweet tradition and did not excuse any lack of modishness on the part of the guests.

Already they were being ushered, by liveried footmen, to the ballroom at the club's main building. They were being served hot spiced punch in little cut-crystal cups, and remarking how transformed the ballroom of Tuxedo was.

Down the middle of its famed parquet dance floor was an aisle, delineated with white rose petals, several inches deep. Bridal arches wrapped in chrysanthemums and lilies of the valley dominated the center of the room. As the guests began to file in, they whispered of the exquisiteness of the display and the high caliber of guests who had made sure of attending, even at such short notice, for the invitations had arrived only a few days before by hand delivery. There was Mrs. Astor, behind her dark veil, present despite the ill health that had kept her in for much of the season and prompted rumors that she was ready to abdicate her throne as queen of New York society. She rested on the arm of Harry Lehr, that winning bachelor, so often spoken of for his flare in leading cotillions and issuing bons mots.

There were the William Schoonmakers making their way to the front row, young Mrs. Schoonmaker—she was the second lady to wear that honorific—blowing kisses and adjusting her blond curls and ruby tiara all the way. There were the Frank Cuttings, whose only son, Edward "Teddy"

Cutting, was known to be such good friends with William's son, Henry Schoonmaker, although since mid-December the two had been seen out together only a few times. There were Cornelius "Neily" Vanderbilt III and his wife, née Grace Wilson, who as a debutante was considered too "fast" and had nearly caused her husband to be disinherited. She looked regal now, in lace-trimmed velvet panne, her auburn hair done up in elaborate curls, as much a Vanderbilt as anyone. But for all the well-born people taking their seats there were several who were notably absent. For amongst those hundred or so guests—a far more selective list than the four hundred allowed into old Mrs. Astor's ballroom—there was one great family unrepresented.

This omission was to many strange and, beneath the gentle string music that announced how very soon the ceremony would begin, one or two of the guests whispered about the absence. Meanwhile, the wind whistled around the building. The icicles hanging from the eaves glittered. The last guests to arrive were urged to take their seats, and then a set of groomsmen in black tails—not the shorn dinner jackets that were the namesake of the resort—moved purposefully to their places.

The last of them, Teddy Cutting, cast a glance back to be sure his friend was ready. As the music rose, the crowd nodded approvingly at the sight of Henry Schoonmaker, his dark hair slicked to the side and his handsome face imbued with a new maturity, taking his place at the altar. Was that a touch of nervousness in his famously rakish features? Was it excitement or was it trepidation? Then he, and indeed every set of eyes in the room, looked down the aisle, where the loveliest debutantes of New York, dressed in glacier blue chiffon, began to emerge. They moved in a slow march, one by one, across the little mountain of rose petals toward the front of the ballroom, trying as best they could to put away their girlish smiles.

When the opening strains of Wagner's processional played, the sylphlike bride appeared in the frame of the first flower-laden arch. The beauty of that girl was remarkable even to her family and friends murmuring in their seats. She was dressed in her mother's bridal lace, and a massive bouquet of frothy whites tumbled from her clasped hands. Her emotions were obscured by her ornate veil, but she moved forward to the altar with a steady purpose.

It was just as she took her place across from Henry that the door swung open and a young member of the staff appeared, breathless, and whispered into the ear of the woman stationed at the entrance. A cold rush of air was followed by a quiet gasp and then an almost inaudible murmur. The intermittent whispers that had begun before the ceremony doubled, then tripled, and now created a low hum in the room even as the reverend cleared his throat and began the ceremony. The

groom's dark eyes roamed across the room. Even the bride stiffened.

The reverend's voice droned insistently on, but the faces of the assembled no longer seemed quite so placid or joyous. A growing discomfort had reached the privileged class even here, where it was warmly ensconced in its winter palace, even on the titillating verge of celebrating the union of two of its brightest members. The eyebrows of the guests were raised; their mouths were open. It was as though, suddenly, the wilds of that city that they'd left behind were not so very far away, after all. Something had happened, and it would forever alter how they remembered the last days of 1899.

One

It has been a dreary few months in New York, given the death of Miss Elizabeth Holland— who was one of society's favorites—and the blizzard that arrived in late November and left the city blanketed for days. But elegant New York has not given up hope for a fine winter season of evenings at the opera and gay cotillions. And our eye has more than once been caught by the newly ladylike comportment of Miss Penelope Hayes, who was the best friend of Miss Holland during her short life. Could Miss Hayes inherit her mantle of impeccable decorum and congeniality?

—FROM *CITÉ CHATTER,* FRIDAY, DECEMBER 15, 1899

"EXCUSE ME, MISS, BUT IS IT REALLY YOU?"

The day was clear and bracingly cold, and as Penelope Hayes turned slowly to her left, where the crowd had massed along the narrow cobblestone street, she exhaled a visible cloud of warm breath. She focused her large lake-blue eyes on the eager face of a girl who could not have been much older than fourteen. She must have emerged from one of those tenement buildings, which rose shoulder to shoulder, at imprecise angles, behind the masses of people. A jungle of black wires was strung from their rooftops, cutting ribbons out of the sky. The girl wore a black coat that had turned almost gray with wear, and her already pinkish complexion had gone patchy red in the cold. Penelope met her eyes and spread her plush lips into their warmest smile.

"Why, yes." She drew herself up, willing the full effect of her slim frame, her elegantly ovular face, her incandescent skin. There had been a time when she was known as the pretty daughter of a nouveau riche, but she had recently taken to wearing the pastels and whites preferred by the demurest girls her age, mindful of their conjugal connotations—although today, given the state of the streets she was traversing, she had chosen a darker hue. She extended her gloved hand and said, "I am Miss Hayes."

"I work at Weingarten the furriers'," the girl went on shyly. "I've seen you once or twice from the backroom."

"Oh, then I must thank you for your service," Penelope replied graciously. She inclined her body forward in a gesture that might almost be called a bow, although the stiff Medici collar of her navy cloth coat with gold piping made it difficult to move her head in a truly humble manner. When she met the girl's eyes again, she quickly added, "Would you like a turkey?"

Already the procession was moving along ahead of her. The marching band playing noels had crossed onto the next block, and she could hear the voice of Mr. William Schoonmaker through the megaphone moving along just behind the band. He was wishing the crowds who thronged the sidewalks a joyous season, and reminding them in as subtle a manner as he was able who had paid for their holiday parade. For the parade had been his idea, and he had financed the band and the traveling nativity scene and the holiday fowl, and he had arranged for various society matrons and debutantes of his acquaintance to pass them out to the poor. They were the real attraction, Penelope couldn't stop herself from thinking, as she turned to her loyal friend Isaac Phillips Buck and reached into the large burlap sack he was carrying.

Even through her dogskin gloves and a layer of newspaper wrapping, she could feel the cold squishiness of the bird. It was heavy and awkward in her hands, and she tried not to show any signs of revulsion as she moved forward with the promised Christmas turkey. The girl looked at the package in a blank way and her smile faded.

"Here," Penelope said, trying not to rush her words. She suddenly, desperately needed the girl to take the turkey from her. "For you, for your family. For Christmas. From the Schoonmakers . . . and from *me*."

The moment lengthened in front of her, and then abruptly the girl's smile returned. Her whole mouth hung open with joy. "Oh, Miss Hayes, thank you! From me . . . and . . . and . . . from my family!" Then she took the weighty bird from Penelope and turned back to her friends in the crowd. "Look!" she caroled. "This turkey was given to me especially by Miss Penelope Hayes!"

Her friends gasped at the prized bird and shot shy looks at the girl in the fitted coat. Already they felt they knew her from seeing her fantastical name so often in the society pages. She stood before them as the rightful heir to the place in the public's heart once held by her best friend, Elizabeth Holland, before Elizabeth's tragic drowning a few months before. Of course, Elizabeth had not drowned, and was in fact very much alive—a fact Penelope knew quite well, since she had helped the "virginal" Miss Holland disappear so that she might more easily be with that member of her family's staff she'd apparently been enamored with. And so that, more importantly, Penelope could reclaim what was rightfully hers: the fiancé Elizabeth had left behind. Her ascension was so nearly complete that already society's most exalted matrons, as well as its newspaper chroniclers, were whispering how very much more Elizabeth-like she seemed now.

This was not something Penelope would have previously found flattering—goodness being rather overrated, in her private opinion—but she had begun to see that it had its advantages.

Penelope repaid the warm embrace of the girl's adulation by lingering a moment longer, her eyes beaming and her smile as broad as it had ever been. Then she turned to Buck, who was highly visible in his gray check suit and amber-colored dress shirt and a coat of beaver fur that covered the length of his generous body.

"You've just got to get me out of here," she whispered. "I haven't seen Henry all day, and I'm cold, and if I have to touch another—"

Buck stopped her with a knowing look. "I will take care of everything."

His features were soft, muted by the fleshiness of his face, and his fair eyebrows were sculpted in a way that lent him the appearance of canniness. A few more ladies, in their wide hats and elaborately lapelled coats, passed by, followed by a marching band. Penelope looked back up the street in the direction of the elder Schoonmaker's voice and knew that his son, Henry, with his dark eyes and his troublemaker's lilt, must be crossing into new streets along with him. Her heart sank a little. Then she turned back to Buck, who had already formulated a plan.

Buck was over six feet tall and his body expanded outward imposingly, and he moved now, as he so often had before, to shield the girl who most benefited from his loyalty. He had not been born rich—though he claimed to be a relation of the famous Buck clan who these days mostly resided in grand old moldering mansions in the Hudson Valley—but was invaluable when it came time to host a party, and as such was often given fine things for free. Penelope pulled the veil of her hat down over her face and followed him into the crowd. Once they had made their way safely through the throng, Buck dropped his cumbersome bag of turkeys and helped Penelope into a waiting brougham.

While Buck said a few words to her driver, she settled into the plush black velvet seat and exhaled. Inside everything one might lean against had the softness of down, and everything one might touch was made of gold. Penelope felt a softening at her temples; the world was right again. She removed her gloves in one deft motion and then tossed them through the open carriage door. Buck glanced at the slushy puddle into which they fell, and then took a step up and into the seat beside Penelope. As the wheels began to crunch against the rough pavement, he leaned forward and pulled a polished wooden box from underneath the seat.

"Kidskin gloves?" he said. "Or would you prefer silk?"

Penelope examined the slender white fingers of her hands as she rubbed them against each other. Most girls like her, whose fathers were industrialists or bank presidents or heads of their own insurance empires, changed their gloves three or four times a day as they moved from teas to dinner parties to intimate little musicales. But Penelope thought her hands were superior, and so preferred to change gloves ten or eleven times. She never wore the same pair twice, though her recently discovered virtue had inspired her to donate them occasionally. "Kid. It isn't warm outside, and you never know who you'll meet on a drive."

"Indeed," Buck replied as he removed a hand-sewn pair for her. "Especially when *I* am giving the coachman his instructions."

"Thank you." Penelope drew the gloves over her wrists and felt like herself again, which was for her always a good thing.

"They adored you today," Buck went on contemplatively.

"If only it weren't all so unbearable." Penelope let her exquisite head rest against the velvet. "I mean really, how many poor people can New York possibly hold? And don't they ever get sick of turkey?" She brought her kid-covered fingertips up to her high, fine cheekbones. "My face hurts from all the smiling."

"It is dull, always keeping up the pretense of being good." Buck paused. "But you were never one to lose sight of a goal," he went on delicately.

"No," Penelope agreed. "And I haven't."

Just then, the carriage came to a stop, and Buck put his hand on the little gold crank to lower the window. Penelope leaned over him and saw that they had come around to the front of the parade and now stood in the intersection looking down at the head of the procession. There was William Schoonmaker, both tall and broad in his black cloth suit. Beside him was the second Mrs. Schoonmaker, née Isabelle De Ford, who was still young, and who was currently a vision in furs and lace. They were framed in the canyon of tenement buildings, and they paused at the sight of the carriage in their path. In a moment Henry came up to their side.

Penelope's breath caught at the sight of him. There had been a time when she saw Henry Schoonmaker almost every day, when they had been intimate with each other and with every secret corner of their families' mansions that permitted behavior not suitable to the maiden daughters of high society. They had done the kinds of things girls like Elizabeth Holland had been famous for not doing—until one day Henry announced that he was engaged to Miss Holland. At a dinner party that Penelope had attended. It was enough to make one vomit, which was in fact what Penelope had done next.

Of course, her violent reaction to that despicable news had since been tempered with understanding. Buck had helped her with that. He had pointed out that old Schoonmaker was a businessman of no small ambition—mayoral ambition—and that he doubtless liked the idea of his son's bride being so pristine and well liked. Penelope felt fairly certain that if Elizabeth was capable of something, then she was, too, and she'd set about making herself into just such a potential daughter-in-law.

She had rarely been near Henry since then, and the sight of him now was like a concentrated dose. He was a slim figure in black, and under the long shadow of his top hat she could see the handsome line of an aristocratic jaw. He still wore a mourning band on his left arm, which Penelope noticed even as she willed Henry to meet her eyes. She knew he would. And in a few moments, he did. Penelope held his gaze with as much modesty as she could muster, smiled an oblique little smile, and then pulled the veil back down over her face.

"It was a lovely parade, Mr. Schoonmaker!" she called out the window, resting her hand on the half-raised glass.

As she settled back into the velvet carriage seat, she heard Buck tell the driver to move on. But she wasn't thinking about where she was going. She was thinking about Henry and how very soon he would be done mourning Elizabeth. He was standing back there now, she just knew, remembering what kind of girl she was under the virtuous veneer, and all that had passed between them. And this time, it wouldn't be just stolen kisses in back hallways. There would be no secrecy and no humiliation. This time it would be for real.

Two

The social leaders of this city have been concerned as of late with one of their own. Mrs.
Holland—whose judgment and taste were once
revered by top-drawer people—has been in
mourning for her husband for almost a year,
but her scarcity has been noticed still. Some
have suggested that the Holland fortune has
dwindled over the years and that the family of
the late Mr. Edward is living in near poverty on
Gramercy Park. With the passing of her elder
daughter, the lovely Elizabeth, who was to
have married Mr. Henry Schoonmaker, Mrs.
Holland will surely be considering matrimonial options for her other child, Diana, who at
sixteen is still very young and has been known
for being seen in public without a hat.

—FROM THE SOCIETY PAGE OF THE *NEW-YORK NEWS OF
THE WORLD GAZETTE*, FRIDAY, DECEMBER 15, 1899

*T*HE MAUVE, LEAFLESS BRANCHES OF TREES ROTATED at a giddy pace around the little frozen pond in Central Park. They moved horizontally between a gray strip of sky and a mass of people whose cheeks had been turned red by the cold. This panorama sped faster and faster until, suddenly, Diana Holland put the toe of her skate down into the ice and came to a dramatic stop. She took an ecstatic breath to steady herself, and felt dizzy and lucky to be alive and in the refreshing winter air.

Then she saw her companion for the afternoon, Percival Coddington.

"Miss Holland," he said as he stumbled toward her. Although Diana felt a strong urge to be far away from Percival, she couldn't help but fear for him a little—and for anyone unlucky enough to be within his wingspan—as he tripped forward on the tips of his skates, his arms flailing in some helpless search for balance.

Diana was trying very hard not to laugh at him. Percival—

as she had already discovered that afternoon—did not take kindly to being laughed at. He had greeted all of her jokes with sourness and ill humor, and had several times pointed out that she was not behaving as he believed a young woman who longed to marry should. There was really nothing to do in such situations *but* laugh, although she was doing her sincere best to resist. To distract him from the pickled expression her face had taken on, she now offered him her hand.

"Miss Holland," Percival said again as his grip tightened. She was glad that two layers of gloves separated her palm from his and made a silent prayer that she would not be pulled down with him.

"Mr. Coddington, my sister was, and still is to me, Miss Holland. I'd prefer Miss Diana."

Percival, whose hair was like a greasy mat and whose nostrils flared in what could only be described as a grotesque way, lowered his eyes respectfully. It was not entirely honest for Diana to have said what she said. Despite the affected pose of extreme mourning and deep melancholy that she had employed for the last two months, she was neither bereaved nor in particularly low spirits. She felt justified in manipulating the storied loss of her elder sister, however, since it was Elizabeth's premature departure from New York that had necessitated a host of afternoons like this one, spent in the company of wealthy and detestable bachelors. For once their

mother had gotten over the initial shock of losing Elizabeth, she had redirected her ambition for an advantageous match from her first daughter onto her second. This despite her poor health, which had afflicted her for much of the fall.

It was Mrs. Holland who had insisted that Diana accept Percival's invitation to ice-skate that day, and she had also been the one—Diana felt she could safely assume—who had suggested the activity in the first place. Percival was objectionable in more than one way, of course, but the most pressing reason that Diana wanted to free her hand from his was that her heart belonged elsewhere. And that was not a thing a woman like Mrs. Holland would have any patience for.

It was, additionally, just like Elizabeth to absent herself from Diana's life at the precise moment Liz finally had an interesting story to tell. For she had been driven to fake her own death by her love for a boy named Will Keller, who had once been the Hollands' coachman and was good looking enough that Diana had wondered on more than one occasion what it would be like to kiss him. The faked death had involved the Hudson River and the assistance of Elizabeth's treacherous friend Penelope Hayes, and then the older Holland girl had gone off to California in pursuit of what must have been a very agonizing, and thus fascinating, love. But since she had learned of her sister's romantic deception, Diana had received only the most limited information about Elizabeth's whereabouts.

And so while Diana supported her sister's quest for true love, and while she remained desperately curious about it, she also couldn't help the feeling that one of its unintended consequences was her own exposure to a matrimonial campaign of which she was neither the ideal nor the intended subject.

She maintained her sad eyes as she skated along with Percival, through the crowds of happy people in bulky coats, betting that if she continued to look abject he would continue to be foiled in his attempts to talk to her. It was with her heart-shaped face and shiny dark eyes focused downward that she first noticed the crack in the ice.

"I'm sorry to have made you think about Miss Holland again," Percival said haltingly as Diana pulled him to the side of the hole along the pond's edge. Already she could feel the dampness of his palm seeping through her knit glove. She could not help but compare him to her bachelor of choice— who was in every way Percival's superior—and this only strengthened her desire to snatch her hand back. "You don't seem so very much like her, but that doesn't mean that you don't deserve as much sympathy as anybody."

"Oh, it's quite all right." Diana quelled her irritation at this comment by reminding herself how insignificant his chances of ever escorting her anywhere again were. Her dissimilarity to her sister had not of course prevented him from surreptitiously glancing over her entire form several times.

She made two strong pushes against the ice. As her speed increased, the deadweight that was Percival Coddington jerked along behind her as they circled the rink. She turned her face shyly in his direction, and attempted a slow, inviting smile. "Surely you can go faster than that, Mr. Coddington."

Percival's father had been an industrialist and his mother the plain and consumptive third daughter of a branch of the Livingston family. It was apparent to anybody who cared to pay attention that their eldest son had come by his personality matrilineally. Since Percival had inherited his father's fortune, he had distinguished himself neither in business nor in society, though he was known to collect the weaponry of foreign cultures. He was not known for being courageous, however, or particularly light on his feet. As Diana moved forward, her awareness of the squealing children and far-off music, of the trees and the sky and even the cold began to fade. She was moving around the rink with purpose now, and she could feel warmth growing in the muscles of her calves as her skates pushed against the ice. They were approaching the crack again now, and she could see the dark water through it.

Diana gave Percival one more faint smile, took two strides forward, and then jerked her hand back. She disguised the intent of this motion by turning on her skates and making a little ta-da flourish with her arms as she began to skate backward. Percival looked at her through pinched, far-set eyes, and for a minute he seemed impressed by Diana's trick. But soon he was wheeling his arms in an attempt at balance, and it became apparent that he did not know how to turn. His skates kept him moving in the same line, and when he saw the direction in which they were taking him his face froze in terror. Diana did not wait to witness Percival's inevitable fall. She continued to move smoothly backward through the crowd, her glossy brown curls blowing forward across her small, pointed chin as she did.

When she heard the cries for help and saw the crowd rush to the place where the fissure in the ice had been, she knew Percival would be all right. She put her knit-gloved hand over her face and allowed herself a giggle. She felt much lighter on the ice now, and very pleased with herself for showing Percival that, even if she was not quite as marriageable as her sister, still she was not for sale. A brief bath in freezing water would remind him that he was quite far from deserving any Holland girl for a bride, and she was only sorry that Henry Schoonmaker was not there to appreciate the orchestration of this quite deserved comeuppance.

It had been over a month since she'd spoken to Henry. He, too, was in mourning for Elizabeth, and though his engagement to her had never been a love match, he did not know that she was alive. For him her death was real, and very sobering. But Diana was the one he truly loved. At least, that was how it had seemed

to her, a month ago, the last time he'd paid her mother and her aunt Edith one of those melancholy visits where nobody said a word as they sat and grieved and looked into their lukewarm tea. He must love her still. Diana was sure of it.

She reached the edge of the pond and took a few choppy steps to a wooden bench. The crowd had formed a dark wall around the place where she'd let go of Percival's hand. Beyond them the landscape was still and white, with the Dakota apartment building rising sternly over the trees. She bent and unlaced her skates with nimble fingers, and before she had even removed them from her feet a boy emerged from a nearby hut with her black leather boots. She reached into her coat pocket to find him a tip, but he must have been eager not to miss any of the action across the ice, because he didn't even wait for it. No one could resist disaster, she supposed.

She had just secured the boots when she noticed a man who had departed from the crowd and was sailing across the ice in her direction. He was wearing a Russian fur hat and a camel-colored suit that didn't look entirely warm enough for a day spent on ice, and he was skating forward with his hands behind his back, which struck Diana as rather jaunty—almost like a pose Henry would assume. When she realized that his shoulders were too wide to be Henry's, that his figure was somewhat more filled out, she felt all the crushing sadness of being woken suddenly from a pleasurable dream.

When he was a few yards away, the man came to a halt, lifted his hat, and tipped his head in her direction. Diana found his appearance, his broad cheeks and sharp nose and brow like some great crouching woolly spider, familiar; his hair was dark and cut close to his head, and he had a certain attentive manner about the eyes. He replaced his hat high on the back of his head and said, "I fear your escort is not going to be able to take you home."

"Oh?" Diana answered innocently. "I suppose that's what all the hubbub is about."

"I'm Davis Barnard," he went on, accepting her comment at its face value and offering his hand. "Would you like a ride?"

"Oh . . . Mr. Barnard." As she pronounced the name, a host of associations came to her. "You write the 'Gamesome Gallant' column, don't you?"

Her new acquaintance smiled faintly and nodded. When he was done changing into his shoes, they walked to his waiting carriage in silence. Diana knew that it was bad form to accept rides from gentlemen she barely knew, but she considered herself unconventional, and anyway, she'd always wondered what a newspaper man looked like up close. It was only once she was situated under a blanket on the leather seat that he began to explain himself.

"You know, I was always a great admirer of your sister,

the elder Miss Holland . . ." he began, as the horses moved forward and jerked the carriage into motion.

"Yes, I remember." Diana knew she should not go on, but did. "You wrote such pretty things about her. Mother always liked that."

"It was a tragedy," he said, which forced Diana to assume the stricken face she had worn so often in the last few months. "I find it very hard to write about your family since your sister's death."

Diana, not knowing what to make of this, remained silent.

"But I still read everything, of course. That piece in the *Gazette* today, for instance, speculating about—" Here he broke off and looked to Diana for her reaction.

She could not stop the heat that was coming into her cheeks and didn't try to mask her irritation. It was true that the Hollands, one of Manhattan's oldest and most genteel families, were at the moment poorly off financially, and while Diana did not think of herself as bound by materialism, she disliked being pitied.

"Speculating about what?" she asked hotly.

"Never mind. It doesn't matter." Barnard rested his chin on his sizable palm and appraised her. "The point is, you come from not one but two of the old lines, and even if some columnists write baseless things about you, the Hollands are still placed amongst the best people. That is why I am very happy to have made your acquaintance. And why I would like to tell you that, if you ever hear any interesting stories, any stories that might be of interest to *moi*, it would be my pleasure to . . . *pay* . . . you a visit." He paused for effect while holding her gaze. "You should know that I am very discreet."

As the carriage pulled out of the park, Diana could feel her lips curling back in amusement. Soon they would be traveling down Fifth. Barnard was returning her smile, and she could not help but toss her head back, in the special way that she had, and laugh. "I hardly think I know anything of interest, Mr. Barnard, though it is very nice of you to have offered me the ride anyway. I will be depending on you to ask me to dance the next time we are in attendance at the same ball," she concluded, which was a nice way of indicating that she had every intention of telling him nothing. This despite the fact that her mind was currently so occupied by secrets of the wild and romantic variety that she had to marvel at herself a little for keeping them this long.

"All right, Miss Diana," he replied with the same mysterious smile. "And I am glad to say that, having seen you so very close up, you are just as lovely as your sister."

They parted cordially in front of the Hollands' home at No. 17 Gramercy Park South; Mr. Barnard helped Diana to the street, kissed her hand, and told her not to forget his offer. He insisted that she take his card, and before leaving he reminded her again of his discretion. As she turned and walked up the stone steps to the enclosed filigreed-iron porch, she couldn't help but smile to herself at the thought that she might need to sell gossip for money. For while it was true that her family's fortune had been reduced to a pittance, there was another secret that Diana was holding close to her chest.

In a letter Elizabeth had written just after her disappearance she had told Diana that she knew about her feelings for Henry. She knew about the night they had spent together in the Schoonmaker greenhouse, and about the flurry of notes that they had sent to each other during Elizabeth and Henry's ill-fated engagement. She had even approved.

And so Diana knew that as soon as it was appropriate—as soon as Henry's mourning period for Elizabeth had ended—she would see him everywhere. At the opera and at the subscription balls and at all the little Christmas parties New York could hold. Soon enough, Henry would propose to her, and she already had permission to accept from the only person who mattered.

Then she would be forever free from those sympathetic frowns, as well as from the coarse implication that she should care about something like money. From these prearranged afternoons with the Percival Coddingtons of the world and the depressing eventuality of a long marriage to one of them.

For it was a lovely auxiliary fact that Henry Schoonmaker was not only very handsome and wickedly fun but also quite rich, and that meant that he could make all of this go away. Although she had to suppose that when she was with Henry her life would be so bright and exciting that she wouldn't find much time for worries or troubles anyway.

Three

There was a time when this state was full of miners panning for gold, but it's nearly a new century, and California is a different place than it was in '49. The new hordes are looking for black gold. The one word on every man's mind is: Oil!

—*BAKERSFIELD SUN*, FRIDAY, DECEMBER 15, 1899

THE GOLDEN GRASSY FIELD LAY AHEAD, PLAYING tricks on the eye so that in one moment Elizabeth Holland thought she was nearly there and in the next knew herself to be miles away. She paused and gazed out from under the brim of her hat, which had done little to protect the alabaster complexion she was once known for. The skin of her heart-shaped face, with its subtle features and small round mouth, had turned a shade of brown she had never before seen on a woman, and her ash-blond hair had been streaked almost white by the sun. She looked behind her, in the direction of the little railroad town of San Pedro from whence she had come. It was impossible for her to tell how long she had been walking, or how close she was to home.

Though home was not the word for it. Home, for the entirety of her eighteen years, had been a stately town house on Gramercy Park. Three generations of Hollands had lived there, filling its wood-paneled rooms with all variety of knick-knacks and objets d'art, with the soft sounds of polite social

intercourse, with the aroma of tea. It was the house where her father had lived all of his too-short life. Through the high bay windows of their parlor, one could see the enclosed and leafy park populated exclusively with well-dressed people of leisure. Home was very far away now.

But Elizabeth had been brought up a Holland, and she carried some of that with her, even in the wide-open expanse of California. She was wearing the same blue-and-white seersucker dress she'd worn the day she left New York, with its narrow waist and three-quarter sleeves and square collar. The white wasn't pure white anymore, but even in this far-off place she did her best to keep it clean. She still walked with her spine straight and her shoulders back, and she clasped her hands girlishly as she moved. Elizabeth had followed her heart, and no one ever regrets that. But still she thought of her mother and sister and her aunt Edith, back on Gramercy Park, abandoned to their poverty. For Elizabeth was the one who was supposed to have saved them, by marrying wealthy Henry Schoonmaker, and instead she had simply slipped away.

But not simply—she knew it could not have been simple. She knew very little else about her family's situation, because her sister, Diana, was a terrible correspondent, and it was much too dangerous for Elizabeth to be nudging her all the time. She had in fact allowed herself only two exchanges with her younger sister, to assure her that she was alive and to give her the address of the Western Union office in San Pedro. Diana had mentioned, in one of her rare and cryptic letters, that their mother's health had suffered. Ever mindful of this, Elizabeth walked all the way into town any day she could, although today there had again been no news from New York. Elizabeth had bought the Bakersfield paper instead, just in case there was a reference or two to doings back east, and begun her long walk back.

Before she arrived in California she had heard of only two cities in the far-off state, Los Angeles and San Francisco, both of which Will had spoken of. She had arrived in San Francisco, unsure of herself or how exactly she would find Will, but determined to do so. And then, there he was—waiting for the train as if he'd known she'd be on it. In truth, he told her later, he'd gone to the station every day, hoping that one afternoon he'd see his Lizzy emerging from a black railcar and stepping toward him through the arriving luggage. Soon after, they rode down through the Central Valley. They had passed towns with names like Merced and Modesto and San Joaquin, which looked as dusty as they sounded, with their sad little clapboard main streets and wooden sidewalks. They hadn't yet gotten as far as Los Angeles.

At first she had missed her home intensely. She had been literally homesick. In New York, Elizabeth had been a girl for whom perfection—of appearance and dress, of etiquette and reputation—had been a kind of habit. She had not let go of these things easily. But now, after two months in the west, where neither dress nor manners were dictated by elaborate rules, she found herself in an almost dreamlike state. There was the great expanse of blue above her—a pure blue unlike any sky she had ever seen in New York—and the sound of warm wind in the ochre grass that she was marching through, and very little else.

She was still unused to hearing no carriage wheels, no far-off El, no rumblings of the laundresses or kitchen girls somewhere down in the house. As she walked, she held her wide-brimmed straw hat to her head, and focused on two things: the arc of blue, and the scarred yellow hills, undulating up and down as far as she could see. To Elizabeth, the noise her own feet made crunching against grass, scattering dirt and pebbles, was almost orchestral.

Suddenly the sound of horse hooves erupted behind her. There was the earthy smell of a large animal, and the loud pronunciation of her nickname.

"Lizzy!"

Her heart seized, but when she looked up she saw Will, her Will, trotting around her on the old dappled horse that he had bought in Lancaster. When she met his eyes, she saw that he was smiling.

"Where do you think you're going?" The laughter was clear enough in his voice.

Elizabeth bit her lip, fighting the impulse to laugh with him. It was not lost on her, the irony that a girl who had been able to read any social situation, from its faintest laugh to its shortest pause, was still unable to read the wide-open country. She should have anticipated Will's approach, and yet she hadn't. "I was going . . . home."

"I was wondering if you weren't running away from me," he went on with the same smile, "when I saw you pass about a hundred yards from camp and keep walking, heading west at a determined gait."

Elizabeth turned around sharply, raising the folded newspaper to her face to keep the sun out of her eyes. She could see it clearly now, over on the bluff, the little makeshift canvas-and-wood cabin that Will had built. It was a ways back now, but perfectly clear.

"You must have moved it!" She looked back at him, shaking her head in mock accusation. "It wasn't there twenty minutes ago! I'm sure of it."

She waited for his reply, and it took her a long minute to realize that he wasn't going to say anything. His pale blue eyes, set far apart in his tanned face, were gazing at her and his thick lips, twisted slightly at their edges, betrayed no sign of movement. He was watching her closely, thinking what, she couldn't be sure, perhaps marveling at how much she'd changed. Before her father died Will Keller had been his valet, and his sturdy features had always distinguished him from the Henry Schoonmakers of the world. But as they grew up, Elizabeth had found Will's good looks surprising, and she considered the pleasant composition of his face her own precious secret.

"You just like me chasing after you, don't you?" he said finally.

"Yes." She smiled. He smiled. Then she took a breath and a step in his direction. "Are you going to take me home then?"

"No," Will answered, swinging his leg over the horse's broad back and landing on its other side. "I wanted to show you something first."

He led the horse with one hand and reached for hers with the other, and together they walked north up a rise. She lagged slightly behind, still holding on tight, the top of her head just reaching his broad shoulder.

"I saw this the other day while I was out scouting," he went on, though in fact Elizabeth needed no explanation. She had followed him across a vast country knowing only vaguely of his plan to seek his fortune out west, and she hardly needed more words to justify climbing to see the view of their rented acreage now. She looked down the gentle slope of the hill and saw a field covered in delicate orange poppies that was as brilliant as any Fifth Avenue chandelier, and clutched his hand tighter.

"So beautiful," she whispered.

"Isn't it?"

"There were always so many flowers at home, remember? But nothing like this."

"That's because these are wildflowers, and anyway, that's not home anymore."

Elizabeth could think of no answer to this, so she simply smiled back. She smiled until he took her face in his hands and kissed her. Then he drew her in, folding her small body into his arms, making her forget that there had ever been any other place.

In New York the time that she had spent with Will, and the affection that they had shown each other, had been secret, stolen from the hours late in the night or early in the morning. Now, in the West, with no one to watch them but the vast sky and the old horse now bending toward the ground, Elizabeth felt drawn to Will with an intensity that was almost frightening. It was a hunger for lost time, she supposed. Already he was hoisting her up, carrying her as he moved toward the horse and opened the saddlebag to remove a piece of canvas.

"Miss Elizabeth," he said, looking up at her with sincere, watchful eyes. He still called her that even though she'd begged him not to. It was a habit he found difficult to let go of. She was still aloft, her body propped against his arms, her own grasp tight around his neck, and as she waited for him to continue he shook out the piece of rough, off-white cloth and let it fall behind her on the ground. Then he bent to lay her down on top of it.

"What were you going to say?" she asked as he came down beside her. She pushed herself halfway up, so that she was lying on her side and facing him.

Will reached over and took off her hat, and began to play with her hair thoughtfully. "Just that I'll build you a real house someday," he said quietly. "With a room to dine in and a room to receive, and enough vases so you can pick all the poppies you want and put them everywhere."

"Oh, I know you will!" She bent her head and laughed, and then gave his arm a pull so that he rose over her, his body blocking out the sky. She lay back, feeling the flowers cushioning her head underneath the canvas, her hair fanning out around her, and smiled up at the serious expression that had come over Will's face. His hair had grown so long that it had to be tucked into the collar of his shirt. The formerly dark color had become almost reddish in the sun. It was as though the city had always been wrong for him, and here, far away, where the land was open, he had arrived at his full strength. He brought his lips to hers with exquisite pressure, and when he drew back again to look at her she couldn't stop the flush that had come across her cheeks and down her neck.

She felt so pleasantly light and empty, and almost over-whelmed by the events that had brought her to this place.

The silence that followed was strangely long, and at first she wondered if he didn't have another surprise. But she had been studying Will's silences for a long time. She knew in a few passing moments that there was something he'd been meaning to tell her.

"It wasn't just luck that we ended up here," he said with the steadfast seriousness that had first endeared him to her. He had pulled away from her and pushed himself up to sitting.

"Oh no?" she answered lightly.

"No. I knew about this place already. Your father told me about this place."

Elizabeth's breath slowed and she felt a momentary dampness along the lower lids of her eyes. The memory of her father was always confused and strong. He had embodied the familial sensibility, its particular grace, but he had never been any good with money. He had made poor decisions about his inheritance and lived largely in a world of his own. She pushed herself up on her elbow to dismiss the emotion. "But how is that . . . ?"

"Back when I drove him everywhere and we would talk"—Will was saying each word carefully, and his speech was terse, as it always was when he had thought something through several times—"he would tell me about the places he had been. He told me about many places that I might want to see, but this was the one he told me to find if I wanted to get rich. He described it exactly. He said that it would be—"

"Oh, Will." Elizabeth felt something like cold in the wind at the bare spot on the back of her neck, just below where her hair rose. "Father said lots of pretty things, but he was a dreamer. You *know* that."

Will continued looking in the direction of the cabin and didn't say anything.

"I just don't want you to hope for something so wild. I was reading in the paper just this morning how difficult it is to find oil, how many men came out from Pennsylvania and fell flat. And those were the ones with experience. They couldn't compete against the big companies; they're the only ones who succeed."

"I'm going to give you just as good a life as the one you gave up." He turned to look at her and then rested his large hand on the curve at the base of her neck. "It was your father who told me how."

Elizabeth never wanted to kiss Will so much as at moments like these. "Oh, I don't need money, Will," she whispered. Then she moved into his warm body and kissed him again.

Later, when they walked back as wrapped up in each other as was possible while still moving forward, she again felt perfectly content. The contented feeling was so overpowering that for a moment she even stopped wondering if that last thing she'd said, about not needing money, could really be true.

Four

DEAR *LADIES' STYLE MONTHLY*: Could you please give me the answer to a question of great concern? What is the proper mourning period for a young person who has lost their betrothed? The etiquette books are undecided on this sad but pressing subject.

DEAR READER: You are not alone in wondering, as a very prominent case like the one you describe is now occupying many in society. While the loss of a fiancée is a grave occurrence, we must remember that engaged couples are not yet man and wife, nor are they technically relatives. And of course, gentlemen in general must observe a shorter mourning period than ladies. So while a respectful, private period of mourning is essential, two months will perfectly suffice.

—*LADIES' STYLE MONTHLY*, DECEMBER 1899

ENRY SCHOONMAKER STOOD AT THE INTERSECTION of two pinched little streets in the old part of town and wondered how soon he could reasonably escape from his father's parade. The carriage from which Penelope Hayes had winked at him had disappeared—it had been heading in the direction of the East River, though its final destination was almost certainly Fifth Avenue, where she lived. Henry's family lived along that string of stocky mansions as well, although their arrival, on the Avenue and in New York society, predated the Hayeses' by many years. But that hardly seemed to matter now. No one particularly cared anymore from where, or when, the Hayeses had come. Penelope had even been able to absent herself from the parade early while maintaining the appearance of some saintly champion of the poor. She was clever—Henry had to admire her for that.

"What a fine young lady Miss Hayes is turning out to be," Henry's father, William Sackhouse Schoonmaker, said as he proceeded through the intersection. Henry watched from behind as his father strode purposefully across the bricked street. "It was so good of her to partake in our little charity, and to stay as long as she did."

"And you know how she must tire so," his wife, Isabelle, put in. At twenty-five, she was only five years older than Henry himself, and she spoke in a high, girlish voice that made her sound perennially giddy. She wore an ocelot coat and a hat that was top-heavy with silk roses and stuffed sparrows, and even with a firm grasp on her husband's arm she still managed to bounce as she walked. "As all ladies do."

"Young Miss Hayes was changed forever, as we all were," Mr. Schoonmaker went on, to the *New York World* reporter who had been trailing along at his other elbow and dutifully writing down his thoughts all afternoon, "by the loss of Miss Holland. You see how transformed my son is."

Both men turned to look at Henry, who was following a few paces behind. He wore a top hat and a black knee-length coat that fit his slim frame well. For while the death of Elizabeth Holland had indeed taken a profound toll on his previously carefree attitude toward life, he had not been so truly transformed as to have given up caring what he wore.

"You see," he heard his father say as he looked away from his son. "He is inconsolable. The current mayor's handling of Elizabeth's death is of course chief among the reasons I intend to challenge him."

The elder Schoonmaker went on, but Henry had heard the speech many times before. His father had recently decided, despite his enormous personal wealth and the power it afforded him, that he wanted to play in politics as well. His desire to be mayor of a recently consolidated New York City was one of the reasons that Henry had been compelled to enter into an engagement with Elizabeth Holland in the first place, and it was thus also one of the reasons that she had come to such a tragic end. For Henry had seen his fiancée on the last day of her life, and the image of her—alone and frightened in the middle of a Manhattan sidewalk—had been simple enough to interpret.

She had stood there for a few moments looking into him. They had been engaged only a few weeks at the time and, under pressure from their families, they were to be married in a matter of days. Henry's behavior during that period was not something he looked back on proudly, although it was one of the few times in his life that he had been completely honest with a girl. Just not the girl he happened to be engaged to. He was not proud, either, of his behavior in the years leading up to his engagement, which had earned him a not undeserved reputation as a cad. Still, he could not bring himself to entirely renounce his behavior the night before he saw Elizabeth on that street corner—the night before she drowned. For that was the night that he had invited her younger sister, Di, to the

Schoonmaker greenhouse. It had been, for him, an uncharacteristically chaste night; she had stayed up whispering to him and kissing him with a sweetness and innocence that could not possibly have survived what happened next. Elizabeth had seen Henry and Diana together the following morning, and he knew from her clear-eyed gaze that she understood what had occurred. That knowledge must have driven her to her death—one did not just *fall* into the river and never return. Henry could not deny that devastating fact.

But Henry did not blame himself alone. He blamed his father, too, which was one of the reasons he could not stomach W. S. Schoonmaker's talking again of Elizabeth as though she were a martyr to his own political cause. He turned and walked back through the marching band that followed in the parade. Above him were tenements, some of them owned by his father's company, with their unimaginative façades and ersatz Italianate ornamentation. Those little plaster flourishes, which were always crumbling, depressed Henry beyond reason. He caught an elbow against a trombone, causing a small collision of musicians, and heard the music quaver for a moment. The band must have known who was signing their paychecks, however, and there was not even a mutter of complaint. They were after all wearing uniforms in the Schoonmaker colors of sky blue and gold.

Henry kept on, through the band, with all its ear-shattering horns, through the clutch of ladies that followed, in their white gloves and weighty hats. He heard the ladies saying his name and knew that they had turned to look at the spectacle of the young man moving downtown, against the traffic of his own father's event. He would hear about it later, of course. His father was fond of threatening to disown him if he did not behave as a future mayor's son should, although these threats had mostly abated since his father had realized that he might plausibly base his campaign on the current mayor's mishandling of a debutante's death and the spectacle of his own son's grief.

"Schoonmaker!"

Henry's eyes moved across the faces of the people massed on the sidewalk and the paraders all around him until his gaze settled, happily, on the face of his old friend Teddy Cutting. Next to Teddy was his younger sister, Alice, who was fair like her brother, with the same gray eyes, which were now focused shyly on the ground. Henry had once kissed her in the garden of the Cuttings' Newport cottage, and she hadn't been able to look at him straight since. She was the youngest of Teddy's sisters, Henry believed, although he could never be sure, as Teddy was the only son among several siblings. To Henry this had always been telling: Teddy was the kind of man who had too many sisters.

"Miss Cutting," Henry said, taking her gloved hand and kissing it. "It is always a pleasure to see you."

Teddy gave him a warning look. "You look like you've had about enough."

Henry smiled with his characteristic charm at both siblings, and said, "I'm full to the gills."

"Let's go, then." Teddy reached out and put a hand on Henry's shoulder. He had been one of Henry's chief sympathizers since the unfortunate events of October. "I know of a lunchroom near here."

They said good-bye to Alice, who joined a group of young women, and then they moved into the crowd of common people with their faces lowered. The shininess of Henry's black top hat and the superb cut of his wool coat would have given them away as members of the city's elite, as would the rich brown check of Teddy's vicuna jacket, or the stamp of the Union Square milliner on his brown bowler. Still, they made no eye contact with the people in the crowd, and when they emerged onto a side street they hailed the first hackney they saw.

Teddy's lunchroom was clean and bright, with a floor of small white octagonal tiles and convex mirrors lining the walls. They sat at a small round table made of sturdy dark wood, and they ordered the German beers that arrived in tall glasses with wedges of lemon. Henry felt quiet after several very public hours, and he was grateful that his friend waited to speak until after they had each sipped.

"How are you bearing it?" Teddy asked, placing his glass back on the table. He had taken off his hat, and his blond hair was brushed neatly to the side. At Henry's wary smile he went on. "I can barely listen to your father's speeches, and I'm not even related to him. I mean, he hardly knew Elizabeth and then to use her death that way, for political purposes—" Teddy broke off, shaking his head in disbelief.

"Let's not talk about that." Henry took a long pull of his beer and then found he didn't feel quite so dark anymore. "It's all hypocrisy and misery if we go that route, and who wants that?"

"Fair enough," Teddy said, returning his smile. "We'll just be happy we're free of ridiculous parades then, and be done with it."

They clinked their glasses and drank, and in the brief silence that followed, Henry found himself wondering how to open a topic that that they had discussed only briefly more than two months before.

"You are really going to have to find a way to put Alice at ease," Teddy offered before Henry could speak. He was trying to give Henry a disapproving look, but he couldn't help a waver of a smile that his friend's old effect was still at work even in gloomy times. "She gets quiet every time she sees you."

"Your sister's too good for me," Henry replied with a

laugh. "She'll see that soon enough, and the problem will be solved."

"She won't want to hear it," Teddy answered heartily, "but I can't say I disagree with you."

Henry paused to drink, and when he placed his beer back on the table he met Teddy's gray eyes. "You know, my official mourning period is almost over."

"I know. Thank God." Teddy drank, and shook his head. "It's been dull out in the world without you."

"We have fun."

"Yes." Teddy's eyes shifted and a memory passed in them. "We'll have a dinner at Sherry's, or maybe a hunting party up in Tuxedo."

Henry twirled his top hat in his lap. "I think I'm going to go to the season's opening at the opera. Even my father likes the idea—the better to drive home his point about Van Wyck's poor handling of Elizabeth's death, when there are sure to be newspaper people around. It's *Roméo et Juliette*, you know."

"Well, we'll have to plan something for afterward, then."

"Yes." Henry looked at his hat and began to twirl it the other way. He brought his eyes back up to Teddy's and returned to the subject he'd so wanted to raise. "There's something else."

Teddy had a fair and distinguished brow, and it rose now, ever so subtly.

"At some point, my father will want me to start thinking about another engagement. . . ." Henry paused to clear his throat. "And the girl I find myself thinking about is Diana Holland."

Their glasses were empty, and one of the waiters in long white aprons appeared to remove them. Teddy asked the man to bring more, and then turned a pained but stern expression on his friend. Henry rarely thought of Teddy as older than himself, but he was reminded of the two years that separated them now.

"That cannot be." Teddy kept his voice low and looked around to see that nobody had heard.

"But *why?*" Henry could not hide the exasperation in his voice. "You know Elizabeth was even less interested in me than I was in her. All those rumors about their money, about it being gone—that must have been the reason she accepted my proposal. She couldn't even bring herself to smile at me. And Diana will be in just the same position as her sister, and, unlike her sister, she has a chance of being happy with me. I would be happy with *her.*"

"You know society will not allow it."

Henry shook his head and cast his eyes about the busy lunchroom. "They will forget."

"I don't want to know what has happened between you and the younger Miss Holland." Teddy paused as their drinks were delivered, and took a quick sip before continuing. "But if you really care for her, and you seem to, then you must stop being so stupid. Her sister was your fiancée, and she has died under circumstances that none of us begin to understand. Circumstances that you yourself suggested might have something to do with her impending nuptials. Diana may be infatuated with you now, but when she grows up, when she understands more about death and family, when she understands how much she has betrayed Elizabeth by taking up with her former fiancé, it will destroy her. And you know perfectly well how often people will remind her. Society does *not* forget."

Henry was taking long sips of his beer and trying not to be angry with his friend for speaking negatively of an imagined future that he had promised himself indulgently during the worst moments of the last few months. He had sat across from Diana in her family's parlor during those first weeks of mourning and imagined the time when she would meet his eyes again, and that eventually all the misery would pass and they could really be together. Diana was the only girl he'd ever met who inspired him to imagine himself as a married man.

"She will come to hate herself, and you too." Teddy shook his head.

For some reason this brought Elizabeth's pitiable visage

on the morning of her death back into Henry's mind's eye, and he began to think of the part his skirt-chasing—however ardent—had played in what she had done next. His fiancée had then seen him with her little sister; perhaps that had been the single event in ending a bright girl's will to live.

"Let's go," Teddy said gently.

Henry finished his beer, and he placed a bill on the table. He had brought the topic up to Teddy once before and subsequently longed to have said nothing. There wasn't a thing left to say now.

In the past Henry had always ignored his friend's advice at his own peril, but still he could not give up the picture of Diana he kept in his mind. Even as he put a resigned sort of smile on his face and placed his hat on his head, he could not help but think of her loose curls and fresh skin, of a gorgeous recklessness that perfectly matched his own.

Five

Women often stop me on the street and demand to know how they can transform their daughters into society ladies, and I always say: If they are not born with position, and if they are not uncommonly beautiful—for few girls today transcend mere prettiness—they will have to marry in where they can. To this mission, clothes are essential. A good place to start, I tell these eager parents, is at a department store in a good part of town, where one can find a salesman one can trust. . . .

—MRS. HAMILTON W. BREEDFELT, _COLLECTED COLUMNS ON RAISING YOUNG LADIES OF CHARACTER_, 1899

$\mathcal{L}$INA BROUD TURNED HERSELF ROUND AND ROUND, overcome with a kind of desire that was still new to her. Everywhere she looked there were objects edged in gold, finished with elaborate hand stitching, or festooned with feathers. They lay in neat piles on tables of mahogany that stretched as far as the eye could see, or at least far enough to reach one of the hundreds of etched mirrors that reflected the opulent scene within the Lord & Taylor department store over and again.

"Tristan," she said in a high, clear tone. She had been working on her elocution, and had lately concluded that the acoustics within the grand department stores of Ladies' Mile were ideal for such an endeavor. In her previous life she had only rarely caught glimpses within such stores, which lined Fifth Avenue and Broadway above Union Square, and attracted the kind of women Lina used to serve. This in spite of the fact that the row of grand retailers and little specialty shops was mere blocks from Gramercy Park, where the women

Lina used to serve still lived. Most of them, anyway. "I adore these gloves."

Tristan Wrigley, who was a salesman at Lord & Taylor and the first friend she had made in her new life, came to her side—perhaps an inch closer than men were supposed to in public with women who were not their relations—and said, "Of course, Mademoiselle Carolina. If I may."

Although Lina was not shy of being seen in public with naked fingers—she had lived most of her life with bare, working hands—she did feel a tinge of embarrassment as Tristan pulled off her gloves and began to draw the new pair on. She immediately noticed how superior in quality the hand-stitched, dove-colored pair were to her own. They fit to her fingers with an almost preternatural closeness, and the smooth softness of the silk against her skin gave her an instantaneous sensation of being very, very rich.

"Does mademoiselle approve?" Like all the Lord & Taylor salesmen, Tristan had been hired for his all-American good looks—the better to lure female shoppers—and he always spoke with an elaborate politesse. He seemed as good a person as any to practice her new persona on, which was why she occasionally let him take her for walks in the park or tea at the hotel. Only occasionally, though—she was merely practicing, and didn't want him to get too close. Her affections lay elsewhere.

"Oh, yes."

Tristan had a long face with an architectural nose and cheekbones that seemed to set him even above his peers. He wore a fitted brown waistcoat and an ivory shirt buttoned at the wrists. His hazel eyes were such a hypnotic color that Lina sometimes found it difficult to look into them for more than two seconds at a time. Looking away from him did not distress her, however. Regularly averting her eyes was in fact useful to the illusion she was trying to maintain: that she was a copper-smelting heiress from out west (Utah, if pressed, though she had not been) and recently orphaned.

At first she had been surprised at how easily Tristan bought her story. The day she had met Tristan had been in the most nascent stage of her new life, and it had included a terrific blunder. That had also been the first day she'd drunk beer or been in a saloon, and it had not ended prettily. The episode might surely have proven what a thousand little missteps suggested: that she was not a lady and that her origins were very humble indeed.

But she had since witnessed—both in her new home, the New Netherland Hotel, and on her visits to Lord & Taylor with Tristan—real western millionaires, and had seen that they were even coarser and more prone to gaffes than she. For Lina Broud—Carolina, as she was trying to refer to herself in her own mind—did know some things about comportment, manners, and dress. She had learned them as the lady's maid of the late Elizabeth Holland. Chief among her observations was how effective an aloof demeanor was in declaring one's personal importance.

It was in fact Elizabeth, whose wealth and reputation for loveliness gave her advantages with which Lina could not compete, who had won the heart of Will Keller—he had been the Hollands' coachman, and Lina had loved him in secret for a long time. This wound was one of the reasons that she had sold her mistress's secret, the one that involved Elizabeth and Will spending nights together in the carriage house, to Elizabeth's sometime friend Penelope Hayes. That information had garnered Lina five hundred dollars, what had then seemed a fortune but had since been reduced by more than half by the dinners and hotel rooms and dresses and trinkets that she hoped would differentiate her from the plain girl she used to be.

It had been a sore disappointment that such an extraordinary-sounding sum didn't go very far in the lifestyle of a girl like Elizabeth. And Lina was not proud, either, that her life as a lady, or something like it, had been made possible by such a sordid transaction. But she had done what she had to do. Her object had not really been to make herself into a society girl—she just wanted to make herself enough Elizabeth-like that, when she was ready, she could go out

west, and then Will would see that it was Lina he'd wanted all along. Or at least, when he heard of Elizabeth's death, that the new, shiny Lina could fill that hole in his heart.

Lina had never been above taking Elizabeth's seconds, even if it was her mistress's death that now allowed the passing down. She wanted to find Will as much as ever. She believed that that time was near—it had to be, or her money would run out first.

Tristan was placing the gloves she had chosen, the little lace shawl, the Persian lamb muff, the new pair of onyx hose that sold for two dollars and twenty-five cents—Tristan had introduced them to her, and now she could not live without them—each in its own box, with the same magical, crinkling tissue. Lina watched with dizzy joy and a vague sense of dread as these objects were folded and placed, wrapped, and then boxed. Once they were boxed, that meant they were hers and that she would have to pay for them.

"Shall I have these sent to your hotel?"

"No . . ." Lina paused and looked away. The late afternoon light was coming in through the high, Romanesque windows that faced the street. Already the day was getting away from her, and she couldn't truly be said to be grander than when it began. When she stepped outside the weather would have dropped, and all the workaday people she so wanted to distinguish herself from would be massed at the store's plate glass windows to gawk at the Christmas display. At moments like these she couldn't help but feel a little sad and recall how devastating it had been when, after years of secret longing, she had one night confessed her feelings to Will and then been sent away. She wanted to be sure that such a rejection wasn't repeated, and reminded herself that she must perfect her transformation before she saw him again. "I'll be taking a hansom, of course—I can carry them myself. But please do send the bill to the hotel."

Lina had recently stopped carrying her new wealth on her person—which had been a kind of nervous obsession when she first went out on her own—and had cautiously begun to embrace the luxury of paying later. She kept her Penelope money in a small silk purse with a leather drawstring buried deep in her drawer of lacy underclothes. In her own experience as a maid, this drawer had possessed a taboo aura; she assumed the maids at the hotel would feel the same way and not go through it too carefully.

"Of course, mademoiselle." Tristan paused and grinned in a way that a real lady probably would have deemed too familiar, and said, "I could accompany you, if you needed assistance."

"That's quite all right," Lina said, looking away from him and subtly turning up her nose. "If you'll just help me on with my coat, I'll be going."

Lina alighted on the corner of Fifty-ninth Street and Fifth Avenue. Once she had firmed up her story and smoothed out some of the details of her performance, she had traded up from a rather seedy hotel on Twenty-sixth Street to the New Netherland, where the bellboys wore royal blue uniforms. It was a wide building of turrets and arched windows with a dignified brown façade, and it loomed over the buildings around it like a terrific sand castle. She had heard somewhere that the Netherland was the tallest hotel in the world, and that was why she had chosen it over the Savoy, its next-door neighbor, or the Plaza, on the west side of the avenue. The three hotels formed a corner around the southeast entrance of the Central Park, and below them stretched the mansions of Huntingtons, Vanderbilts, and Hayeses. The thought that she lived so near people of that caliber still gave Lina a pleasant little electric shock.

Her room was not the best, and still it cost twenty-nine dollars a week. She couldn't go on like this forever, she knew that, but it hardly mattered, since she would soon be with Will. Strong, capable Will—he would take care of her, and in the meantime, she hoped some of the elegance of hotel life would rub off. That, and she liked returning to her room to the surprise of a swept carpet and a bed remade by some invisible mechanism. She liked stepping out and seeing that a cab was waiting on the street, as though her arrival had been anticipated exactly.

Lina looked at the driver, and gestured that he should help her with her purchases. She threw her shoulders back and walked, in her practiced way, toward the arched entrance. Despite her freckles—which spread across her nose and darkened her complexion even in winter—there was a natural dignity to her appearance. Her mouth had the effect of pouting, and her eyes were the color of lichen, and there was an upturn to her nose. She wore a fitted tan coat with dramatic lapels that flattered her waist and somewhat unfeminine shoulders, and a little matching hat with a black plume that bounced as she approached the desk.

"Miss Broud, good afternoon," the diminutive clerk behind the massive mahogany desk greeted her.

As she usually did at such moments Lina concentrated on hiding the pleasure her new surroundings caused her. For the floor was an opulent mosaic with a shiny finish, and the electric light of the chandelier reflected off the marble stairway as though it were the entrance to a grand court in Europe. The lobby smelled of perfume and coffee, and it quietly suggested to anyone who entered that there was no place else to be. *If only Will could see me at just this second,* she would think when she was standing there, he would forget that he ever

loved Elizabeth; he would see the perfect girl who had been hidden right in front of him, disguised in the rough.

Lina tipped her head in muted acknowledgment. "My key, please, Mr. Cullen."

It was when the clerk turned away that she became aware of the presence close behind her. She brought her head around sharply—she thought she had been clear that the driver should wait near the door until one of the bellboys came for her things—and came face-to-face with a far better-dressed man. He wore a burgundy velvet smoking jacket and black slacks, and his ivory collar came all the way to his carefully shaved chin. His features were fine, except for his nose, which belied a taste for the drink, and he was grinning at her in a way that might have been flirtatious. She couldn't be sure of this, however, because he was older—too old a gentleman to be flirting with a seventeen–year-old girl, she thought. But then, there was so much she didn't yet understand.

The clerk had returned with her key, but he was watch-ing the man in burgundy deferentially and made no move to hand it over to Lina. She waited for the gentleman to speak, and when the seconds had added up, her heart began to pound for fear he knew her secret.

"Are those your things?" he asked, pointing to the driver, who had in fact been waiting patiently near the door with his hat in his hand and his eyes focused on the arched ceiling, according to her instructions and with appropriate awe. "Because the bellboys here—forgive me for saying so, George— are inexperienced and cannot be trusted with such finery."

Lina had never been in a situation like this one and was without any idea of the proper response. The clerk wouldn't meet her eyes.

"My apologies." The gentleman inclined forward in a kind of bow without taking his gaze off Lina. "Mr. Longhorn, at your service."

The full name was Carey Lewis Longhorn. She knew it from her sister, Claire, whose favorite pastime was reading society columns. He was older than she had suspected then, and richer too—the heir to a banking fortune, if Lina wasn't mixing him up with someone else. He was known for a string of broken engagements in his youth, and a series of attachments to countesses and fashionable matrons in middle age, and for currently having a large collection of portraits depicting the beauties of the present day. Lina was amazed to see that he was still grinning at her. His eyes were a pale blue that suggested the liveliness of their owner, and his gaunt cheeks rose sharply with the smile.

"Thank you," Lina finally replied. She knew her hesitance and confusion showed but there was nothing she could do to change it. Beyond Mr. Longhorn, she could see that his valet was already collecting her boxes and paying the cab driver. The clerk offered the key to Mr. Longhorn—still with immaculate deference, and without even acknowledging that it belonged to Lina—and then she found herself following him away from the desk.

"Are you staying in the hotel with your parents?" Mr. Longhorn asked as they stepped into the elevator. The attendant was closing the mahogany and stained glass door. Lina's gaze had floated upward to the iron lacework of the ceiling as the ornamented cage jerked and drew them higher. The movement of her eyes had more to do with a continual wonder at the mechanics of vertical conveyance than sadness, but she was not entirely displeased by what Mr. Longhorn said next. "No, I didn't think so. I have seen you here several times, and always alone. The world is never easy, but orphans are a special case. I am sorry for your loss."

Lina lowered her eyes to the black-and-white-tiled floor. "He died in the mines," she lied. "A routine inspection. Father always insisted on doing them himself rather than trust an underling. Copper smelting, that was his business, and he had several mines of his own, too. My mother could not take the shock and her heart gave out within a month. They worked so hard so that I might enjoy this. . . ." She paused to gesture at the gilded elevator, and let her lower lip just quiver. "And though it's not always easy for me, I think they would want me to enjoy it still."

Mr. Longhorn's gray eyebrows rose slightly, and for a moment Lina feared that she'd been improper. For though parts of Lina's story were true—both of her parents were dead, making her technically an orphan—she was no heiress, and there were moments when she felt like a tremendous fraud. But apparently Longhorn did not think so, for he concluded, with a compassionate smile, "A girl after my own heart."

"Ninth floor," the attendant announced as they jerked to a halt. He drew back the door, and as they passed into the hall Lina noticed that he too averted his eyes from Mr. Longhorn. She couldn't help but be a little impressed by all the awe this nearly gray man inspired, even as he offered his arm and began to escort her down the plush carpeting of the hall to her room. She could hear the footsteps of the valet close behind, carrying her precious boxes.

When they reached her room, Mr. Longhorn leaned forward to unlock the heavy oak door. To her relief he made no attempt to enter. He handed her the key, and said, "With your permission, Robert will put your things on the table."

Lina's room was too small to have a table, and she was relieved to hear herself answer with an alternative: "He can put them on the settee by the window."

The valet moved quietly and efficiently to do as he was told.

"It has been a pleasure to meet you, Miss . . ."

"Broud. Carolina Broud."

"Miss Broud." The old gentleman leaned forward and took her hand to kiss it. The valet exited her room and waited patiently in the background. "You have been very kind allowing me to accompany you for a few moments, and I hope you will be willing to repeat the favor this evening."

Lina looked back at the valet, as though he might confirm that all of this was very unexpected and perhaps a little inappropriate, but he did not meet her gaze.

"You see," Mr. Longhorn went on, with what Lina thought might have been a twinkle in his eye, "I have taken a box at the opera for the season, and tonight is the opening, and I have nobody but Robert here to share it with. Would you mind terribly if I asked you to join me?"

Plain little Lina Broud in a box at the opera; she could not have been more surprised if he had presented her with a diamond tiara and crowned her the queen of Persia. She had spent all morning dressed as a society girl, but tonight, rather than remain invisible in her room as she usually did, she was being offered the chance to walk among them. She would be brilliant and looked on, just like the girl Will had believed himself to be in love with. Her first thought was to apologize to Robert for taking his seat, but then she told herself to smile, and realized that she already was.

"Oh, yes," she said. It was far beyond her control to sound less eager. "I would love to."

Six

After years where everyone wanted to over-bedeck themselves in the ultra-new, it seems that simplicity may again be in vogue. The best people are having quiet little dinners and cutting their day dresses from plain muslin. But remember: There is simplicity and there is simplicity, and the elegant variety is not always as easy as it sounds.

—*DRESS MAGAZINE*, DECEMBER 1899

HERE WERE ONLY A FEW THINGS IN THE LITTLE cabin on the Keller lease, but what was there Will had made a point of acquiring for Elizabeth. In the middle of the dirt floor was a square table that Will had built, and over to the side was an old brass frame bed that he had bought off a wildcatter gone broke up in Lancaster, the same one who had sold them the horse. There was the brass-framed oval mirror that was hung over the tin water basin—both of the same provenance—and it was there that Elizabeth still arranged her hair before dinner every night, usually in a little bun high in the back, like the center of a pincushion. Hair done, water brought up from the well, she had now turned to a task she knew very little of. Elizabeth Holland was attempting, once again, to make dinner.

A clutch of the orange poppies that she had taken from the field yesterday sat in an old mason jar at the center of the table, which was covered with the same canvas they used for everything. Beside them was a little pile of Will's books—

Geological Techniques for Locating Petroleum Beneath the Earth's Surface and *How a Man Digs a Well in the Wild.* She had managed to get a fire going in the little iron stove in the corner, but opening the cans of baked beans was proving too difficult for her. The opener was rusted, and she suspected that Will had found it somewhere—a bit of thrift that she would have considered admirable at any other moment, but was currently so distressing to her that she wanted to scream.

This was in fact what she did next. She let out a cry that might very well have been—it occurred to her even as her throat began to vibrate and her lungs became empty of air—the loudest noise she'd ever personally made. When it was over she was still alone, although she felt better. She put her hand on her abdomen and closed her eyes. Her lips turned upward in a slight smile; it was, after all, amusing to think that she was so far away from all those fine things she'd so worked to be and finding herself unequal to even small tasks. To be incapable was as new to her as vociferous outbursts.

She put down the can and sat at the table. It was that part of the day when she usually became conscious of having been alone for a long stretch, after Will had stayed out in the field for many hours with Denny, the partner he'd found in Oakland. Those were hours beyond her realm, and she didn't try to understand what they did out there. The world of labor had always been Will's world, and a mystery to her, and while

this had once seemed like a plain fact, it did make her feel a little guilty lately. She knew he had spent time setting up their home—which would have been a natural task for a different kind of girl—that he could have otherwise used to explore the field. Elizabeth wanted nothing more than to be with Will, but she couldn't help but wish—at moments like these, late in the day, when, in New York, the sun would have already gone down—that she could better keep up with him. It was the perfect society girl in her, and she only longed to prepare a frontier supper with half the aplomb she used to deploy chatting with visitors on Sunday in her family drawing room.

She sat there for a while thinking of those people she'd left behind and of those several thousand miles that separated them. She wouldn't miss them so if only she could see into their lives a little more, if only that distance were slightly more conquerable. Every now and then she would read a week-old newspaper that mentioned some New York news, but that mainly stoked her worry, for it was inevitably about how her mother wasn't her old self or how Diana still was.

"Lizzy!" Will called before he was even through the door. Elizabeth looked up from the table, and already she was up in his arms. She was in the air and being swung around. Her arms were tight at his neck, and she clung to him, feeling again how right it was for her to be in this place at this time. She was taking in his scent—that mixture of sweat and plain soap and some other musky quality just beyond her grasp—when he spoke in a quiet voice. "Today we had luck."

He set her down, and as her feet touched the floor, she looked up into his face. It was full of sun and light, and his pale blue eyes looked lucky indeed. "What kind of luck?"

"Oil luck." He paused and pressed his thick lips together and watched her. His breath made his chest rise and fall under the threadbare collared shirt rolled to his sleeves. His hair was dark from the sweat where it hadn't been bleached by the sun. "Denny and I, we found it. We found oil—shiny, black oil. You can smell it out there. I just know there's lakes of it underground. It's seeping through the rocks. The air is full of sulfur. We're going to follow what my book says and dig a well and sell it to the refinery in Lancaster, and then we'll be able to hire more workers. For a while we'll have to spend everything we make. But it's right here—we're just sitting on it, the thing that's going to make us rich."

Will had been speaking so quickly and with such excitement that he had to stop and take several breaths. But the energy was in his face and body; he was heaving with it. He took off the serge trousers, which he wore every day when he left home, because they were smeared with the sticky black stuff. He put on the long underwear he wore to sleep in, all the while telling her how oil was extracted and how much he thought would be there and what barrels of crude were selling for these days. She hung the trousers on the back of the bed, so they wouldn't soil anything else, and watched Will as he went to open the can of beans and continued talking about the team he would need to hire and what the returns would be.

Elizabeth's cheeks had risen in one of those radiant smiles that used to be wasted on brocade, or the gift bags at balls, or salmon mousse. She was surprised to find it was not for this mineral wealth, however—all that still seemed like some far-off fantasy. It was for Will as he would be. There would be successes, whether they began with the oil field or not, and after that he would become one of those men they wrote about in the adventure magazines—about his mythic youth and his great business acumen and all the intelligent choices he had made along the way. He would be shrewd and hard with people who needed it, but he would be fair and looked up to. He would be the head of a family, and he would help those people who were deserving and in need.

The softness would go out of his face, but the crooked nose would remain the same. They would grow older and see the world change together. They looked at each other for another long moment, and then she moved in, pressing her body against his body, feeling his heart beating in his chest.

Seven

I have heard from several sources that Mr. Henry Schoonmaker will make his first social appearance since the death of his fiancée, Miss Elizabeth Holland, at the opening of the Metropolitan Opera's winter season tonight. Though the proper mourning time has been observed, some suggest that he may be stepping out a little too soon. . . .

—FROM THE "GAMESOME GALLANT" COLUMN IN THE *NEW YORK IMPERIAL*, SATURDAY, DECEMBER 16, 1899

"YOU DON'T JUST THROW A PERSON THROUGH A crack in the ice," said Mrs. Edward Holland, who was born Louisa Gansevoort and still retained some of the inimitable social presence that the joining of those two surnames implied. She was garbed in black mourning clothes twice over, first for her husband and again for her elder child, and she sat in the corner of Diana's gaslit bedroom with darting and watchful obsidian eyes. There was something physically reduced about her, however—a shadow had been cast over her former imperiousness. She was ill, Diana knew in certain moments, although in others she told herself it was no more than a mood that would be dispelled just as soon as Diana agreed to be married.

"*Threw* is rather an exaggeration," Diana answered blithely. She was seated at the vanity, her attention fixed on the dark ringlets that edged her heart-shaped face and its wild-rose complexion. Her lady's maid, Claire, who had been helping her get dressed, stood at her shoulder. Diana was not going to great lengths to seem interested in her mother's concerns. "I can't be held responsible for the clumsiness of a Percival Coddington," she added, turning just slightly to meet the gaze of her aunt Edith, lounging on the bed with its pale pink headboard in an ivory shirtwast and skirt.

"It's a miracle it didn't make the papers," her mother went on sharply. "Or that he wasn't too severely injured. But there are plenty of eyes in this city, Diana, and plenty of mouths. They will be saying soon enough that you don't know how to behave. Once a reputation has been too often confirmed, society cannot forget it." Her eyes took on a faraway look, and she paused to sink deeper into the wing chair with the worn gold upholstery. It was the chair that Diana curled into when she stayed up reading novels of heroines beset by wickedly handsome men, and it was until recently the place of her most dramatic flights of fancy. But no longer. Recurrent memories of Henry Schoonmaker were the most exciting thing to happen in her conscious mind these days.

She smiled faintly at her reflection. Then, checking herself, she met Claire's eyes in the mirror, and gave her a little look in anticipation of Mrs. Holland's next argument.

"When I was a girl," it began, "they used to tell us that a woman's name should appear in the papers three times: on the occasions of her birth, her marriage, and her death."

"Well," said Edith, pushing her head back into the arm

that was folded as a pillow behind her head, "our generation did away with that old adage."

Diana's name had already appeared in the columns several times—more often for something that brought embarrassment to her mother than not—but this did not stop an imaginary photograph of Henry and her descending the church steps from popping into her head under the banner headline YOUNGER HOLLAND SISTER WEDS SCHOONMAKER.

Claire moved forward and finished Diana's hair with a honeydew-colored ribbon that matched the honeydew dress she wore. The dress whittled her waist and revealed her clavicles and was decorated at the shoulders with little poofs of honeydew-dyed feathers. It was from Paris, and had been purchased by her sister during the previous summer season, which she had spent abroad. There had been a macabre element to the remaking of the departed sister's dress, and no one had liked it. But there was no money for a new one, as her mother mechanically reminded her both by implication and outright, and in the end the tailoring had been ordered.

"If your name should appear in the papers after tonight," Mrs. Holland returned, ignoring her sister-in-law's comment, "let it not be because you have managed to half-kill Spencer Newburg."

Diana stood at this and turned to her mother, her face

imbued with the curious light of two divergent emotions. She would have liked to tell the petite matriarch that if she was not so ham-fistedly trying to marry her daughter off, then she wouldn't have to worry so for the safety of these gentlemen. This seemed irritatingly obvious enough to Diana. But the mention of Spencer Newburg's name was like music. Not because of any innate characteristics possessed by Mr. Newburg, who was a widower of twenty-seven, and whose face, always long, had grown ever longer since the loss of young Mrs. Newburg to rheumatic fever. Still, the sound of his name had been sweet to Diana since that morning when she'd read the papers and realized that her evening of listening to opera with him would afford her the first chance to see Henry in weeks. Her heart thrilled at the thought that she might be under the same roof as him that night, that their eyes might meet, that perhaps their hands might even touch. Spencer Newburg's bit part in all this afforded him a special grace.

Her mother rose from her chair now too. Stern veins stood out along her neck, and the bones of her face pressed against the skin.

"Anyway, Mrs. Gore is my host, and I'm not even sure I will meet Mr. Newburg," Diana said, somewhat disingenuously. For though Mr. Newburg's elder sister had been the one to officially invite her to sit in their family box, she had made clear on the two occasions she had visited the Hollands that it was for her brother's sake that Diana should come. Moreover, it was well known that Grover Gore's wife had made it her mission for the season to find her brother a good match who might mend his broken heart. Mrs. Holland—it was not lost on her younger child—had been allied with the Gores for several decades. "But if I do, I will handle him delicately."

The length of Mrs. Holland's neck seemed to grow and her chin gestured toward the white plaster filigree of the ceiling. Diana watched her, waiting for some sort of rebuke, but the tension in her mother's face disappeared then, and her whole body seemed to slacken. It was as though she were going to faint. "I think I'll be going to bed," she said abruptly. "Be good, Diana."

She left a pall in the room even after the door had shut behind her. Diana blinked and then turned to her aunt. "Look, I frighten even my mother."

"You look beautiful, Di," Edith answered from the bed with a sympathetic little wink. The late Mr. Holland's younger sister shared several facial features with her nieces, and had been known for being rather passionate in her youth. She had made a bad marriage to a titled Spaniard, which had ended in divorce, and she was now known by her maiden name. She had always liked sitting in while Diana played dress-up. "And I don't think you have to worry about Mr. Newburg being the only one who notices," she added with a purposeful inflection that made Diana wonder briefly how much her aunt intuited about her desires.

Diana leaned back into the mirror to check her reflection a final time, and found that she agreed that she wouldn't have to count on Mr. Newburg alone for attention. Her eyes were hazy and dark, her mouth tiny and plump. The only anxiety she felt was that some of the loveliness might fade before she found Henry. She was in a fine mood again, and she maintained it by reminding herself that once her mother understood that Henry loved her and that she loved Henry, then all this anxious nonsense about a swift match would finally cease.

They arrived late to the Metropolitan Opera at Broadway and Fortieth, as was the prevailing custom of their class. The street was still crowded with carriages when Diana and Mrs. Gore alighted on the pavement and joined the other women in their brocade wraps making their way to the ladies' entrance on the side. They missed the masked ball scene entirely but took their seats—happily enough for Diana—just as the baritone began "Mab, la Reine des Mensonges." Her father, who cared deeply about such things in life, had considered Gounod's *Roméo et Juliette* not to his taste, but Diana liked any and all varieties of

stirring music, particularly when it touched on lovers cruelly divided by circumstance.

Diana's gaze swept across the auditorium—the rows of seats below, the tiers of less-coveted boxes above, all filled with rich fabrics and bright jewels and flushed faces partially obscured by fans. She sat down beside Mrs. Gore, who wore a dress of blue velvet, which she filled out in a way that no one could have imagined when she was still lithe Lily Newburg. Her younger brother had said little on the way over, and did not now travel farther than the inner room of his family's box, where he rested on the couch and smoked moodily.

His young guest did not pay him any mind. She could barely contain herself from leaning against the polished brass rail to look down on the stage below. The music was surging and lively; she had always liked the sad mystery of those words in Shakespeare, and she loved them now in opera, too. For a moment, with the rise and fall of the orchestra, the prospect of seeing Henry almost slipped from her mind. But only almost.

"I'd heard that Henry Schoonmaker was going to be out tonight," her hostess said, lowering her diamond lorgnon from her eyes. "But I don't see him in the Schoonmaker box."

Diana felt the urge to lift her own glasses so she might investigate the view herself, but managed to replace the desire with a demure "Oh?"

"Pity your sister wasn't able to marry him. He is a very charming, very *marriageable* young man," Mrs. Gore clucked, unaware of the wounding potential of this comment, so consumed was she by the wasted currency of a handsome groom without a bride. Then she brought the lorgnon back up to her nose and began to survey the other boxes, in which sat all the New Yorkers of their kind, spying on one another and looming over the stalls below, where a very different sort of people went to enjoy music.

"You know," Mrs. Gore went on with the same tactlessness, "I heard a rumor that your sister hadn't died at all, that there certainly would have been a body, and that none of the rest of the story adds up, and that she's perhaps forgotten her identity or been taken up by a band of thieves. . . . I don't suppose there's any truth to it as far as your family knows?"

Diana shook her head faintly and resolved not to look in the direction of the Schoonmaker box for at least another ten minutes. She was trying to appear a little scandalized, in the hope that this would prevent any future speculations on the part of Mrs. Gore about Elizabeth not being dead. She kept her eyes focused on the stage, where Juliette had now entered with dark curls cascading down her back. The chandelier glittered from the center of the room, illuminating the many diamond tiaras and chokers in the boxes, complementing the sumptuous silks of the dresses and the pale skin of their

wearers. Diana felt the glow upon her skin too, and longed to be looked at. And so, after the passing of a lonely minute, she found herself turning to her left to see that, in fact, the Schoonmaker box showcased only Mrs. Schoonmaker—resplendent in petal pink—and the dowdy visage of Henry's younger sister, Prudence. There was nothing to suggest movement in the crimson penumbra behind them.

Diana looked away and tried not to feel disappointed. Her eyes were then drawn from the diva onstage, whose ample white bosom rose and fell with a passion that Diana felt sure she alone in the audience could comprehend, to the lithe form of Penelope Hayes a few boxes to their right.

The lids of her enormous blue eyes were lowered in ennui, and her head was tilted just slightly to the side. She wore a black aigrette in her hair and a dress of black jet that was trimmed with black ribbon at the décolletage. Her long white arms were folded at her lap in a prim way, which must have been part of the saintliness the gossip columns had recently made such point of. Nonetheless, Diana was reminded—as she always was when she saw Penelope—of how Henry had described her on the evening when they'd talked all night. *Savage* was the word he'd used. Her sister, too, had warned her to watch out for Penelope. But what she felt at that moment was not distrust, but vulnerability.

For she could not help but think that Penelope, sitting in

the Hayes family box in the new black dress made especially for her, and her hair set high and back without a silly curlicue anywhere in sight, had known Henry much more than she had. Not better, perhaps, but for longer, and more physically. Down on the stage Roméo had espied Juliette; the tenor was singing of his instantaneous enchantment. Diana's eyes drifted to the stage for only a moment, but when they returned to Penelope, an entirely different look had come over her face. The boredom was gone, and there was a confidence and purposefulness in every aspect of her pose. Just then a barely audible murmuring rose amongst the people in the boxes. The collective gaze had shifted to Diana's left; she looked too, and that was when she saw him.

Henry was taking the seat directly behind his sister. His father moved, at a heavier and slower gait, to the seat beside him, a lumbering performance that was given little notice by the son.

"He does still look sad, I'll give him that," said Mrs. Gore, who had somehow restrained herself from using her glasses for a more privileged view. "But it does nothing to obscure his handsomeness, I'm sure you'd agree, even if he was nearly your brother."

Diana could not find the breath to answer. Nor was she particularly cognizant of the movement in the back of the Newburgs' box, where Webster Youngham, favored architect of New York's nouveau riche, had appeared, diverting, for a moment at least, the attentions of Mrs. Gore.

"May I present Miss Holland," Diana heard her hostess say. This meant that she must, reluctantly, look away from Henry, whose stiff white collar contrasted against his gold-touched skin. "The younger daughter of Mrs. Edward Holland."

"Miss Holland," Mr. Youngham said, kissing her hand. "My condolences for your sister. What a surprise to see you out and about. But I will have to send my compliments to your mother—you are just as lovely as I have always heard."

Diana smiled and lowered her eyes. Back in September she had kissed his assistant in the coatroom during a ball at the new Hayes mansion—a fact she was pretty sure he was unaware of, given his consumption of wine that evening. Of course, that had been before her whole world changed. She peeked in the direction of the Hayeses' box, and found to her dismay that Penelope was gazing across the opera house with the same imperturbable erectness as before.

The murmuring in the boxes had either died down or been buried by the music, which was now loud again. Diana turned, nodding to their visitor as she did. "You must excuse me for a moment—the music is a little much for me," she lied.

As she moved away from her seat, she looked back once,

and saw that Henry's face was turned in her direction. She went faster now, up into the inner box—where Mr. Newburg's eyes fluttered open long enough to give her a reproachful look—and then up into the curving corridor. It was dark, illuminated occasionally by dim wall sconces, and she passed only one or two men making their little visits to their friends' boxes. The corridor brought her around quickly to Box 23, which she knew from the program was the one occupied by the Schoonmakers that season. She paused there to smooth herself over, but already the crimson curtain was being drawn back from the other side.

The shadows fell across his fine, sculptured features, and she could scarcely see his eyes or what was in them. Her chest was as loud as a steam train in her ears. In her imaginings she and Henry had been as intimate as two people had ever been, and so she whispered the line that she had practiced for the last two months:

"I was wondering, Mr. Schoonmaker, when I might again have the pleasure of visiting your greenhouse." Her voice was as faint and delicate as she had ever heard it; the word *greenhouse* was lush in her pronunciation. It had been a word with magical connotations for her ever since she had spent the night in his.

"Di . . ." Henry began at last. She took a little step forward and smiled just slightly in hope that he might return the gesture, might confirm how fully her memory had obsessed him. But her footing was off. "Miss Diana." His voice grew quieter with every word. She noticed that his standing collar was so high that he could not comfortably hang his head. "You know that cannot be."

Suddenly the floorboards below her, the gallery underneath, the subterranean caves holding props and rats and who knew what else—none of it was steady. A heat had come into Diana's cheeks, and she thought of the blue-eyed sureness with which Penelope had looked across the house. "I don't understand," she whispered.

"Perhaps you thought we might—" Henry broke off again, and shook his head as though he were shaking away a fly. There was coldness in his voice when he spoke again: "But you can't think that anymore. No matter what pretty things I said to you, you must know now that they can never come to . . . fruition."

Diana frowned at the curious formality of his phrasing and took a step backward. Henry had had several lovers, by his own admission, and Diana felt herself suddenly to be one of many. She wasn't even sure anymore if she could technically be *called* one of his lovers. "Is this because of Penelope?"

Henry's brow relaxed and he almost smiled. "No . . . not at all. Why would you . . . ? No."

Every word was a struggle for breath "Then why . . . ?"

"I meant all those things, Di." Henry reached and took her hand, which did nothing to bridge the already impassable distance she felt between them. He was a charmer—of course he would try out all his charming gestures on her now. "It's not Penelope. It's not any other girl. But it would be wrong. You might think you wouldn't care about the impropriety now, but I was your sister's fiancé. And your sister"—here he closed his eyes and swallowed—"is dead."

As Henry trailed off, his friend Teddy Cutting appeared in the corridor. He had been Elizabeth's friend, too, Diana knew. His blond hair was parted at one side and slicked to the other, and he came upon them slowly and with a look of concerned disapproval in his face.

"But . . ." Diana stopped herself and the flicker of a smile was put out on her face. *But Elizabeth isn't dead,* she wanted to tell Henry. She would have liked to shout it. She couldn't, of course—she had promised her sister that she wouldn't tell. Telling would ruin everything for Liz.

It was the entr'acte, and now there were dozens of men wearing their black waistcoats passing through the halls on visits of all kinds. Their cigar smoke had filtered out with them. When she felt Henry withdraw his hand she knew there was nothing else for her but retreat. She turned quickly enough, she hoped, that neither man saw the fallen expression on her face.

Diana walked as proudly as she could in the direction of the Newburg box, though she knew already her capacity for smiling was entirely gone. The dress swerved behind her; it had so recently seemed to make her beautiful, but now it was an enormous encumbrance. Weeks of heightened anticipation had been decimated in mere moments, but as she took her seat she felt mainly stung.

Later, at night, in her own room, with the salmon damask darkest in the places from which pictures frames had disappeared, she would see how far this unraveled all her hopes, all the assumptions on which she had based her idea of the future. Only then would she begin to feel so awful and desperate that it was as though, curiously, an enormous cavity had formed within her that could never possibly be filled.

For now, sitting in the opera house, numb to the vibrations of the music, she thought of her mother, and lowered her eyes, and hid her wounded pride. She murmured demurely, just as Mrs. Holland would have liked, for Mr. Newburg and Mrs. Gore and all the rounds of guests who came to their precious opera box. On stage Roméo began to sing, "L'amour, l'amour!" but her enjoyment of the music was entirely gone.

Men at the opera are always promiscuous with their visiting of other people's boxes. It is one of the things that make such evenings tolerable.

—MAEVE DE JONG, *LOVE AND OTHER FOLLIES OF THE GREAT FAMILIES OF OLD NEW YORK*

ENRY HAD WATCHED DIANA'S STUBBORN LITTLE
walk as she went away from him before, but he
did not find any humor in it now. There had been other wom-
en, too, who had walked away from him, but at that point
Henry had always already become bored with them and found
his gaze focused in some new, more desirable direction. He
didn't want to look away now and so remained still, experiencing a sensation of loss that was new to him, and pitiful. He
was grateful that Teddy, still at his side, allowed the moment
to come to its sad end without words. The taste in his mouth
was unbearably bitter.

Men in high collars and white tie were emerging from
the boxes, and he realized that they must have reached the
entr'acte. The men were off to find themselves a drink or perhaps a female companion whose delicate feelings, moved by
the sweep of music, left her open to sweet-talking advances.

"Shall we?" Henry said, turning and meeting Teddy's sea
gray eyes.

"Shall we what?" Teddy answered.

There was a certain involuntary violence to the shrug of Henry's shoulders that followed. He had never in his life experienced such a disconnect between the thing he wanted to do and the thing that he did do; for him his desires had always been a kind of moral compass that led him happily, unquestioningly, to ever more fantastic locations. He was not, like the stage hero, a lover of love. He had sought novelty and good times from his affairs. But in Diana he had found an object for his affections who was earthly beautiful but still light as air. She was as quick and ever changing and as game for anything as he was, but he had dismissed her, and she had not done anything to protest.

"To the bar?" was his eventual answer, and Teddy, like the old friend he was, led him there. The little bar was tucked in the back of the gentlemen's smoking lounge, and old Sam with the drooping mustache waited there under the globe lights in his paisley waistcoat and black bow tie to give refugees from the chatter and surveillance of the boxes their much-needed respite.

"Two whiskey and waters," Teddy said as they approached.

"No water for me."

"All right, Mr. Schoonmaker," Sam answered, with a knowing look. "Mr. Cutting, should I charge this to your box?"

"Yes, Sam, thank you."

They leaned against the bar, and when their drinks came they raised them up. Henry sensed that Teddy wanted to say something, and after he'd placed the glass down on the bar and gestured for a refill, he turned to his friend. "Why are you looking at me like that?"

Teddy ignored the irritation in Henry's voice and responded with characteristic mildness. "You did the right thing."

Henry nodded stiffly, conveying neither conviction nor disagreement. He would have to take Teddy's word for it, since he himself had little to no experience with doing the right thing. He knew it didn't *feel* good, though. Doing right was supposed to be its own reward, that was what his governesses always told him; it was supposed to fill one with inner light.

"It's a simple thing for a man to forget his nature," Teddy was saying, "to get lost in the present and forget how he was, and how he will be. But I know you, and I'm here to remind you what you're like. You lose interest, Henry. Whatever you feel for Diana now, the chances that it will fade . . . and what will be left of her spirit when it does . . . you could ruin the Hollands, Henry, if you're not careful."

Henry acknowledged Sam as his glass was refilled. "You don't know that."

"No, I don't," Teddy said. He was rushing his words,

and Henry knew that he felt bad. He was trying to justify it for both of them. "But I'm being cautious for you. You might think it could be all fun and games, but the way you're connected . . . She'd need more from you than the random girl who catches your eye. There will be others, Henry, and if we were betting on it, my money'd be on your attention span for women growing shorter and not the other way around."

Henry drank. He couldn't argue with this, because it was speculative, and for a moment it even gave him heart. Indeed, his attention to any particular girl was famously short, and soon enough the rotten feeling he was currently experiencing would wane. There would be other distractions, and his life—the one he'd had before he became engaged to Elizabeth Holland—would resume. But, like the suggestion that he had done right, this line of thinking led nowhere, and he was left with the same desire to go to Diana and tell her he'd been an ass, that he hardly knew himself, that she had to forgive him, and a million other little thoughts that popped into his head.

"Elizabeth had restraint, but Diana's too hot. If you make her love you, Henry, there's no telling—"

"Teddy, can't we just . . ." Henry interrupted, gesturing at the refilled glass at his elbow. It was his third or his fourth, he couldn't remember anymore.

"Yes."

They clinked classes dully and then finished the drinks

in silence. The third act had already begun by the time they stumbled back to Box 23. The visiting between the boxes was in full swing, and no one was pretending to listen to the music anymore, except perhaps Diana Holland, situated with the Newburgs, whose box was in the middle of the grand horseshoe of boxes, on the first tier, where all the people like them sat. She inclined forward slightly, her shoulders uneven, her lips slightly parted, and she gazed at the singers on stage as though they were the ones responsible for crushing her heart.

Teddy was sitting behind Prudie and dutifully trying to make small talk, which was what Henry had told him he should do before they left the gentlemen's salon. Prudence had recently turned seventeen, and it hadn't made her any prettier—her appearance as well as her manners suggested many hours spent out of sunlight. Her replies were largely composed of single words, and Henry wondered if he had encouraged this particular conversation as some sort of punishment for Teddy. If his friend thought so, he certainly didn't show it, and when he leaned back into his chair, he turned to Henry and said lightly, "Your sister does know a lot about the stage."

Prudence turned her feral, dark eyes at Henry, making sure he'd caught that last bit.

Henry, who was having trouble focusing his eyes after the whiskey, murmured his assent. Then he looked across the great auditorium and saw Penelope Hayes. She was looking at him with a whisper of a smile, and when she saw that his gaze had fallen on her, she raised her eagle feather fan to the level of her eyes and beat it several times. He looked beyond her, down the wide vista of boxes, where ladies in pairs whispered to each other behind fans or peered through opera glasses while their male escorts, standing behind, offered dry asides. They were looking at him, he felt, scrutinizing him to see whether he looked sad enough about Elizabeth, wondering how broken he was, how long until they could again return to the epic topic of who would marry into the Schoonmaker fortune.

Henry raised his hand in what he intended as a sarcastic gesture, and called out "Hello!" loud enough for the Schoonmakers' neighbors to hear. It was a cry for something Henry could scarcely begin to identify, but it didn't really matter, since onstage the performance continued, and in the seats around him there was only silence.

Nine

Won't you pay a visit to

my box tonight?

—*P*

"*W*AS THAT FOR ME?" PENELOPE WHISPERED. SHE didn't waste time turning toward the person for whom her question was intended. She looked instead across the opera house at Henry, who had just called out a hello loud enough for all the people in private boxes to hear. He'd slumped back into his chair now and, as his gaze was focused on the arms he'd folded across his chest, there was no way to determine whom he'd meant to address.

"Perhaps," Buck answered. He was sitting in the seat just behind Penelope, to the right of her grandfather Ogden, who could no longer hear well enough to appreciate the music, but whose eyesight was sharp enough—when he wasn't drowsing—to comment authoritatively on all the best bosoms in the house. He had never bothered learning the table manners of the Manhattan upper class, despite his lifelong effort to join it, but he had seen that the fault was corrected in his son. Richmond Hayes, Penelope's father, had been a quick study in business as well as personal comportment, which was why he stayed in the inner box at the opera—or better yet, in the gentlemen's smoking room—and kept his eyes to himself.

"No, it wasn't—you're a horrid yes-man," Penelope lashed back affectionately. "He's just giving everyone something to talk about."

"Is that what you children call it these days?" said Mrs. Hayes, who sat beside her daughter along the rail. For a moment Penelope just looked at her mother in surprise—she was usually too concerned with what other people were doing to listen in on her daughter's conversations—but then the older woman's opera glasses were back to her busy little eyes, and she was again looking for some glimmer of scandal out in the audience. Penelope reflected for a moment on the unfortunate number of chins possessed by her mother, on the lackluster quality of her hair that was the result of many years of dyeing it, and on the garish appearance of her too-made-up face.

"Giving all of *them* something to talk about, I should say." Penelope lowered her eyes and tried to force a blush. Her skin had the sheen of china naturally, and embarrassment was not a feeling easily induced in her, but after a few moments she managed something like a petal shade to rise in her sharp cheekbones—not much, but enough, so that if the right matron were looking through her eyeglasses at just that moment, she'd see how ashamed young Miss Hayes was of her grotesque mother. Or the right gossip columnist, for that matter. Then she twisted around and directed her words into her fan. "Buck, could you do me an itty-bitty favor?"

"But of course."

She had written the note hours ago—in fact, she had written it four times, trying to make sure that the paper looked casually ripped enough, that her penmanship was clear enough not to be misunderstood while still suggesting spontaneity. As she had pressed her pen down to produce each letter of those nine little words, she had thought of him. Now she palmed it, and reached behind her to take Buck's hand in hers.

"Please take this to Box 23," she whispered.

Buck inclined his head gently and rose up behind her. Just before he blocked her view of the doings in the inner box, she saw a young man in a black jacket and wing collar enter. She knew it was Henry, come to save her the trouble of sending Buck around with notes, and the skin of her shoulders tingled. But then a second passed and she saw clearly that the features above the little white bow tie belonged—horribly—to Amos Vreewold.

"Mr. Vreewold," Buck was saying. "I have a few visits I have to make. Please take my seat and keep Miss Hayes company."

Amos shook Buck's hand, and then refocused his slightly

downturned eyes on Penelope. He was tall and possessed of a prominent nose that swelled at the center. His dark hair never seemed to agree on quite which direction it was going. There had been a time—a long time ago, it seemed now—when he and Penelope had occasionally disappeared behind trees at garden parties together, and so there was plenty of reason for him to be looking at her that way, as though her demure posturing were for his own particular amusement. Still, his familiarity irritated her; she extended her arm in his direction.

"Miss Hayes, it is always a pleasure," he said, bending to kiss her hand. He sat down behind her, with a flourish of tails, in the seat where Buck had so recently been. "Mrs. Hayes, you are looking lovely this evening," he added, though she was wearing a dress of red satin that, in her daughter's and everybody else's opinion, clung unflatteringly to an excess of flesh.

"Thank you, Amos," Penelope's mother said, without looking away from her opera-glass view. "Is that stomacher on your mother made of real diamonds?"

"Oh, yes," he answered, managing somehow to keep his smirk brief.

Penelope pitied herself that her new persona did not allow for public rudeness to her mother and smiled dewily up at her visitor. "Mr. Vreewold, whatever brings you to our box?"

"Why, you, of course. I haven't seen you out and looking so beautiful since the unfortunate events of October."

"No, I suppose you haven't."

"You must have been very stricken—that's what they all say."

"Well," Penelope turned her eyes back to the stage in a delicate, pained sweep. "I was."

"If you are ever in need of someone to remember Elizabeth with . . ."

Penelope manufactured a little choking sniff. "Thank you."

"I hear other things, as well. . . ."

"Oh?"

Penelope managed to keep her head steady and her gaze on the stage, though she could not help a little shine coming back into her wide blue eyes.

"Yes, all the girls are talking about it. About how brokenhearted Henry is and how melancholy you are, and how it would be the perfect end in a novel if you were to end up married to him. My sister has sent me round to find out if it's true." He leaned forward here, and spoke the next bit into her ear. "I was hoping not."

Penelope brought her fan up over her smile and hoped that the warm feeling of triumph that this had provoked in her was not somehow evident in her posture. "Of course not," she replied in a lowered voice. "It is awfully inappropriate of you to talk so soon of any romance concerning Henry Schoonmaker."

Here her mother's small eyes shifted in her daughter's direction, and Penelope experienced a moment of conflicting emotions. For she knew that this rumor, so satisfying to her ears, was also satisfying to her mother's sense of social ambition, and she found herself inwardly joyful and irritated over the same tidbit.

"All right, then. We'll talk of something else," Amos answered mildly as he leaned back in his seat without the smallest sign of discomfort. And then he did: of hunting dogs and notched lapels, which only reminded Penelope why she had tired of him in the first place. As he droned on, as her mother winked her little eyelids mercilessly at anyone who met her stare, Penelope saw, in the far corner of her vision, that Buck had entered Box 23. She innocently raised her glasses to her face. It was the first time she had indulged the impulse all night, and it took her a few moments—in which she was terrified she'd miss everything—to find the pertinent box in the magnified view.

Then she had Henry very close indeed, framed in a black circle. She watched him greet Buck with characteristic aloofness. Her view was too narrow to know when the note exchanged hands, and Henry must have maintained a straight face as he opened it, because even when he lowered his gaze, he registered no change in expression. But she knew when he realized who its author was, because at that moment he looked up and directly at her.

Penelope let out a tiny involuntary gasp and dropped her opera glasses into her lap, which did nothing to prevent her viewing what happened next. Henry raised his hand to dismiss Buck without even looking him in the eyes and then, his gaze still focused on Penelope, he shook his head twice slowly. He might as well have ripped the little note to shreds. It felt as though he'd slapped her in the face.

"I had better be on my way . . ." she heard Amos say.

Though his presence had receded in her consciousness, she was deeply sorry to hear this. She felt suddenly the importance of Henry, and everybody else, seeing her receive the attentions of bachelors, especially those with old Dutch names and new industrial money. Her whole campaign to seem like a potential bride was forgotten in the wake of Henry's snub. Now all she wanted was to seem an object of desire. But Amos was standing. He had taken her hand to kiss it good-bye.

"Thank you for visiting," she said, fighting to maintain a quiet frailty. "What a relief to have friends like you at times like these."

Amos winked at her, which was not the response she had intended to elicit, and then said a few words to Mrs. Hayes before absenting himself from their box. Penelope tried to lean in the opposite direction of her mother, making the most of the advantageous shadows falling across her pale, soft chest.

She directed her face to one corner of the stage so that she could sneak a few looks over at the Schoonmakers.

She wanted badly to seem elegant and aloof, but there was something like a fever of urgency inside of her that she couldn't bring down. She put one hand over the other in her lap and then reversed them. It would be forever before Buck could make his way back through the corridor and tell her exactly what had happened. But she could see for herself and she knew plenty already. Henry wasn't understanding her plan; he was indifferent to her artful maneuvers. She rearranged her hands again and then fidgeted with the gold chain of her opera glasses until her mother told her to stop, which she did.

"It's official. There are many fine gowns in the audience this evening, but none as fine as those seen in the Hayeses' box," Buck said when he eventually retook his seat. Penelope sensed that he had more compliments at the ready, but she signaled their superfluity with her hand. What did it matter anyway that she was so much lovelier than the other girls when Henry was so blind. The wretched tick of her heart was unbearably loud in her ears, but she could not fidget and she could not frown. She was realizing for the first time in her life what agony it was to experience such unquiet beneath an impeccable veneer.

Ten

With the opening of the opera tonight, we can again expect to see many of the city's most lamentable invalids, those suffering from that insidious disease called *social aspirations,* who will no doubt be trying to elbow their way into making new friends in high places by renting a box, no matter the cost, as have so many strivers before them. We can at least be assured that the crowd they move in is already inoculated.

—FROM THE SOCIETY PAGE OF THE *NEW-YORK NEWS OF THE WORLD GAZETTE,* SATURDAY, DECEMBER 16, 1899

"*A*ND WHO IS THIS?"

Lina put away the view through her opera glasses—which held Vanderbilts and Livingstons and Vreewolds, not to mention gowns by Worth and Doucet, and diamond tiaras, and gentlemen pouring sweet words into the pink-tipped ears of ladies whose names were always in the columns—and turned to see the new arrivals in Mr. Long-horn's box. They were hovering over her in their black jackets and white ties, their beards flecked with gray. They were not, she was a little sad to realize, her peers.

"I present to you Miss Broud, a new addition to our fine city," Mr. Longhorn said with a little flourish. "She comes to us from out west."

Lina lowered her eyelids and hoped that he had not mentioned her geographic origins to account for a dress that was clearly out of date. It used to belong, like all her dresses, to Penelope Hayes; it was of blue chiffon and flounced around her shoulders and neckline in tiers. The color complemented her skin and hair, at least, and now that she'd altered it, the skirt swerved elegantly down past her toes. She had had to borrow one of the laundry girls to help her with the corset, explaining again that she simply could not find a maid whose manners she approved of.

"This is Lispenard Bradley, the painter," Mr. Longhorn went on, indicating the taller of the two men, who was also the one in the brighter shirt. "And this is Ethan Hall Smith."

Lina smiled a little at the visitors and did her best to appear shy, which was more or less the case. She could not help but feel a little quiet surrounded by people who ordered girls like her around from their first waking moments, though shyness was also a precautionary measure to keep her from saying anything that might betray the truth of her biography. Her older sister, Claire, who still worked for the Hollands, loved to read about such scenes in the newspaper, but Lina knew it would be even better if she got to hear about it first-hand. So she concentrated on silently collecting anecdotes.

She turned away from the men bashfully—although she was pleasantly aware that they continued to look at her—and rested a bony elbow on the brass rail. Down below her, on the first floor of the opera house, were all those people in rows. Only a few weeks ago—perhaps only a few hours ago—they had been her betters. And now she floated above them, watching and being watched on another tier. She could almost feel the warm embrace of a highborn viewership; all around her they were looking and wondering who she was.

"Perhaps I may paint your portrait someday?" Mr. Bradley leaned toward her from where he stood, at the entrance to the inner box. He smiled and his mustache spread toward his ears. "You have a most unique look."

"Thank you," Lina answered. The idea of a rendering of her features on canvas was almost too grand to get hold of, though a practical element did enter her thoughts: She would need a new dress for that, too. She remembered quite exactly how Elizabeth always wore a new dress for a sitting. "I'd like it very much."

Mr. Bradley nodded as though to say it were confirmed, and from the expression on his face Lina could see that he liked the idea of it. There was a silence that followed in which the four people in Mr. Longhorn's box looked from one to the other, and though they were all smiles and the general mood never reached a level of awkwardness, Lina began to feel just slightly exposed. After all, the great Elizabeth Holland would certainly not have appeared in a venue like this with three men and no chaperone. Perhaps Mr. Longhorn, who was of an older generation, might be considered a chaperone of a kind; yet her instincts told her that now was the time to rise, make a demure little gesture, and go to the ladies' lounge for a while.

Mr. Longhorn and his friends responded with loud encouragements for her to stay, and she promised a quick return. As she walked, at an even, straight-backed gait, she congratulated herself on knowing when to absent herself, when to make herself rare. She was developing the instincts of a lady—that was what Elizabeth had possessed, the thing that had drawn Will to her. But Liz was dead, and Lina was learning more every day, and when she saw Will next, she would have that something, and it would draw him to her instead.

If she had imagined that she would get to practice her new mien in the ladies' lounge, however, she was disabused of the notion upon entering it. The women who rested there, on low velvet couches, glanced up at her entrance and cast looks in her direction that were quite the opposite of the appreciative glances she had received from Mr. Longhorn's friends. Their expressions were blank and their shoulders turned away from her at unwelcoming angles. The color rose in Lina's cheeks, and she found herself for the first time longing for the invisibility that came with being a lady's maid. Her mouth opened, but then she realized that she didn't even begin to know how she should start a conversation with any of these women. She was an outsider again.

"Excuse me," Lina heard herself say. There was a heat rising in her chest, under all those layers of dress and underthings.

A woman in pale red with fluffy blond hair and black lashes pushed herself up on her elbow and said, "Are you lost?"

Lina's blush flamed up, and when she heard the twitters this inspired, she decided to leave. She had only just turned her back on the laughter, however, when another girl came rushing through the heavy damask curtains and ran full into her.

"Oh," Diana Holland said. She appeared stricken— Lina noticed that even as her own breath shortened and she began to realize, with no small amount of agitation, how one mistake had piled on another. Diana's expression had already changed into one of recognition; in a moment, the truth would be out. Then the younger Miss Holland—the only Miss Holland—blinked and looked out at the other ladies, and when she looked back at Lina her expression had changed again. "Oh . . . I was hoping I would run into you," she said loudly as she took Lina's arm and steered her toward a private little settee covered by silk cushions in the corner.

Lina's breath came back to her as she sat. She might have felt relief if she hadn't been so confused. There was a long pause in which Diana closed her eyes and let some private pain pass across her features. She was wearing a dress of pastel green that Lina remembered unpacking from Elizabeth's trunk upon her return from Paris at the end of the summer, and her brown curls were falling out of place as usual. When

Diana's lids fluttered open again, she didn't look exactly overjoyed, but there was a certain gladness in her expression.

"Oh, Lina," she said quietly. "I'm so happy to see a friendly face right now. But what are you doing here?"

"I'm a guest." Lina looked out across the room and saw that several ladies were pretending not to watch them. They were all far away enough, however, that if she kept her voice low she wouldn't be heard. "Of Mr. Longhorn's."

"Carey Lewis Longhorn?" Diana asked, her eyebrows arcing upward.

"Yes, and actually"—here Lina's voice broke a little, though she forced herself to push on—"I like to be called Carolina now, if you don't mind. It's my given name, what they call me out west, where I'm from," she concluded, her voice now becoming almost inaudible. She willed Diana to understand her intent and play along.

The light danced in Diana's wide, dark pupils. The women across the room shifted in their seats, rustling their gowns and murmuring to one another. "I like the sound of that better, actually," Diana said after several moments.

"You do?" Lina tried to look more serious than surprised, though she had in truth lost all sense of what her face must look like. She had left the Hollands on the worst possible terms, and though she and Diana had never fought, she had also never considered that the younger Holland might have an opinion about Lina that was separate from her sister's. "Father was in copper smelting, out west," she heard herself say, "but they're both dead now. That's why I came here."

"Ah, yes, I remember." Diana nodded seriously. "You met my sister, Elizabeth, in Paris—she told me your story."

"Yes." Lina hurried to make herself say a phrase she never thought she'd utter: "Dear Elizabeth."

"You're like the heroine of some novel." Diana paused thoughtfully and took Lina's hand. "Be careful of the tragic fall at the end, though—anyone who rises too quickly is supposed to get one, and I wouldn't want that for you."

"Thank you, Miss. . . ." As Lina trailed off she noticed that one of the ladies across the room, who was dressed in spangled gold satin, was smiling at her. Diana was being so nice about everything, Lina almost wanted to tell her about the rest of her plan, and meeting Will. But some superstition rose in her, and she decided she might jinx it if she revealed too much. "Thank you, Di."

Diana leaned her head of curls back against the cushions, but Lina could not possibly help but look across the room of women who a moment ago had been thinking unkind thoughts about her and now considered her one of them. She was overcome by the frightening exhilaration of having gotten away with something that was near impossible.

In an instant she was brought back to a luxury store for

ladies of years ago where her mother, when she was the Holland girls' governess, used to run errands. On one occasion Lina had been so taken with a set of hair combs that they had appeared in her dreams, and on the next trip to the store, she had reached out and tried to grasp them from the display table. She had been too furtive, too uncalculating, to grab both, but it hardly mattered. The thrill she'd felt on possessing even one of those gilt filigreed objects could not possibly have been increased by the finding of a practical use for it. She would sneak little looks at the glittering comb from time to time, when she was alone, and the sight of it always inspired that same dangerous sensation inside of her. It was the same with her now, except that the feeling was more tangible and the thing she had gotten away with far more important.

She carried the feeling with her back to Mr. Longhorn's box, after she and Diana had parted in the hall, where he continued to introduce her to whatever friends stopped by even as the performers below reached their sad, feverish end. She could see her prettiness reflected in these visitors' eyes, and knew that she would appear that way to Will when she was with him next. Lina's confidence grew with her sense of elation, and she felt even more acutely the glimmering golden light of the chandelier as it fell across her forehead and clavicles, the gay fizz of the champagne that Mr. Longhorn served her, the vast grandeur of the auditorium, which already felt like one of

her places. She had been a success at the opera—it was almost like an object she could hold, a piece of evidence that suggested she might almost be ready to go west.

"Thank you, Mr. Longhorn," she said when she had finally, regretfully reached the door to her room in the Netherland.

"It is I who should thank you," he answered, with a gallant tip of the head and a kiss on her gloved hand. He stood back and waited, with the lines from his nostrils to the corners of his mouth becoming a little extra pronounced and a sharp twinkle in his eye. She smiled back at him—she could hardly have stopped—before slipping past the door.

The night was still far too vivid for her to have slept, but that wouldn't have happened anyway. No sooner had the lock turned in its groove did she became aware of a scene that would haunt any potential dreams. The magical transformation of her room had occurred—the bed made up, the floor swept, her breakfast things long gone and fresh flowers appeared in their place—but there was still one troubling detail.

Her little silk purse with the leather drawstring was lying in the middle of the floor. The purse itself never moved from the drawer in her wardrobe, where it slept under a heap of stockings, but there it was, on the plum-colored rug, perfectly evident under the bright new electric lights. She might have dashed to it, in the hope that everything could be explained by absentmindedness, but she knew already that its contents were gone.

Eleven

A great many servants are necessary to run an elegant house these days, and in New York a fleet of twelve is considered rather modest. Those unfortunate ladies who make do with fewer—or, heaven forbid, can only support one or two—must expect that they will take on some of the housework themselves.

—*LADIES' STYLE MONTHLY*, DECEMBER 1899

$\mathcal{D}$IANA WOKE ON THE MORNING FOLLOWING THE opera with the same feeling of emptiness and a need for a several other things besides. Her mouth was dry and her hair was a fright, and she didn't feel that it was at all within her power to make the bed. Ordinarily Claire, in her capacity as Diana's lady's maid, would have brought her water and hot chocolate in the morning, but that whole routine seemed a little silly once their money started running out and they were forced to let some servants go. Mrs. Holland still viewed Will's disappearance as a defection based on some knowledge of the family finances, and since then they had had to let go of their laundress and scullery girl; and Mr. and Mrs. Faber, who had been the butler and head housekeeper, respectively, had left only last week when it had become apparent that payment would be from then on an uncertain prospect. With all the extra work this made for Claire, Diana had heroically relieved her of any extraneous cosseting duties.

But on this Sunday morning, Diana did not feel in the

least bit heroic. She didn't feel like anything. The sensation of being hollow showed no signs of abating, and even so, eating was not among her multitude of wants. She wanted water, she wanted to look pretty, she wanted to be embraced and petted. Though she did not want to see Henry in the least—the very idea made her stomach feel weak and her eyes burn—she would have liked a better explanation of the rejection he had served her the previous night. She would gladly have had something that sounded like good news to share with her mother. But most of all she longed for her older sister, who had so often been an aloof, judgmental girl when she had still lived in the Holland house, but who now seemed like the only person really qualified to assess Diana's situation.

Eventually Diana forced herself up. She found some strength and used it to make herself look presentable. She put on a long black skirt and an ivory shirtwaist with tiny pearl buttons—a uniform that would have made any girl less combustible than Diana look put together. But her character was of the sort not easily dominated by clothes, and so it was in a mildly disheveled state that she went down the main stairs of her family town house and into the shadowy tranquility of the front hall. The Persian carpets that ran down the stairs to the front door remained, though many of the little pictures that had once dotted the walls had been removed, leaving sad little holes in their place. At that very moment there were several

frames stacked near the front entrance, a sure sign that the dealer would be by again soon.

Not long ago, the selling of material objects had seemed to Diana a romantic shedding of things, a return to essentials, but her mind had since changed. It had been easy to be careless about things when she thought she had the love of Henry Schoonmaker; she saw that the disappearance of bric-a-brac was a more painful business now. Such were her thoughts as she drew back the heavy, polished pocket door, which caught a little in its track, and entered her family's parlor.

"Good morning," her aunt Edith said, standing upon Diana's entrance. She was wearing an old white dress with a narrow waist and somewhat more volume in the rear than was the fashion anymore. It caused Diana to imagine Edith as a young woman, when her hair still fell in dark little curls and when she still thought of the world as wide with possibilities.

"Good morning," Diana answered, crossing to the little grouping of bergère chairs where her aunt had been sitting with a tray of tea things.

"You had better go straight up to your mother." Aunt Edith's eyes shifted downward, as though she disliked dwelling on what she was about to express. "You know she sometimes tends to the dramatic, but she has a bad look about her."

"Oh," Diana said, receiving this comment as more of a rebuke than it had been intended.

If she had been looking more closely, she might have seen that her aunt's face in fact showed signs of real fear and distress for her sister-in-law. Although Edith did not share her brother's wife's love for a rigid social code, the women had been living under the same roof for some years and had come to a kind of mutual understanding. For Mrs. Holland's part, she had always liked Edith as much as she liked anyone possessed of an important surname and a much-admired face, and of course she believed, like all the Old New York people, that family should have a united front and that any differences were to be kept to oneself.

"Is she ill?" Diana asked after a pause. She was thinking of how little she had tried to engage Spencer Newburg last night, and how casually she had dispensed with Percival Coddington the day before, with a tinge of regret. Of course she could never love either of them. But the idea of having disregarded her mother's desires so completely seemed less funny today.

"I don't know." Edith observed Diana and spoke slowly. "She just says that she can't leave the bed. I think you had better go now."

Diana nodded, though her feet were heavy. When she had at last reached the door, Edith added: "Don't forget to tell her how much you charmed Mr. Newburg."

The way the older woman continued to look at her—

hopefully, encouragingly—made Diana wonder, as she lingered on the threshold, if she looked as much like a girl in trouble as she was. For it was beginning to dawn on her, despite the clamoring of her wounded feelings, that if Henry wasn't as in love with her as she had thought—if he wasn't in love with her at all—then she was going to have to face some truly unappealing choices.

It had never taken her so long to climb those stairs, and when she reached the second floor she slowed to a stop. The heavy carved door to her mother's room was ajar, and she could see the diffuse light coming through the crack.

"Diana . . . ?" her mother called from inside the bedroom. Diana stepped forward. She leaned against the door and peeked past it. Her mother's eyes were closed and her head rested back against a pile of white pillows. Her hair, which was usually so carefully arranged, if not also covered by a widow's cap, now streamed down across her shoulders. Her face was very pale. "Are you there?" she called again, her voice still a little sharp even when it strained.

A kind of agitation had come over Diana, and she knew that she couldn't face her mother. She was being counted on to give assurances, but the reality of Henry not loving her was too new for her to hide; the rawness of her abject position would foil any attempts to conceal it.

Elizabeth would have been able to maintain a façade.

Elizabeth would have put her mother's mind at ease, however temporarily. Diana, doubtful of her ability to do either of these things to even a slight degree, was already hurrying down the stairs. She was wrapping herself in a coat and scarf. She was moving past the front door onto the enclosed iron porch and down to the street, all the while fixating on the idea that she must get a message to her sister.

Coming out of the downtown Western Union office a few hours later, Diana hardly felt any better but was slightly warmed by the sense that she had something to look forward to. She had cabled her sister, via Will Keller, all the latest traumas and was now somewhat comforted by the vague notion that she might receive an inspired response. Perhaps Elizabeth would know a reason her little sister's life was all coming apart at the seams. At the very least, Diana's many weighty problems no longer felt like her problems alone, and for this reason she was moving with some of her characteristic chin-up confidence. She was also in a part of town where she was unlikely to meet any of her acquaintances, and she felt somewhat freed from her own identity and so quite able to walk without subterfuge.

This assumption was swiftly put away by the sound of her own name, spoken not particularly loudly but with perfect clarity by someone following her through the brass-framed plate glass doors of the office and into the bright, cold afternoon. She paused before turning to face the stranger. The sun was in her eyes, and it took a few more seconds before she recognized Davis Barnard. He was wearing the same fur hat as the last time they'd met, and one of his sharp dark brows was cocked.

"Good afternoon, Mr. Barnard," she said. The spirit of her sister must have arrived somehow, for though she had no more happy faces, the corners of Diana's mouth sprang up into something like a polite smile. "I'm surprised to see you so far downtown."

"I had to send a telegram. Can't be too careful of spies in the newsroom, my dear. Anyway, I was about to say the same thing to you," Barnard answered dryly, with an amused twist to his thin lips. "Maybe the rumors are true, and you are cabling Elizabeth in London, where she has run off to marry the fifth in line to the British throne?"

Diana had always considered herself a good fibber, but she knew that the expression she wore now could disguise nothing. She turned her face to the street, with its worn cobblestones and indifferent midday traffic.

"Oh, Diana." Barnard lowered his eyes, in which Diana momentarily caught a glimpse of something like shame. "I didn't mean to make light about Elizabeth."

His voice quieted when he pronounced the name, and he watched two men in frock coats pass. They were dressed for business, but they were as plain as the buildings with their workaday painted wood signs and small glass storefronts that lined the street.

"It's all right." Diana met his eyes to show him that what she said was true.

"But I'm glad to have caught you—I think you have some information that I would give a great deal to know. . . ."

Diana, sensing that she was again nearing the topic of her sister and thus a position requiring a level of deception that she was not currently capable of, quickly turned hot. "I really don't know what you mean."

"The young lady accompanying Carey Lewis Longhorn at the opera last night?" Barnard urged gently. "I heard you were talking with her in the ladies' lounge. Everyone was buzzing about it, and of course they all want to know who she could be."

"Oh." Diana bit her lip. With all the other heartrending going on, she had nearly forgotten about running into Lina, and had entirely neglected to tell Claire how grand her little sister looked. But reading it in the columns would be even better.

"I'm sure it feels a little uncomfortable, for a lady like you . . . but perhaps this will help." Her interlocutor produced an envelope. It was edged with gold, and when she peeked inside, she saw a twenty-dollar bill.

"Thank you," Diana said, taking it. So this was how life was, she thought with a faint smile: It wore you down until you emerged at its wildest, most unexpected ends. "I believe the young lady you were speaking of is named Carolina Broud," Diana began cautiously. "She met Elizabeth in Paris in the spring, and was offering me condolences." Once she had begun telling the lie, Diana found she didn't mind at all and even wanted to spin it further. "She's an orphan, you know, and they quite understood each other, having both lost fathers. The Broud money was from copper smelting, I believe, and it has brought Carolina to the city with the idea of seeing something of society. . . ."

"And is the old bachelor looking for love again?"

Diana tried her best to look scandalized and then replied that she hadn't the faintest.

"Ah, well. It's an excellent item just the same. Can I offer you a ride home, Miss Di?"

Diana knew that it wouldn't look right, but then she told herself that things only looked wrong when there was someone to see you. The air was bracing and the walk back uptown would take far more strength than she had. Barnard gestured to his phaeton across the cobblestone street and, with the memory of the gilt-edged envelope still fresh in her mind,

Diana found herself disinclined to flat-out refuse any of his offers.

"Thank you," she said. "Though I must insist that you not be too familiar. Diana is my given name."

Barnard tipped his head, as though to say, "As you wish," and then Diana accepted his proffered arm.

Twelve

TRANSCONTINENTAL CABLE MESSAGE

THE WESTERN UNION TELEGRAPH COMPANY

TO: *Will Keller*

ARRIVED AT: 25 *Main Street,*
San Pedro, California
1:25 p.m., Sunday, December 17, 1899

*Henry is not in love except perhaps
with Penelope—think I may have been
very selfish—two servants left—no monies
whatsoever—Mother won't get out of bed—
she's not well and I don't know what to
do—help me—D*

THE DINNER ELIZABETH SERVED THAT NIGHT would be far superior to the scarcely touched beans of the previous evening. For one thing, there would be real meat—steaks bought that day in town—and potatoes roasted in a pan over the fire and Waldorf salad. She had gone and purchased these items herself, that afternoon. She'd purposefully avoided the post office, which had previously been her single, obsessive destination.

"Did you get a letter today, Mrs. Keller?" they had asked her at the general store. They believed that she was Will's wife, which was what she had told them to explain her presence out there alone with two men, and they knew how frequently she asked if there was anything for her or her husband in the mail. She didn't like this lie—it was against everything she had been brought up to believe to live as man and wife without being married—but it was preferable to publicly appearing to do so.

"Oh, no," Elizabeth had replied, blushing under her hat. "I'm just here for groceries today," she added softly.

The other reason was that Will was going to help her with the cooking, which he seemed to know something of, since his living quarters had been so close to the Holland kitchen and because, when he was thirteen and growing so quickly, it had been necessary for him to become good friends with their cook and learn from her. It was Will who insisted they should celebrate. Finding oil meant that soon they would be living at a whole new level, and this made him feel much better about spending some of his savings to have a real dinner. Elizabeth had gone to pick up those necessary things while he and Denny began to put together their makeshift rig, trying to make it just as safe and effective as one of those huge ones the big oil companies used.

On the long walk back to the cabin, she had reflected on Will's ability to save. He was always working hard, she knew that, but it was an irony she could not fail to appreciate that he had accumulated money while the family that employed him frittered theirs away. And then he had worked to save more while he waited for her in San Francisco. There was money for steak, when it was called for, and she mused in a far-off way about how Will, not Henry, would have been the better person on whom to pin the family's hopes for salvation.

That hardly seemed to matter anymore, though. Now that she saw how assuredly Will would make her rich again, she found she didn't even need it. She knew what money would mean for her mother, for the rest of the family, but for her it no longer held any power. It almost made her laugh—she found herself smirking as she pulled back the canvas flap that served as a door to the cabin—how much she had worried over losing her dresses and her objects and all her trinkets and jewels. Now that they were gone, she never thought of them.

She continued thinking about all that constituted the boy she loved until he returned, his eyes bright with excitement and his whole body animated with the work of the day. There was that usual smell of sweat and soap when he came through the door, and a new one—it was something like sulfur, and it reminded Elizabeth of intense industry and all the other things he was cut out for.

"Lizzy," he said. He took the paring knife with which she had been removing the skins of the potatoes out of her hand and laid it on the table, and then his arms took her up. After the kiss he met her eyes, and his lips were drawn back so far it was impossible to think he might ever frown again.

There was a new shine there and a new buoyancy in his step that reminded her of that time in their lives when they first admitted they were in love. That it was not some childhood game in which they imagined being married as grownups but something far more real. That was when she had ordered a delivery entrance installed between the kitchen and the carriage house so that she could slip down to see him at night. Neither of them had yet turned sixteen, and the complications of their situation had not fully dawned on them.

"Where's Denny?" She rested her head on his chest and took in a warm breath. He was holding her to him with his hand and had turned to assess what still needed to be done for dinner.

"I sent him into town for whiskey." Will picked up a piece of chopped apple from the table and put it in his mouth.

"Oh, I could have gotten that!"

"A real lady, buying alcohol like any roustabout?"

Elizabeth pursed her lips. "I'm not sure they have those scruples out here," she said.

"No, but you do." He swallowed the apple and then gently tapped her nose. There had been moments since Elizabeth's arrival in California when she felt self-conscious about all her old manners, which were more difficult to discard than the desire for things or the instinct to marry where money already was. But then there were moments like these when Will put her at ease and when she knew that all the things that constituted her self were as sweet to him as he was to her. He kissed her forehead, and then they continued to work at the celebration dinner without words in the flickering lamplight.

It was into this pleasant silence that Denny Planck returned. Elizabeth turned and acknowledged him with a small smile and nod as he came through the door and thought, as she often had before, how he might be handsome if it weren't for the skin of his cheeks, which were pitted with smallpox scars, and his somewhat oversize ears. For his height gave him natural advantages, and there was a sweet willingness to follow others in his brown eyes. He was heavier than Will and less articulate, but Will liked and trusted him, and that was enough to make her like him, too.

"Smells good," he said with a grin.

"Denny!" Elizabeth's laugh rang out. "We haven't even started cooking yet."

Will went over and threw an arm over his friend's shoulder. Elizabeth wasn't sure she'd ever seen her sweetheart in such a state of conviviality. There was confidence in his every movement and a looseness in his limbs.

"Looks good, then," Denny replied, wearing the same grin. "Here," he went on, removing a bottle wrapped in paper from the crook between his arm and his side. "I brought the whiskey."

"Bravo!" Will took the bottle and unwrapped it and threw the paper into the fire. Grabbing three of the little mismatched mason jars, which had once held small amounts of jam or sardines, he poured them each a finger of brown liquid. Then he passed the jars around and raised his high. "To our success!"

They clinked their glasses and drank. Elizabeth had been known to drink a moderate amount of champagne at balls in New York, but she had never tasted whiskey, and it burned her tongue. She didn't mind, though. It all felt like part of the lucky new sunlight that had fallen on them.

"To our success," Denny seconded as he placed the little jar back on the table. "Oh, and Will, there was this for you at the post office. They told me Mrs. Keller"—here Denny winked in a way Elizabeth would have preferred he'd not— "might have missed it on her earlier foray into town."

Elizabeth pretended to go back to mixing together the walnuts and apples and celery in the chipped blue tin bowl as Will set down his glass. He moved away to rip open the sealed yellow telegram, and she turned to watch him even as Denny sat down at the table and picked up a handful of walnuts, which he began shoveling into his mouth. She wanted to stop wondering what the contents of the telegram said, but found that she couldn't bring her attention back to the salad. After a moment, Will looked up at her and she saw that the celebration had gone out of his face.

"Oh, Liz," he said.

"What is it?"

Will looked at Denny, who was absorbed in pouring himself a second glass of whiskey, and back to Elizabeth. He tilted his head toward the door, indicating that she should follow him. "Denny, we'll be right back, all right?" Then, summoning some of the previous gaiety: "Slow down with the whiskey or we won't have anything left to celebrate with."

Denny acknowledged this comment with a laugh, and then they left him and went out into the darkness. They walked for several moments, away from the low light of the cabin, before either of them spoke. All of the orange had gone out of the sky while Elizabeth had been inside, and where the purple up above had turned to black, pins of light had started to emerge.

Will's voice was the first to break the quiet. "I knew this would happen," he began quietly. "I just didn't think it would be so soon."

"What did it say?" The look on his face provoked a feeling of dread, and she could barely even whisper now.

"It was from Diana. She says she needs help, and that your mother is not well."

Elizabeth felt the cold sweep over her body. "Is it serious?"

Will shook his head firmly. "It just says that she's ill, Lizzie. It's pretty brief, and you know your sister isn't a realist. There's no way to know exactly what's happening."

All of a sudden Elizabeth flashed on a vision of her mother, broken and bedridden. The thought of her so reduced was more terrible and heartbreaking than she could have begun to anticipate. "I have to go to her."

Will's eyes were wide and watchful as he nodded. "I'll go with you, then."

Elizabeth put her hand over her mouth and tried to keep herself from crying. There was that bruised feeling in her chest that always preceded tears, but she told herself that would be very selfish, that her mother was too far away to see how she felt and she would only be crying over her own guilty behavior. "Oh, Will. The oil."

"It's been there a long time." A smile wavered on his lips, and then he reached out for her. She felt the whole spread of his palm against the small of her back; his other hand lightly brushed the hair back from her face. "It will be there when we come back. The train leaves San Pedro at noon tomorrow."

Elizabeth let her body relax into his. All of her fears for her family, which she had been keeping at bay, were back with her now. She wondered if she would be able to sleep that night, or any night before she was with them again. She tried not to think the worst, but already her fretful imagination had gotten away from her.

Thirteen

Of all the misfortunes that seem to have befallen the Holland family as of late, no rumor has stuck so painfully as the one that Miss Elizabeth is alive and being held by some nefarious cabal or other, which some ladies might view as a fate worse than death. Of course, if it is money that her captors want, they will be sorely disappointed in their ransom. . . .

—FROM *CITÉ CHATTER*, MONDAY, DECEMBER 18, 1899

"AT LEAST YOU LOOK VERY WELL," AGNES JONES said, with a furtive look at the dark green velvet jacket that Diana was wearing. This was a non sequitur as far as Diana was concerned, as there had been no mention of what exactly Diana's appearance was a silver lining to. Previously they had been talking about the weather, which was bright and brisk. If she had not been annoyed, she might have considered that Agnes was politely alluding to the continual disappearance of objects from the Holland parlor, or the recent untoward rumors about Elizabeth, or the lack of a fire going even when there were patches of ice on the sidewalk.

"Thank you," Diana replied, haughtily arranging the lapels of her jacket. It was voluminous in the upper sleeves and narrow at the wrists and waist, and the color brought out the russet tones of her dark curls. She had bought it yesterday, with her gossip earnings, and though even a ready-to-wear piece was an extravagance that she could hardly justify, it was turning out quite useful in an unheated house. She needed it to make her feel better in more profound ways as well, which was not something she expected her guest to understand. Agnes, Diana thought rather ungenerously, knew nothing of the sorrows of beautiful girls. "As do you."

Agnes shrugged modestly. She was wearing a walking dress of moth brown cheviot that did not fit her right in the least and a bonnet that entirely overwhelmed her square little head. Diana noted these facts without remorse. Agnes had been one of Elizabeth's friends—a pity project of Liz's, really, as Agnes had had an unfortunate beginning in life and was now an orphan of minor financial independence—but none of the other Hollands had ever had the patience for her. She still insisted on coming by for tea even after the Hollands had suspended their "day" for visitors, a few weeks after Elizabeth's passing, ostensibly because it reminded her of her lost friend. Even before Mrs. Holland had turned ill, she'd taken to hiding upstairs on these occasions.

"This room isn't the same without Elizabeth," Agnes presently observed. She cast her eyes over its oak pocket door and wainscoting, its embossed olive leather paneling, its scattered antique chairs. The room was more sparsely furnished than before, it was true.

"No, nothing ever will be," the younger Miss Holland replied with an impatient wave of her hand. The girls had finished their tea, which Diana had made herself to save Claire the trouble. She had steeped it perhaps a little too long, and the strength of the tea, combined with her utter lack of appetite over the last few days, had given her the jitters, which had the not unexpected side effect of making her conversation more flip than usual.

"I must be going," Agnes went on after a pause.

"Yes, I guess you'd better."

At the door, Diana managed to feign a little politeness and urge her guest to come again. Elizabeth would have liked it, she told herself, which was more or less true. Then she turned, into the dark foyer, and looked down at the unpolished silver tray on the floor—the ornate piece of furniture that it used to sit on was apparently another casualty of the Hollands' current lack of funds. There were a few cards there. She picked them up out of a vague curiosity—after all, if she were to keep doing business with Barnard, she would have to pay more attention to the comings and going of the sorts of people who left cards—and came to a stop at the one with Teddy Cutting's name on it. She turned it over and saw the words:

Miss Diana,

I am sorry to have missed you,

but it has all been arranged

for Monday night. I will

come by in my carriage
at seven o'clock for you.
Yours, Teddy

Diana had always found Teddy rather dull—he was the sort of boy who worshipped sweetly pale things like Elizabeth—but he held a special interest to her as one of Henry's particular friends. It drove her up to the second floor, holding her long black skirt back from her quickly moving feet. She rapped twice on her mother's door and then entered without waiting for an answer. Since Diana had last peeked into the room, the white curtains had been drawn down from the canopy, and the heavy chintz drapes of the north-facing windows had been closed. This change in atmosphere did not deter Diana, who continued on to the bed and perched on the white matelassé bedspread.

She wasted no time before saying, "Mother, I'm glad to hear you're feeling better."

Mrs. Holland, whose head was resting on a pile of pillows and whose shut lids were veined with blue, paused a moment before replying: "I am not feeling very well at all. I have been worrying about you all night—where did you run off to yesterday morning?"

"I only went out for a little air," Diana said in a moment. She wondered if telling her mother the truth—that she had been sending a telegram to her living, breathing sister—would have alleviated all of the gloom.

"After what happened to Elizabeth, one would think you would be a little kind and wouldn't give me so much cause to worry."

She opened her eyes then and gave Diana a look that was very difficult to meet. The daughter held it as long as she could, and then moved her hand across her face to tuck a few hairs back into their upward arrangement. "Sorry, Mother," she answered grudgingly. "But what does this note from Mr. Cutting mean?"

"Ah, Mr. Cutting..." Mrs. Holland's eyelids drooped closed again. "Well, my dear, since Mr. Newburg and Mr. Coddington do not seem to have taken any interest in you, I thought you might do well to see one of Elizabeth's old friends, and it happens that Mr. Cutting was looking for a young lady to accompany him to a dinner that his married sister is giving this evening."

"How did you arrange . . . ?" Diana began, mystified. At that particular moment she wasn't sure whether to believe in her mother's illness or not.

"You have not forgotten who you are, I hope, Diana." Here Mrs. Holland's eyes opened as she turned her face at such an angle that what light there was in the room caught against the underside of her sharp chin. "Who *we* are."

Her gaze fell to the fitted waist of the new jacket, and for a moment Diana's breath caught at the thought that she was about to be asked where it had come from.

"I'm sorry it has been so cold, Diana," her mother nearly whispered. "Claire told me that the firewood deliveries have stopped, and I have given her funds to pay the bill."

With that her eyes closed again and Diana took her leave. As she returned to her room she could not help but wonder what this Teddy business meant. It was curious and inscrutable news, and what it indicated about her mother's state was even more obscure. Clearly Mrs. Holland had been out of bed the day before and with enough of her old influence to arrange for her daughter to be escorted for an evening by one of New York's most eligible. But that she had looked at the brilliant green of Diana's jacket and felt sympathy for her daughter's being cold rather than growing suspicious over an unfamiliar piece of clothing was strange and alarming. That was not Louisa Gansevoort Holland at all. Ordinarily she was an obsessive cataloguer of material goods. That something new and fine had escaped her notice did not in the least bode well.

Diana sat in the gold wing chair in her room, unsettled and a little restless. She pushed her head back into the chair's cushioned upholstery and ran her fingers along its mahogany arms contemplatively. After some thought, she came to the conclusion that there was nothing to do but choose a dress impressive enough to catch Teddy's eye. That was the way to make use of the evening. He would have to more than notice her—he would have to be taken in by her beauty. Then he would feel compelled to immediately describe it, in lavish terms, to his friend Henry.

Fourteen

Many have already noted that the elder states-man of New York bachelors, Mr. Carey Lewis Longhorn, was sighted for the first time with a young lady of unique but undoubted pretti-ness at the opening of the opera on Saturday evening. Some have speculated that she is the one to finally tame that eternally unattached fellow. But it is I alone who have exclusively learned her identity: She is Miss Carolina Broad, a western heiress to a copper-smelting fortune, and she intends to grace our city for some time. I will inform as more becomes known of this enchanting young lady. . . .

—FROM THE "GAMESOME GALLANT" COLUMN IN THE *NEW YORK IMPERIAL*, MONDAY, DECEMBER 18, 1899

$\mathscr{L}$INA SHOULD HAVE KNOWN THAT THE ADVENT OF her first true moment of glory would coincide with the complete annihilation of all her dreams. Also, that were her name ever to appear in the columns, it would naturally be misspelled. If Will happened to glance over the columns he likely wouldn't even wonder if the girl mentioned was the one he used to know. She had been born into the plain world, and it now seemed very likely that she would die in the plain world as well. She had taken her desire to be grand one step too far, and now the sight of her full name, *Carolina*, in print made her feel a little sick with herself for having dared to imagine such a fine future for someone so clearly destined to be common. She had paid through Friday at the hotel: after that would commence the long descent Diana had warned her about.

There had first been the fact of her money being gone. This had been an eventuality, of course—it was more than half gone in a short period of time. But it would have lasted her a little longer, and then it would have taken her away from the city and all of its expenses to find Will out west. She had been planning to carefully budget out the remainder any day now, exactly how much it would cost to travel to Chicago and from there to San Francisco. Then she might need more, to travel down the coast to one of those towns she had heard Will speak of before, places he'd no doubt read about in one of his books. And of course she had hoped to arrive in Elizabeth Holland–style grandeur. For all of it to be gone at once, and for it to have taken all her plans with it!

She had sat with this new fact for a good part of the night, and that was when the anger came. For the money had not disappeared into thin air. Someone had it. Someone was already spending it, and probably on something much less important than finding the love of one's life. Surely whoever had it was someone whose name had not just appeared— correctly or not—in the "Gamesome Gallant" column in the Monday early edition.

She wondered, at first, if the thievery weren't somehow Mr. Longhorn's doing. It was a little too good to be believed, after all, that her first trip to the opera should bring her into such a very fine box. But he was enormously rich—that fact was in no way in doubt—so why would he bother with her paltry fortune? Then she thought of Robert, Mr. Longhorn's valet, but of course Robert had been waiting at the carriage outside the opera house the whole evening. She thought of

the front-desk man, and of the maid, of all the invisible parts that made the hotel function—but she stopped herself there. She had been lying to them so consistently, and she had been so artful in her vagueness, that to bring a precise complaint felt impossible. Later, when she was older and grander, when she had proved herself as a lady, this illogic would seem like the comical thinking of a frightened child. But at the moment the idea of causing any kind of scene was nearly as terrifying as the loss of the money itself.

If only she could raise half the stolen sum, she told herself, she would go to Will straightaway. These thoughts circled her head all morning, and then, around noon, she remembered she still had one thing left to sell.

"Miss Carolina Broad," the Hayeses' butler announced from the corner of what appeared to be a vast drawing room. Lina, hovering behind him, caught a glimpse of the girl who had first given her hope for a new way of life. She was perched on the corner of a divan and wearing a displeased expression as well as a skirt of dusty pink silk. Penelope looked up at the sound of the name and turned her head to the side contemplatively. Perhaps, Lina thought, she had noticed the changes to the name since the last time she'd heard it, or maybe she hadn't—it was impossible to know. "I would have presented her card, mademoiselle," the butler went on, not assuaging the visitor's discomfort in the least, "but she hasn't got one."

It was through a forest of blue-and-white-upholstered Louis Quinze that Lina had to walk—her nerves raw and her courage flagging all the way—to get to the young lady of the grand new house. Although she had met Penelope before, it was hardly the kind of interaction that might lead to further genteel visits. Lina had to force her leather lace-up boots—a gift from Tristan, the day after they'd met—across the black walnut floor. She was finding it awfully difficult to appear natural.

Penelope looked up at Lina only after she had paused a few feet from the divan. The young lady of the house was drawing her long fingers over the head of a small black-and-white dog. "That dress used to be mine."

Lina looked down on the pale red fabric with the Swiss dot pattern, which she had worn quite a few times over the fall. She remembered Penelope telling her, when she handed it down, that it had been one of her favorites—Lina wondered now if anyone at the hotel might have recognized its provenance.

The large man with the feminine brow and soft skin, who had been reading the columns in a chair just behind Penelope—though she'd never met him, Lina assumed he was the Buck Elizabeth used to speak so doubtfully of— commented without raising his eyes from his folded paper, "She certainly doesn't wear it as you did."

"Oh . . ." Lina looked down at herself and wished she hadn't come. It had been a mistake, as she would have realized earlier if she hadn't been desperate. But she *was* desperate, so she moved a little closer to her onetime patroness.

"I can't imagine what brings you here," Penelope put in sharply.

"It's quite irregular," Buck added.

Lina's cheeks turned the color of claret. "Perhaps I could speak to you about that in private?"

Penelope looked as though she had just been asked to make her own bed.

"Anything you can say to Miss Hayes, you can say to me," Buck said finally, ending a pause that had done unkind things to Lina's already suffering nerves.

She looked several times from Buck and back to Penelope, and finally resolved to go forward with what she had planned to say. "I thought we might be able to arrange another trade."

"Another trade?" Penelope exclaimed. There was disbelief in her wide-open eyes. "I hope you haven't told anyone about all that."

"Of course not." Lina drew her lower lip under her teeth

and wondered just how evident the despair was on her face. "But this is a bit of news I think you'd find most interesting."

Penelope's gaze turned neutral and she moved her elbow—its sharpness obvious even beneath the tight-fitting pink silk—a little forward on the armrest. "Well. What is it?"

"It's about the Hollands," she forced herself to say. "I discovered it while I was still part of their staff. You see, there was a man, I think he dealt in antiques and things, he would come by the house and take pieces of theirs away. The bills were really piling up then. That's how I realized . . . me and my sister, Claire . . . that they'd lost their money. And Claire still works there, so I know that they've had to let most of their staff go."

"Carolina Broad, is it?"

Lina nodded.

"Carolina . . ." A dry smile had crept onto Penelope's face. Maybe this was a good sign, Lina thought. For a brief moment she felt at ease in that vast room with its ormolu-encrusted mirrors and old master paintings and its blindingly shiny floor. "Are you saying that the famous Hollands are poor?"

Carolina smiled back a little now. "Oh, yes. I am absolutely sure of it—"

"Lord, get out." Penelope's face fell and she waved her hand impulsively. She turned her whole body away from her

visitor now, even as Lina bent toward her, wishing to know what she had done wrong.

"But before you said that—"

"The Hollands are poor?" Penelope went on in a voice that even the little dog, struggling to free his tail from under her skirt, seemed to find discomfiting. "Everyone *knows* that one already. If you'd come here with a reason Henry Schoonmaker hasn't fallen back in love with me, then perhaps . . . but that's a riddle that people far smarter than you are stumped by. You stupid girl, did you really think you were going to come into my house and sell me old news?"

Lina's lips hung open slightly and she took these words as though they had been a physical reprimand. She was indeed a very stupid girl. "I was only trying to help," she said faintly.

"Oh, tsk, tsk," Buck admonished from the background. "You were trying to sell something, dearie."

Lina felt so miserable and confused, there in the middle of that once-again hostile room, that she was almost grateful for Penelope's next stroke.

"Rathmill!" she called. Lina turned and saw the butler appear in the doorway. "Miss *Broad* was confused about whom she was calling on. You can show her out now."

The butler understood the implications perfectly, crossed to the helpless girl in the lesser shade of red, and took her by the arm. Lina went without protest, hanging her head on the long walk back across the floor.

"That was unpleasant," she heard Buck say as she was pulled forcibly into the hall. "And just when you were about to go out."

Lina closed her eyes as the butler drew her roughly toward the front entrance. She had so recently crossed its black-and-white-checked floor in hope and trepidation, but she returned to it with all her hopes dashed. Penelope was right: She was a stupid girl who would never find her way.

Fifteen

It is no surprise, given her popularity as a debutante, how lively the new Mrs. Schoonmaker's
Mondays are. One can count on seeing everyone one might want to see there. . . .

—FROM THE SOCIETY PAGE OF THE *NEW-YORK NEWS OF
THE WORLD GAZETTE,* MONDAY, DECEMBER 18, 1899

T HE SECOND MRS. SCHOONMAKER WAS KNOWN not only for her Mondays but also for her Louis Quatorze, which was a mix of her own collection of antique furniture and that of the first Mrs. Schoonmaker. Isabelle was known for her miniatures as well, and for her facial features, which were diminutive and exquisite, and of course for the company she kept. Lydia Vreewold and Grace Vanderbilt— who were of the same generation and shared some of the youth and vivaciousness that characterized their hostess—were sitting on a little settee upholstered in pale turquoise silk and discussing the clothes they planned to buy in Paris that spring; James De Ford, Isabelle's younger brother, was standing by one of the tall windows that looked out onto Fifth Avenue and listening to the painter Lispenard Bradley pontificate about nudes. (The second Mrs. Schoonmaker was further known for having somewhat irregularly allowed an artist or two into her circle.) Penelope Hayes—dressed impeccably in a dusky pink silk day dress, a new set of tiny dark bangs just intruding onto

her high white forehead—stepped into this scene of superior furniture and celebrated names.

"Penelope, my dear, you look good enough to eat," Isabelle said, lacing her arm through that of her guest and steering her across the carpeted floor, which was populated by gleaming chairs and various marble statuary and a few top-notch people, comfortably positioned for conversation. Penelope wouldn't have disagreed, though she was satisfied in the event to lower her eyes and murmur a shy thanks. She looked around—subtly, her face turned toward the dark purple patterns of the Hamadan carpets—with the idea of seeing Henry.

"Poor Henry," Isabelle went on, apparently sensing in which direction Penelope's thoughts were running. "His father was furious with him over that little outburst at the opera. Which is so *silly*! Weren't you and I and everybody else dying for a little diversion at precisely that moment?"

"Oh, I probably was, though I can't remember the outburst you speak of," Penelope replied, trying to edge a little bit of chumminess into her shy tone. She took her hostess's small, soft palm into her own and leaned toward the older woman intimately. "Was Mr. Schoonmaker terribly harsh?"

"He was. There was so much yelling when poor Henry got home." Isabelle lowered her voice to a confidential pitch as they moved slowly and regally toward the tea things.

Several of the guests had taken notice of the new arrival, but Henry, reclining on a chaise longue in the corner by himself, was looking rather moody and staring at the ceiling. He had not noticed Penelope, a fact that she comprehended with a slight tickle of rage in her throat. "He's quite worried that Henry'll do something that might make the family look bad now, when he's just received so much enthusiasm for his mayoral campaign," Isabelle went on in the same tone. "But of course, most of the support has come because of sympathy for *Henry*, losing Elizabeth and all . . . so it's a fine line for Schoonmaker—he can't punish him *too* much."

"No, I suppose not." They had arrived at the refreshment table, and Isabelle wasted no time in putting a small collection of petits fours glacés onto a small plate. Penelope allowed herself a long, unabashed look in Henry's direction, which he did not return. He was wearing the usual black jacket and slacks, and the skin around his eyes, which were pretty in an almost feminine way, was touched by a purple fatigue.

Isabelle poured tea for both of them, examining her new friend as she did. She brushed a golden curl away from her eyes and lowered her voice. "Schoonmaker has actually been rather gentle, compared with his usual fury. *I* think Henry has such a long face because of how terribly he's taking Elizabeth's death." The ladies took their teacups and moved toward a set of chairs by a window, which would allow them to appear with the full benefit of the afternoon light; Penelope and Isabelle comprehended the advantage of this spot with unspoken collusion. "You know, I think when a man loses a wife it's less of a blow, because he has already had a little bit of life with her. But to lose a fiancée is like having a meal presented to one and then whisked a way before even a single bite can be had. . . ."

Penelope nodded compassionately, although she felt certain that Elizabeth was not a dish Henry would have ordered in the first place. Isabelle sighed and put the little sea-foam green pastry half into her mouth, her eyes rolling to the coved ceiling as she did. "It seems that Henry was greatly matured by the loss of his fiancée," Penelope said delicately, if completely disingenuously, looking over her teacup to confirm that the subject of their discussions had still not looked in her direction.

"Oh, I should say so, though Schoonmaker doesn't think so at all." Isabelle leaned forward and put a hand on Penelope's arm. "He is petrified that at any moment Henry might cease to appear sad about the whole miserable affair."

"That's rather mercenary." Penelope felt that the new her would react in this way, though as soon as the statement had escaped her mouth, she wondered if it might sound critical of her future family-in-law. It wasn't easy, trying to make friends as a Little Miss Goody Two-Shoes.

"Oh, yes, of course that's a terrible way to put it.

Especially since you were such a particular friend of Elizabeth's." Isabelle put the rest of the petit four in her mouth remorsefully and swallowed it. "It's such a pity for Elizabeth, too, and for her family. What a thing it would have been for them if she *had* married Henry. Have you heard the stories about their situation?"

Penelope nodded gravely, keeping her smile safely at bay. She had almost put the pathetic visit from the Hollands' old maid out of her mind but recalled it now with a certain satisfaction. There was nothing so richly pitiful as the help turning against their employers.

"But of course, it would have been quite the thing for Elizabeth to have been Mrs. Henry Schoonmaker, too. A good married lady she would have made." Isabelle sighed and put her empty plate down on a small, marble-topped table with an exuberantly curved base. Then she leaned back against her chair and turned her face in Penelope's direction. A girlish color had come into her cheeks, and where there had been concern in her eyes before, now there was a gleam of mischief. "You know what they say, that a lady's life really doesn't begin until she's a married woman? I had no idea how true that was until *I* was married."

"Really?" Penelope responded with a matching sparkle in her eye. She had always felt a little sad for Isabelle, who seemed like fun, and who had had so many beaux as a debutante—including, Penelope believed, her own brother, Grayson—for being married to a controlling, humorless old man. She was glad to hear that being Mrs. William Schoonmaker was not as suffocating as she had imagined. "But I'm so afraid that marriage will mean I must always do only what my husband wishes, and *that* doesn't sound terribly fun."

"Oh, *no*, my dear, you must stop thinking that way. Once you are married, no one can suspect you of anything." Isabelle followed this statement with a long wink and then a pause, in which she rearranged her hands and watched Penelope with cautious eyes. Penelope felt herself to be on the receiving end of the kind of evaluation of which she was ordinarily the author. It was as though Isabelle were trying to look through her. "You know . . . I always thought Elizabeth would have made a lovely Mrs. Henry Schoonmaker, just as I said . . . but she wouldn't have been my first choice for a daughter-in-law."

Penelope could not help but spread her plush red lips into a full smile at this statement. She looked away, so as not to seem too eager, and rested her pale fingers on the shiny oak finial of her chair. "What sort of daughter-in-law would you have preferred?"

"Oh . . ." Isabelle shifted thoughtfully in her chair. "One who wasn't so very . . . *very* good, I suppose. Elizabeth would always have been checking in on the linens and chiding me for being rude to some old bore—don't you think so?"

Penelope nodded, perhaps a little too quickly.

"Not to speak ill of the dead," her hostess went on. "But someone a little . . . a little more like you would add to the Schoonmaker family in the way that would most please me."

The pair looked at each other for a long moment, a glimmer of understanding on both their faces.

"Now, tell me what has become of your brother? We do miss him in New York. . . ."

"Oh, Grayson?" Penelope smiled and complied, giving her hostess as much information on her older brother, who had been seeing to the family business abroad for some years, as she possibly could. The two ladies continued to engage each other in affectionate conversation, their long silk skirts adjoining on the carpet, until the butler appeared in the doorway and announced Teddy Cutting's name. At this point both Isabelle and Penelope looked up and watched with interest as he crossed to Henry and began to talk to him in hushed tones without bothering to take a seat.

"How rude of Mr. Cutting not to greet you first," Penelope murmured.

"I quite agree with you," Isabelle answered, sounding not offended in the least, "though I suppose it is Henry's home too."

Meanwhile, Henry had stood; something, apparently, had been agreed upon.

"Oh, Mr. Cutting!" Isabelle cried. Everyone in the room turned to look, a fact to which their hostess appeared entirely indifferent. She had taken Penelope's hand again, as if to imply that this was all for the younger woman's benefit. "I'm sure you aren't going to leave without greeting me!"

The attention of the room was now fixed on the pair of chairs by the window; Penelope leaned forward so that the late-day sun would illuminate her best angle. She watched as Teddy, remaining awkwardly in his spot, adjusted his jacket so that it hung just so on him. It had already been hanging just so. The moment lengthened, and Teddy looked to Henry as though he might know what the appropriate thing to do was. But Henry—to Penelope's mute fury and suffocating disappointment—closed his eyes in impatience and turned toward the ornate oak door frame.

Penelope barely registered Teddy as he moved, with some embarrassment, to his hostess and greeted her with a kiss on the hand.

"My apologies for not coming to you immediately, Mrs. Schoonmaker," he said. The contractions around his gray eyes indicated he was sincere.

Had Penelope not been so stunned by Henry's continual lack of interest in her, she might have wondered why Isabelle's eyes had become dewy and flirtatious in the presence of boring old Teddy, and if this was perhaps all she'd meant when she said married women had more fun. But for Penelope, at that particular moment, Henry's baffling indifference was all-consuming.

"Miss Hayes," Teddy was saying, "it is a pleasure to see you as well."

"Oh, hello, Teddy," Penelope answered, extending her hand so that she could feel the soft impress of his lips through her glove. "Where has your friend gone to?"

"Oh, Henry? Some of us are off to race four-in-hands in the park, and Henry has agreed to come along. He has just now gone to give his instructions to the stable."

Penelope could only manage to maintain a faint smile while Teddy exchanged a few obligatory niceties with Mrs. Schoonmaker. Then he took his leave and with it any hope of seeing Henry for the rest of the afternoon.

"You see," Isabelle said, once again taking Penelope's hand. "Henry is so curiously devastated by Elizabeth's passing. It reveals itself most especially in the deterioration of his manners."

Penelope would not before that moment have credited any of Henry's inexplicable behaviors to Elizabeth's death, but she found herself wondering if this could in fact be true now. Isabelle, as her tone and winking glances indicated, was fast becoming her ally, and *she* apparently believed it to be the reason. Penelope closed her eyes and remembered Elizabeth, so cold and determined as she'd laid out the plan that would remove her from New York and Henry's attentions forever. It had not been something she would have previously thought Liz capable of, and that was the least of what Penelope had been surprised by that day. She had had to confront several holes in her knowledge of the world, and she supposed that late in December, in the Schoonmakers' drawing room, there might still be one or two things she was wrong about.

"But don't worry," Isabelle was saying. "We will make him see that although Elizabeth had her charms, there are other ladies who would perhaps be a more ideal match for him."

Penelope nodded and gave her the smile of a confidante. She found that she no longer minded the idea that Henry's enduring melancholia might have something to do with the fact that Elizabeth was dead, because if that were so—if Henry was too depressed over Elizabeth's "death" to see that Penelope was the girl for him—it was based on a misconception that she herself could easily dispel.

Sixteen

It is not unheard of for bachelor twosomes to keep one or more young ladies up in the air for years and then wed titled British girls with fine houses and deficient bank accounts whom no one has ever seen before. . . .

—MRS. L. A. M. BRECKINRIDGE, *THE LAWS OF BEING IN WELL-MANNERED CIRCLES*

"ARE YOU ENJOYING YOURSELF, MISS HOLLAND?"

Diana looked up from the oyster-colored sofa on which she had arranged herself and into the eyes of Teddy Cutting. Her elbow rested high on one of the three mahogany crests of the piece of furniture's arched back, and her milky skin glowed in the rose-colored light emanating from a nearby lamp. The walls of the room were a deep plum, and the mood was that of the pleasurable sleepiness that always follows a long meal. Diana, cinched into ivory chiffon, looked very bright in the dark room and low light. Her dress collected in many folds to a V-shaped point both at its neckline and in the back and her skirt overflowed the seat. She was lovely, as everybody at the Ralph Darrolls' small dinner party had noticed, but she knew this was of no particular interest to Teddy. He had mentioned her sister seven times over as many courses.

"Very much," she answered with a flirtatious smile; she had not given up her goal of appearing beautiful to the man she couldn't help but consider Henry's proxy. It was like some wound that she could not help but pluck at.

"I'm glad—may I sit with you?"

"Yes." Diana was in fact genuinely glad for Teddy's company. Though his presence held no romance at all for her, she had discovered that evening that she did like him. There was something in his sincere gray eyes that suggested a vast sadness and sense of guilt for the absurd good fortunes of his life. This was not a sentiment Diana shared—she could not stop herself from feeling unlucky—but she found it interesting. "Your sister's home is very fine," she went on.

Florence Cutting, Teddy's oldest sister, had become Mrs. Darroll only a month ago. She was currently sitting near the fire talking to a man who was not her husband and looking rather larger than she had at her wedding.

"That is not the kind of conversation the Diana Holland I know makes." Teddy smiled. "But yes, it is very fine. Of course, it was my uncle's house before, and he gave it to them at the wedding, furniture and all, so I can't say Mrs. Darroll has had to do much."

"Still, I'm sure she's given it her own touches. *She* looks beautiful—you can still see it even under all that jacquard. I suppose you will be an uncle in under half a year?"

"Ah, that is the Diana I remember," Teddy replied, now

disguising his smile with a sip from his snifter. "But I am not going to respond to such a supposition."

"Tell me how Henry is, then." The pain and pleasure of saying his name out loud were almost equally intense.

Teddy's smile faded, and he looked at her with the same concern he had shown when they'd discussed her mother's grief over dessert. A lamp with a hand-painted porcelain shade lit up his blond hair from behind, casting shadows under his facial features. "I saw him this afternoon."

"And he is well?"

"He doesn't seem terribly happy," Teddy answered stiffly.

"I imagine you mean he takes my sister's passing harder than I do?"

"He takes it hard," Teddy said, looking at her and then looking away. "Though I'm sure it cannot be as difficult for him as it has been for you."

"No." Diana paused and placed her hands in her lap. She decided that she might as well ask the questions that came into her head, since the worst Teddy could do in response was not answer them. Still, she had to summon some courage to say, "What was he doing?" and even so her voice came across a little plaintive.

"We raced four-in-hands in the park. I won, which is rare, and leads me to conclude that his thoughts may have been elsewhere." Teddy stared into his drink and related these facts in a businesslike tone. "Before that, he was in his stepmother's drawing room—she receives on Mondays, you know."

"Who doesn't know?" Diana tried to smile, but she was aware that this must have appeared little more than the mechanical lifting of her upper lip. "Were there many people there?"

"Yes."

Across the room, gowns shifted and light played against china teacups and crystal glasses. There was laughter of the faint, urbane variety, and the crackle of a large fire. "Who, I wonder?"

"Oh, that painter Bradley and one of the fashionable Vanderbilt women and—"

"Penelope Hayes?"

No one in the room was paying attention to their little corner, and even if they had been, Diana felt herself completely absorbed, half out of dread, in the conversation. Teddy sipped from his drink, but that was as long a pause as he could conjure. "Yes, she was there."

A mute anger came over Diana as she received this information. Of course Penelope had been there. Elizabeth had warned her to watch out for Penelope, but she had been passive, believing all the time that Henry's love for her was true and lasting. She had been hot and instinctual—she had forgotten that all the while Penelope would be looking out for her own desires, just as she had when she drove Diana's sister out of town. When she changed the subject, she was unable to thoroughly disguise the bitterness in her voice. "I wonder if you mentioned that you would be seeing me?"

"No," Teddy replied in a kind tone, "it never came up."

She nodded and tried not to feel disappointed by the news that Henry had not been talking of her.

"But Teddy, I know so little of you . . ." Diana went on, summoning all of her resources for one brave smile and a comment that she hoped would save her the struggle of talking any more. Teddy returned it and then went on to tell her about the poetry he used to read at Columbia College, from which he had graduated in the spring, and how he planned to be a lawyer and work for a living, even though he was supposed to inherit so much from his father. Diana half listened and nodded along. She watched the gentlemen in tails come in and out of doorways and greet the ladies who grew rosy sitting in their tufted corner chairs.

She tried to keep Teddy talking, and when it was necessary, to answer his comments in monosyllables. Anything more would have revealed how weak she felt again, how rent in two she was. At any moment, she feared, her chin might begin to tremble like a little girl's. She had been a fool, she now knew. She had believed that Henry's love was simply hers and that she didn't have to do anything for it, when in fact all the young unmarried girls were ruthlessly advancing across the chessboard of Manhattan to make him theirs. One of those girls was Penelope Hayes, whom her sister had specifically warned her about, and who was well known to be the queen.

Seventeen

To those who say it is irresponsible to spread rumors of Elizabeth Holland's possible continued existence on this earth, we say it is irresponsible to categorically deny them. After all, her body has never been found. Her carriage accident could indeed have been the work of kidnappers—they may have intended to ensnare Miss Hayes, too, and not fully realized their plan—and she may have been plucked from the water as soon as she fell and now be living in captivity in some remote state of our union, or even in one of the lesser-visited wards of our teeming city. . . .

—FROM THE SOCIETY PAGE OF THE *NEW-YORK NEWS OF THE WORLD GAZETTE*, MONDAY, DECEMBER 18, 1899

$\mathcal{T}$HEY'D WOKEN UP IN THE MIDDLE OF NOWHERE— well, in an oil field, which looked on the face of it very much like nowhere—but by late afternoon Elizabeth and Will were moving steadily northward to San Francisco in a first-class car. There had been several delays at the station in San Pedro, and for a time Elizabeth had given up hope of her pulse returning to a normal rate. The first-class car had been Will's idea. It was an extravagance she wasn't sure if they could afford—how deep could his savings run, anyway? But he'd insisted that this was the way to celebrate the imminent change in their lives. Elizabeth might have protested more strongly, except that her worries lay elsewhere.

"Where do you think we'll be by tomorrow?" Will asked, taking her hand, as their car hurtled through the middle of California.

"I don't know." Outside, the sun was going down. Elizabeth pushed her head back into the red velvet cushion of the car and shifted her gaze from the rapidly changing landscape

in the window to Will. The names on their door read ELIZA-
BETH AND WILL KELLER, and they were keeping up the ruse of
being a married couple so that they could share a berth without suspicion. He had apologized to her, once they'd taken
their seats, and promised that he wouldn't make her lie about
something that important much longer.

"I slept all the way cross-country last time," Will said.
She winced to think what must have been on his mind during that trip, even though his tone was a happy one. He was
worried about her, she could see that—his light blue eyes were
wide and observant against his sun-darkened skin. "I plan to
take in more of the view this time."

Elizabeth pressed her palm into his and tried to smile.
They were both wearing their coats for the first time since
they'd left New York—this despite the heat of the railway
cars—because she believed it made them look more put
together. She felt a little ashamed to be tawny and dirty, so
simply dressed, amidst all these trappings of travel gentility,
but at least she could believe that her fellow travelers were
merely rich and not yet distinguished by taste or class. Still,
Elizabeth would have done anything to cover the yellowing
her seersucker dress had taken on. In Will's case, however, the
black smears on his serge trousers seemed to garner as much
murmured admiration as his fitted brown coat.

Three chandeliers illuminated their car, and a carpet ran

down its center. They were on their way to New York, and the air around them was all warm and perfumed, but still, Elizabeth's mind was restless.

"We'll be with them soon enough," Will told her gently, as if reading her thoughts.

Elizabeth nodded and rested her head against his shoulder. What Will said was true, but it did little to comfort her, because the question that had interrupted her sleep the night before was not how soon she could be with her family, but what she could do for them once she arrived.

Will believed that they were sitting on vast wealth, and she believed him, but she knew it would take time and effort to turn that into cash. Her family needed money now, or preferably yesterday. But Elizabeth owned something that could be turned into cash, though she could hardly think of it without a sheen of sweat collecting on her brow. That thing was Henry Schoonmaker's engagement ring, a Tiffany diamond set in gold.

The ring was in her pocket, wrapped once in tissue paper and then in newspaper and then finally in a piece of canvas. She hadn't yet told Will that she had brought it with her from New York. It was such a talisman of her past betrayals, she didn't even like to think of it. But she reminded herself that it might do her family a world of good—it might hire the necessary doctor, or put Diana in the right dress—and she had already been selfish enough. She would feel better, she told herself, once it was out of her hands and she had its worth in bills.

She had a plan for that, too—she knew that the train was to stop in Oakland for several hours, to pick up new passengers and cargo. There were places near the station where things could be pawned, as Denny had told her once. She would slip out on some excuse and would be done with it quickly.

"If you don't stop making that distraught face," Will said, interrupting her agitated planning, "I think I might start to cry."

She leaned into his shoulder and told him she would try. Her eyelids were heavy, and in a moment they fell closed. She let the train's northward movement rock her, and Will, too, and in a little while she did manage—however briefly—to let her family's troubles fade from her mind. As she fell into sleep, she told herself that she was capable of executing her plan. It was would be easy, and then she would be able to repay her family for all the distress she had caused.

Eighteen

Everyone knows a girl who made a good start to her social career and became compromised by being seen too often alone in the company of gentlemen or perhaps going too many times out of that hallowed sphere in which our young goddesses are meant to walk. . . . If she plans to live a long time in society, a girl cannot be too careful which streets she strolls upon and in whose homes she is a guest.

—MRS. L. A. M. BRECKINRIDGE, *THE LAWS OF BEING IN WELL-MANNERED CIRCLES*

"WHERE ARE YOU GOING?"

Diana turned slowly from the front door and looked back into the afternoon shadows that fell across the foyer behind her. She felt a small tug of conscience as Claire came forward in her simple black dress. Claire was her friend, after all—her best friend, she might have even said on some occasions. The maid was looking tired and a little worried now, and though Diana would have preferred her to be neither of those things, the guilt she was feeling was more likely based on the fact that the next words out of her mouth were going to be a lie.

"Outside for a little air." Diana thought she managed to sound breezy enough.

"But it's freezing outside, and from the way the sky's looking there may be hail and—"

"I'll bring an umbrella, then." Diana looked into Claire's wide, fair face, which was framed in reddish hair, and tried to look like someone above questioning.

"I won't be able to make a fire, though, when you get back, since we've got no firewood, and if you should catch a chill . . ."

So her mother hadn't managed to give Claire the money to keep the cold out.

"Dear Claire," Diana said, releasing the brass doorknob for a moment and moving toward her friend. She took Claire's hands in her own and kissed her on either cheek. "Order the firewood."

"But they said they won't defer payment any longer and that—"

"Tell them we shall pay on delivery. When I get back I will have money for them. . . ."

She smiled, kissed the other girl's milky forehead, and hurried out the door and down the stone steps to the street. "But you must wear a warmer coat!" she heard Claire exclaim as she hurried east.

Diana did not turn to acknowledge this last admonishment, even though she knew Claire to be correct on her final point. Clouds were forming ominous slate gray armories in the sky and she had not, as promised, brought an umbrella. There were still coats in the house, of course. Her mother had not yet stooped to selling off their wardrobe. But Diana was on a particular mission, and she wanted to look a certain way. She was wearing the new green velvet jacket that fit her so perfectly, and a long skirt of houndstooth check with black buttons that brought the fabric close to her hips. She was walking at a determined gait that would not have won the approval of any society matrons, and repeating to herself, *Davis Barnard, 155 East Sixteenth Street, Third Floor.* The wind was sharp and icy, but she hardly thought of it. Her skirt fluttered behind her as she went.

The building was a plain four-story apartment house with a brown face and two unblinking windows per floor. There was no answer at first, and as Diana stood still on the pavement the cold started to set in. The address hadn't meant anything to her before a few days ago, but, as she waited, it occurred to her that it might have significance for others. Indeed, for all she knew, the ladies passing in their cold-weather hats and plain skirts were fully aware of the meaning of No. 155 East Sixteenth Street. This thought made her uncharacteristically self-conscious, and she pulled her conspicuous green coat close to her body as though it might somehow disguise her. Elizabeth would have thought of this possibility. Elizabeth would have considered who might be watching, instead of charging ahead on a whim.

"Hello down there!"

Diana craned her neck back and looked upward. She kept her hand on the straw top of her brimmed hat and squinted—for even a moody sky contains some light—at the head of Davis Barnard protruding from a third-floor window.

"Ah, Miss Truscott!" he called.

She spun, looking around her, but there seemed to be no other girls interested in that particular window.

"I mean *you*," Mr. Barnard went on, in a somewhat more circumspect voice.

"Oh," Diana said, turning her gaze on the third floor again. "I wanted to come up," she added simply.

"Of course."

A few seconds later a key attached to a large silver ring came clattering to the ground, and then Diana let herself in and climbed the stairs to the little apartment inhabited by the writer of the *Imperial*'s society page.

"Miss Holland," Mr. Barnard said, ushering her in, "how bold you are."

"If you'd thought I was a priss, I doubt you would have approached me in the first place," Diana replied, fixing her hands in the pockets of her skirt and looking around her. She took in the long and slender room and noted that its twilight blue paint had been applied some time ago; its walls were dotted with framed prints, and the floor was covered with layers of carpets. A cut-glass punch bowl figured prominently on the cabinet, the table was a mess of papers and notebooks and books, and the daybed seemed to have taken on a similar desk-like function, save that there were more pillows involved. "So this is what they mean when they say 'bachelor apartment.'"

"Oh, yes, I am the ne plus ultra of bachelors."

Diana's cheekbones tinged red at the sound of a phrase she didn't recognize. "What is that supposed to mean?"

Davis smiled where he might have laughed. "It means I have achieved the most profound degree of bachelorhood."

"Is that so?" Diana replied aridly. She moved to the table and drew her fingers across the spines of a pile of books.

"Ah, I did not say the ne plus ultra of playboys or the ne plus ultra of roués. Only of bachelors, and you can see that my room will give you plenty of testimony to that end."

Diana nodded, understanding but not wanting to seem too friendly, and moved closer to the fireplace, which was roaring cozily and decorated with a pair of boxing gloves strung up like Christmas stockings.

"Would you like some coffee?"

"Please." Diana turned and observed her host, whose appearance was somewhat more rumpled than when she had met him out in the world. He wore a salmon-colored shirt under a dark gray vest, the forward curve of which suggested good living on the part of its wearer. A belly was contained there, like the back of an upholstered chair that has been a little overstuffed. His dark hair was cut so close to his head that it seemed to form three separate sections, one on the top and two on the sides, and below the unique brow was the same attentiveness in the eyes that had first tempted her to entertain his suit.

"How do you take it?" he asked as he poured the dark liquid from a silver pot on the side table.

Diana bit her lip. She was a tea drinker, most days. "However you do."

"Well, then." Davis reached to the shelf above him, where several bottles crowded out the reflection of a long, thin mirror, and he took down a decanter of brown alcohol, from which he poured a shot into each of their cups. "Please sit, Miss Diana," he said as he handed her one of the cups and perched on the edge of the daybed.

She settled into the cane-backed chair and put her hands against the warm sides of the white cup. The sting of whiskey mingled with the steam of the coffee in her nose. Even on that historic night in Henry's greenhouse, Diana had not felt quite so conscious of breaking the rules as she did now. *Mother would die if she knew I was here!* Diana thought, before realizing that that particular phrase wasn't so amusing, given her mother's current state of health, and banished the small smile that had crept onto her face.

Perhaps Davis sensed that her thoughts had turned to the impropriety of her visit, for he went on to say, with the same sly expression: "I never thought I'd see a Miss Holland here in my rooms."

Diana shrugged evasively and took a sip of the heady coffee. Then she met his eyes and, letting her moods break across her face like fast-moving weather, smiled. "This is the best coffee I've ever had," she said gaily. "Anyway, I haven't come to talk about me. I have something to sell."

"Oh?" The dark brow jutted upward, before Davis tilted his coffee cup and drained it. He placed the empty cup on the edge of the cluttered table and crossed his wrists on his knee. "What is it?"

"Well," Diana began, switching the cross of her legs and rolling her warm brown eyes to the ceiling, "If I were the writer, I'd phrase it thusly: 'The new Mrs. Ralph Darroll was seen giving an intimate dinner party in her new home on Madison Avenue, a gift from her paternal uncle for her marriage just last month, and is reported to already be wearing dresses in the style they call *empire*.'"

"I think I see your point." Davis paused and knit his fingers together so that he could rest his chin on them. "But it's a little subtle for the common reader, don't you think?"

This stung slightly, as Diana had been working out the wording all morning, but, not to be hindered, she pressed her hands into her thighs, exhaled, and tried again. "Then what if you added: 'Could it be for the same reason that good Empress Josephine favored the style? In which case, there may be a Ralph Jr. in less than half a year.'"

"Very *good*, Miss Di. I see you're a fan of my columns."

Diana smiled happily at the compliment and chose to

ignore its second half. She looked at the old family daguerreotypes on the mantel, and then let her eyes fall on a vellum-bound book of poems on the edge of the table nearest her.

"I'll run it this week," Davis told her. Diana's gaze snapped back to her host. She wasn't sure why this news gave her such pleasure, but she found herself clapping her hands together like a giddy little girl.

"It's at the same rate," Davis, his dark eyes ever watchful, continued. "Of course, I could double your money."

"How?" Diana asked, lowering her hands and trying to look like a person who drove a hard bargain.

"The readers of the 'Gamesome Gallant' column are always interested in the doings of the Hollands, and surely they'd like to know what Miss Diana Holland was doing at the Ralph Darrolls', when by all societal measures she should be in black at home, still mourning for her sister, or perhaps tending to a mother whom people say isn't well. . . ."

Diana had to look away from Davis. She had never been a good girl, and yet sitting in this small, cluttered room, drinking whiskey in her coffee, and telling secrets about her people was beginning to feel something like exposure. But it was also, in its way, exhilarating. She stood and walked to the window, with its faded velveteen cushions and old lace curtains, where she paused to let the last of her coffee burn a streak down her throat and into her stomach.

"You're a very special source to me," Davis went on in a more serious tone. "I'd never write something about you unless you allowed me to. And I know your mother is very old-fashioned. But I also know you've been out with three gentlemen in hardly more days, so I think she's got an objective that wouldn't necessarily be impeded by my mentioning your name. . . ."

Of course Diana, looking down on the huddled crowds who were now leaving work en masse and traveling home wrapped in their bulky dark garments, was not wondering what her mother would think when she saw the item. She was imagining Henry, reading about her with his friend, ideally turning purple with rage and then, perhaps, challenging Teddy to a duel. Oh, she wouldn't want anybody getting hurt, of course, but there was nothing like a little chest-beating to remind a man where his true feelings lay. Not that she even knew exactly what to think of Henry, if he cared more for Penelope than for her, but she did want him to regret losing her. She wanted his regret to equal hers. She wanted it to be greater.

It occurred to her, standing at the edge of that little room and looking down, selling observations that were supposed to evaporate in the air so that they would be laid down in print instead, that she was no longer an innocent. She was always doing this of course, feeling one day that she was experienced and then waking up the next and realizing how naïve she had been. But she was pretty sure she had now crossed some line.

"I think that would make a very interesting item, Mr. Barnard," she said, turning away from the window and perching against the sill. "And if you'll pour me a little more of your magical coffee I'll tell you how I'd put it."

Davis gave her his crooked smile and went back to the cabinet.

Diana looked across the warm little oblong room, which she had decided fit perfectly her idea of a literary garret, and sighed contentedly. "I'd begin: 'The enchanting Miss Diana Holland was seen chatting intimately. . . .'"

Nineteen

It is common knowledge that at every dinner party ever given since the dawn of time, the guests have been sat such that the sexes alternate: male, female, male, female, etc. This is the way nature intended it, and it has allowed many a happy hostess to claim some kind of credit in the forming of romantic alliances that otherwise outshine them.

—*VAN KAMP'S GUIDE TO HOUSEKEEPING FOR LADIES OF HIGH SOCIETY,* 1899 EDITION

"*D*ID YOU NOTICE SOMETHING DIFFERENT?" ISABELLE whispered to Penelope, seated beside her at the long Schoonmaker dining table, just as the venison in port wine sauce was being served. She was wearing a dress of pale yellow tulle finished with antique lace that flounced around her shoulders and came, once or twice when she was bending forward to whisper girlishly, a little closer to the buttery platter of pommes parisienne than Penelope would have wanted her own dress to. "A little rule I've broken?"

Penelope had in fact noticed that all of the ladies were seated in a row, and though she would have preferred to have been sitting right next to Henry, she saw the genius of having them all on display. There were few comparisons that did not flatter the young Miss Hayes, and sitting next to Prudence Schoonmaker certainly set off her attractive qualities as sitting next to a gentleman might not have. Isabelle, on her left, had kept her engaged in a conversation about dresses through the early courses, which was a subject that Penelope found acceptably diverting on any given day, but particularly enlightening when it turned to Henry's favorite cuts. Prudie, on her right, happily had not been moved to say anything as yet.

"It's *so* much more fun this way," the hostess went on, gushing.

"Divine," Penelope replied, sipping her champagne. "Soon all the other hostesses will be imitating you. Of course, you must be careful, or all the men in New York will blame you for having corrupted their wives."

Penelope gave the full benefit of her sharp white shoulder to Prudie—who had just made an unattractive noise in response to this comment—and offered up a discreet laugh in Isabelle's direction, who in any event had already turned to her friend Lucy Carr, the wraithlike divorcée who was seated on her other side. "Lucy, you've got to hear what Penny just said. She just said that all the men in New York will say I've corrupted their wives and . . ."

Across the table, through a bower of orchids, Penelope glimpsed Henry. He was talking more than usual, perhaps because he was seated next to Nicholas Livingston, who could be expansive on the subject of yachts, and he had not looked at her all evening. This had provoked a dull ache in the back of her throat but did little to dim the sense of mission that she had brought with her to the Schoonmakers'. Indeed, her whole body tingled with it. She had dressed for triumph in a garment of gossamer, which framed her bustline in filmy layers, and crepe de chine, which cascaded down toward her high-heeled slippers and overwhelmed her toes. The dress was so pale a pink it was virtually white, though her favorite color was represented in the small red medallions at the shoulders and a hundred little bows down near the hem. It fit her exceptionally well; Penelope had spent all of yesterday at the dressmaker's making sure that this was so.

The waiters were still fussing around the epic table, and the smell of the venison was turning Penelope's stomach. She wrinkled her nose, despite the risks this posed to her skin, at its rising fumes. She'd never imagined she'd agree with the old hostesses and their draconian dining rules, but she had begun to conclude that it really was more proper to alternate the sexes—being so completely in the company of women was not a thing Penelope had ever been fond of. The only one in that row of ladies whose friendship she cared about just then was Isabelle. She could not complain of Isabelle's efforts to bring her close to Henry. Complain she did of course, if only in her own head, for though Henry was ideally positioned to make eyes at her, his attentions remained stubbornly elsewhere.

Penelope waited patiently through the cheeses. She checked her reflection in the polished silver ice bucket that lay amongst all the flowers and heaping serving trays, gently evening the line of small dark bangs on her high white fore-head. She moved the food on her plate around, and turned her denuded shoulders so that they most ideally caught the light. She squeezed the hand of her hostess once or twice and allowed Mrs. Carr to go into raptures about Penelope's bright future in society and what a lot of good it did everybody to see a fresh face.

"Wherever has that brother of yours been?" Mrs. Carr asked, segueing awkwardly, as though the question had been on her mind for some time.

Penelope noted Isabelle's blush, and then gave her the abridged version of what she had told her hostess on Monday. She had just received a telegram from Grayson that afternoon, however, and so she was able to add, "He's on his way back to New York now, though, so you'll soon be able to ask him all these questions yourself."

At last the dinner was over, and the whole party—forty or so stuffed and tipsy people—moved to the ballroom.

"How ever are you going to cheer your stepson up?" Penelope asked, with a little sympathetic waver in her voice, once she had settled herself between Mrs. Schoonmaker and Mrs. Carr on the rust velvet causeuse at the center of the ballroom. Her position in the middle was calculated, for the divorcée—with her ringing laugh and head of lioness curls—could only accentuate the younger woman's virginal façade.

She risked a look out of the corner of her eye at the elder Schoonmaker, who was standing just below a large, Gallic-looking mural and talking with a man of too advanced an age to be of much interest, and concluded that he had taken note. Dull Spencer Newburg was standing in their vicinity, and Penelope noticed that his sister Mrs. Gore had been watching her as though she were considering her for a part in a play.

"I don't know! Lucy, how are we going to cheer him up?" Mrs. Schoonmaker leaned across Penelope's lap as she spoke, resting her silk fan against Penelope's skirt.

"If I were you," Mrs. Carr answered confidentially, "I'd contrive to have him dance with Miss Hayes."

Mrs. Schoonmaker clasped her hands at this suggestion, which was just the one—Penelope felt sure—she'd been fishing for.

"Oh, but if he isn't in a dancing spirit . . ." she demurred.

"Nonsense." Mrs. Schoonmaker gave her a look that indicated they understood each other and then rose and went, with casual purpose, toward her husband, yellow flounces rustling in her wake.

Penelope watched as the hostess brushed aside the older man—it was Carey Lewis Longhorn, she saw now—and said a few pointed words to Mr. Schoonmaker. Then she shifted her eyes to the many large paintings in huge gilt frames, which were arranged salon style on the opposite wall, in time for her host to look over and note her discomfort at being left alone with a gaudy divorcée in the middle of a public room. She brought Isabelle's abandoned fan up to shield her mouth.

"I wonder what Schoonmaker has to talk about with Carey Longhorn. Mr. Longhorn's my friend, of course, but they've never been in the same circles . . ." Mrs. Carr was saying, but Penelope hardly registered it, for she was keeping careful track in her peripheral vision of what Henry's father and stepmother were doing. They had come to an agreement, and they were excusing themselves and then going jointly across the floor to the corner where Henry was, somehow or other, still engaged in a conversation with Nicholas Livingston. Penelope steeled herself. She willed the full, dewy, attention-getting affect of her physical appearance. She batted the fan and waited.

"He was seen with some young thing at the opera the other night—can you imagine? It would be something if he married at this point, and to a girl who might be his granddaughter!"

Penelope was only half listening. She had become aware of the music, which emanated from a quartet in the next room. She took a breath that brought composure into all corners of her body. She let her eyelids quiver shut, and when she opened them, Henry, dressed in the usual tailored blacks, occupied the central position in her view. Over his shoulder Mr. and Mrs.

Schoonmaker were visible, watching; Mrs. Carr rose, winked showily, and allowed herself to be taken into conversation by Mr. Longhorn. All around the room, Penelope thought, people were aware that Henry Schoonmaker was about to ask Penelope Hayes to dance.

"Hello," Henry said simply.

Penelope kept her chin down even as her lake-blue eyes rolled to meet his. "Don't nights like these make you miss Elizabeth so?"

Henry shifted his jaw and appeared to consider how best to answer this. "It's not nights like these that do it."

"Oh, what I wouldn't give to have her back," Penelope sighed, putting a little misery into the rise and fall of her shoulders.

"You forget, I know you," Henry replied quickly. There was a certain fire in his eye. "And I think honesty becomes you much better."

The reference to their former intimacy felt nearly as good as the touch of his hands on her would have, and she looked back at him baldly.

"That's better." Henry wore a smile of knowing resignation as he reached for Penelope's hand. "They say we should dance."

Then she really did feel his hands, ever so lightly over her gloved fingers, as she allowed herself to be helped up and swept through the polished oak archway and into the adjoining room, where three or four other couples moved in subdued circles. Henry was looking at her as though he were trying to figure her out, and after his last comment she made no effort to disguise anything in her reciprocal gaze. There was a woodenness to his movements that was new since the last time they'd danced, so many months ago, but still she could feel the distant press of his leg through her skirts.

"I think you really are broken about it," she said finally. She tipped her head thoughtfully to the side as they turned.

"About Elizabeth?" Henry closed his eyes and lowered his voice, although there was no real need. The musicians in the corner played loudly enough that the other couples would not hear them as they moved, their bodies rising and falling, across the room. "How could I not be, over something so awful. But I suppose it would be like you," he went on, almost affectionately, "to be black-hearted about it."

"On the contrary, I miss my friend tremendously. But you forget how she betrayed me."

"Oh, Penelope," Henry answered, in a veritable whisper. The room, with its peach-colored flocked wallpaper, moved around behind him. "It hardly matters now."

"No, what matters is that she's dead. Which is a tragedy."

Henry was silent, considering his answer. "Yes, that's exactly it," he said eventually.

"That's why you don't flirt anymore? Why you never look for fun like you used to? Why you don't look at me in that particular way?"

"It just wouldn't be right," Henry responded with quiet intensity. The touch of his hand at her lower back was so faint she could hardly stand it.

"Ah, no." Penelope felt the low light of the room landing on her high cheekbones like so many particles of gold. She tried to tell herself not to say it all at once, though already her lips burned pleasantly with the information. "But it wouldn't seem that way if you knew what I knew."

They were now speaking in such low voices that they were by necessity drawn closer into each other. "What do you know, Penny?"

"That Elizabeth is alive." Penelope was surprised, even after all the planning, by how much pleasure that phrase could give her.

Henry's left eye twitched and his grip on her tightened involuntarily, but he managed to keep dancing as before, if a beat faster. "What are you talking about?"

"She faked her death to escape marrying you." Penelope's smile had achieved its most full and glorious expression. They were moving faster now, across the floor, without any thought to Adelaide Wetmore and Regis Doyle, whom they nearly cut when they turned. "I *helped*."

"You . . . where is she?" Henry's eyes were wide and full of fire. He was watching her, trying to decide what to believe.

"In California. It seems she wasn't in love with you at all, Henry. It seems she might have been—"

"You mean she didn't fall in the river?" Henry interrupted. He was blinking rapidly and speaking in a slower, stupider voice then Penelope had ever heard him use.

Penelope gave a slow satisfied shake of her head. *There,* she thought. *I have really stunned him.*

"You mean she's all right?"

"*Yes,* she's—"

But if Henry had registered the irritated tone creeping into Penelope's voice, he did not have time to show it. The world-weary face he had been wearing around for months was gone and the old roguish gleam had come back into his eye. He stopped dancing and let go of her, which caused everyone else in the room to stop dancing too—to Penelope's great horror—the better to watch what was unfolding. Henry looked briefly at the other couples and did not bother to hide the smile on his face. He reached for Penelope's hand and kissed it. "I am needed elsewhere . . ." was the only excuse he gave, before quickly exiting the room.

"Oh," said Adelaide, her right hand still held aloft by her partner, Mr. Doyle. "I hope he's all right," she said out loud, but the way she looked after him indicated she was more concerned with losing her chance to dance with the young man of the house over the rest of the evening.

Penelope's dark lashes fluttered and her irritation rose up. All around her people were staring in amusement. She couldn't remember a time when her wishes had been so continually thwarted. There was still the smell of Henry, his cognac and cigarettes and a slight whiff of the cologne he wore, and the faint impress of his hand at her back. But what she felt most acutely was the humiliation of being left on the dance floor, amongst her inferiors, with only a smarting heart and the ruins of a grand plan.

Twenty

The elements that make an ideal bride are manifold: her looks, her manners, her father's money, her mother's people all play a part. But of course she is nothing without that air of purity which surrounds the most desirable debutantes.

——MRS. HAMILTON W. BREEDFELT, *COLLECTED COLUMNS ON RAISING YOUNG LADIES OF CHARACTER*, 1899

*O*UTSIDE OF THE SCHOONMAKERS' FIFTH AVENUE mansion it had begun to snow. The air felt warmer than Henry had expected, and the flakes were so gentle that they melted on his nose as though it were nothing more than a fine mist. The sidewalk was taking on a patina of lacy white, upon which Henry's dark footprints fell with exuberant lightness. In a few minutes the whole world had changed. Now he knew what that last, clear-eyed look his fiancée had given him had meant—not that she chose death, but that she chose another life, one that would allow her little sister to be with the one she loved. He was already past the clutch of waiting coachmen warming themselves from their flasks by the curb, and heading toward Gramercy Park.

No. 17 had been Elizabeth's house to him, a place where he went at first with a lukewarm sense of obligation and later with a weighty sense of his own poor behavior. Before that it had been just another well-appointed landmark on the tour of properties owned by the Old New York families whose gentility was becoming more and more outdated every day. On that Tuesday evening, it was only Diana's house to him. All the rooms but hers could burn for all he cared. That low feeling that he had been living under was gone. The central facts upon which that feeling was based—that Elizabeth was dead, that he was to blame, that youth was fragile, that he could not be with the one girl who made matrimony seem attractive—had been dispelled by a few words. There was only one person with whom Henry might have wanted to share this great good news, and, conveniently enough, she was the sister of the girl who wasn't dead.

He could not have been sure how long it took him to arrive there. It felt like no time, and yet it must have been forever, because somewhere in between the limestone edifice on Fifth and the simple brown town house on Gramercy, all of his mistakes had been erased and he was again a man without regrets. The last and only time he had seen Diana's bedroom he had reached it by the trellis, but he had now so fully recovered his uncircumspect self that he walked straight up to the front door and found that it opened easily at his touch. This was all the invitation he needed, and into the darkened foyer he went. He continued on to the second floor, taking no notice of details, and there he chose the door with light under the jamb. There was no knocking this time, either. He turned the knob and went in.

The little room was cast in warm lamplight, which

illuminated the damask walls and the bookshelves and the bear rug by the unlit fire. Beside it was an old wing chair, where Diana sat in a pile of white laces with her dark ringlets in heaps, looking fixedly at a book. Perhaps she assumed that the open door meant only the intrusion of her maid, for she didn't immediately look up from the page. Her legs were disguised under an old quilt and her eyes continued along the lines of her novel as though nothing in the world were so important. When she reached the end of her paragraph she laid the book in her lap and looked up. She realized that it was not her maid, and then the whites of her eyes expanded and her mouth opened as though she might scream.

Henry was at her side immediately, his hand over her mouth. "Don't," he said in a gentle voice.

Her eyes widened, but he must have conveyed something to her with his tone, because some of the anguish and surprise went out of them. There remained, in her great brown irises, a kind of apprehensive wondering, however, and at last she said, with quietness to match his own: "I can't imagine what you would be doing here."

"I am here." His voice was full of absurd good luck, and he gave her a lopsided smile that he thought might convey how pleased he was by this fact.

She only went on staring at him in the same way. "I can see that."

"Di . . ." Henry fell to one knee and reached for her hand, but she was quicker than he and drew it away.

"Our last meeting didn't leave much room for friendliness, Mr. Schoonmaker. If you really think you have a chance of seducing me on any random dark night you choose, I can assure you that you are wrong."

Henry was confused by this hard, cold version of Diana, and he paused and tried to draw on his vast experience, hoping he somehow already knew how to deal with such a situation. But he had never had an experience like this one before. He opened his mouth a few times but failed to produce any sentences. He decided to try taking up her hand again, and at last she allowed him to—albeit with a certain cold disinclination—and then he finally found the words. "Elizabeth is alive," he said.

Diana closed the book in her lap and sat up straight. She left her hand in his—a positive sign, which he found himself ridiculously pleased with—but she went on staring at him searchingly. When she at last whispered, "I know," some of the thaw was off her voice.

"You know?" This was a shock, but Henry was too elated to really parse it. "But that morning, after you came to the greenhouse . . . I saw Elizabeth . . . I thought she . . . might not have wanted to live—"

"No," Diana said cautiously. "She's alive. And quite happy, I think."

"Well, it's all right, then, don't you see? I mean, if she's all right, if she isn't dead, if she never wanted to marry me anyway and that was some colossal mistake, then you and I can be together. You and I can—" Here he broke off and allowed the arch of a dark eyebrow to complete his thought. He realized that his knee, digging into the floorboards, pained him, and he sat down on the floor beside her chair. "You should have told me a long time ago."

The rose was returning to Diana's cheek, but the way she was looking at him still suggested caution. There was something almost unbearably poignant about seeing her here in her small room, with its salmon-colored walls and books, the room where she had been a little girl. "It's a secret. I promised Elizabeth. If anyone were to find out . . ." She pulled back her hand again all of a sudden and brought the lace collar of her dressing gown in close over the skin of her neck. "How did you find out?"

"Penelope told me. She just told me, less than an hour ago. My stepmother was giving a dinner party—"

"What is it between you and Penelope?" Diana had stood up, and she moved away from Henry across the floor toward the narrow bed, with its headboard upholstered in pale pink silk.

That Diana might feel jealous of Penelope had not occurred to him. Still, his sense of lightness and emancipation had not diminished and he stood and placed his hands in his coat pockets. He gave her a long, serious look, holding her gaze with composed affection. "There is nothing between Penelope and me," he enunciated.

"Nothing?" Diana answered bitterly. "How could I possibly believe that? I'm not blind, you know, and I'm not totally out of things. I see how she looks at you. And I know what you have been."

"The way she looks at me doesn't say anything about my feelings for her, which are exactly as I've told you. They are nothing. Haven't I always been honest with you?" he went on in a softer tone. "I was the one who told you what had passed between Penelope and me, so why would I lie now?"

"Because you're a bounder, I suppose."

Diana's face was full of outrage, but her breath was stuck and her heart seemed to be almost visibly beating. Henry could see plainly that she was at war with herself and that she didn't know what to believe. He went on looking at her with all the weight of his sincerity and then he moved toward her. He took her little face in his hands and kissed her open mouth.

The kiss lasted a long time, and when it was over she whispered, "You're not a bounder."

"It's all right." Henry began to play with one of the curls behind her ear. "Your sister's alive, Di, which means there's no tragedy here, no grand betrayal. If we wanted we could—"

He was interrupted by the sound of the doorbell from below, which was faint but definite, as it repeated itself over the silence in the house.

Diana's eyes went around the room and then met his. There was trepidation in her gaze, and when the bell sounded a third time, she said, "Maybe it's Elizabeth?"

"Elizabeth?" This seemed unlikely to Henry, but then, his expectations were being so quickly overturned that he was disinclined to fully dismiss any possibility. "Wouldn't she just let herself in? That's what I did, and I'm not even related. . . ."

Another girl, coming on the possibility of being discovered with a man to whom she was neither engaged nor married, would have gone into an agony of self-recrimination and wrung her hands at the specter of her coming ruin. Not Diana. There was a bite of the lip and an extension of her white neck and then she took Henry's hand and led him to her door. She opened it deftly and they moved out of the room in silence. Down the hall they went, her arm extended backward to pull him, her hand gripping his with affectionate confidence. She stopped them just before the top of the stair, so that they were obscured from down below by a wall. A light had gone on in the foyer.

"Mr. Cairns," said a female voice that Henry didn't recognize, "we haven't seen you in such a long time. What brings you here, and so very late at night?"

Diana looked back at him, and through the darkness he saw that the perfect roundness of her lips was mouthing, "Aunt Edith."

"I'm very sorry for the impropriety, Miss Holland. I've just come from Boston and I would have arrived at a much more acceptable hour had not the weather taken a turn for the worse. I have been meaning to pay you a visit since I heard of Miss Elizabeth's unfortunate passing, but business detained me. I have recently been hearing reports of your family's distress and I—"

"Mr. Cairns, please, there is no need for you to explain yourself. I will have the maid make up a bed for you. In the meantime, go into the drawing room. Mrs. Holland is ill, far to ill too receive you. But I will get Miss Di and . . ."

Edith continued her speech downstairs, but at the mention of her name Diana turned, startled. She moved in close to Henry without any definite purpose and lifted her little chin upward. The shadows falling across her features only made him yearn to see her more clearly, and he had to look away to keep himself from lifting her up and pressing her small body into the wall with his.

"You have to go," Diana whispered.

"I know. I'll come back soon. I'll come back every day hoping to get you alone."

"Good." She gestured unhappily toward her room. "The trellis . . ."

Henry had met before with the trellis to Diana's bedroom, and it had ended with bruises and scratches and a wedding date being moved up. "No, not that again." He could not stop himself from giving her a knowing little grin, despite the danger.

Diana pressed her lips together and her eyes darted. "The servants' stairs, then."

She gestured to the door. Henry had been so absorbed in the facts of her skin and the glitter of her eyes that he did not notice, until just then, that the conversation downstairs had come to an end and that there were footsteps falling on the stairs. He moved quickly to the door Diana had indicated and without even the luxury of a backwards glance went down the narrow, dark servants' stairs. He was concentrating on the sounds of feet above, going up, and so didn't consider what he might find at the bottom. That was how he came stealthily into the kitchen and saw the back of a maid in a coarse black dress, bending over a stove.

She was tired—this was evident by the stoop of her shoulders—and her red hair was only partially restrained as it fell down her back. She must have been awakened by the bell, and seemed to be going about her task of making tea and setting up a tray with a slowness that would not have been tolerated earlier in the day, or in another house. Henry crept along the wall, stepping mindfully across the old wooden planks of the floor. His thoughts were moving so quickly and his blood was so astir that he was shocked that his presence wasn't deafening to her. But she kept at her work with a sleepy diligence, and Henry managed to go out into the hall without her noticing him.

The foyer was lit by a gas lamp but was empty of any human presence. Henry was swift, and in a moment he was back out in the night air, moving steadily north past the iron gate of the pleasant park, which was now covered in a thickening blanket of white. He was breathing rapidly. He had escaped unnoticed. A few moments ago he and the girl who owned all of his affections had been at great risk, but the risk had passed. The improbability of this only lightened his mood and reminded him that the world was his to play in. He hadn't felt so free in a long time.

He crossed the street, its white sheet of new-fallen snow reflecting the purplish light of the street lamps, and walked north along the park. It was at the northwest corner that he came across a small band of men wrapped up in coats and scarves and caroling with all the power of their stout bellies, "And heaven and nature sing! And heaven and nature sing! And heaven, and heaven, and nature sing!" He paused and watched them, feeling in the moment as though they had been placed there with the express purpose of voicing his inner exaltations. One of the men noticed Henry and immediately laced arms with him, pulling him along with the group as they headed toward Fifth.

"I had no idea it was so near Christmas," Henry said, when the song was over. He didn't recognize any of the men, though they were dressed well enough. They had apparently been to another party before this one.

"Oh, yes, it's the twentieth tomorrow," replied the man who had drawn him in jovially. He reached into his coat and produced a metal flask. "Any excuse for some brandy—do have some," he added with a slight slurring of the final word.

"Much obliged." Henry took the flask and happily swigged to the lifting of his cares and the restoration of his girl.

"Say, friend," the man went on genially, "do you know any other carols?"

Henry had suffered through caroling several times in his life, but at that moment he was unable to remember any song besides "Joy to the World," and said so.

The little band roared at this, and then picked up the song again from the beginning. They were louder this time and Henry felt its message all the more. He took another swig and began to sing along, too, as they moved joyously onto the avenue, thoughts of Diana and her glossy lips and their future together dancing in his head.

With our many modern conveyances, arrivals late at night and early in the morning are highly avoidable, as any polite house guest well knows. A hostess cannot always select her guests according to their manners, however, and should make herself presentable and gracious at whatever hour is required.

—*VAN KAMP'S GUIDE TO HOUSEKEEPING FOR LADIES OF HIGH SOCIETY,* 1899 EDITION

$\mathcal{W}$HEN DIANA ENTERED HER FAMILY DRAWING ROOM late on a Tuesday evening it was with a composed appearance her older sister might have strived for. She wore a simple black dress that circled in to display her small waist but disguised her other physical gifts, and her hair was more neatly in its place than it had been all evening. She carried herself with quiet dignity across the carpet to the unlit fireplace where her aunt Edith was waiting as though engaged in some kind of performance, and indeed it seemed to Diana that several layers of artifice would be required to disguise the emotions she felt within. Henry loved her again; her whole body was beating with it.

"Mr. Cairns," she said, extending her hand but letting go of his grip before he could kiss it. Snowden Cairns had been her father's occasional business partner and sometime fellow adventurer. *The poor man,* she thought. He was looking at her so earnestly, and she knew that her skin was lit up like some Hudson River sunset and that her pupils were dark and wide. "It's been so long."

"It has, a fact I regret. I hope you received the letters of condolence that I sent after your father's passing? And news of your sister's untimely end has recently reached me. You must accept my deepest apologies for not being here for either funeral. . . . I have been traveling, and there are times when returning to the eastern seaboard is too complicated even on the gravest occasions."

Diana gestured for him to sit, and she herself moved backward into the faded bergère chair beside the one in which her aunt sat. Snowden went on saying kind things about her family, but she was having difficulty following every word. It wasn't that Snowden didn't seem earnest and well meaning, and though she had always thought of him, when she thought of him at all, as a friend of her father's, he did not look nearly old enough to play the part. His nose was short and blocklike and his eyes, which shifted from green to brown, were set far apart under straight, thick brows. His face was not unhandsome, despite its appearance of having weathered a great deal of time out of doors. He had thick, preternaturally blond hair that rose back from his forehead on either side of a middle part, and he made a nice presentation of himself. But he was not Henry. He was only the reason that she was not with Henry now.

She had been reliving the sensations of that unexpected kiss when she noticed that her visitor was still standing. "How is your mother?" he asked, his tone gentle and considerate.

"She is very ill," Diana replied, perhaps with more irritation than she had intended. She looked at her aunt for confirmation of this fact; Edith's concerned eyes moved from Diana's to Mr. Cairns and then she nodded gravely.

"Well, no wonder . . ." he answered, with a dismissive wave of his hand. "It's freezing in here. I am surprised you are not taken ill yourself."

"We . . ." Diana colored and paused. "We hadn't been expecting anyone this late in the day."

She saw Snowden looking at the empty brass rack where the firewood was usually stored. She wanted to tell him that she was taking care of it—that in fact a fire had been built in her mother's room and the kitchen and even her own room that day, thanks to *her* ingenuity—but of course, that would only lead to questions about where the money had come from. And her trip to East Sixteenth Street was not something she could reveal. They had owed so much money to the wood company that her earnings really hadn't gone very far, so it was true that Claire was rationing it and was probably waiting to see how long Snowden planned to stay before she wasted any of it on a fire so late in the evening.

"Miss Diana, if I may," Snowden went on, moving toward her and crouching at her side. The proximity of his face did not make it any more attractive to her. "I have heard reports of your family's misfortunes, and while I can scarcely believe it, having been so closely allied with those fortunes in the past, I am here to help in any way I can. You need not be proud with me."

Then he rose and moved swiftly to the bay windows that faced onto the street. He rapped on the pane, and Diana caught a glimpse of a private coach outside. A few minutes later Snowden's valet was making a fire. Diana's thoughts were too scattered, in that particular moment, to dwell on the peculiarity of Mr. Cairns's traveling with firewood. The valet was dressed similarly to his employer, in workaday brown trousers and a waistcoat of worn black leather. Snowden's shirt, however, was of slate gray silk, rather than thick, utilitarian cotton, and Diana could not help but note a gold bracelet at his cuff catching the light.

"There," her guest declared when a full fire roared under the large, marble mantel. Diana was indeed warmed but the change in temperature did little to help her focus her thoughts away from their reinstated magnetic pole. "Obviously there are other things that are needed around the house, too—I will see to them. But just now, I must see your mother."

Diana looked up from her folded hands mistily. "Oh?"

"It is of the utmost importance."

"What is?"

"That I see your mother."

"Oh!" Diana stood, a little startled by how far her thoughts had strayed in the presence of a near stranger and her aunt. "Well . . ." she went on, more to pave an exit for herself than for any other reason.

"I don't think Mrs. Holland is well enough for that," Edith said, rearranging her aubergine silk sleeves against the chair's padded armrests.

"I'll go see if she's well enough to see you," Diana put in before Snowden could say anything more. Here was an opportunity to leave the room, and she intended to take it.

"Thank you." Snowden made a little bowing motion.

Diana found her mother in the same position as when she had last seen her. She was in her bed, the curtains drawn down, her head resting on a pile of white pillows. But she had somehow contrived to get her hair into some semblance of purposeful arrangement and back under her widow's cap. Her eyes were open.

"What is it, Diana?" she said without pretense of surprise.

"It's Mr. Cairns, Father's friend. He's downstairs and he wants to see you—" Diana was here interrupted by the sound of the door opening again. She turned with some impatience to see the man she had just been talking of, in all his rustic-gentleman trappings, coming into the room. For a man to see into a woman's bedroom was such an assault to decorum that even Diana herself felt a touch scandalized.

"Mrs. Holland," he began, "I cannot tell you how abjectly sorry I am for not having been able to extend my condolences for the passing of both your husband and daughter in person."

"Thank you, Mr. Cairns. I read your letters, however, and I know your feelings."

"Good. I hope you will not consider me overly forward in telling you that I have been hearing of your financial woes and I have come here to tell you that I do not believe any of it. If I may, Mrs. Holland, it is really not possible. I'd like to offer my services in this matter." He paused and withdrew an envelope from inside his waistcoat. "I have brought you a check."

Diana, who had been standing dutifully by her mother's bedside, felt her temper flare at this. It really wasn't necessary, she would have liked to have said, since a solution to all of their problems had very recently presented itself. And that solution was far handsomer than Snowden Trapp Cairns. She would have liked to dismiss his offer fast and sharp, but she found herself silenced again by the fact of her own indiscretions.

She was happy, however, to hear that her mother's thoughts were not entirely divergent from her own. "We can't accept your charity, Mr. Cairns, though it is very kind of you to come to us."

"But it isn't charity," Mr. Cairns said seriously. "It is in fact money that I have owed you for some time, and isn't in truth so very great an amount. Your father's percentage from a modestly successful claim we shared in the Klondike. So you see, if you don't take it, you will be forcing me to be a thief."

Diana found the smile that followed to be unbearably ingratiating.

"Mr. Cairns—" began Mrs. Holland, in a tone of unconvincing protest.

"I insist," Snowden interrupted with finality.

"Thank you." Mrs. Holland accepted the check with a touch of humility that, even in her diminished state, must have been difficult for her to affect. As she leaned over to place it on the night table a look of relief passed briefly across her face. "How long do you plan to be in town?"

"I am presently without duties elsewhere, and if you will allow me, Mrs. Holland, I would like to have a look at your papers. It is preposterous to me that you should be as bad off as they say. . . ." Snowden paused, and his eyes flashed. "Or as you seem to believe you are."

"That is very good of you, though I assure you I have been through the papers and the situation is quite dire. No matter—while you are in town you must stay with us."

Snowden gave a quick bow, his boots closing in on each other at the heels.

"Thank you, Mrs. Holland. We will talk more tomorrow.

But for now I have disturbed you long enough. I will go down and find the maid. She will find a place for me where I will be of the least trouble." He paused to take Diana's hand, though he did not again attempt to kiss it. He held her gaze instead. "Good night, Miss Diana."

"Good night," Diana replied faintly. His exit from the room was a relief to her. It meant that very soon she would again be alone with her thoughts, which was the nearest she could get to again being close to Henry.

The door closed, and she felt her mother's cold hand on her wrist.

"Di?" she said.

"Yes, Mother?" Diana leaned against the bed and watched her mother relax back into her pillows.

"You're tired now, dear, but tomorrow be a little good to Mr. Cairns, would you?"

Diana hardly knew what expression she made. She understood of course what her mother meant by being good. She wanted her to be to Mr. Cairns as she had not been to Mr. Coddington or Mr. Newburg or Mr. Cutting. But at that moment Diana couldn't imagine any man but Henry ever holding her interest again.

Twenty
Two

Good girls hold their heads high by daylight,
Their grace and their virtue soaring with kites,
While bad girls slink along in their shame—
Everyone stares at them, everyone blames.
But those bad girls sleep soundly at night,
Ne'er do their consciences wake them in a fright,
While our good girls toss and they turn—
They lay awake for those who will burn.

—*A SEAMSTRESS'S VERSES*, 1898

THE ROCKING OF A TRAIN WAS EVIDENTLY SOMEthing that calmed Will, for Elizabeth, lying in the crook of his arm, woke up to see that he was perfectly, angelically asleep. The remainders of the lunch they'd eaten early that day had been removed from the little table in front of their red velvet upholstered seat, and the view through the brass-framed window showed that darkness had almost completely fallen. Or was it the first light of dawn? The hour was either very late or very early, but in any event the porter had not disturbed them to make up their berth. She had slept so little the night before that it was natural she would have fallen so completely into dreaming on the train. Elizabeth closed her eyes and then opened them again.

She sat up suddenly and stood. Will shifted but did not wake up. Her shoulders were tight and her mouth was dry. Had they slept through the Oakland stop? If that was true, her chances to save her family were behind her—she knew, from Denny, where the pawnshops were there, but how would she find such places in other cities? She didn't know how long they would stay anywhere else. It seemed impossible that she would now be able to carry out her plan.

She moved down the train, looking for some friendly face, but all was quiet. As she reached the observation car, she saw through the glass that a well-dressed man was sitting there, smoking. She was so preoccupied that she went through the door and addressed the stranger with an abruptness that she would have termed rude in her previous life.

"Have we passed Oakland?" she said.

"Yes, some hours ago," the man replied, turning. This answer distressed her so thoroughly that she did not recognize the man until he pronounced her name.

"Miss Elizabeth Holland," Grayson Hayes repeated with emphasis.

She looked up into the man's face and knew that she had not mistaken Penelope's older brother. Though she hadn't seen him in almost four years, his was a face she knew well. He had high, flat cheeks like his sister and a nose like an arrow pointing downward and a thin pencil moustache. His eyes were blue like his sister's and were positioned just slightly too close together—for some reason that Elizabeth had never fully understood, this gave him a wily rather than clownish appearance.

Then she remembered that she was supposed to be dead.

He was looking at her as though he knew the whole catalogue of her secrets, but that might have just been an old Hayes intimidation technique. He had been abroad, after all, and had always had the family trait of self-absorption. He might have known anything about her or nothing at all. The only thing Elizabeth was sure of was that she disliked the way his eyes were on her.

He had hardened since she last saw him, which was at a small dance at the Hayeses' old town house on Washington Square, where he had flattered her by asking her to dance— she had been very young then, and he had been the pick of the bachelors—but then he'd abandoned her midwaltz to dance with Isabelle De Ford. He was larger now, no longer someone you could describe as a boy. He wore his hair in a way that reminded her of Henry. It was the way they all wore their hair, those boys who cast proprietary glances at the whole world.

"You must have me confused," she said coldly.

Then she turned and ran back through the cars until she reached Will. Grayson Hayes did not follow her, although she kept looking back to be sure, and when she reached her own compartment she shook Will awake. He opened his eyes slowly, lazily, and when he made her out he smiled. A few seconds passed and then he asked her what was wrong.

"We have to get off this train." Her voice trembled, and she knew that if she did not manage a deep breath soon, she might collapse. Will must have realized her state of agitation, because the happiness went out of his face. "We have to get off as soon as we can."

Twenty Three

A young woman who is new in town and wants to make an entrance in society is in an unenviable position. Of course, if she comes with letters of introduction or her family has excellent connections, she will not want for company. But it is unacceptable for a young lady to call around where she has not yet been introduced.

—MRS. L. A. M. BRECKINRIDGE, *THE LAWS OF BEING IN WELL-MANNERED CIRCLES*

FTER THE CRUSHING VISIT WITH PENELOPE Hayes, Lina had hardly left her small, perfect hotel room. It was more perfect to her with every passing hour. She sat at the little polished lady's writing desk and looked at the matching polished bed with its blue spread that went so nicely with the fleur-de-lys wallpaper. She thought with growing sadness of how soon she would have to fall asleep without the shelter of its gilt-edged ceiling. She shot poignant little looks at the elegant ceiling lamp with the U-shaped white shades, which looked like a bouquet of tulips with stems of brass. She had only left the room to eat breakfast and read the paper, but found that her name had not again been mentioned. To punish herself, she went to bed hungry. She had been reaching for too much, by fistfuls. If she had simply acquired the dress and manners of a lady and then gone straightaway to Will, none of this would have happened—but she had wanted to be seen and admired too, and that vain desire had caused her to let her guard down.

It was Wednesday. On Friday she would be homeless.

Now every sound seemed, however irrationally, to prefigure her swift expulsion from the hotel. Even the most gentle knocking. She looked up and blinked in the direction of the sound. For a moment she wondered why the management hadn't already charged in to remove her, and then she realized that she was going to have to let them in. She went to the door and opened it cautiously. There was no one from the hotel staff out in the hall—just Tristan, looking at her with those warm hazel eyes. He took his bowler off so that she could see his light hair, which was overgrown a little and pushed backward rakishly. His height filled the entry and he was smiling at her out of the corner of his mouth.

"They just let you in?" She was unable to mask her surprise. How he had gotten this far unannounced was beyond her, though the affection in his face made it so that she didn't care particularly. She had not wondered until that moment whether or not Tristan was the thief—but the look he was giving her, and the memory of his previous attentions, made her dislike that theory intensely.

"I thought I'd bring your bills in person."

"Oh." The despair was as plain in her tone now as surprise had been a few seconds before.

"That's no way to greet a man who comes bearing gifts," Tristan answered as he produced a long brown box with the

Lord & Taylor logo on its front. He had disguised it under his cloth coat, which he carried thrown across his arm.

This caught Lina's attention and—feeling that desire for gorgeous objects rise in her again, despite all the degradations of the week—she reached for the box. Tristan smiled at her grab but let it pass into her hand easily. When she lifted the top she saw a pair of white suede opera gloves cushioned in deep red tissue. They were elbow length, with a row of small pearl buttons that extended from just below the wrist. "They're beautiful!" she whispered.

"A gift from your greatest admirer; I thought you should have them now that you're going to the opera."

Lina looked up and met her guest's eye. So he had seen the column, too.

"I assume you are the Miss Broad who was in the papers. Surely you're not too fancy to let me in?" Tristan said, already closing the door behind him and tossing his coat onto the foot of her bed. "I hope you're not in love with this old man," he went on casually as he assessed her surroundings. "I got worried when I realized you had been away from the store for so long."

Lina turned her body toward him but did not respond to his last comment. Her attention remained fixed on the gloves. They were such a wretched little reminder of everything she had muddied up, and a wave of self-pity came over her. All of a sudden she knew she was going to cry.

"What's the matter?" Tristan's voice had grown concerned, and he laid a reassuring hand on her shoulder. The kindness of this touch made her situation feel even more pathetic, and she put her face into her cupped hands to hide the hot tears that were now streaming involuntarily down her face. "Don't do that, Miss Broad," Tristan went on. "You don't think your reputation has been ruined, do you? It hasn't in the least. I was only kidding when I said that. *I* know you're not in love with him, and so does everybody else. If you were seen often with different men of the kind, then you might be in danger, but one little piece like that won't do any harm. And besides, everyone will be so distracted by your newness that they won't even think about the propriety of it."

"Oh, it's not that," Lina answered miserably through her sobs. She longed for Will, to be able to confess all of her imperfections and missteps to him. But it was Tristan who was there with her now.

"What, then?"

Lina caught her breath and looked up at the salesman. Her face was red and her eyes were puffy and bright, but there was still so much kindness in his posture that she couldn't help but want to tell him everything. "My purse has been stolen."

Tristan's smile fell a little. "Your purse?"

"Yes, from my room, the night of the opera. It had over two hundred dollars in it, and it was taken—all of it!"

"You must tell the management then."

"No, no," Lina said quickly. She was too ashamed to look at him. "Not that."

Tristan reached forward and took both her hands. The rare gentleness of this human touch only made her want to cry more. She had not been touched in a long time. "Why? Is it because you suspect someone close to you . . . or someone who would be severely punished?"

Lina shook her head firmly.

"But even so, so many tears over so little money." He laughed awkwardly, clasping her hands with his own. "Of course, it's a great deal of money—to someone like *me*. But to you, dear Carolina, that can't be such a loss, can it?"

"It's all I have!" she blurted. It felt almost good to have said so, to let someone in the world know how destitute she was.

Tristan stepped back. Despite the narrowness of the little room in hues of blue, he seemed to have gone a great distance. "But your inheritance . . . ?"

"I'm not an heiress," Lina wailed. The truth was coming out now, and there was no way for her to stop it. She looked into Tristan's eyes, which were still solicitous under an increasingly furrowed brow. "I'm a maid, or I was until the Holland family fired me. That money was all I had. I got it by—never mind. But now I have nothing."

The moment that followed was long and full of tension, and it ended when Tristan removed his hands. Lina hiccupped a final tear as he moved farther away from her and threw himself down contemplatively onto the small velvet settee by the window. "That's why you hated Elizabeth Holland." He turned back to her with a face that was entirely transformed. "You're a maid," he said disgustedly.

She blinked and put one of her hands into the other.

"I thought you were a lady!" he continued, his voice rising to an almost angry pitch.

"I . . . I . . ." Lina stammered.

For a moment she thought she was going to see Tristan in a fit of temper, but he surprised her by putting his face into his hands and starting to laugh.

"What's so funny?" Her heart was pounding in her chest, and she could scarcely summon the breath for even that question.

"Oh, you really fooled me, Miss Broad—*Broud*—whatever your name is. You really pulled one over on me." For a moment she thought his eyes were wet, too, from hilarity or sadness, she wasn't sure. He was smiling, though, and that seemed a not entirely bad thing. "Congratulations. You got me good."

Lina went over and sat down beside him on the settee. She perched on the corner, not wanting to come too close, and tried to meet his gaze. "Don't be angry at me, Tristan," she said in a quiet voice. "I couldn't stand that right now."

"I'm not angry at you. In fact . . ." Here he paused to laugh, as one laughs at absurdity rather than humor. "I have something to confess to you."

Lina's nerves were tender and her pulse was now frighteningly quick. She tried to draw her lips back in a smile to match his. "Oh, yes?" she prodded.

"You see, I'm not what I seem either."

"Oh?" Lina was still attempting lightness, but she knew that her smile had gone brittle. "You mean you don't work at Lord and Taylor's?"

"No . . . no, of course I work there. But you see, I'm just like you. I'm from nothing, and I decided nothing wasn't good enough for me. You aren't the first heiress I've known— you're just the first fake heiress I've known. There's a lot to be gained from being kind to ladies like you—or the kind of lady you were pretending to be. That's my racket, my pretty girl."

"Oh" was all Lina could manage in reply. She was now feeling intensely stupid. It occurred to her for the first time that the fallacy of her claim to be an heiress did not protect her in the least from being preyed on, as true heiresses were. That would be funny someday, she imagined. "Well, goodbye, I guess," she went on eventually. She didn't want to be alone, but she supposed it was what she deserved. "There's nothing to be gained for you here."

Tristan pushed himself up and looked out the window. Her view showed the façade of another hotel, with all its little picture windows into other peoples' ambitions, and down below the carriages depositing the kind of ladies she'd aspired to be like on the walk. They would soon be off to yachts on the Mediterranean or weekends at Tuxedo, and their hats had all been imported from France. "Oh, I wouldn't say that."

Lina flushed. "There's really nothing more to take."

Tristan's hazel eyes moved slowly back to meet hers. "I don't want to *take* anything from you, Carolina. But as far as I can make out, you've got quite a nice little con going already. You have the interest of Carey Lewis Longhorn, not to mention Mr. Gallant."

Lina didn't think the columnist's surname was really Gallant, but she was in no position to correct anyone just then.

"You'd need my help, of course. For protection and guidance. You have been doing an all right job so far, but you would have tripped up and revealed yourself soon. For instance, you're going to have to be careful about only being seen out with perpetual bachelors. If you don't make friends with a girl or two, the ladies will never accept you, and that will mean certain social death." Tristan paused and put his mouth against a contemplative fist. "That's priceless advice," he went on in a moment.

"But for now what really matters is that Mr. Longhorn is rich and he likes you. This means jewels and presents will follow, and those are just as valuable as any inheritance. . . ."

The beginnings of hope were branching through Lina's mind, but she was still wary. She had believed recklessly before, and look where that had gotten her. "I wouldn't have to . . . ?"

"No! No, no, no." Tristan moved closer to her on the settee and gave her a reassuring look. Down below, people who could not afford to stay in the hotel but still wanted to look grand were arriving for luncheon. "That would be a bit like killing the golden goose, wouldn't it?"

Lina blinked thoughtfully, turning this over. It still seemed too wild. She had labored since childhood to win the attentions of a boy who worked in a carriage house—how on earth would she hold the interest of a man whose love life was the stuff of gossip columns? In a few days, no less. "But how can I go on without any money? The bills you brought me alone, not to mention I'll be removed from the hotel on Friday when I can't pay. . . ."

"You are too easily defeated. *That* we will have to cure you of. I really should have caught you earlier and saved you from yourself—*nobody* pays on time. They must consider you a very eccentric heiress indeed here at the New Netherland!

This is one of the chief characteristics of rich people: that they don't know what things cost and forget all the time that they are supposed to pay for them. With just a little gall you will be able to put them off long enough to find yourself in a position where Mr. Longhorn is footing your bill. And then you—and I—will really be in the money."

Lina nodded, a little confusedly. She couldn't help but feel somewhat nervous and exposed listening to this plot. But it was some kind of relief that Tristan was still there, even though he knew her real identity. She didn't mind entertaining his schemes, however crazy they were, just for a little while. It made her feel not entirely destitute, listening to his ideas for her, and she began to feel that perhaps there was a way for her to get just a little of that money back. Not all of it, just enough to buy a ticket west. Then she would go off to find Will, and leave all of her mistakes behind her in New York.

Twenty Four

Property has ever been a fluid concept—
just ask the wife of the Wall Street specu-
lator who writes her party invitations on
Marie Antoinette's escritoire.

—MRS. L. A. M. BRECKINRIDGE, *THE LAWS OF BEING
IN WELL-MANNERED CIRCLES*

HE WHISTLE BLEW, AND LOUD SHOUTS OF "ALL aboard!" could be heard up and down the platform. Inside the simple wooden waiting room, in the small mountain town where Will and Elizabeth had disembarked, benches emptied and hats were clutched as travelers ran for the lumbering iron beast that was preparing to depart again. The table between Will and Elizabeth had uneven legs, and every time one of them put an agitated elbow on its unvarnished top, their glasses of lemonade threatened to spill over. Finally the train left the station, causing all of the windows to shake in their frames but bestowing some quiet on Elizabeth's thoughts.

Will stood first and went to the window, where he took his time assessing the length of the platform and anyone who remained on it. He waited until the steam cleared and then he turned to where Elizabeth sat, folded into the camel wrap with flannel lining that she had worn the day she left New York. He stretched his long, taut arms over his head before moving his hands to the back of his neck, where he collected his overgrown hair and tucked it into the collar of his plaid shirt.

Will made a whistling sound of relief and smiled so that his fine, strong teeth showed. "He's gone, Lizzie," Will called, "so you can stop looking so frightened."

Elizabeth tried to smile. She stood and went to him, and then looked out the window as though Will's statement needed some kind of verification. She did feel less frightened, but it hardly settled her mind. On the other end of the room the lunch-counter workers, who had been selling pie and sliced-chicken sandwiches, were closing up. The newsagent was counting his take.

"Thank goodness," she said finally, wishing her relief didn't sound so thin.

"And now we have twelve hours before the next train comes. Just time enough to find a little chapel and get hitched, I'd say." Will laughed, although she knew he was at least partially in earnest. That moment back in New York when he had knelt to propose to her—this was just after she had become engaged to Henry—was still wincingly fresh in her mind. "You could be Mrs. Keller for real on the next car we ride."

Elizabeth lowered her eyes and swallowed, the sound of which was unbearably loud in her own ears at least. A few days ago this would have seemed a very romantic suggestion, but at the moment it brought back all the old feelings. The old guilt, from the days when Will was so desirable and true and she was the hypocrite favorite of New York's ruling class. She put her hand into her pocket and folded it around the ring.

"Or we could go on living in sin." His voice was softer this time, but had not entirely lost its humor.

"No, I—"

"What's the matter?"

"It's that I don't know what we'll find in New York. Or how Mother really is or what kind of trouble Diana has gotten into." Elizabeth had to close her eyes to keep herself from crying. She drew the wrap closer around her with one hand and tightened her fist over the ring with the other. "I've been imagining the worst. And I'm worried about money. What if we get there and they're going to be thrown out of the house, and they can't afford any medicine, and—"

"Hush. There's no reason to think things are so bad. All we know is what the papers say, and you know that they exaggerate. And anyway, I have some money."

"I know, but Will . . ." Elizabeth looked at him and then shifted her eyes to the rough-hewn floorboards. She ran her fingers along the table that they had just been sitting at. "I have something I didn't tell you about. Something I was planning on selling, in Oakland. Something that might make all the difference to my family."

She looked up at Will, who was watching her and waiting. Besides the faint chatting of the newsagent and the lemonade salesgirl, the room was silent.

"My engagement ring." Her voice broke over the word. "From Henry Schoonmaker."

Elizabeth had avoided even saying that name out loud to Will since they had left New York. She disliked doing it now, and it was plain on his face that he found the sound of it distasteful too. "Oh."

Now she spoke fast, hoping to bring him away from that maudlin precipice he was surely now approaching. "Not because I want it, Will—because it's worth a great deal of money, because I thought maybe we would need it and I didn't know how I was ever going to find you and . . ." Her voice trailed off. "But I did find you."

"I wouldn't have let you get lost." Will still hadn't met her eyes yet, and his jaw was set so that it emerged prominently over his neck.

"I know," Elizabeth replied. She didn't like how small her voice had gotten, but she couldn't help it.

"I'm not angry, Lizzie, don't be like that. It's just not a nice memory is all. I would have liked to have been the one to give you that ring."

It was late in the afternoon and the light coming in from the windows on either side of the station was moody and blue, but Elizabeth found that she was radiating in her old way despite all that. "I don't even like that ring."

"You don't?" Will met her eyes now, and there was the suggestion of a smile just waiting to emerge.

"No." She reached for his hands and took them both up, swinging her arms to lighten his mood. "I would have thrown it in the river with my old self if I didn't have a practical streak. But I do—that part of me wants to sell the ring. Just in case my family really needs that money. Just in case."

The arc of a line had emerged between the left corner of Will's mouth and his left nostril. His large hands were holding on to her dainty ones, and they swung their arms back and forth a few more times just thinking of what they would yet do together. "Someday I'm going to buy you just the kind of ring you want."

"I know," Elizabeth whispered. "I know you will."

"In the meantime, let's go sell that ring, get it off both our minds." Will dropped her hands and put an arm over her shoulder, drawing her toward the far door of the waiting room, which led away from the train platform and into town. "That way you can stop worrying, putting lines in that famous complexion of yours."

"But how will we know where to go? We've never been here before," Elizabeth said, even as they moved across the floor.

"All train stations are the same," he answered, his jovial tone fully restored to him. "Surrounded by saloons and pawnshops, so that people desperate to get away can sell what they have. Or have a drink while they wait. We aren't desperate, though, neither of us. We're going to get a good price for that ring. It's caused enough trouble, and now it's going to give us something back."

Elizabeth, tucked in under Will's shoulder and headed into a snow-covered place she had never seen before, began to feel all right again. She felt truly calm for the first time since Diana's telegram had arrived. They were wrapped up in their coats, which made them look a little put together despite everything, and they could already feel the bracing air just outside and the whole future just beyond it.

D—

I am so sorry I wasn't able to
visit you yesterday or the day before.
My father has placed me on house
arrest. I would have written sooner,
but even my correspondence is being
monitored. Will you come tonight?
Nine o'clock, the same place as before.

—HS

"$\mathcal{W}$HO IS THE NOTE FROM?"

Diana, who was sitting too close to the fire in her family drawing room, raised her eyes as though she were coming out of a daytime sleep. For a few moments her thoughts had been entirely elsewhere, further uptown, in the greenhouse where she'd once spent the night, in that perfect presence. The most exciting presence she'd ever known. Her lids fluttered and she realized that the side of her body facing the flames had grown hot and red. She folded the note hastily and put it in the pocket of the honeydew-colored dress she had worn only the week before. The dress, which had been a witness to feelings entirely opposite of what she was experiencing now, had been her mother's decision that night and this evening, as well.

"Oh, it doesn't matter," she told Snowden, who was sitting across from her in a dull black jacket that seemed deliberately chosen to accentuate his less urban qualities. "What were you saying . . . ?"

"I was saying that the ways in which I am prepared to help you and your family are not a charity . . ." Snowden went on, looking vaguely pleased with himself. It was a point he seemed at pains to make, and to which Diana was surely obliged to listen, as she feared Edith, stationed in the near background and pretending to read from a book of sermons, might remind her if her attention lapsed. For he had bought more wood than they could burn all winter, and stocked the pantries, and erected in the corner of the room a Christmas tree that brought a sense of festivity to the Holland house that would have been unthinkable the day before. "Your father and my business interests were of course entangled, and our holdings in the Klondike were for a time difficult to decipher. . . ."

Diana smiled mistily and focused her eyes on the dust brown collar of Snowden's shirt so she would appear to be paying attention even as she allowed her thoughts to drift. She had been dreamy and agitated since their guest had arrived, trying not to seem rude or dismissive but unable to banish the image or idea of Henry for even a moment. Of course, when he had not come to visit on Wednesday and then again on Thursday—as he had so clearly promised on Tuesday night—her yearning had grown and she had not been able to eat, and by evening she had felt tingly and weak. It had been a sweet, almost unbearable state of confusion. She was certain that this time she had not misjudged Henry, however, and his note—

which had been delivered by some anonymous man, just as darkness was falling, and then brought to her by a distracted Claire—had finally vindicated this assumption.

She was lucky in a way that Snowden was there, because all of his projects to make the house better kept her busy and prevented her imagination from wandering too far in any direction, although she did not in truth want to be distracted.

"What a time we had on the Klondike, though . . ." Snowden was saying.

She did not ask herself why Henry's father had put him on house arrest. She only imagined that he must be experiencing a kind of torture, as she was, and that his intentions and desires were also shifted to the greenhouse with the simple brass frame bed. Diana wondered if there were a way to calculate this division of self—what percentage of her body and spirit was there in the drawing room of No. 17 Gramercy Park South, what percentage was transported to that perfect place with the arched glass ceiling where she was close enough to Henry that she could smell his clean, faintly cologned skin. Certainly more than half. The arrival of that note, which was now safely hidden in her pocket, had so captured her senses that she could almost feel the delicate play of Henry's fingertips along her arm.

"Of course, that was only one of our adventures. We went looking for fortunes in South Africa and Cal-ee-for-nye-ay."

Diana shifted in her seat and nodded vaguely. This weak attempt at humor did not please her. Meanwhile, the line of Henry's chin was as clear in her mind as the white line of the mantel on which Snowden rested his stubby elbow. She could see the exact shade of his eyes, although she would not have been able to answer whether Snowden's were blue, green, or brown. The objects in the room she occupied—a room she had seen daily for all of her life—were indistinct, but she was already mentally mapping the route she would take out of the house, the route that would take her to Henry. She had already planned what she would wear and what she was prepared to give him.

"Diana, are you well?"

"Yes," Diana answered, startled. She decided she should appear convincing and so reiterated the sentiment. "Very well."

"Good. You looked faint for a moment, but if you are feeling well, then there is something your mother and I have discussed. We have talked about how well I knew your father, his affections and hopes for his daughters—hopes that now fall exclusively on you. We have discussed what Mr. Holland thought appropriate and true, and we decided that at this juncture it would be wise to show the world how lovely—and how well—you are. We shall dispel the rumors about the Hollands having to hide in poverty. You and I will thus have dinner tonight at Sherry's, with your aunt Edith as chaperone. The world will see how beautiful you look—have I told you, by the way, how beautifully you wear that dress?" Snowden reached inside the breast of his jacket and removed a small oblong box. "It will go very well with this, don't you think?"

Diana watched as he pulled back the black velvet lid and revealed a delicate pearl choker that, on another day, she might have readily agreed would go very well with her dress.

"But—tonight?" she started, her cheeks slackening. She was all of a sudden back in the parlor with all the dark wood-work and the olive-colored walls. Her skin was being scorched by the fire, and, try as she might, she could not recover her flight of fancy. She was only, horribly, here. A quiver of disappointment shot through her. Tonight she was supposed to be with Henry, in his greenhouse, but she would not even have time to send him a note explaining her absence.

Snowden, if he noticed, was not deterred. "Yes—has there ever been a more perfect time for it? The reservation is for nine o'clock," he said as he moved to hook the double string of pearls at the nape of her neck. Diana's face was cast into shadow as Snowden's torso moved in toward her and she took the opportunity to grimace for all the things she would miss. The pearls were cold against her skin, and the clasp made a sound of sick finality as it snapped shut.

. . . at the same gathering, the enchanting Miss Diana Holland was seen chatting intimately with Mr. Teddy Cutting. She's also been spotted recently at the opera with Spencer Newburg and skating in the park with Percival Coddington. One might infer that Mrs. Holland is looking to make a match? Of course, Cutting's position, fortune, and age make him the most suitable of these suitors. . . .

——FROM THE "GAMESOME GALLANT" COLUMN IN THE
NEW YORK IMPERIAL, FRIDAY, DECEMBER 22, 1899

ENRY CROSSED HIS LEGS AND SHIFTED IN THE
wooden rocker that was positioned so as to casually access a view into the long main room of the Schoonmaker
greenhouse. He was wearing trousers with whisper-thin pin-
stripes and a cream shirt fastened at the wrist with cuff links
that bore his initials. Dressing well was a habit for Henry, but
he had put extra care into what he wore that particular Friday
evening. This despite the fact that he was on house arrest, after
celebrating his renewed hopes for a life with Diana Holland
with a group of drunken Christmas carolers. He had brought
extra blankets to the gardener's old bedroom himself and lit
the small wood-burning stove, but still he was concerned that
Diana, when she came, would not be warm enough.

He had been stuck inside the house for two days, during
which time he had done little but experience a building frustration and dream of Diana. He had rallied all his ingenuity to
find a way to slip her a note without his father getting mind
of it.

Of course now it was well past the appointed time, and there was still no sign of her. He had gone out twice to sneak along the gate and look for her, but a prolonged presence there would only have given him away. Since then he'd had a good hour to contemplate whether this was the longest he had ever waited for a woman. While it far outdistanced the third occasion, it only came in second, after an evening one summer in Newport when he waited for a woman whose smile gleamed with the same pristine glory as her wedding ring and who, the hours finally proved, was never going to show up. He had already known in his heart that she wasn't coming, and as such was so thoroughly boozed up that he wouldn't have been allowed to return to gentle company anyway. He instead lay back in the grass and thought maudlin thoughts about love and matrimony and how he would never engage in either.

His mood was different now. He was entirely sure that Diana was on her way to him, that he was in her thoughts as she was in his, and that the time before they were again together was finite. Quite finite.

Still, waiting was not something he was used to; he was not, in any event, doing it very gracefully. He stood, walked around the bed, arched his neck to look at the curved ceiling with its glass panes in their white iron web, which hung over the simple bed buried in quilts. He breathed in the rich, earthy air and straightened his collar. He checked the smoothness of his vaguely golden skin over his high cheekbones in a small mirror and wondered if he had time to get a bottle of wine from the cellar. He turned, finally, back to the chair, where he crossed his legs in the other direction and then began rustling through a pile of newspapers on a wrought-iron table that had been painted white. He supposed the gardener brought them there so that he could read something while he was taking lunch. Henry reminded himself that he should check with the gardener, who was now living with one of Isabelle's seamstresses in the main servants' quarters, to see how much time he spent there before he planned another rendezvous, as he was already planning for many more.

Of course, that was an attitude he had before he began idly flipping through the old newspapers in a vain attempt to pass the time. Henry was not naturally interested in world events or stock crises or theater reviews or the problem of public drunkenness amongst the city's coachmen and cabdrivers. He was interested in yachting and horses, topics amply covered by that week's papers and that he might have read about on another occasion. At that particular moment, with the stars positioned as they were, he was only really prepared to read to the bottom of a sentence that contained the words *Diana* and *Holland*. And after a few moments of shiftless reading he did find one.

The paragraph began innocently enough with some

account of a dinner party of Florence Cutting's—she was Mrs. Darroll now; a few other details followed, but Henry wasn't reading that part so carefully—which apparently Diana, his Di, had attended. Not only attended, but spent in the company of his friend Teddy. The "intimate" company. This word conjured for Henry all the irritating ways his friend behaved when he took a special liking to a girl—stroking her hand and fetching anything she might have a vague desire for and generally being overly solicitous in a way that no man in his right mind would ever have the patience to be. Henry read the item again four times but found the account unchanged.

Now he saw why Teddy had been so against his relationship with Diana. It was because Teddy wanted her for himself. Henry balled up the paper and threw it onto the bed.

He walked through the long central passageway of the greenhouse, surrounded by year-round hyacinths and orchids, and into the main house with a single thought. He must find Diana and demand to know what had happened. Before she told him too much he would explain how insufferable Teddy was, what a do-gooder, how often—against his own sense of style and his best friend's frequent cajoling—he succumbed to decorum. He would tell her how Teddy, like an old matron after too much tea, had discouraged their love. . . . But of course, this line of thinking only made Henry realize how much his friend had gained by stalling him.

Henry continued through the small first-floor galleries with the idea of finding a servant who might be able to help him locate a coat. It was cold, he knew that much, and he had no time to ascend the stairs to his own suite of rooms. He was thinking about the coat and whether he should in fact go to Teddy first when he stumbled into one of the private drawing rooms and saw that it was occupied. By his father, stepmother—though he still had a hard time thinking of her that way—and Penelope Hayes.

"Oh, Henry!" his stepmother gasped, turning in her chair and batting her fan with some mixture of cunning and glee. She was wearing a dress of black chiffon that gathered in folds at the bust like a Grecian gown and cascaded from her shoulders like wings. White lace covered her slim arms and her neck all the way up to her chin. "So glad to see you. We are having one of these private little quiet evenings, which we fashionable people are being said to prefer this season, and it's boring me half to death. Since *you* were the last one to bring shame on the family, the very least you could do is join us."

"Oh, *do*," Penelope seconded in a voice that subtly contained—he knew it well enough—the intention to seduce. She was clothed all in off-white. It was not her color. She was cold, and there was something about her skin that suggested death.

"You must excuse me," Henry began, backing for the

door. Isabelle arched a blond brow, and Penelope's fan came down to her lap in a swoop. He saw in an instant that the women were colluding with each other. "You see, it's that I've got to—"

Henry was cut off by the sound of the carved and polished legs of his father's chair as they screeched backward against the floor. The man's solid frame came to standing and then crossed the parquet, where he grabbed Henry by the arm and said coldly, "Oh, no. You're not going anywhere. Or have you forgotten the fact of your house arrest?" Henry looked at the roaring fire and the ladies by it as he was forcibly brought back into the room. "How poor your memory is," his father continued, almost as an aside, as he pushed him into the settee by Penelope.

This closeness to the Hayeses' finest product was a thing he once sought out, but he felt a strong disinclination to it now. She had seemed, then, like the perfect partner in crime—a girl who shared his contempt for all the rules everybody else was so terrified of breaking. Now he saw that she was happy to break them only when it aligned with her other calculations. She might have shared his contempt for everybody else, but she still wanted their adulation. This seemed a very bloodless, unimaginative kind of desire now that his heart was so full of Diana Holland. He clenched his fists and glared at the people who were keeping him from her.

Twenty
Seven

Of course a girl may have multiple beaux, but she should not appear to have too many and should be careful what she promises them. She will have to be especially careful of appearances when she is older and can no longer explain away her behavior as naïveté. And of course she should be considerate, and make sure that two beaux do not meet.

—FROM THE "DEBUTANTE" COLUMN, *DRESS MAGAZINE*, DECEMBER 1899

"MISS BROAD, HOW LUCKY CAREY FOUND YOU!" Lucy Carr, the merriest divorcée in New York society, cried happily as the older gentleman's brougham came to a stop in front of her apartment house in the East Forties. Over dinner, she had told Lina ostensibly everything there was to know about her, and on the ride home she had kept her arm laced in the younger woman's with a tautness that seemed to resist any potential letting go. The night air was chill and their breath came through their fur wrappings in mystical white gusts. "We are so in need of new blood in our set. And everybody but me is married, which gets *awfully* dull."

"You forget me," Mr. Longhorn put in from the opposing seat.

"Oh, surely *you* don't count," Mrs. Carr replied with a brassy laugh.

"You're right, dear. I'm so old I sometimes forget that Central Park is a park at all and not some great wasteland of swamp and rock. But I did throw a lovely dinner, didn't I?"

If Lina had once thought it would be difficult to catch his attention a second time, she had been disabused of this notion as soon as they crossed paths in the lobby and he asked her to dinner. She'd said yes, after which he apologized at length for having misunderstood her name at the opera. "It was a lovely good time, Mr. Longhorn."

She said this with a shy sweetness that was the mode of flirtation for girls her age—or at least, it was the mode of flirtation she had seen employed by Elizabeth Holland in her own drawing room—although her feelings fully backed the sentiment. It had been a lovely day. They had raced sleighs in the park and dined in one of the private room at Sherry's, which she had read about but never entered, and her nose was still a little red from the exertion and the champagne and she felt almost giddy at having met so many new people. She had caught her own reflection in plenty of mirrors and knew her eyes to be very bright. The ease with which she had been swept up by Longhorn's circle startled her, but she didn't mind. Anyway, their association was bound to be brief. The world seemed good after all just then, and very likely to supply her with the means to buy a ticket west any day now.

"Mrs. Carr," Mr. Longhorn prompted. "Your apartment?"

"Oh, yes!" Lucy kissed Lina on the cheek and made her promise that they would soon be in each other's company again. Once Mrs. Carr, and the long furs she was trailing, disappeared into the brightly lit lobby, the carriage jerked into motion. Mr. Longhorn and Lina did not speak again until the horses came to their final stop at the New Netherland.

"My dear," the older gentleman said, as he came down to the sidewalk, "I haven't had you to myself all evening. Won't you come up for a brandy?"

"Of course, Mr. Longhorn." Lina remained aloft for a moment on the carriage's backseat. All was very still and quiet on the street, but those heroic buildings with their gilded flourishes rose above her, twinkling at the windows. She sighed, and then took Longhorn's man's arm so that he could help her down. "I'd be delighted."

"You go on in then," he said kindly. "I won't have anyone talking about you going to an old man's room late at night. Go to your room and take off your coat, and I'll send Robert for you in a little while."

Lina's bottom lip trembled up under her teeth and she nodded. She went into the grand lobby, her feet falling lightly across the mosaic floor. She requested her key with such entitlement that she wondered briefly if Mr. Cullen wouldn't mistake her for someone with a grander room. Then she crossed to the elevator and told the attendant what floor she was on without making the mistake of looking at him. The iron door closed and she felt herself rising. *I'm rising,* she thought, *I'm rising, I'm rising.*

"Carry yourself awfully high, don't you?"

Lina's breath stuck at the impertinence. Her cheeks flamed up as she waited for the attendant to turn. When he did she saw a reckless smile and a pair of hazel eyes that she recognized as Tristan's. The light of the chandelier was suddenly blinding. She stepped back instinctually.

"Where did you get that uniform?"

"Ah, you underestimate me, my Carolina," he answered with the same smile. "It seems you had a successful evening."

"Yes." Lina took a breath and began to recover herself. "He's asked me up for brandy."

"Good! He'll soon be ours. But be careful—give him too much, and you'll be as useless as any maid."

"I won't."

"And for God's sake, keep on the lookout for a new friend. Being seen with divorcées like Mrs. Carr is worse than having no friends at all."

Lina didn't ask herself how he knew about Mrs. Carr. "I'll remember that."

"And be careful not to say too much, or you may give yourself away." Tristan moved his hand to the elevator's lever.

"No, of course not."

"And if it's the only thing you remember: Pretend to drink, but in fact take little. He may get drunk, but be careful you do not."

Lina nodded and continued nodding until he told her to stop. She would not have predicted what he did next once if she had been asked a thousand times, which was that he stepped toward her and tilted his head. She felt the leather-padded wall of the elevator against her back and his lips against hers. The skin of his face was rough as sand; her chest swelled up and it touched his. It was her first kiss, and it was both hard and soft at once. She had imagined Will doing this to her a hundred times, but imaginary kisses were nothing compared to the real thing. It felt like a whole bouquet of flowers opening in the light.

When the elevator jerked to a stop everything about her dress was in order and she stepped onto the ninth floor without looking back.

"Be ready, Miss Broad," she heard Tristan say as she walked toward her room. "My next move comes soon."

Lina was surprised at herself. For a girl who had just experienced her first kiss, her nerves were remarkably steady. She was careful not to take too much brandy even as Mr. Longhorn enjoyed his. She smiled charmingly as he told her stories about his country estate and his yacht and which of his business associates bored him particularly. Despite the cues Tristan had just given her, she was certain that everything she knew about sitting still and appearing entranced she had learned from Elizabeth, but she didn't mind this. Elizabeth had taken plenty from her. It was only fair to take a little back.

"I would like to take *you* to Paris . . ." Mr. Longhorn was saying. He had been talking about Paris quite a bit. His long limbs jutted out lazily from his rather full center, which a velvet smoking jacket, of a slightly deeper shade than the one he had been wearing when they met, encased richly. He had put off his cigar for the moment, which Lina was thankful for. No one in the Holland household had ever smoked them—except, occasionally and in secret, Edith, old Mr. Holland's sister—and so she was unused to their odor. "Paris," he went on wistfully, "is where every good thing happened to me."

They were situated on rich brown club chairs in front of a roaring fire in the sunken sitting room of Longhorn's suite. The cut-glass decanter sat between them, and Longhorn's man hovered in the background. It was impossible to know what the hour was, although Lina wasn't sure she had ever been awake so late, at least not this way.

"Surely not *every* good thing," Lina said.

"No, not every good thing," Mr. Longhorn returned gaily. The lines of his well-lived-in face deepened, and he tossed his head back. His gray hair grew most thickly on the sides of his head and over his ears, Lina noticed, although it was still an impressive head of hair. "Not everything at all! But I was there when I was a young man, so I can't help but associate it with the best times."

Lina smiled blandly at this. She wasn't sure how else to respond and so she did as Tristan had instructed and kept quiet, which the passing seconds proved to be a reaction of which Longhorn approved.

"See how young I used to be!"

Lina looked around her, almost expecting to see some apparition of his younger self. She saw him gesture, instead, toward a wall of portraits that she had glanced at cursorily on her entrance and taken to be nothing more than his famous collection of beauties. They were all portraits, it was true, but as she rose and approached she saw that one of the thick gold frames contained the likeness of a man in his twenties. He had a mane of black hair and a nose still fine and sculptured. But she recognized the high cheekbones and the playful eyes, and she saw clearly enough where Mr. Longhorn got his taste for old-fashioned collars. She looked at the painting and felt a passing longing for her first kiss to have been with a gentleman like that.

"This was you?" she whispered.

"Yes, back when all the girls would have had me." Mr. Longhorn paused and took a sip of his brandy. "I hope you don't think me immodest, Miss Broad, to say so. But that was how I was then. I sometimes wish—several times a day even—

that I'd not been so taken with myself and had chosen a wife. Then I wouldn't be so alone now. But I also can't help being a little impressed by myself when I look back."

"Oh, I don't blame you," Lina said, flushing a little at the sincerity in her voice. She looked away from Longhorn's portrait, and across the framed depictions of beauties past and present. There they were in rosy watercolor or in broad, colorful strokes of oil, with their painted cheeks and fitted silks. She felt a kind of longing to be among them, to be considered so beautiful that some painter would want to immortalize her. For a moment she forgot that she was not alone and lost herself in staring at the portraits. That was when her eyes fell on Elizabeth Holland.

Her portrait was small and framed in simple black tole. She was positioned so that her body faced away from the viewer, but she looked back over her shoulder with a look of utter self-possession. The strokes that rendered her were light and airy, but everything about the likeness was Elizabeth: the small, round mouth, the innocent, wide-set eyes, the pale, clear skin with touches of apricot coloring at the nose and pointed chin. She was wearing a dress of pale pink silk that Lina remembered dressing her in.

Lina turned away, hoping it wasn't obvious to her host how badly she wanted to be like the girl in the painting, and walked toward the high casement windows that looked down on the park. She could see now why her room cost only what it did. Mr. Longhorn's suite had several rooms, with antique furniture and a fireplace that would have dwarfed the Hollands'. More impressive yet, it looked not over a street but over a park. A huge and elegant park that spread below them: bare, purple trees in the snow contained neatly by a rim of buildings on each side as though it were Longhorn's own personal flower bed.

It was the end of an evening in which she had known what it was to be envied and admired. Gazing down at that view, she found that these experiences only made her long for more. When she left the window, she couldn't help but glance one last time at Longhorn's portrait. Oh, if only she could have known him *then*.

"Mr. Longhorn." She had turned away from the youth in the picture and was now looking at the real thing. His heavy lids had closed while she was at the window, and they reopened only slowly now.

"Oh . . . Carolina," he replied after a minute. He seemed to have forgotten himself, but when he recognized her, he smiled contentedly. "How happy you make me, my dear," he added, a little sadly.

Lina's gaze drifted to Robert, in a black swallowtail coat and pants of the same color. He was watching her. Even his brass buttons shone in her direction.

A moment ago, Lina's opinion of herself had been quite high. It sank a little now, when she saw how Robert was looking at her. His face was placid, and he was observing the scene as though it were one he'd witnessed before. Her sense of herself as a success might have been further reduced had not a sound at the door called him to attention. When Robert opened the door she found that the winds had changed direction again.

For there was Tristan, wearing the brown suit of a Lord & Taylor salesman and wielding a rather ominous collection of oblong envelopes. She could feel the impress of his lips on hers, as though the kiss had occurred only seconds ago—as though it had left a mark. He brushed past Robert and stood looking down on Mr. Longhorn.

"I am sorry to interrupt, but I have been trying to find Miss Broad everywhere."

"What seems to be the matter?" Mr. Longhorn replied coldly. He sat up now, alert.

"I've never seen this man." Lina's voice was hoarse and she felt very much like a skiff battered in a gale. Tristan had mentioned a next move, but this seemed awfully soon. Her confidence began to erode. She seemed again very close to being exposed.

"Surely, Miss Broad, you remember me from Lord and Taylor's department store?" Tristan pressed.

"Oh! But I go to so many stores. . . ." He was looking at her intensely, which only worsened the heat rising in her cheeks. "I guess my memory gets a little bad sometimes."

"Miss Broad can forget department store clerks just as often as she pleases," Mr. Longhorn cut in. "I really don't see how that justifies your interruption. It is very late, and this is my private room, so state your business or get out."

A few moments ago, Longhorn had considered her one of the bright young things. But here was her friend, the con artist, come to dispel any of those notions. Lina closed her eyes and waited for things to fall apart.

"I apologize for the hour, but I have been waiting in the lobby for Miss Broad since six. It's about these bills—"

"Bills? You bother me with *bills* so late in the evening?"

Lina opened her eyes. The older gentleman had drawn himself up. Even though he leaned against the arm of the chair for support, the derision in his voice was biting, and she actually thought she saw Tristan shrink backward a hair.

"I'll thank you to have Miss Broad's bills sent directly to my office on Prince Street from now on, and that you molest the young lady herself no further. You know the address? Good. My man will make sure you find the way out."

Breath returned to Lina's body, although she was still unsure whether to be relieved or devastated. She felt sure that Tristan's appearance had broken her spell. Mr. Longhorn turned away from the door, and she could see that he had been angry—really, truly angry. He brought his balled fist to his mouth and coughed into it violently several times. As Tristan backed into the hall, he winked once at Lina and then turned.

"Thank you, sir," he called before he disappeared down the far stairwell, with Robert following watchfully behind.

When Mr. Longhorn's fit of coughing ended, he paused and let his eyes linger on his young guest.

"That was so . . . odd." She was stumbling over her words, and she could not look up from the table. "I can pay you back, of course, just as soon as—"

The old gentleman made a gesture with his hand as though he were batting away a moth. "I don't want you to pay me back, my dear."

"But I *could*," she persisted stupidly.

"No, you couldn't. I know what you've been up to, or do you think I made all my money by trusting every huckster that came along?"

"No." The truth of what he said set in for Lina a few minutes too late. She had been anticipating those words, "I know what you've been up to," and it was almost a relief to hear them. "I suppose you didn't," she offered finally.

"No, I knew just what you were up to that first day in the lobby."

She began to fidget with the lace detail of her dress. The shame was almost overwhelming, but in a few minutes, she told herself, it would all be over.

"And I thought to myself, A girl that lovely shouldn't have to degrade herself just because she wasn't born into anything. It's different for a man with talent. A man with talent can work hard and make some money and marry himself a name. Not so a girl, not unless her pa works hard. And I suspect you never had much of a pa."

Only now did Lina allow her gaze to rise a little up. "No." Her voice was a cautious whisper.

"Don't look so scared, dear. I don't want anything more from you than your company, and you don't need to worry about my being a lecher like they say. I don't want to take any of the glow off you. I waited too long to marry, and now it's too late for me, but I'd still like someone to go to parties with and to tell me how the young people do things. If you'd be that girl for me, I'd see that the department stores and the hotel clerks don't bother you anymore. Your bills would go directly to me—you could hire yourself a lady's maid and your own coach. I would see that they give you the best."

Lina was so stunned with gratitude she hardly knew what to do. So she was worth immortalizing, after all. Or at least dressing up. A calming warmth was spreading all over her body, and she had to remind herself to smile. "Thank you,

Mr. Longhorn," she said as the smile suffused her face. "That sounds nice."

"Good. Tomorrow you'll go get yourself some new things. I want you to attend the Schoonmakers' annual Christmas Eve party with me, and you'll need a gown nobody has seen before for that."

Lina knew her nodding was a little profuse, but already she was picturing the cut and hue.

When he spoke again, there was a new gentleness in his words. "I'm sorry for that ugly little scene, my dear. We needn't dwell on it anymore."

"Oh, I am, too," she said softly. But Lina wasn't sorry at all. For Lina, the waters had unexpectedly turned tranquil, and she found herself floating under a bright, warm sun.

Twenty Eight

No man ever believes his depiction in the press to be accurate.

—*SOCIETY AS I WROTE IT*, BY "THE GAMESOME GALLANT,"
DECEMBER 1899

ATURDAY WAS THE DAY BEFORE CHRISTMAS EVE, and it passed quietly for smart New York. The sun went down early and, for Henry, it was as though daylight never happened. He brooded all night in his own room, slept fitfully but late, and by five o'clock darkness had completely fallen. It seemed one continuous night, for here he was again, in the same drawing room with the same people. There were a few extras, too—Lucy Carr and Mr. Gore. Apparently, Isabelle couldn't go without entertainment for two nights together and had put her foot down, since ordinarily old Schoonmaker would not have let a divorcée into his house twice in one week, and especially not at the same time as a man who was seen so regularly without his wife. They were playing bridge, the four of them—Mrs. Schoonmaker, Mrs. Carr, Gore, and Penelope Hayes, who was watching Henry, bird of prey–like, without ever seeming to turn her eyes in his direction.

"Bridge," said Henry without moving his nose too far

from his waiting cognac. "Isn't that one of the unladylike pursuits?"

"Only when you do it in large parties or the big hotels or in foreign places," replied his father, who had been sitting next to him getting red-faced on his son's favorite after-dinner drink and saying very little.

"In other words, only when you get seen?"

"Exactly. Not everybody is so pathologically *seen* as you, my boy."

Henry nodded and drank. He tapped his fingers on the ormolu-encrusted arm of his chair and considered the fact that if he had not been seen on one recent evening in particular, he would be free to go find out exactly what had happened between Teddy and Diana. Instead, he sat in the parlor of his family's Fifth Avenue mansion, growing older by the minute just like everybody else.

He could hear, in the adjoining galleries and parlors, the servants preparing for the Christmas Eve party Mrs. Schoonmaker was planning—she had complained of the ruckus, and of the strain the preparations put on her nerves, several times already. It occurred to Henry that he was sitting in that same enfilade of rooms where his engagement had been announced, some months before, and it seemed to him that from that original act of cowardice came all his current misfortunes.

"Miss Hayes is such a lovely good girl." His father took

a drink when he had finished speaking but did not otherwise pretend that this was a random observation.

"You didn't used to think so."

"Tragedies change people." Henry's father shifted his bulk in his antique chair, which sighed, and moved his snifter from one hand to the other. "Some people," he added pointedly.

Henry took a bitter sip and propped his head against his fist, shifting his body as he did away from his father's. He looked across the floor, the polish of which was obscured by the dark carpets, at Penelope, who was posed against the little card table in her pale yellow dress with the gold beading around the bustline. Her dark hair was swept up into a high sculpture, and the glow from the next room gently outlined her long, curved neck. He had kissed that neck, but he felt very far away from a desire to do so now. It was arched just so for him, he knew, but also for his father, and this thought gave him a deep feeling of disgust.

Henry's attention was sharply diverted when the butler appeared in the door and announced a name that had been much in his thoughts. Before the final syllable of the name "Teddy Cutting" had been uttered, Henry was out of his chair and across the floor. He met Teddy as he entered, looked him in the eye and stated a sharp and simple: "You."

"Hello to you, too," Teddy replied with mild amusement. "I was just dining at Delmonico's. Everybody missed you."

"I've got to talk to you." Henry's eyes flashed around the room even as he roughly linked his arm through Teddy's. To his great irritation, Teddy released himself and moved to the card table, where he made his hellos. Only after he had gone around the circle did he allow himself to be drawn forward into the galleries. He wore a bemused twist to his smile and a dinner jacket that Henry noticed as being distinctly borrowed from his own style. His blond hair was darkened with the pomade that held it parted on the side.

"I saw the paper," Henry hissed when they were out of earshot from the others. The walls of the room were deep red, and copper pots in the corners overflowed with ferns.

"What paper?" Teddy asked. He was maintaining a stance of vaguely amused innocence that did nothing to calm Henry's ire. He tapped his top hat, which he was still holding, against his thigh as though he were bored. "It's really a shame you're on house arrest so soon after you ended your mourning period . . ." he went on. "The fellows miss you."

"The paper with the item about you and Diana Holland."

"What are you talking about?" Teddy said, halting by a marble nymph and finally looking his friend in the eye.

"That 'Gallant' column," Henry replied hotly. "The one that mentioned you being intimate with my—with the young lady with whom you thought I shouldn't be engaging in a romantic relationship at this particular historical moment."

Teddy paused and his gray eyes shifted back toward the room where the others were laughing over something or other. All amusement had washed out of his face. He tapped his foot against the parquet floor and considered for a moment how best to reply. "Oh, Henry, you can't believe—" He broke off, shaking his head. "That thing that had Florence so upset? Did you read what it said about *her*, Henry? How could I have been concerned about what it said about *me*, when . . ."

Henry's face was stuck in a furious frown. His rage had built up without his control, and it had no route of escape. Teddy was watching him in that quiet, serious way he sometimes had late at night after too many drinks had been spilled, and Henry could almost see his own frightful visage reflected in his friend's. The fun that was being had down the corridor of rooms seemed a thousand miles away.

"I didn't notice about Florence," Henry said finally. His throat was tight.

"Henry . . . it was arranged by my sister's mother-in-law and Mrs. Holland that I would escort Diana to a little dinner. I enjoyed her company very much, just as I always enjoyed her sister's, but you know there is nothing between us." He kept on with those eyes, and Henry felt his rage subside an inch. "Don't make yourself ridiculous with accusations," Teddy concluded sharply.

"All right, all right." Henry sighed and covered his face

with his hand. He was about to ask why then, if there had been nothing between his friend and Diana, she had not come to him last night, but stopped himself—not because he was afraid of shocking Teddy, but because he felt suddenly protective of her again. And of her sister, wherever she was, guarding her secret just as he should.

"You love her," Teddy observed quietly.

Henry replied with an uncharacteristic lack of irony: "Yes."

Teddy's eyes shifted to the plaster interlacing that decorated the ceiling in curlicues. "Lord, you never make it easy, do you."

"No."

"You are aware of that."

"Yes." Henry paused. He had known Teddy a long time, but he had never had a conversation with him quite like this one. "But I've never felt like this, either."

His friend regarded him. Moments passed, and for the first time Henry was afraid to hear his friend's assessment. "You'll have to get her, then."

Henry let out a breath he hadn't realized he was holding. "I can't even leave the house."

Only now did he move his hand from his eyes, and saw that his friend was nodding. Teddy touched his arm and leaned in for a view of the room where a fire was crackling and cards were being loudly played.

"Your father's gone out for a minute," Teddy observed.

The two men looked at each other and then turned and started back toward the others at an inconspicuous pace.

"What a bore he is," Teddy mocked, with a little jab in Henry's direction, when they were again beside the card table.

"Oh, I know!" Isabelle spoke with enthusiasm but barely glanced up from her hand. Cards were, as his father had observed several times—erroneously, in the son's opinion— her only vice.

"I rather like our new Henry," Penelope said in a soft voice that, if Henry had heard it from behind a door, he would have sworn belonged to some other girl.

"I'm going to bed," Henry went on, trying not to betray the new energy that was already making racehorses of his thoughts.

"And I'm going to see what the city at night has to offer a young man like myself."

Both men stepped away from the marble-topped table across the deep purple carpet. The light from the fire played across Penelope's slim, yellow torso and on her stunned features.

"Good night to both of you then," Mrs. Schoonmaker said, only now turning her focus away from the cards. She shot a look at Penelope. "Apologies from Mr. Schoonmaker; he was called to the club unexpectedly. Some political bore or other."

"Good night," chorused the others.

The two men walked toward the door. Once they were out in the hall, Henry turned to his friend as though he were bidding him farewell. Teddy risked a look backward and nodded as he handed Henry his hat. The two men shook hands and then walked past each other, Teddy moving in the direction of Henry's rooms and Henry, the hat pulled down over his face, toward the Cutting carriage that was waiting by the curb.

Twenty Nine

Perhaps the Holland family is not so bad off as they say, for the late Mr. Holland's business partner—Mr. Snowden Trapp Cairns—was seen squiring Miss Edith Holland and her niece Diana at Sherry's last night. The light from their windows has, neighbors report, been uncommonly bright in the last few days. But will these developments stamp out the rumors of Elizabeth's unfortunate fate, or will it fan them higher?

—FROM *CITÉ CHATTER*, SATURDAY, DECEMBER 23, 1899

"LADIES USUALLY DO NOT BELIEVE ME, BUT THE Yukon can be quite lovely in summer," Snowden Cairns was saying as the remains of the broiled squab were being removed from the Hollands' table. "The drifts of fuchsia fireweed, the lavender lupins, the daisies, the arnicas, all of them giving off their pungent perfume . . . and meanwhile the robins and woodpeckers making their music . . ."

Diana's softly rounded cheek was rested on her balled fist, and her lids were heavy. Her drowsiness was not, she was vaguely aware, what her mother had meant when she asked her to be nice to Snowden. But drowsiness was the only alternative she currently knew to a kind of wild agitation. She could hardly swallow a bite of food, her skin felt cold despite the many fires now burning in the hearths of No. 17, and her head was encircled in feverish heat. She was lovesick for any sign of Henry, and she now understood—as she had never before understood—how literally true that phrase could be. Snowden, her constant companion, did not make not seeing

Henry any easier. He was a dull and repetitive conversational-ist, she had decided over dinner the night before, and she had not yet revised her opinion.

"Of course, that was before the stampede, before the boomtowns started appearing and the unsavory characters spilled off the ships in droves. . . ."

Snowden's man had finished clearing the dinner things, and Edith, who was positioned on the other side of the table from Diana, was giving her a look. There lay between them new candles and piles of oranges and the old crochet table linens and what was left of the family silver.

"Are you tired, Di?" her aunt asked her, interrupting their guest's soliloquy. They had tacitly agreed to let him speak, since his retinue had gone about repairing the house, securing the kind of fare the Hollands had not consumed in months and positioning a decorated tree in the parlor and locating new pictures to fill the unfaded squares in the wallpaper. It would have taken something more than indifference to politesse not to listen to whatever he wanted to say.

"Yes, Miss Di, you do look weary," Snowden seconded with a tone of concern that she would have given many things not to be the beneficiary of.

"I am," she lied. "I am entirely fatigued. Perhaps it is the weather, or perhaps I am worn down by my gratitude," she said with a sincerity that was strong but not strong enough to

escape Edith's notice. "So many things you have done for us!" she added quickly. "It rather overwhelms."

"Then you had better go to bed," her aunt went on with a warning eye. Diana could never tell if it was the facial resemblance between herself and her aunt that made her feel understood at moments like these, or if she really was being empathized with.

"Indeed, you have listened to enough of my boring stories." Snowden gave her a smile that she supposed she might have found generous if she did not find his every gesture a tiresome intrusion on her thoughts. "Please don't weary yourself further on my account. You were such a pleasure to dine with last night and tonight. I hope you will have the strength for many more meals in my company."

Diana managed a kind of smile and left the low-lit dining room with lowered eyes bearing only a lazy implication of regret. Though her emotions had not deviated from a jittery frailty, she knew that in her own room she could at least attempt sleep, and that if she dreamed, she might then finally be with Henry. Earlier in the day, when Snowden's retinue was carrying in crates of produce and bundles of firewood, she had managed to slip a bottle from one of the cases of wine. When she reached her own room, she thought, she would have a glass of it, and then she would become giddy and then hazy, and she would drift off soon enough. It had not occurred to her that she had no means of uncorking it, or that she didn't even know how.

She climbed the stairs indifferently, holding back her skirt. She paused with her hand on the brass knob and considered going back for a corkscrew but decided against it. If she ran into Snowden, there would be more odious conversing, and then she would never get back to her safe little room. When she opened the door she saw that such a trip had already been made unnecessary.

For there Henry sat next to the opened bottle of wine. He had been so present in her thoughts that it seemed entirely rational for him to now be present in reality. It was only how much better he looked in person that needed getting used to, and that she absorbed soon enough. His face was set in a subtle, familiar smile, and his eyes were full of fire. He was wearing a black dinner jacket, and a shiny top hat rested in his lap. He was still, watching her, and yet every inch of him was animated. Diana leaned against the door behind her to close it and felt for the lock without diverting her gaze. She would not have trusted him to stay there if she had looked away.

The light in the room came entirely from one lamp by her bed and the dying flames under the mantel. Henry was sitting next to the fireplace, in the wing chair with the worn gold upholstery, where she had imagined herself reading a few verses before that hopeful sleep. The embers lent his skin even more of a metallic glow than usual. She did not think that his dark eyes had blinked even once since she entered.

"You're in my chair," she whispered.

Then she gave up the support of the door and crossed to him, her feet falling across the white bearskin rug. She plucked the hat from his lap and placed it on her head, jauntily, and then she sat across Henry's legs sidesaddle. He brought an arm around her and fixed his palm on the high, flat part of her thigh, his gaze unwavering. When she realized that she could smell him, she finally knew he was real.

"I'd like to reply that you're wearing my hat," he said, "except that it's not mine."

"Oh?"

"It's Teddy Cutting's."

His expression was unchanged, but she could hear the difference in the way he pronounced the name. It was not how he ordinarily would have pronounced it. Diana's confusion was momentary, and then she remembered, in a rush, a room on East Sixteenth Street, a desperate feeling, and a gossip item that she herself had spitefully composed. She took the hat off.

"Oh, you can't *think*—"

"No, but still I'd like you to tell me."

"That was a silly prank, Henry." She tossed the hat toward the bed and fussed with her long, white skirt. "There's nothing. It was when I thought that you and Penelope—"

"Enough."

She watched the play of light in his eyes and decided that if Henry had felt jealousy over the Teddy incident, then she could truly let go of the emotions his past involvement with Penelope had caused her. She bent her face toward him and waited until his lips met hers. He brought his mouth to hers again and again, slowly and softly at first, but then with a growing urgency. His hands were in her hair, they were at the most siphoned part of her corset. She was only vaguely aware of the sound her heeled slippers made when they fell to the floor, one and then the other. It seemed very natural that, as she knew somewhere in the margins of her consciousness, her hair was spilling down around her shoulders. Minutes had passed, but she had no idea how many, when he pulled her face back from his.

"I love you."

He said it simply, quietly. He didn't say those words as she had imagined them said so many times by characters in novels. He didn't say them with desperation, with pleading, with futile rage or florid persuasion. He spoke without lasciviousness; he spoke only with the intention of being understood.

Diana's response was a smile that was radiant and beyond her control.

"You know I never loved Penelope, and I never will." She

wasn't sure she had ever seen his black eyes so devoid of mischief, so sincere. "It won't seem right to people, you and me.
They don't know Elizabeth is alive—they'll just think that I've
replaced her with another horse from the same sire. Whatever position your family is in now, our affair won't make it
easier."

Diana raised her chin and held his gaze. "It's right to me."

"I wouldn't want you to do anything that made you feel—"

But Diana had heard enough. She stopped Henry with
a lasting, humid kiss. When it was over, she drew him down
backward onto the bearskin rug. He propped himself on his
elbow and looked at her for a long moment, in which she
felt she knew what it was to be an artist's model as she was
studied. He reached for the open wine bottle, which had been
sitting beside the chair, and took a long sip. Diana took it from
him, and she too sipped, and after that there was no more
discussion.

Henry rose over her with careful hands and watchful eyes. He took off his jacket, and then he rolled back her
stockings and examined her small feet. He kissed her on the
ankles, and then he planted kisses up to the insides of her
knees. She was trying to keep herself very still, and she found
she had to remind herself to breathe. By the time their mouths
met again she had lost all sense of the outside world, but she
hardly cared.

He asked her once more if she was sure, and she nodded that she was. She told herself she was.

There was a stabbing kind of pain at first, and Diana briefly wondered if she were perhaps the first human woman born physically unable to commit original sin. But then Henry whispered to her and time passed—she would never know how much—and she found her body wanted to move against his in a way that she had never, even at her baddest moments, imagined herself moving.

Later, at some remote part of the night, she woke to find Henry examining her naked shoulder. He watched her and she watched him back. She went down to the kitchen to get them water, but she mostly spent the rest of the hours before morning curled against his chest as tightly as possible.

She couldn't remember when her thoughts merged into sleep, but she knew exactly when she was awakened. There was the sound of the door handle turning in its groove, and then she opened her eyes to see her own bedroom bathed in morning light. It was sparkling white all around her, but all Diana could think was: *I am not a virgin anymore. I am no longer a girl.* Her body was different, too; it felt sore but experienced, like a body prepared for everything the world had to offer.

Then the door swung against the warped wood planks and she looked up and into the face of her lady's maid. Claire was holding a blue-and-white porcelain pitcher. Diana turned to where she was looking and saw Henry's handsome, sleeping face beside her on the bearskin rug. His face looked even better in the morning, at close range. The fire had died down in the night. By the time she looked back at the door, it had been drawn shut. Thank goodness it was only Claire, she thought, and moved back into the warm, sleeping form beside her and let her eyelids flutter contentedly shut.

Thirty

The value of secrets is ever fluctuating, although ladies who have been in society for a long time learn that a secret kept can be worth more than a secret told.

——MAEVE DE JONG, *LOVE AND OTHER FOLLIES OF THE GREAT FAMILIES OF OLD NEW YORK*

*L*INA WALKED BETWEEN THE WHITE AND BROWN patches of lawn and the sparsely leaved trees of Union Square at a pace that was neither hurried nor careless. She walked like a girl wearing a new fur coat, which in fact she was. It was made of broadtail, with a high chinchilla collar. Tristan had helped her pick it out that morning. And she was trying to walk as she remembered Elizabeth Holland walking: as though she were sublimely indifferent to the cold, and to the passing, bundled girls who looked in wonder at the rich pelts she wore when out for a stroll, trailed by an obedient maid. She wasn't really a maid, of course. But Lina had instructed her sister to walk behind her today at a cautious distance.

"What if we see Mrs. Carr or one of the others?" she had explained, and Claire, giddy at the thought of her little sister socializing with such fine people, had agreed.

"That is a very fine muff," Claire said now. She was referring to the Persian lamb muff that Lina had purchased, what seemed a lifetime ago, with her Penelope money. Lina's hands were protected by it now, as protected from the chill wind as a fine pair of white hands that had never seen a day of work might be.

"Isn't it?" Lina replied over her shoulder. The muff didn't seem so special to her now that she had the coat. She liked to think that, framed by the collar, her neck appeared longer, more imperious, like the neck of a girl named Carolina. At moments like these, her feelings for Will dimmed slightly, and she thought that she could stand to be in New York just a little longer, to practice her manners that much more. Certainly passersby, noting the quality enveloping her long body, would read her faint freckles as exotic and her sage green eyes as too aloof to be categorized as green or gray. But it was the muff that Claire had noticed—and Lina, sensing a way to begin telling her tales of all her fantastic new friends, had lied. She'd said that Longhorn had given it to her, like he'd given her the coat.

"You will have to be careful to take good care of it."

"Oh, I will." For a reason Lina couldn't quite pinpoint, this comment gave her a little shiver. Claire could not have meant to, but her warning reminded Lina how tenuous her grandeur was, even now that she had accepted Longhorn's proposal. Tristan had admonished her again that morning for a failing she was beginning to care more about; he had reminded her how short-lived her social career would be if she did not win the friendship of some female other than Mrs. Carr. "I know how, after all."

"That is true." They were moving forward, past wrought-iron benches, across the octagonal stone pavement, and Lina could hear the crunch of the remains of the last snow under her feet. It was too cold that day for a stroll, and so there were few people in the park. "I only wonder what Mr. Longhorn will expect in return for such a present."

"Oh, no, you don't have to worry about that. Tristan says—"

"Who's Tristan?"

Lina stopped walking and her irises rolled to the sky. The sound of his name was both confusing and pleasing to her. She hadn't told her sister about Tristan when he was just a department store salesman, she certainly didn't know how to explain now that she knew what he truly was. Or, rather, now she knew that he was more than he seemed. And also now that he had kissed her. When she imagined how she would begin such a story, she wondered if the whole thing didn't sound a little mad. No, better not to bring up Tristan. She turned and took Claire—who looked almost surprised to have come face-to-face with her newly grand sister—by the arm.

"I've talked so much about me."

"Oh, but I like hearing about all your new friends." Claire, who was wearing a black cloth coat and a hat that matched it in color and age if not in style, smiled through her shivers. Her nose had grown almost painfully red. Lina drew her toward one of the benches and removed her muff. Over the tops of the leafless trees, they could see the high stone roofs of the buildings on the east side of the square.

"Try it on," she instructed. When Claire demurred, she continued with an "I insist."

Two female servants in plain coats were passing with goods from market, and it was only once they had passed that Claire took the glossy black piece and considered it. She was slow to put it on, but once her hands had disappeared inside, a pleased expression began to take hold of her features.

"You should keep it," Lina said impulsively. As soon as she had spoken, the thought of losing the muff, which now seemed sentimentally like one of the first fine things she had purchased for herself, was terrible to her.

"Oh, no, I couldn't, Lina, it's yours—and anyway, what will Mr. Longhorn say when he sees you're not wearing it?"

Thus reminded of her lie, Lina began to feel that she didn't deserve the muff to begin with. "He will wonder what's happened to it," she replied darkly, "and I will tell him that I must have been silly and left it somewhere, and then perhaps he will buy me a new one. Or perhaps he won't. It will be a little test to see how deep his affection goes."

"Oh, Lina! You mustn't be like that." Claire smiled through her disapproval. "That would be such a Penelope Hayes thing to do."

Hearing that name out loud did not, at that moment, improve Lina's idea of herself—in fact, it raised a glowering shame for being so recently in a position of peddling secrets—and so she brought the conversation in a different direction in the only way she could think of. "How is Diana? You know, I ran into her quite literally at the opera."

"Oh, yes, I know. I didn't believe the Carolina Broad in the paper could possibly be you, until she confirmed it for me." Claire looked around her, at the small park in its shades of gray with the skinny trees casting shadows even at midday. There was no one near them, and those at a distance had wrapped scarves and hats around their ears to protect themselves from the cold. She lowered her voice even so. "But you know, I am worried about her."

"About Diana?" Lina said. "I can't imagine why—she never worries about anyone else." Her sister gave her a look and she grudgingly added: "I only mean that she'll be all right because she's always been so good at watching out for herself."

"Perhaps not anymore . . ."

"What could you mean?"

"Well, I'm not saying anything about *her* at all. It's just something I saw. Something that might not reflect well on the Hollands . . ." Claire shifted on the bench and curled forward a little as though she might somehow hide what she knew with her body. "Well, it was *one* of the Hollands, and I saw her with a young man. A young man who used to be very intimately involved with the family, so much so that he was likely to have married into it."

Lina was irritated by her sister's obfuscation, and couldn't help but reveal a little of it in her tone. "You saw her *with* him?"

"*Yes,*" Claire answered miserably.

"But what do you mean by 'with'?" Lina experienced a tingle of interest now, although it would be too wild if her sister was saying what she seemed to be saying.

"Well, you know . . . *with.*"

Lina's eyes had grown wide. "No, I don't know. With each other in the parlor yesterday afternoon?"

"With each other this morning, in each other's arms, with their clothes in disarray." Claire put her whole face into the muff and made a distraught sound from the back of her throat. "What can I tell her? I just wish I had never seen it. I wish it had never been."

Lina could scarcely believe the story—it was too audacious, really. But Claire would never have dreamed such a thing in a million years, and Lina found herself unable to stop picturing it, as though she had come across an overturned omnibus in the middle of Broadway and was suddenly surrounded by a gawking and inert crowd, unable to look away. It was disgraceful but also romantic enough to make Lina's heart turn. She pressed her lips together and watched her sister, who was quite visibly more ashamed of what had transpired than Diana Holland ever would be.

"I don't think you need to tell her anything," Lina began. She had not—for all her mixed emotions, for all her fascination, revulsion, jealousy—missed what acquiring this knowledge might mean for her.

"You don't?" Claire's features were scrunched together in a kind of moral agony.

"Surely just being seen will have made her realize how careless and dangerous her behavior has been." Lina spoke slowly and tried to catch her sister's eye, which she was unable to do. "Just knowing how easily she could have been caught by you or her mother or aunt will make her more circumspect."

"Do you really think so?"

There was sudden moisture in the air. Lina observed her sister. She was so good with the Hollands, so selfless. It had always seemed wrong to Lina how they could spend all their hours treating Claire like their inferior and she could still behave toward them with the loyalty of blood relatives. That was why they showed her so much. That was why she saw into their bedrooms early in the morning, when they were not at all the kind of family that the world believed them to be. Of course, Claire would never use such information. But Lina, sitting on a wrought-iron bench in a nearly empty park on a wintry morning, knew that she could. A few days ago, she certainly would have.

"I'm convinced everything will come out right in the end." Lina touched her sister's shoulder, indicating that she should go, and they both stood. It had begun to snow, and tiny white flakes were catching in Lina's coat. She looked at her sister in the shiny black muff, and said: "You must keep that fur, though. It will be my Christmas present to you."

The furrows in Claire's brow disappeared, and she smiled down at her new possession. Lina's mind was occupied by this latest, outrageous information, and as they walked— arm in arm this time—to the northern entrance of the park, she found that she no longer minded the loss of the muff at all. The story she had just heard had reminded her that there were far more important things that she should concentrate on acquiring.

Thirty One

THE WILLIAM S. SCHOONMAKER FAMILY
REQUESTS THE PLEASURE OF YOUR COMPANY
ON THE EVE OF CHRISTMAS, 1899
AT NINE O'CLOCK
416 FIFTH AVENUE

*T*HE VANITY MIRROR IN DIANA HOLLAND'S BED-
room, with its oval mahogany frame carved at the
edges to evoke putti and seraphim, had sat in the same place for
the better part of a decade, but it had never held such beauty.
There, close to the mirror on the table, amongst combs and
pins and powders and face paints, was a simple vase jar filled
with purple hyacinths. They had arrived that morning with a
reminder that the Hollands were wanted at the Schoonmakers'
Christmas Eve party, even though the families were no longer happily to be joined in marriage, and their fragrance filled
the air. They had been a symbol that Diana had read in plain
English, and she had claimed them for her room with an off-
hand comment about hyacinths being her favorite flowers.

In any event, it was chiefly her own beauty that filled
the mirror on that particular Christmas Eve. Her pupils were
as wide and black as midnight, and her cheeks had the sweet
flush of a summer sundown.

The face of her lady's maid, hovering in the background

as Diana's dark curls were pinned upward, was looking a little gaunt by comparison. Her eyes flickered everywhere but did not meet those of her mistress. She was uncharacteristically quiet.

Diana pursed her round little mouth and let her own gaze rove about the room. All the details were the same as ever: the salmon damask walls, the white bearskin rug, the small mantel, the white chenille bedspread; and yet it was a room forever altered. Diana almost wished she lived in the kind of world where a plaque could be erected—small, subtle, definitely of weathered copper—that would record for posterity the momentous event that had occurred there. What had happened between her and Henry.

Diana decided that the only way to break the silence was all of a sudden. "I'm glad you saw us."

Claire's blue eyes darted to the mirror and met Diana's before she went quickly back to her work. "I don't think I know what you mean."

"It's all right, Claire, I'm not angry." Diana paused to examine the swath of pale skin at her chest that the white gown, trimmed with dark green, left exposed, and how it caught the low light of her bedroom. The electric light in Henry's ballroom was sure to be brighter, but she felt confident that that could only be in her favor. "I'm glad."

Claire's sigh filled the room. "Miss Diana, if anyone finds out they'll—"

"But you won't tell anyone. And me, *I* was bound to tell someone just to be able to talk about it. But now that you know, someone knows, and I won't have to worry about blabbering on! Except to you, which I'm afraid I may be doing."

Claire sighed again, although more softly this time—soft enough that Diana could sense she was ready to relent.

"Really, Claire, has anything so exciting ever happened in the history of this household? Me and Henry—"

"You and your sister's fiancé."

Diana brought her lips together. She had forgotten herself. She let her gaze float up and saw that Claire was looking her directly in the eyes now. "Oh, Di, just be careful. Be careful!" And then she allowed herself a little smile. She was weaving holly into Diana's hair, and as she worked her smile grew. By the time all the holly was gone from the tray in front of them and Diana's hair was festive with green, the smile had overcome her face, and she and her mistress met each other's eyes like the giddy romantics they were.

They didn't speak again until Diana had stood for Claire to give a final powder on her nose. "So you'll be able to see him tonight?" she almost whispered.

"Snowden is escorting me, of course, so I won't really be able to see him." Diana's heart sped at the slightest mention of Henry. She had tried not to think of him too often that day. "But just to be in the same room with him, Claire! I'll be able to look at him at least. I'm sure I'll know how he is feeling from a single glance."

From that moment forward she thought of nothing but Henry. As she went to her mother's bedroom to bid her good night and as she walked down the stairs to admire the Christmas tree with Snowden and her aunt. Then they drove, in Snowden's carriage, to the Schoonmakers' limestone mansion on Fifth near Thirty-eighth Street, and by the time her father's old partner had extended a hand to help her up the steep steps to that cheerily lit entryway, her thoughts of Henry were so all-consuming that it was a kind of miracle that she did not stumble on the new-fallen snow and that she did not respond to Snowden's pleasantries with sentences that were composed of nothing but Henry's name.

In through the greeting line she went, down the halls crowded out with potted poinsettias, thinking all the time that her heart was swollen to the point of bursting. The ballroom chandelier illuminated countless male faces bobbing on their standing white collars like soft-boiled eggs, but no matter how quickly her eyes darted, no matter how many smiles she shot to her familial acquaintances, still she could not locate Henry in the crowd. She felt on the verge of betraying herself by bringing up the distressing absence when Snowden saved her the trouble.

"Which one is young Schoonmaker? The man Elizabeth was to have married . . ."

Her aunt had been whisked up by one of the Gansevoort cousins, and a waiter had brought them glasses of warm winter punch. Diana sipped from the little cup to steady her nerves. *Why was Henry not there?* she wanted to scream. *And who is he with?* went the echo in her thoughts.

"I don't see him," she said, as indifferently as possible.

"Well, that's very odd, that the young man of the house should be absent on an evening that is so important to his family."

"Yes, I—"

Diana broke off. She had noticed how many eyes in the room were on her. The Misses Wetmore, in hues of lavender, were whispering to each other from the rust velvet causeuse at the center of the room, no doubt wondering about the stranger Diana had entered with and what his marital status was. Amos Vreewold and Nicholas Livingston stood in the shadows of the arched entryway to an adjoining gallery, watching her with fervid eyes that made her wonder if they weren't comparing her appearance to that of the elder sister they had danced with so often. There was Davis Barnard, hiding behind his punch, his brows rising like two flying buttresses at the glimpse of the mystery person she had brought. And entering from the main hall was Penelope, preceded by a fluid skirt of deep red silk, looking Diana over once before she turned her face on the crowd. Penelope was also accompanied by a stranger—at least, he was strange to Diana. Yet the tall man who held Penelope's arm seemed entirely at ease in the room and nodded to a few people he evidently knew well, before turning in the direction of the younger Holland, where he was far less economical with his gaze than Miss Hayes had been.

Diana wasn't sure she had ever seen Penelope not accompanied by that heavyset party-planning fellow, and wondered who the new arrival could be.

If she had been asked before that moment, she would have said that she was indifferent to being looked at. But she was the youngest of the family, and she had never borne the brunt of society's proclivity for gawking. There, in the Schoonmakers' ballroom, on the eve of Christmas, she experienced a revelation: Being looked at circumscribed one's movements. It could really hem a girl in, she realized, as Elizabeth must have realized two years ago at least. She desperately wanted to seek out an explanation for Henry's absence tonight, but her many observers, seen and unseen, made that impossible.

She couldn't shake the feeling, either, that she had been so physically changed that her transgressions were plain on her body. She felt so much aware of her own beauty, it seemed inconceivable that everybody else wouldn't notice the difference, too. And she also couldn't help feeling that she was marked.

"He—" she began again. She hoped it wasn't clear from

her tone that, to her, this was *the* he. "He took Elizabeth's passing very hard. I'm sure it is difficult for him to think how this would have been their first Christmas as—as man and wife."

Snowden nodded faintly at this explanation, and then he went on to ask her milder questions about the other guests, and what part of town they lived in, and what sort of structures they occupied, and Diana obliged as much as she was able. She did not bother trying to keep her thoughts calm, of course. It was far too late for that.

Living too much in one's head can be dangerous, her father had liked to tell her. He had always said it lovingly and with some amount of pride, when he had occasion to compare his and his daughter's personal traits. But Diana remembered it now, in the margins of a ballroom decorated with hundreds of little pictures in big frames and filled by a crowd of faces upturned grotesquely with holiday cheer, with a kind of dread.

The racket her heart was making in her ears was now drowning out all the rosy thoughts of Henry, and she began instead to fear that she had somehow or other been a fool again. That was the way love was, she guessed—it left you always unsteady on your feet. But something caused her to turn her head, before that feeling of vulnerability grew too strong, and that was when she saw Henry staring at her with such affection and desire that it made her lips quiver open. He was across the room, near the entrance. There was nothing unsteady about his gaze, which she held for several seconds. By the time two large men moved to either side of him, blocking her view and drawing Henry deeper into the ballroom, she knew that she had not been a fool. She knew that the evening would be a success based on that look alone, and the shine came back into her eyes.

Thirty Two

H—

I don't even know if this will get
to you, but you must accept my
apologies. I guess I dozed off last
night. I will be hoping to see you
soon, one way or another, but in the
meantime, good luck.

—T

*H*ENRY WAS A REMARKABLY WELL-FED BACHELOR, and it had been some years since the absence of a lady had caused him anything like discomfort. Still, on Christmas Eve, with a fresh snow still settling into the panes of the Schoonmaker windows and onto the sloped mansard roof above them, he could not help but feel a little hungry. When he had slipped back into his bedroom late that morning, he'd found his friend Teddy already gone, and then he'd slept until the sounds of party preparation woke him with a start. Then his imagination turned directly to the pink skin and reckless curls of the young Miss Holland. The most important thing he'd accomplished all day, by far, was having the hyacinths sent to her home. It was with these thoughts that he began to feel a pleasant kind of anticipation for an event of his father's that he would not otherwise have cared about remotely.

He rang to have his dinner in his room, which he picked at indifferently, and then he dressed in his customary black dinner jacket with tails and white tie without summoning the assistance of a footman. He didn't want to be pampered. He didn't want to be spoon-fed by all the liveried manservants his father could afford. He was thinking about the plush neckline of Diana Holland and the bright knowingness in her eyes, and having another man fussing about his waistcoat would only interfere with such thoughts. How brave she was, how fearless in the face of every expectation she was supposed to meet. Being near her made him feel brave too. It made him feel as though he needed, beyond her, very little indeed.

He took a final sip of the coffee that had been resting on a sideboard and fixed the last strands of his hair into place. Then he looked down from his bay windows onto Fifth Avenue, where all those his father deemed worthy or useful were being helped down to the sidewalk. The snow glistened as bright as any of the diamonds, and it even necessitated the carrying of one or two of the ladies who feared for their gowns. Henry smiled ruefully and thought to himself that Diana would never have done such a thing. She would have inhaled the cold and gone up the steps as indomitably as she did everything. Then he turned and stood, under the great mural of picnicking bons vivants that decorated the ceiling of his rooms, and checked his tie a final time in the full-length mirror with the copper snake ensnaring it.

He walked toward the door with airy purpose, and it seemed to him that he would have reached the main floor of his family's house in a few, blithe steps. The reason he did not was entirely to do with the two men standing at his door. They were wearing the black tails and dove gray slacks of butlers, although their faces seemed to have known rougher things than drawing rooms and pantries. Their features, like their hands, were thick and chapped.

"Excuse me," Henry said hotly.

"Oh, no, sir," replied the first.

"Excuse us, sir," seconded the other. "We'll be escorting you downstairs, then."

"Why?" Henry's voice was indignant. "I hardly need—"

"Your father's orders," answered the first.

"Seems you broke house arrest—your father found your friend Cutting dozing off in there early this morning, and figured out that you'd given him the slip."

"Wasn't too pleased," added the other, lowering his eyes at his charge.

"No, not at all."

"Speaking of Mr. Cutting," said the first man with a gap-toothed smile, "this note came for you earlier."

A folded, cream-colored piece of paper was extended toward him. Henry snatched it. He opened it slowly, and as he read he began to see what had happened. He looked at the two men in disbelief, and down the long corridor to where the guests were arriving. The floor had been polished that day, and the light of the entryway was visible down at the end, spilling across the boards like daylight at the end of a cave. He could hear the shrieks of delight as the droves came in, and he took a step in that direction. The two men moved to either side of his shoulders, close enough that Henry smelled the smell of men who did not spend their days looking after hereditary silver. He took another step, and the men followed him exactly. As Henry went forward, the men matching his movements, he realized that he was in another of his father's traps.

The three of them went down the grand stairway in absurd lockstep, Henry fighting—not very successfully—his caged feeling. The shiny floors of the hall were almost all crowded out by the arriving guests, who filled the air with silly exclamations and loud prattle. Several of them turned, without much subtlety, to look at Henry as he passed. They went under the wide oak entryway and into the ballroom with all its paintings high on the walls. Henry felt the men fall behind him for just a moment, and that was when he caught a glimpse of her.

She was a vision in a white gown, her dark hair forming a hazy halo around her rosy, heart-shaped face. Her long lashes fluttered to touch her cheeks, and then her eyes opened fully in his direction. Her small, round mouth flexed in an immediate and knowing smile. *That's the girl I'm going to marry*, Henry thought. Then the shoulder of one of his father's men obstructed his view, and he heard the other one say: "Mr. Schoonmaker wants you going this way."

Thirty Three

Returned from Europe: Grayson Hayes, only son of Mr. and Mrs. Richmond Hayes, via Asia, the Pacific, and the transcontinental railroad. Young Mr. Hayes intends to stay at his family home, 670 Fifth Avenue, for the rest of the season.

—FROM THE SOCIETY PAGE OF THE *NEW-YORK NEWS OF THE WORLD GAZETTE*, SUNDAY, DECEMBER 24, 1899

ENELOPE CROSSED THE THRESHOLD OF THE Schoonmaker ballroom with all things necessary for a notable entrance. She wore a new dress from the Parisian couturier Doucet, who kept a dossier on her measurements and fabric preferences. It had arrived just that week, and it was made of a garnet-colored silk faille in rows of tucks and volants that brought it close to her body in the hips and ribs and flowed outward at the knee and was garlanded at the neckline and hem with yards of white point d'esprit. She was glad it was Christmas, if only for the excuse to return to her favorite shade. Her dark hair was done up with simple height, and it was ringed with real pine and pearls. And if her natural stature and glow were not enough to win attention, she had on her arm the returned prodigal, Grayson Hayes, the older brother everyone was always asking about.

Of course, the entrance proved a useless and petty endeavor. Henry was nowhere to be seen, a fact Penelope grasped in a few unquiet moments.

They glided into the room, in advance of their less comely parents, slowly, letting the light catch against the architectural planes of their faces. Penelope resented her brother, in a mild sort of way, for his prolonged absence and for taking some attention away from her. But she knew that everybody thought of her as the bright sibling, the sibling who would make a more brilliant marriage, the sibling who would propel the family name to new levels of social exclusivity. It was only that he had made himself scarce that made him so exciting now, and she was inclined to let him have his moment. She clung, sisterly, to his arm as they moved forward along the green velvet wall hangings.

"Is that little Diana Holland over there?" Grayson asked in a low voice.

"Little is the right word. Her sister may have been a prude, but at least she had the proper finishing and coming-out. Diana really is an untrained thing." Penelope cocked an eyebrow and drew herself up to her superior height.

"You know, I saw a girl who looked just like her sister on the train from California. . . ."

"Elizabeth Holland is dead," she replied sharply. Only after she had spoken did the chill set in. Whenever she heard a rumor about Elizabeth being still alive, she felt a touch of fear that her former friend might be returning to New York to take away all the things that were rightfully Penelope's. It was true that she had left with utter determination, although Penelope sometimes wondered how long a girl used to servants and satin underthings could last in the dusty West. But it was easy enough to dismiss what was written in the papers as fantasy, and harder to hear the observations of her always exacting brother.

"I *know*, Penny, but this young lady looked uncommonly like her. And when I approached her, she dismissed the notion just the way you would. The way a girl from New York would. Whoever she was, she wasn't western bred."

"Grayson." Penelope's voice had fallen to a gravelly whisper. "Not now."

"In any event," her brother went on, his voice light with understanding, "her sister will be quite pretty when the edges come off."

Penelope might have sniffed, but she was distracted from her brother's distressing comments by the sight of Mrs. Isabelle Schoonmaker moving toward them at a barely disguised charge. She was wearing a gown of gold lamé with a tremendous bronze bow at the neckline and a large sash of the same color demarcating her waist. Several peacock feathers bounced in her waves of blond hair. Penelope was pleased to note her friend's approach, and was already planning a neat segue to Henry's whereabouts, when the rosy hostess was intercepted midstride.

"Mrs. Schoonmaker," old Carey Lewis Longhorn was saying. He had stepped out of the crowd accompanied by a brunette whose broad back was turned toward Penelope. His companion's hair was pinned to the back of her head in the shape of a big, wooden spoon. Mrs. Schoonmaker's blue eyes rolled yearningly in the direction of the Hayes siblings; Penelope winked at her in sympathy.

Penelope leaned in toward her brother's ear. "Mrs. Schoonmaker and I have lately become fast friends."

"Is that so," he replied dryly.

By the time they arrived by the Hayeses' side, Penelope had realized who Longhorn's young friend was. She couldn't help but huff a little at the sight of the Hollands' old maid, her hair so clearly done by her own hand, and in the company of that randy old bachelor. She really was an idiot. If she went on being seen only with that man—and no doubt the likes of his famous friend, old divorced Lucy Carr, too—then people would begin to talk. And it would be the kind of talk that would doom her even more quickly than her plain face.

"Isabelle!" Penelope cried, blowing kisses.

"Penny!" Mrs. Schoonmaker rejoined. She looked at Grayson and turned a color of pink that brought out the turquoise in her eyes. "You know Mr. Longhorn, of course, Mr. Longhorn, this is Mr. Hayes and Miss Hayes. And Penelope,

Mr. Hayes, this is Miss Carolina Broad of Utah, who is a new friend of Mr. Longhorn's."

"Charmed," Grayson said as he leaned forward and kissed "Carolina's" gloved hand. "Mr. Longhorn," he went on, "I believe you have the portrait Sargent did of our lovely Isabelle in your collection."

"Indeed I do." Longhorn permitted himself a wink in the other man's direction. "Although I have to say that she has only grown lovelier since then. Perhaps, if her husband permits, I will have another commissioned. . . ."

Mr. Longhorn continued praising Isabelle's beauty, but Penelope was having trouble focusing on their little group's conversational direction. She was doing her best to appear to pay attention, when Lina disengaged herself from Longhorn and moved in Penelope's direction with a confidence of gait that she had not heretofore exhibited. Because—and only because—it was not currently in her interest to appear outwardly rude, Penelope allowed herself to be drawn away from the others and back into the marbled hall. Once they were out of earshot she resumed a cold tone. "I suppose you've got something to sell."

"Oh, no." The former maid looked around the room and then directly into the other girl's eyes. *Eye contact,* thought Penelope. *How* very *novel.* "Not in the slightest, although I do have a story to tell you that I think you'll find very amusing."

Late guests were still trickling in at the entryway down at the end of the hall, and the air was colder here than in the ballroom. Isabelle's intrusion had made Penelope forget, however temporarily, Grayson's comment about Elizabeth, but now the specter was back. Penelope's features hardened.

"It's about Henry," Lina said. The clicks of the girls' high-heeled slippers echoed in the hall several times before the former help made a needless clarification: "Henry Schoonmaker. You wondered out loud to me once why he wasn't in love with you, and I think I might have an idea," she went on baldly.

Now it was Penelope whose arm tightened against Lina's, and she drew her away from the entryway and across the gleaming, cream-colored floor. They moved along the walls, which were decorated in the richly colored tapestries of the ancestral home of some old, fallen European family, and out of earshot.

"Yes, but it's a rather personal story, and I really wouldn't feel comfortable telling someone who wasn't my friend." The former maid paused for an effect that was not altogether necessary. "My very good friend. You are my friend, aren't you, Miss Hayes?"

Penelope couldn't help but feel a little impressed by this. So Carolina knew there were more important things than money if she were going to make it in New York. "Yes," Penelope replied slowly, trying not to seem too eager. After all, she didn't yet know whether this information would be useful to her or not. "You are my friend. Though of course, my best friends are the ones with the best stories."

"Oh, I'm sure they are." A waiter with a tray of hot-spiced punch in little crystal cups passed them, on his way from the kitchen to the main site of the party. Once he had passed, Lina took a breath. She seemed to be stitching the words together in her head. "You wanted to know why Mr. Schoonmaker doesn't love you, and while I can hardly pretend to answer that, I can tell you where he woke up this morning and with whom."

Penelope felt a sudden rage burning at her ears and down her throat. She had to set her teeth to keep her temper from reaching the boiling point. Since she knew she could not then be trusted with words, she gave her new friend a look and waited impatiently for her to go on.

"So, would you like to know?"

"*Yes.*" Penelope had to close her eyes for a minute to disguise her seething. She needed to know who this person, whom Henry erroneously believed to have some quality that might recommend her over the girl in whose embrace he'd spent the entire summer of 1899, was. She needed to know now.

"But I'll need guarantees, specific guarantees."

Penelope's eyes were tinged red, she knew, but she opened them and stared into Lina's. Her pale green eyes were so open and steady, as though she really believed that whatever she was about to ask for could rival Penelope's goal in importance.

Penelope would have called her expression stupid, except that the girl seemed to have been clever again in collecting information. "What? Anything."

"I'll need to be invited on your family's days of course, and welcomed as your friend." Lina spoke carefully, laying out a plan she had apparently spent much obsessive thought on. It was as though she were looking at sweets in a glass case and saying, *I'll take that, and that, and that*. "And as your friend, I will be expecting to be invited to any balls that might also be thrown at the Hayeses' house. And since our friendship is indeed so dear to both of us, then would I be too forward in expecting an invitation to stay in Newport during the summer season? And when there is a wedding"—Lina paused to smile confidentially at her new friend—"I would be so very honored to be among your bridesmaids."

"Yes, yes, for God's sake. All of it. I promise that I will take you up." Penelope's throat was entirely dry, and she had to pause to swallow. She would have promised anything at that particular moment. "I will make you. Only tell me now."

Penelope became aware of the sounds of revelry back down the hall again as Lina paused to catch her breath, and then the horrid story came out.

"He woke up in my former mistress's house, in the room of her younger sister. With her younger sister. They were—"

"How do you know?" Penelope's voice was dark, her

words strained and chosen for utility. She could picture this scene, of Henry and that impetuous little girl, and she was struggling not to.

"Because my sister, Claire, who still works there, saw them. She walked in on them—"

"That's enough. I believe you." Penelope closed her prettily painted lids and tried to regain herself. It was too idiotic to be believed, and yet it all perversely fit together. In one moment her body felt chills and in the next unbearable heat. "I cannot tell you now," she pronounced slowly, carefully, "how very much I appreciate your sharing this with me. You have become a very close friend. You are always welcome at my home when we are receiving, and you can count on invitations to our gatherings and any weekend parties out of town we might hold. Now, however, as my friend, please go back and tell my brother and Mrs. Schoonmaker that I am not feeling very well and that I had to go to the ladies' dressing room to regain myself. You'll see my gratitude later."

Penelope kept her eyes shut and listened as Lina's footsteps fell away. She sank a row of teeth into her plush bottom lip and turned her face to the wall. She rested her forehead against one of those precious tapestries, with their antique threads and grand depictions of the heroism of old. She raised her fist and pounded the soft side of it against the thick fabric five times until her heartbeats began to slow down.

Thirty Four

There are those girls who will choose friends only for the other girl's brothers. One must be chary of such friends, but one cannot avoid them entirely—it is, after all, a very useful tactic that your daughter may someday rightfully employ.

—MRS. HAMILTON W. BREEDFELT, *COLLECTED COLUMNS ON RAISING YOUNG LADIES OF CHARACTER,* 1899

*T*HE GIRL WHO RETURNED TO THE MAIN SCHOON-maker ballroom was indifferent to the lack of ornament in her hair or relative sparseness of baubles on her person. She didn't worry about the modesty of her posture or the kindness of her expression. She was unconcerned with whether she had been nice or not. She was not nice. She did not want to be like her childhood friend Elizabeth Holland anymore. She wanted to be like her new friend Penelope Hayes, and Penelope had promised to show her how. At least, she had promised to lend the glow of her presence, and to invite her along to all the right places, and that would be enough. That was really all she needed. When she reached the spot where she had left Mr. Longhorn, she saw that he had just engaged Mrs. Schoonmaker for a dance. She found that standing there patiently for the right length of time was sufficient to persuade Mr. Hayes to ask the same of her.

"Carolina, are you and my sister very good friends?" he asked as they moved onto the dance floor. Lina's dress, which she had charged to Mr. Longhorn's account at Lord & Taylor, moved along behind her. It was made of a flattering navy that encased her arms and waist and was embellished at the bust-line with tiny pearls that offered a pleasing contrast to the skin below her collarbone.

"Yes, very good friends," she answered. Having said it, she smiled. "Though of course we haven't known each other long. I'm new to the city."

She had dreaded the idea of dancing, although she knew that if she really did begin traveling in the moneyed world, she would have to eventually. She had gone so far as to prance around her hotel room trying to remember the steps she had helped Elizabeth practice when she had first started lessons with the finishing governess. Carolina was surprised to find that now, with the glow of confidence that came from having new friends in excellent positions, it was easy enough to reference her western origins as an excuse for any lack of polish and allow herself to be led. When she was led, Carolina Broad danced just fine.

"I hope you aren't planning to leave us any time soon," her partner said with an upward twist to his full, shiny lips. It occurred to her that this, her first dance at a society function, was with a bachelor close to her own age. How preferable that was—for the first time, anyway—to old Mr. Longhorn, how-ever kind he had revealed himself to be.

"Oh, I think not." Carolina's eyes grew wide, and she allowed herself to feel the full weight of her answer. The room, with its gilded decorations and painted faces, with its high laughter and low murmurs, with its bowers of pine and glittering Christmas stars, was circling around her at an exhilarating pace. That pace, she thought, could be the pace of her life. It would be a shame to leave the city now, she reasoned, when she was just getting somewhere. Staying a little longer, and really polishing herself, would be the smarter thing to do. "I like it here, and anyway, where else is there to go?"

Grayson looked into her eyes with perfect understanding. "Having spent some four years abroad now, I cannot say I agree more. And I'm glad you'll be staying. If you're a friend of Penelope's, then there are some gentlemen to whom I will have to introduce you. . . ."

And later on he did. By the end of the evening her feet were sore from dancing, and her cheeks were permanently flushed from all the compliments she had received. She couldn't help but think that if Will Keller had been there, she wouldn't have noticed him in the crowd and that he would have seen clearly what an idiot he'd been for passing her up that night in the carriage house. For she had been partnered with Nicholas Livingston and Abelard Gore and Leland Bouchard, an heir to the Bouchard banking fortune, whose hand sat very low

on the small of her back and who demanded several times to know when he would next see her out.

Later, in the carriage on the way back to the hotel, Carolina would remark with full honesty that it had been a very merry Christmas indeed. The street ahead was covered in a layer of white that had only been disturbed by one or two vehicles ahead of them. The wide mansions, made of imported stone and festooned with all sorts of architectural flourishes, passed slowly as they moved up the avenue. Light flooded their entryways, and seasonal decorations could be seen in their windows. It seemed to Carolina at that moment that, if things kept going her way, Will would see her name in the paper for sure, and then he would have to come looking for her, instead of the other way around. She had to put her hand over her mouth to hide the smile, for she was thinking how bright the New Year would be.

Thirty Five

The trains that arrive daily now from out west bring not only those who have been revived by their sojourns on the frontier states but also the broken spirits of those who have lost fortunes in the so-called boomtowns. Their hawked things come back too, by the crateful, to be repolished and set by New York's jewelers and sold at handsome profit to the newest millionaire trying to buy his wife class. No doubt many a Christmas gift with an untoward past will be given in our fine city tomorrow.

—FROM THE EDITORIAL PAGE OF *THE NEW YORK TIMES*,
SUNDAY, DECEMBER 24, 1899

THE MANHATTAN THAT ELIZABETH STEPPED BACK into could not have been more opposite of the city she'd left nearly three months ago. There was no bluster or busyness. There was barely a person on the street. All around her was a kind of deathly quiet, and for a long moment she wondered if she hadn't truly died and the afterlife wasn't somehow a New York stripped of its population. There was a new-fallen snow, not yet riven by carriage wheels, and here and there the warm light from inside a window reflected onto a white bank. She would never know for sure, but she thought that this must have been what the city looked like half a century ago: dark, silent, and still. Will kept his arm firmly around her shoulder as they walked, although she wasn't sure if it was to steady her or to keep her warm.

"You're cold," he observed.

She nodded but couldn't respond further. She was too full of nerves at the prospect of seeing her family, or what she would say to her mother and aunt as a way of explanation. The only thing keeping her quiet and steady was Will's presence at her side. They had the ring money—had, in fact—gotten quite a good price for it—and Will had wanted to take a hansom from the station. But Elizabeth had insisted that walking a circuitous route home under cover of darkness was the safest thing to do. Having seen Grayson Hayes on the train was enough of a shock to make her homecoming a very circumspect one, and she reasoned that returning slowly and on her own two feet might also bring a trace of calm.

"We're almost there," he added reassuringly, although he knew perfectly well that they were now close enough to Gramercy that she could have found the house blindfolded.

"It's not the cold," she said.

"I know that." His voice was so gentle it was almost like he was holding her. "But being inside will help anyway."

When they came to it, they stood for a long moment in front of No. 17 Gramercy. Although the brownstone façade stared back at her with the same placid composition of windows and doors as ever, the view through the plate glass was darkened. She had expected some sign of life, and the lack of it gave her a small terror. It was only at Will's urging that she walked up to the door and, taking the key from its hiding place, unlocked it.

The foyer was unlit, but as her eyes adjusted she saw that the old piece of furniture where visitors used to leave their cards was gone. A darkened parlor was visible through the wide door frame, and she could tell by the smell that there had been a fire there recently. She clung to Will's hand as she went up the stairs, and as she did, she saw that the walls were decorated with pictures in frames that were not the pictures she remembered hanging there before. The sound her feet made as they touched the stairs surprised her until she realized that the Persian runner, which used to flow from the second-floor hallway down to the door, was gone.

She soon found that her own room was missing much of the bric-a-brac that had once made it so light and lived-in, although the robin's egg blue wallpaper was the same, and the great mahogany sleigh bed on the risen platform was made up the same way as it had been made every day for years. She was not nearly as shocked to be back in this room where so many of her days had ended, as she was by the fact that Will was there with her. She had followed him into the unknown, and yet he had never seen her bedroom. It was still her bedroom.

"Will," she said, turning around to look at him, "I'm glad you came with me."

He looked down on her with those large, sweet eyes. Strands of hair were out of place, falling over his forehead and around his ears. His brows separated just slightly, and there was movement in his full lower lip. "I know. I am too."

She moved toward him and he let her in, folding her up

in his taut arms. She propped her chin on his chest, lengthening her neck, and looked up. "I hope I didn't ruin anything."

"I don't think you ruined anything." A smile had crept onto Will's face. Then he bent and brought his mouth to hers, their lips touching again and again so lightly the touches could just barely be called kisses. She began to feel warm again for the first time since they'd left the train. When he stopped, she lowered her chin and put her forehead into his chest.

"Do you think she's . . ." Elizabeth caught her breath, not wanting to say *alive*. She certainly didn't want to say *dead*. That would be letting her thoughts rush to the worst, and Will had warned her that that wouldn't help. "All right?"

"Yes." Will's hand moved over her forehead and over her hair. His fingers rested on the tendrils at the nape of her neck. "Yes, but you should go to her."

Elizabeth pressed her eyelids together. "I'll go now," she said, although it took her several moments more to lift her forehead from its solid resting place and look up at Will with a wan smile. He was looking back at her with those same eyes, full of pure intent, which had always affected her so. They were looking through her. They were a reminder that she knew what was right and good.

She found candles in the closet and lit them, although as she left Will in the room he was already lying down on the bed. He had not slept well on the train the night before as

they approached New York. She imagined that by the time she reached the end of the hall he would already be asleep.

The door to her mother's bedroom, on the east side of the house and facing the street, seemed as fearsome to her as when she lived there. It was perhaps for this reason that she went there first, and not to Diana or her aunt Edith. She pushed back the door with the same trembling approach as when she was a child, needing to face what frightened her the most, and went in. There was no light in the room, but long before her eyes adjusted, she recognized the sound of her mother's breath. Her mother was breathing. The shore-like sound of her inhalations and exhalations was as natural a thing as Elizabeth had heard, and for a moment she was again a little girl.

"Mother," she whispered, reaching out for the hand resting nearest her on the bedspread. It was cold but familiar, those long nimble fingers, so useful in the writing of all those notes of thanks and condolence and gossip and spite. Elizabeth could make things out now from what light came through the windows, and when she repeated the word *mother,* she saw a pair of dark eyes slowly open. There was no recognition in them yet, although they gazed stolidly in Elizabeth's direction.

"Are you all right?"

There were more shadows in the room than light, but

still she could see that the grooves under her mother's eyes were turned a dark purple.

"Do you recognize me?"

It took some time, but her mother, without breaking the blank stare, gradually brought herself up on her elbows. She blinked and watched the younger woman. Elizabeth wasn't sure if she was holding back her fury and disbelief, or even if she saw her at all. A few moments passed before her mother said, in a voice that clearly had not been used as much as it was accustomed to: "Is it Christmas?"

"No," Elizabeth whispered. "Not yet. Not until tomorrow." She wanted to cry and stopped herself by saying: "Tomorrow is Christmas."

"Today is Christmas Eve?" Her mother's eyes had grown so wide they could not possibly have been taking in what was real.

Tears were now streaming down Elizabeth's cheeks and, fearing audible sobs, she simply nodded. She was crying for all the things she used to want and all the things she'd given up and all the people that she was going to have to leave behind again. She was crying for Will's perfect vision, which he had included her in, only for her to muck it up with all her old responsibilities.

"Today is Christmas Eve and you're an angel come back to me in the form of Elizabeth?"

Elizabeth forced her small, rounded lips together and held on to her mother's hand. "No," she said when she was able. "I am Elizabeth. It's Christmas Eve and I'm Elizabeth and I'm not dead—that was all a kind of mistake. I've come back from—"

"My Elizabeth is an angel." The elder Holland woman's eyes shut and she fell back on the pillow, her dark hair forming a puddle around her white face. "She's an angel and she came back to me."

For a long time Elizabeth stood by the bed wondering what she had done to her mother and how she would ever make it better. When she had left, she saw clearly enough now, she had taken the last of what her mother lived for.

Eventually she climbed up on the bed and rested her head on the pillow beside her mother's and began to wonder, instead, how she was going to tell Will that they couldn't go back to California until she'd somehow managed to make her mother well again.

Thirty
Six

Social observers cannot have helped but notice the recent alliance between Mrs. William Schoonmaker and young Penelope Hayes, and those of us of the analytical persuasion have wondered if the former lady isn't being so friendly to the latter on behalf of her stepson. Could young Schoonmaker be in love again?

—FROM THE SOCIETY PAGE OF THE *NEW-YORK NEWS OF THE WORLD GAZETTE*, SUNDAY, DECEMBER 24, 1899

$\mathscr{B}$ Y MIDNIGHT ON CHRISTMAS EVE HENRY WAS entirely sick of the two goons who were now his constant companions. If there had been some absurd humor to these shadows early on, he could no longer see it. They had monitored his champagne intake, though not as carefully as they had his movements—he had had several glasses, and his tie was now a little off-kilter, and the strands of his shiny dark hair no longer fit so neatly together. That wild urgency to escape had faded, if just slightly, into a wincing, futile need. He knew Diana was in the room, and he felt desperate to catch whatever glimpses of her he could. He had, over the last hour, become obsessed with the idea that she dance with no one else.

And—it wasn't his first thought—the realization was beginning to dawn that, wherever she was among the crowd that filled his family ballroom, she probably could have used a reassuring look or two. She had risked everything for him— this was something he was just grasping, the self-recrimination rising in his throat—and he couldn't even ask her to dance. It was not his finest moment. He knew that she was out there, along the wall somewhere, surrounded by all those social harpies with their expectations and narrow definitions, with their fans and cutting remarks, with their meager hearts. She would be looking about her with a certain trembling innocence. She would sigh in that way that moved her whole body.

When he saw her next, she was leaving. The man she had come with—it must have been the old business associate of her father's she'd told him about—offered his arm to escort her out, and she managed only one glance across the ballroom in Henry's direction. He stepped forward, from the place in the arched doorway where he and his father's men had been loitering silently. There was the dew of evening in her wide eyes and a gloss on her lips. Before she left the room, his view was blocked by another woman whose hair was done up in festive green. Penelope Hayes was walking toward him. Directly behind her was his stepmother.

He tilted himself, trying to see around her, and then tried to pretend the movement had been a kind of bow in Penelope's direction. She was holding two champagne flutes.

"Mr. Schoonmaker says that you fellows can have a ten-minute break if you like," Isabelle said, as she swept toward him with all the metallic shimmer of a vault full of bullion. She paused, a blond curl bouncing against her cheek, and straightened his tie. When the two large men had taken up her offer and headed for the door, she squeezed Penelope's wrist and winked at Henry before taking up the arm of some passing matron with exclamations of her finery and slipping back into the main room.

Henry leaned against the oak frame that separated the main ballroom from the series of little galleries. He looked back into the room, with all its light and noise and shimmering headpieces, wishing that Diana were there but knowing she was already gone. "I can't play any games with you right now."

"No games," Penelope replied lightly. She raised one glass up, gesturing that he should follow if he wanted it. Then she walked, as fluidly as she was able, given the restrictions of her red dress, which buckled in on her from all points, into the galleries. For reasons that he did not fully comprehend—though he hoped it was not for champagne alone—Henry followed. There was some terrible purpose in her posture, which he knew he could not afford to ignore. "Anyway, you should know by now that it was never a game for me, Henry."

They moved from one gallery to the next, past old Dutch paintings of gleaming black grapes, skulls, and half-filled wine jugs. He looked back, where all the movement was, hoping nobody had noticed them slip away. He made himself look at

Penelope and then saw her eyes, fevered, over the rim of her glass as she sipped. "It was for me," he said. If she flinched, it passed quickly.

"It was a fun game, for a while, and then all the fun went out of it. I haven't been playing for a long time, Penny."

Penelope's lacy shoulders rose slightly and fell, and then she drained her glass. She tossed it over her shoulder, and when it shattered against the oak wainscoting, it jolted something in Henry, although he tried to keep the reaction out of his face. There was so little reaction in Penelope that it might as well have been rose petals falling against snow.

"I thought you might want to play again." Her voice was low but decidedly not quiet, and there was something in it that made Henry's stomach turn.

"I'm pretty certain not," he answered definitively.

She gave a little laugh from the back of her throat and then stopped walking. She tilted her head in a number of directions; she was looking at her hands now, but that wasn't what amused her. "Oh, *Henry*, don't you know by now that when it's me you ought to pause a minute and try to see what you're missing?"

He was tired suddenly. He had never been so tired. He wanted to be anywhere but where he was. He could scarcely put the words together. "What am I missing?"

She put space between her words and let each one fall

with purpose. "I should have known it wasn't Elizabeth you cared for."

Henry looked at Penelope, but her lids were low and her gaze evasive. The room they were in had deep blue walls above the wainscoting and was full of paintings his father knew he was supposed to admire but in fact found too glum to look at very often. They both moved, away from the far-off view of the ballroom, colluding for a moment in a measure of privacy. "Pardon?"

"I should have known, as the whole town knows by now, that with you it's always a brunette."

Henry's instinct was to reply with a joke, although he could not for the life of him have sounded amused at that moment. "I do have a type."

"Yes, and a plan of attack."

"If you're suggesting that I—"

"Oh, *suggesting*. I'm not suggesting. I wouldn't waste either of our time with suggesting."

Penelope did now meet his gaze. She was looking at him with eyes a little rabid and very proud. There was a terrible defiance in them.

"I know about you and Diana Holland, Henry."

"I have no idea—"

"The maid saw you, Henry, in the morning, in Diana's bedroom. Rather compromising, isn't it? You've gotten sloppy, Henry. You were never that sloppy with me."

Henry could not nod at the veracity of this statement. He clung to his champagne glass, as he might have at any socially awkward moment, waiting for what would come next.

"The maid is in my pocket, you see. She's a good girl and she doesn't want to say anything, but everybody has a price and it's a piece of information that some people would pay very highly for. Some people who put out papers."

"They wouldn't publish—"

"Oh, maybe they wouldn't publish it. Maybe they would. But once they knew it, they wouldn't be able to stop themselves from talking about it. And talking is just as bad. Then, Henry, my friend, the fun really would be over for you. And for a little girl we both adore . . ." Penelope left off speaking and ended her threat with a subtle roll of her shoulders.

"You can't do that, Penny." Lines had emerged in Henry's forehead where they had never been before. He was taken by the desire to find Diana, wherever she was, and hide her. "It would ruin her."

Laughter came next. It was high and throaty and not very different from the laugh he used to hear when Penelope had seemed his ideal match and was more often in his days. "Oh, Henry, for someone who's known me so well, you understand me very little. The ruination of Diana Holland! That would be *fun*." Penelope clasped her hands. "Finally, a little entertainment. But I think you've already done the hard part. It would really just mean letting everyone else in on your handiwork."

"It's my fault, Penelope, my doing." He was as alert as one only becomes after full days of sleeplessness. He could see now, plainly, that this was his chance to do something gallant. He had Penelope here, and her secret hadn't gone anywhere yet. He knew her, he reminded himself—he could figure out how to stop her. "It's me you want to punish, anyway. Punish me."

"Of course I want to punish both of you," she replied with a blithe wave of her hand. "But I'm not a bad person, Henry. I know it's your fault. I'll let you be a man and take care of it."

Henry's whole body was taut with fury, and he had to close his eyes to hide all his violent feelings. It took him a few seconds before he even managed to nod.

"The first thing is that you won't be seeing Diana anymore. But that won't be difficult, because the second thing is that you'll be proposing to me."

Before he could think, he took an impulsive step, and all of a sudden he was very close to Penelope. His breath was coarse and furious. He was not prone to anger—not a very useful emotion, he might have observed in another mood—but when it came it was sudden and irreversible. It was hot, and he was now close enough to Penelope that he knew she felt the rise in temperature. For her part, Penelope shrank back coquettishly against the wall, one shoulder rising and the other falling, although the sum of her reaction was the half-moon crease that emerged at the right corner of her mouth.

"Oh, you don't like that, do you?" she whispered. There was a terrible light in her eyes, and her lips hung open as she watched him. Her blue irises moved right and left. "But consider a minute, Henry, how preferable it would be to marry a girl everyone wants to see you with already—how lovely and gay, how glittering and fine, how infinitely preferable that would be to the ruination of your *last* fiancée's little sister. But I would oblige, if that's what you truly want." She shrugged. "I'll give you a little time to think about it."

When Penelope went out of the room, she took all the air with her. Over there, in the direction she had returned, under the coved ceiling of the ballroom, the voices had grown shrill, and the guests had forgotten that it was Christmas Eve, and now it was just like any party. But of course, it wasn't Christmas Eve anymore, Henry thought darkly. It was Christmas Day, but for Henry, there was no joy in it: In a matter of minutes, his life had arrived at a crushing and impassable stretch.

Thirty Seven

It is Christmas, with snow lying all around. But when the snow begins to melt, and takes with it all the cares and distractions of the holidays, we wonder if this story, which a little sparrow whispered to us, of Elizabeth Holland being yet among the living, will pick up speed. Or might the news come early and prove a true Christmas miracle? For now, we will just have to regard it as idle rumor.

—FROM THE SOCIETY PAGE OF THE *NEW YORK RECORD-COURIER*, MONDAY, DECEMBER 25, 1899

*I*T HAD NOT BEEN THE TRADITION OF THE GAN-
sevoorts to make Christmas a formal affair. They had
always found it perfectly sufficient to prepare a large urn of
hot buttered rum for whichever of their cousins might happen
to call at their Bond Street house, and later on, they would
send one of the young men out to bestow gifts on those family
members who lived within walking distance. They treated it
as a day to drink a little more than usual, in the Dutch way,
and to remark on one another's children. They were unlike
the Holland family, who were known to "do" Christmas. That
family held a musical evening with a Christian theme for a
hundred or so, and later there would be broth served in a dining room so crowded with poinsettias that the guests' faces
would reflect the red glow. Everyone in New York knew that
Louisa Gansevoort only kept those Holland traditions that
she liked when she became one of them, and that their way of
Christmas had not been among those that won her favor.

This was a rare point of agreement between Mrs.

Holland and her younger child, and it was perhaps for this reason that Diana's memories of Christmas were fond. It had been a day when she was encouraged to recite her favorite poetry, when her appearance only had to be good enough for the family, when neatly wrapped boxes of bright new things were exchanged, and when her father—having not been asked to spend time with anyone but those he most wanted to spend his time with—was in high spirits. Perhaps it was for this reason that Diana woke, on the twenty-fifth, looked down on the sun beating on the new layer of snow in the back gardens, and felt a breath of optimism.

This despite the fact that she had been a very bad girl and still had no marriage proposal to show for it.

The previous evening had given her only a taste of what she most yearned for, but she woke with a sense of pleasant anticipation, which the holiday always brought, and she found that it stayed with her even as she put on a dressing gown and pinned up her curls. Although Snowden's presence at the Schoonmakers', and that of the two large men who had trailed Henry, had made it impossible for them to spend even a few minutes in each other's company, still, they had exchanged glances, and she had felt loved. She even wondered if Henry wouldn't find some way to be with her again later that day. She went down to the parlor with the idea that she might spend a few minutes by herself by the tree, breathing in the pine, and if

Claire happened by, she would ask her for a cup of chocolate. But when she entered the parlor she saw that the chocolate had already been made and that she no longer wanted to be alone.

"Elizabeth!" she cried at the sight of her sister, sitting in her same favorite chair by the fireplace, which held a few modest flames. Her hands fluttered involuntarily to the lace that was buttoned close to her neck and all the way up to her chin. More sounds came out of her mouth, although they were more or less unintelligible, and then she ran to her sister's side and threw herself down at her feet and rested her head against her knee. Diana closed her eyes and just let herself feel that her sister really was there, body and all. It was a struggle to contain the news of what had happened with Henry, because Will was there behind her, sitting on a tasseled ottoman, still holding the iron poker, and his presence made her feel uncharacteristically shy.

"Diana!" Elizabeth brought her sister's face up by the chin and looked at her. She bent and gave her a kiss on the forehead.

"I can't believe you're really here!" Diana now acknowledged Will, whose long legs in their serge trousers jutted outward so that his elbows rested on his knees. It was funny, but not unpleasant, seeing him here amongst the crowded antiques and layered Persian carpets of their family home. They both looked thinner and like they'd taken a lot of sun. "But I'm so glad. Everything's just a mess, Liz, and we need you, and I know it's probably just terrible going all the way across the country and—"

Elizabeth interrupted her with a smile and a gentle "Aren't you going to say hello to Will?"

"Oh, hello, Will!" Diana stood and went over to the family's former coachman and kissed him on the cheek. "I *know*," she said conspiratorially and felt her cheeks scorch a little. "And I think it's terribly romantic."

"Did you ever think you'd see me in your parlor?" Will's mouth was stern and his eyes very, very blue. His hair had grown longer since the last time she saw him, and the baby-roundness had been rubbed off his face somewhat. The green branches of the tree behind him made his hair look a little reddish by comparison, and over the mantel Mr. Holland's portrait stared down at him.

"Oh, of course I did! And . . . and . . . you must have been in here lots of times before, weren't you? When we were little and—"

Will kept the corners of his mouth down, but the joke had broken in his eyes.

"Anyway," Diana went on with a laugh when she saw that she was being teased, "I'm glad you're here now. And you, Liz, you have to tell me what I can do, because things have moved so very quickly with Henry that it's a little frightening and—"

Patience had never been one of Diana's virtues, and she was so eager to get her sister's advice that she almost forgot herself and her shyness about Will in the moment. When Snowden came in through the pocket doors—which his men had not yet managed to oil, leaving them susceptible to loud catching in the groove—she quite remembered what she ought not to say. She spun away from her sister, and the pleasure drained clear out of her features.

"Miss Diana," he said mildly as he crossed toward their little group. "Don't let me interrupt you."

"I . . ." The words stuck in her throat. Several irrational plans sprang to her mind: Maybe she could claim Elizabeth was someone else, and not the sister whose death she had so often lamented to her family's guest. Or maybe he hadn't noticed Elizabeth, and if Diana created some distraction, she might slip out of the room before he did. It was with this half-insane idea in her head that she went on, somewhat defensively: "You haven't interrupted anything at all."

"Oh, no?" For a man to whom she had so repeatedly lied, he seemed neither outraged nor astonished by the sight of the dead Holland girl in their midst, a fact Diana, still so totally stunned by the whole situation, was more relieved than confused by. His gaze went from one sister to the other, but he waited patiently for an explanation, and this kindness only worsened Diana's sense of having been caught in an enormous untruth. He must have also seen Will, but Diana was too terrified to look and see how *he* was handling this intrusion. Her fingers went to her reddening cheeks.

"It's only that I'm hardly dressed for company," she stuttered, still avoiding a fact that was becoming more obvious as the seconds passed.

"You must not stand on ceremony with me, who as you know has come to love your family as my own." Snowden bowed his head a little in expectation and moved the heels of his scuffed, well-traveled boots together. Surely he must be feeling ill-used by this same family, who had so benefited from his largesse and who had misrepresented their woes to him.

But of course, Diana had been the only one who had known their woes were a falsehood.

Just when Diana was starting to feel a little desperate, wondering how she should handle this situation, Elizabeth stood behind her and came to her side. She placed a gentle hand on Diana's shoulder, the touch of which seemed to encourage calm.

"Elizabeth, she's alive!" Diana said then, waving her hands as though the illogical nature of the event had just occurred to her. Maybe, she thought in a moment of pure lunacy, if she seemed to have just realized herself, he wouldn't be so angry with her later. She punctuated this statement with a laugh that contained not nearly enough amusement and sounded unpleasant even to her own ears.

"Yes," Snowden replied. "I can see that."

A silence followed in which Diana fidgeted uncontrollably and then turned her vexed expression on her sister. Finally Elizabeth said, "I know it must seem very odd to you that I'm here, given the reports of my death."

"Odd," Snowden repeated. His thin lips settled slowly around the word. "It's not odd. It's miraculous! I'm so pleased that I was here for this tremendous moment. I knew your father very well, Elizabeth, and I owe him quite a lot. I don't know if Diana has told you . . ."

Diana shook her head, feeling very ashamed. She found herself hoping that he wouldn't mention to Elizabeth how indifferent to him she'd been, and how generally poor as a hostess. *Elizabeth* would never, after all, have let someone give the family so much without the return of great heaps of charm and attention. And what must he think of Will, standing back there behind Elizabeth, still in his workman's clothes?

". . . but I have some small holdings of your father's that have been wrapped up for a time—I won't bore you with the details, but I have just recently been able to liquidate them, and I have come to help your family put itself back together. I hope you won't find me overly forward, Miss Holland, if I observe that your family has found itself in financial straits and that such a situation ought to be corrected."

Elizabeth went forward to the place on the carpet where Snowden stood and took his hand. Her sister could sense, even looking at her back, that she had summoned all her old warmth and radiance. The sun coming in through the high windows shot through her pile of blond hair, illuminating it. When she spoke, it was with the sweet, low tone of a much older girl. "I thank you for that, Mr. Cairns. It is unbelievably kind. I know how much affection my father had for you, and I can plainly see how much you want to repay that. My whole family and I are deeply grateful."

"It is an honor." Snowden held on to Elizabeth's hand even as he made a little bow. "And I will continue my presumptuousness by telling you that my men have brought some presents that I would like very much to give you, and later on I hope you will allow me to provide your kitchen with what is necessary for a proper Christmas dinner."

Diana looked back at Will, who was standing at attention with his hands behind his back and whose shirt of blue and black plaid was a handsome contrast to his suntanned skin. All of her embarrassment and confusion must have been evident on her face because he winked at her in a way that momentarily alleviated her tension.

"Oh, Mr. Cairns, such kindness." Elizabeth's hands

remained in his, and her tone was full of honey. "I cannot imagine a better way to celebrate the holiday and—"

Diana saw the figure in the hall around the time her sister stopped talking. Her gaze drifted, and she noticed that the woman watching them through the partially open doors seemed to have tried to do her hair, although the effect was messier than if she had simply left it down. The long nightgown, which was fitted in the bust and neck but flowed outward from the elbows and the waist, gave Mrs. Holland the look—it occurred to Diana, before the gravity of the situation settled in—of a rather mad member of a Greek chorus. She was small of body, but she was watching the scene with eyes that were large, the irises like black pools in a forest, and rimmed with alert anxiety.

That's what real surprise looks like, Diana thought to herself a little regretfully, just before she realized that she and her sister were going to have a lot to explain.

Eight

Grandes dames do not let go of their grudges willingly; I have known some to cherish a resentment for twenty years or more, against their rival social arbiters but also against their own sisters and children. Such is their privilege, though there are those of us who wake up on Christmas morning hoping that this year it will be a day of reunion.

—MRS. L. A. M. BRECKINRIDGE, *THE LAWS OF BEING IN WELL-MANNERED CIRCLES*

HE SILENCE MIGHT HAVE LASTED HOURS, ALTHOUGH it was difficult to be certain. Elizabeth realized that her mother was watching her from the foyer, and then, before anyone made a sound, there was time for her to recall all the things that used to be expected of her and to turn, slowly, to face the petite matriarch. She felt plainer and less adorned than she ever had. She was wearing the same worn dress—she had looked in her closet for something else, but all the old things were gone—and she felt denuded. Mrs. Holland's mouth hung open, and she hardly seemed to be breathing as she remained in the doorway with a steadiness that, given her behavior the night before, Elizabeth would not have thought her capable of. She appeared to be using the moments of silence to check every inch of her daughter. When they were over, she took two long strides to the center of the room and pulled Elizabeth to her breast.

"Oh thank God, thank God, thank God," she repeated over and again.

Elizabeth hadn't been so close to her mother's body since she was a child. The moment passed, however, and quickly. Mrs. Holland kept a hold on her daughter's elbow as she stepped back. "Claire!" she yelled. The force of her voice somewhat calmed her daughter's worries about her health. "Claire, come here!"

Claire came hurrying in, her wide cheeks pink with exertion. She placed a hand on the stomach of her plain black percale dress with the wide boat neck and looked around the room. Elizabeth tried to smile at her reassuringly, and after Claire had looked back for a few long seconds, the tip of her nose began to turn red and her eyes started to well.

"Claire," Mrs. Holland said sharply. She kept one hand at her daughter's elbow, and the other went to the back of Elizabeth's head, where it rested, firm and loving. "Draw the curtains. Miss Holland has come back to us, as you can plainly see. You will be able to talk with her later. Mr. Cairns, forgive me, you will think us a very odd family. I do hope you will stay on for Christmas dinner. Diana—"

Everyone looked at Diana, who brought her arms up over her laces, suggesting deep discomfort and a barely controlled impulse to go off and hide.

"Yes?" Even in the morning with her hair hardly done and her face nothing more than washed, she shone with a loveliness that was new to her, more grown-up. She seemed to know what she had now.

"Diana, you shall help Claire prepare luncheon for Mr. Cairns. You will see that he is entertained." Mrs. Holland's eyes flashed about the room, as though she were assessing the extent of her resumed authority. Claire had drawn the curtains, which brought shadows back into the room. It was now the parlor that Elizabeth remembered. Without the natural light you hardly noticed the missing Asian vases or the one or two landscapes that had been taken down from the walls. It was again the dense and richly colored collection of objects that had always represented the Hollands. "And you, Keller."

Elizabeth felt a little quickstep of panic. "Mother, he's not to blame. He—"

"I don't know what you're talking about, Elizabeth." Her mother's grip on her head tightened, and she could feel the command to silence as though it were emanating through her palm. "I was asking Keller where he's been. It's been damned hard for me to find someone who knows as much about horses since you've gone," she went on in Will's direction, "and I frankly blame you that I had to sell them."

"I'm sorry, Mrs. Holland." Will looked into his old employer's eyes as he might look on a frigid morning that there was no choice but to go out into. He moved his head just slightly but kept his gaze steady. "But you knew I couldn't stay here forever."

He blinked, and then his gaze was on Elizabeth. She wanted to go stand beside him, to show everyone just how she felt, but she knew from the way he was looking at her that this was unnecessary.

"Keller, we'll discuss this at a later hour."

Mrs. Holland's hand now went to Elizabeth's wrist, and Elizabeth felt herself being drawn out of the parlor. From the four others there was plain silence. Elizabeth could only note the piney smell of the tree, the soft snap of the fire that Will had built that morning, and the faint and reassuring smile that he managed to give her before she was pulled from the room. Then she was going up the stairs. She felt the old fear of her mother's temper, and was nervous about how she'd ever explain where she had been and what she had done. But her mother's strong grip, which indicated how very much among the living she was, was some kind of consolation.

They had just reached the second-floor landing when she saw her aunt Edith's head emerge over the rail. "Elizabeth!" she shouted. She held on to the banister, but otherwise her body moved downward at a run. When she came onto Mrs. Holland and Elizabeth, she threw her arms around the younger girl. "How can this be?" she whispered, pulling back. Her cheekbones protruded, shiny and definite from her thinning skin, but she otherwise retained that Holland beauty she had been known for in her youth. Elizabeth looked into the small, round eyes and saw that she was overcome.

"Perhaps we all should sit somewhere?" Elizabeth suggested, and then the two older women ferried her into the master bedroom. Elizabeth and her aunt went to the armchairs by the fireplace, and Mrs. Holland went to the window, where she pushed back the calico valance and peered down on the street. She continued to fuss with the lace undercurtains as she did.

Words still had not presented themselves. The Elizabeth whom she'd been taught to be was back with her now, and to such a girl as she had been there was no way to explain what had taken her west. But her aunt was urging her with a look. Her mouth flexed as though she might cry, and there were stars of light reflected in her eyes. The moments stretched out in front of them, and then Elizabeth saw that she would have to be the first to speak. Once she began, she found that she couldn't stop.

"I couldn't marry Henry Schoonmaker. I couldn't do that. I couldn't be married to him and I had to stop it. I love Will, Mother." Elizabeth looked but saw no change in her mother's expression. This revelation was apparently too much for Edith, however, who now lowered her eyes. "He had already gone when I realized it. That is, I knew I loved him already, but he was gone when I realized that I couldn't live without him. That I couldn't marry Henry. So I followed Will and I found him, in California. He was working in a shipping yard and saving money to lease a piece of land down near Los Angeles. He always works so hard for things, and he had saved a lot. Even from before, from out here in New York. He had a hunch there would be oil there, and now we've found it. Will says there's so much of it we'll be rich . . . and then we can help you, Mother. Will wants that too."

"Oh, Elizabeth." Her mother let out a breath that might have sent a hot-air balloon soaring. "I had such hopes for you."

"I know." Elizabeth's eyes stung, and for the first time that day she found herself unable to look at her mother. She looked around the room, which she had barely entered since her childhood, with its imposing four-poster bed and flocked, wheat-colored wallpaper. The room was not large, and the women were situated close enough to each other that Elizabeth felt their discomfort and confusion almost physically. "I know you did."

"It sounds like one of your father's schemes," her mother went on dismissively.

There was the suggestion of a reply on Edith's lips, but in the end she said nothing.

Mrs. Holland let go of the valance, and when she spoke, her voice was bitter. "You could have married anyone."

"I might have," Elizabeth carefully corrected her. "But when it came to it, I couldn't."

"I see." Her mother turned away from the window and looked at her for a long, sad stretch. The dust was streaming down, visible in the light. "Oh, Elizabeth," she said finally. "To have you back and find that it isn't you."

"But it is me, Mother, and we're going to be rich again. We all are, because of Will."

Mrs. Holland was unmoved by this. She had begun shaking her head back and forth, and her hands were working together nervously. "It's all too wild, Lizzie. I don't know where you got the idea that you can just do as you please. Running off. Do you know what you've done to this family? Do you know what you've done to me?"

Elizabeth's voice might have been coming from the other room. "I do know."

"Well, you're not going back to California, not as I live and breathe. You're not seeing Will Keller again—"

"Louisa." Edith could not bring her eyes to meet those of her sister-in-law, but the tone of her voice signified real conviction. "My brother always liked the boy, and anyway, you know nothing good ever comes of separating lovers."

Elizabeth was fairly certain the word *lover* caused as much discomfort to her mother as it did to her. The pause that followed was so long, however, and the change in her mother's

face so significant that she wondered if they hadn't touched on some corner of family history that she wasn't privy to.

"Oh!" her mother said after a time. She put her hands over her face, and her shoulders fell. "Oh, Elizabeth."

Meanwhile, downstairs, the Holland house was thrown into movement. Diana was relieved to see that Snowden didn't seem to have noticed that he had been so calculatedly deceived. "What a miraculous day this is," he said as Diana descended the stairs from her bedroom, where she had changed from her dressing gown into a skirt patterned with many stripes of horizontal green, and a black chiffon shirtwaist. "How lucky I am to be here for Miss Holland's return."

"And how lucky we are to have you here to celebrate with us," Diana said. She was still feeling a little guilty over her falsehood, and so was trying to be especially respectful of him. "It wouldn't have been much of a celebration without you," she added, truthfully, since his entourage had made itself busy carting in the necessary foodstuffs for a proper Christmas feast. They were all over the house, shaking out old linens and polishing what silver was left. They crisscrossed the floors with new candelabras and vases and chair cushions.

"Since your mother and sister are busy, perhaps you could

consult on the dinner menu with Miss Broud and me before it is finalized?" He paused and gave her a shy smile. "As long as we're waiting for the others for luncheon."

"Of course, Mr. Cairns—" Diana broke off when she saw a figure through the door glass. Her body grew buoyant and inclined in his direction when she realized who it was. "Mr. Cairns, would you excuse me just one moment?"

"Of course."

Diana walked quickly to the door and went out onto the enclosed filigreed-iron porch where Henry stood, three steps up from the street, in a black coat and hat. She pulled the door behind her, but when she looked back, she saw that Snowden had not moved from the place in the middle of the foyer.

"We're being watched, Henry." She tried to speak with composure and not to smile too much. The air came right through her thin shirt and chilled her skin. "So don't do anything rash," she added with a wink, and so playfully that she might almost have been encouraging the opposite.

"I have to talk to you," he said. He was looking at her intensely, and his eyes were round with feeling. They were worried, sleepless eyes. She had found their separation to be so agonizing that it was almost a physical affliction, but now she saw that for Henry it had been much worse. She had heard that lack of gratification could be very hard on men, and she supposed that explained the difference.

"I can't *now*, Henry," she replied. She felt naughty, just standing with him this way in public, and she thought that she could hear his pulse even with so much space between them. It was getting harder by the second, standing right in front of him and not reaching out to touch his face. "There's such news, and the house is full of activity. I will be missed now."

"But Diana—" Henry took a step toward her, and she almost moved in to kiss him despite everything. But Snowden was still there in the hall—she could feel his eyes on them. She knew that she would betray herself some way if she went on talking to Henry, so she stepped away and put her hand on the door handle.

"Henry, come later. Come tonight. But if you stay now, you will only get me in trouble!" she hissed. Then she drew back the door, so that he would be unable to say more. He did go on looking at her, however, his dark eyes searching her with so much desire that she felt a little weak. That look made her feel so delightful that she couldn't help but hold it a few seconds too long, before she stepped up and back into the house, ready to deceive Snowden a little more.

Several hours and a lot of talk later, Elizabeth emerged from Mrs. Holland's bedroom and saw that Will was waiting for her. Not in a place where he might have heard the conversation, but near her bedroom, so that she would know he was there when the discussion was over. They met in the middle of the hallway, where she took his hand and brought him into the servants' stairs. It was all darkness there, and the ceiling was low. This was the path she had always taken to visit him, when desire had first begun to outweigh consequences, and before any decisions had to be made.

"What did she say to you?" Will asked finally.

"She gave us her blessing." Elizabeth's breath was broken, short, and loud in her own ears. There was so much relief to be found in seeing her mother alive, in seeing the family provided for by some act of providence, but she had also found it exhausting being so truthful in this house where she had once lied so impeccably. What she and Will did next was going to be real in a way it hadn't been before, because she had proclaimed her intentions out loud. She pressed her forehead against his.

"Oh." Will's tone was as full of gratitude as if he had used actual words of thanks.

"Yes." She was becoming aware of the salty liquid from her eyes and from her nose, collecting above her top lip. "She gave two conditions. The first was that we were to be married."

Will pulled her tighter. She felt almost crushed against him, which was just as she wanted it.

"The second was that we leave. She said that if anyone found out, that would be the end of the family forever. Maybe she'll come visit us, she said. But we can't stay here."

Their breathing was slow and their inhalations came at the same time. There was the creak of feet falling on the main stairs, and the sound of instructions being given down in the kitchen. "What do you think?"

"I think," she said, pressing her lids down hard against each other, "that you need to go buy a suit to be married in."

Downstairs, Claire was already giving directions for how to set the table and making lists of what was still needed for a proper Christmas dinner. Later, when the late part of the afternoon began to fade into evening, there would be young turkey with chestnut sauce and potatoes whipped with cream and champagne punch. There would be gifts and toasts and prayers. But for now, Elizabeth wanted nothing but to stay in the dark and be held just as she was.

Thirty Nine

It is by now well known that William S. Schoonmaker wants to run for mayor, although he has thus far based his candidacy on little more than the unfortunate loss of his only son's fiancée. The young man has lately been seen out again and dancing with young ladies, however, prompting rumors of new attachments. If his first fiancée is in fact alive, as the appearance of her engagement ring might indicate, will young Schoonmaker renew his suit? Surely the would-be mayor could put quite a bounty on the head of her supposed captors. . . .

—FROM THE FIRST PAGE OF THE *NEW-YORK NEWS OF THE WORLD GAZETTE*, DECEMBER 26, 1899

"I'D LIKE A DOZEN WHITE ROSES, A DOZEN WHITE freesias, a bunch of baby's breath. . . ." Diana Holland paused and frowned. She hadn't made a list, and she was now forgetting all of the things that her sister had asked her to order.

Yesterday, after her brief encounter with Henry, she'd run upstairs for a private moment in her room. That was when she came upon Elizabeth and Will embracing, and she learned their good news. She'd been so swept up in the general exhilaration of love—hers and Henry's, Liz and Will's—that she'd volunteered to go to the florist herself when her sister told her the list of things to be done. This was, after all, far preferable to remaining in the house and being "nice" to Snowden. Here she was free to imagine the flowers she'd one day pick out for her and Henry.

He hadn't come to her last night, but even seeing him on the porch had been enough to consume her thoughts and destroy her concentration. Landry the florist smiled at her from the other side of the marble counter in his Broadway shop; as he had already told her, it was not a busy day for flowers. "Oh! And lilies of the valley! Do you have any of those . . . ?"

"Sounds like a wedding."

Diana looked up and into the mirror behind the register. The place was all mirrors where it wasn't white porcelain tile. She looked into the inquiring eyes of the gossip columnist for a few uncertain seconds, and then she turned so that Mr. Landry wouldn't note the playful nature of her smile. "Mr. Barnard, are you following me?"

"Not at all," he answered in a tone that left her entirely in doubt.

"Well, nor are these flowers for a wedding," she shot back blithely. "We always celebrate a white Christmas at the Holland house. You can print *that* if you like."

Then she turned back to Mr. Landry and asked if she could pick up her order on Thursday morning.

"Weren't you here to get flowers, Mr. Barnard?" she asked as he moved to follow her back onto the street.

"I found my daily requirement for visual beauty has unexpectedly been filled by a different source," he replied, holding the door for her.

Outside the sun was shining, which did nothing to mitigate the icy cut of the wind. Dead leaves reeled in the air and skittered across the sidewalk as Diana brought her camel coat in closer to her chest. "That's quite a dose of flattery. Pretty soon I'll have to start wondering if you don't have an angle."

"I hope you won't think me somehow not in earnest about your beauty if I do."

"Ah, well, that I can't tell you." Diana ducked her head so that the brim of her bonnet covered her face. "Some things must remain a mystery, and for now, I think I'll keep my opinion of you and your compliments to myself."

"I'll have to look forward to that another day, then. Though I do of course have an angle." He pushed his hat back on his head and arched a dark brow.

"Of course you do!" They were walking up Broadway, and though the cold was biting at her, Diana felt a peculiar elation at being again in the gossip columnist's company. Perhaps it was knowing that she held a few secrets greater than he could imagine, secrets she could never reveal to him. He walked along on her left, so that he shielded her from the view of anyone passing in the street, and he was looking at her in that way that made her feel as though he might have noticed some attractive quality of hers that had escaped even her own notice. Of course, she glowed whenever she thought of Henry, and Henry was always in her thoughts. "Well, do share."

"The public is hungry for news about you, Miss Diana," he went on in a voice that didn't quite touch down on seriousness. "Can't you tell us something? Perhaps there's wedding news? Or maybe something about this Snowden Cairns fellow."

"He is not a beau, if you're wondering that," Diana answered quickly, remembering how poorly the last report of her possible attachment had gone over.

"No? Hmmm . . . and your Christmas dinner?"

"Oh," Diana replied gaily. They were moving forward, up the avenue, at a good pace now. "We had turkey with cranberries and asparagus points on toast and hothouse lettuce with mayonnaise and, later, plum pudding!"

"Don't tease me, Diana. I meant, were there any special guests? Perhaps one with the first initial E.?"

Diana smiled her elusive little smile. She was surprised to find within herself a small inclination to tell him, although she wasn't certain if it was because she wanted the record set straight, or because she enjoyed telling her own story, or if it was simply that she liked manipulating what the papers printed. "I really don't know what you mean" was her eventual reply.

He sighed. She had never seen him disappointed, and it only made her wish she could tell him more. But he was looking away from her now. He was trying to get a cigarette going even as he walked into the wind.

"Are there really no other stories for you to write?" Diana affected a sympathetic face.

"There are," he said, his eyes meeting hers in a passing moment. The cigarette was evidently lit, and he exhaled a cloud of smoke. "But I just don't want to pursue either of them."

"And why not?" The rhythm in Diana's chest had slowed to an occasional thud. Was it possible that Davis Barnard was jealous over her? Because he had heard that Henry was in love with her and that perhaps there was a wedding on the way? It was a little wild, Diana had to admit to herself, that news would have traveled so quickly, but he had, after all, been prodding her about a wedding, and it would maybe explain Henry's keeping himself scarce on Christmas Eve. . . .

"Because they are neither of them are very good for the Hollands, and, as you know, I never want to write anything that might hurt your family." They had come to East Twentieth Street, and Diana looked to see if his face didn't betray some of his meaning. She had to turn there—she was almost home. "The first is about Elizabeth; that's why I was asking about her. Seems her engagement ring turned up in a pawnshop out west and now everyone is speculating if she isn't alive somewhere."

Diana's heart sped, and she gave a loud laugh that she hoped distracted from the color going out of her face. "Surely I'd know if that were true," she shot back, without the slightest idea whether she was convincing or not.

"It would be a wonderful thing of course . . ." Davis said

earnestly. "Although the pawnshop isn't a very nice element of the whole story. People wonder, if she is alive, what sort of ordeal she's been through. I know it would be devastating to get your hopes up and then find out that she's still dead."

"Yes." There were few people on the street, all of them too cold to observe what passed between a young lady from a good family and a newspaper writer on a Broadway street corner. All of the sudden, Diana wished to be home already. "I suppose Tiffany makes a lot of rings."

"Well, they're just rumors. No one knows for sure. Though there has been talk of tracking down the man who sold it and having him arrested." He paused and looked Diana over. "I suppose you gave that up long ago."

"I wonder what the other story is?" Diana was almost afraid to ask, but the cold was setting in now, and she was growing more antsy with every passing moment. She feared that if he went on about Elizabeth, she would surely betray something.

"Ah! Well, that's not so bad either if you look at it from a certain angle, though some people would say that Henry Schoonmaker getting engaged to Penelope Hayes at this particular moment signifies—"

"What?" Diana had lost any capacity for coyness or subterfuge. Her vision had gone spotty, and it was all she could do not to reach up and put a hand on the columnist's wide shoulder to steady herself. Gramercy was only a few blocks away, but she was stuck there, at that asymmetrical street corner with its high buildings and noisy street traffic.

"Yes, I didn't like it either. But that's the story. That Buck fellow who Penelope is always hanging around with told me. He's my cousin, I'm ashamed to say, though I like to think of him as at least a second cousin. . . ."

"Is it to be announced?" So this was betrayal. It was like being left alone in the desert at dusk without water or warmth. It left your mouth dry and your will broken. It sapped your tears and made you hollow. The news sounded impossible until she remembered the look on Henry's face yesterday, when he'd come to her door, which she had so naïvely explained away. Perhaps he had been coming to tell her yesterday, or maybe he had wanted to take her and run away. None of that mattered anymore. Now she knew what cowardice he was capable of.

Davis shrugged. "I suppose everyone likes attention. Probably I'll run it myself. . . . It's a good little piece of news, if you get over the distastefulness of it all—"

Diana wasn't sure what else he said. She was running down Twentieth Street at an absurd gallop, her whole body lunging forward and swaying as she did. The cold was so far under her clothes that she could hardly feel her feet. She certainly couldn't feel her heart. All she hoped for at that particular moment was that she might be able to reach home and her sister before the sobbing started.

Forty

The Schoonmakers gave a delightful Christmas Eve fete, at which the copper-smelting heiress Carolina Broad was universally liked by everybody. She has the simple manner of our western states, but her natural beauty was still very much admired by all the young gentleman, in particular banking heir Leland Bouchard, who was accused by one or two of his fellow bachelors of filling up her dance card far too early. . . .

—FROM THE "GAMESOME GALLANT" COLUMN IN THE *NEW YORK IMPERIAL*, TUESDAY, DECEMBER 26, 1899

$\mathcal{D}$ EPARTMENT STORES NO LONGER LOOKED THE same to Carolina. She had been told by Tristan that she had better get a dressmaker: Girls of her sort were not seen in ready-to-wear, he said, and she knew this must be the truth, since he told her so even to his own detriment. After all, *he* worked in a department store, and this would mean fewer sales for him. But it was only the day after Christmas, and all of the best dressmakers would be unavailable until at least the New Year, he had warned her when she arrived on a mission to purchase shirtwaists and accessories and skirts and a lace or two on Mr. Longhorn's account.

The arrangement with Mr. Longhorn felt entirely easy and comfortable to her, she told Tristan when he asked. Though the older gentleman did not seem to want to hear any facts of her previous life, he did—when she hinted, over Christmas dinner in the hotel's grand dining room, that she might have a sister in the city—say that the elder Miss Broad ought to have some presents for the holiday as well. And so

Carolina had entered Lord & Taylor and looked across the rows of tables with their precious objects and felt neither fear nor unquenchable desire, but rather that she could simply have any of those things that interested her.

"At any rate, Miss Broad, you are looking very well taken care of today. . . ."

Carolina twisted about, catching her reflection in the mirror, imagining that her contortions presented a view of her in which she possessed the long neck, the plush lips, the hazy eyes and fluffy hair of a Gibson girl. "Tristan," she remarked with a certain languor, "I am going to need all your help today."

Tristan watched her, drawing his hand along the edge of the polished cherry table as he did. He was in shirtsleeves and a brown waistcoat, and his chin looked soft, as though it had been shaved that morning. "Today," Tristan replied, "there is no one else to serve. You, my lovely, are a success."

Carolina's cheek bent toward her shoulder. She wondered if he might try to kiss her again. Not that she supposed she should really be doing any of that anymore—but she couldn't help but find the memory a little exciting. It was nice, she now knew, to be touched.

"It really worked, didn't it?" Tristan's voice had lowered, although she still wished he wouldn't talk about it in public. "You didn't think it would . . . I could tell. You looked so scared in the hotel that night. But I knew. I've been around, I know when to play a card."

Carolina nodded faintly. She found she didn't want to acknowledge the thrust of this conversation out loud.

"Before we go looking for things for you, though . . ." There was a quality in Tristan's voice that she had never heard before, and it made her turn toward him. "The high-class ladies I've befriended in the past, when I've had a small debt to pay or some other expense, I've filched a little here or there and nobody has ever noticed." He paused and looked away. Behind him, shopgirls hurried back and forth. "I have a confession to make. I took your money, but I didn't know it was all you had."

Before Carolina knew whether she should be angry or frightened or grateful for this news, whether her impression of Tristan was that he was more or less trustworthy now, he gave her a wolfish grin and went on.

"But you see how much better it worked out in the end? I hope you feel I have repaid my debt."

Like any society girl confronted with an uncomfortable fact, Carolina felt overwhelmingly now that she simply didn't want to have to think about it anymore. "Oh, let's not talk about all that hash," she said. Then she thought of something pleasant and smiled. "Let's see what pretty things Mr. Longhorn doesn't want to buy me today."

His response didn't come immediately, and she wondered in the interval whether he wouldn't keep trying to bring up the past. But then a smile came, spreading steadily under the neat mustache, and there was that flash in his hazel eyes. "Yes, let's," he said, and offered an arm. As she took it, they moved forward across the floor, each one playing their part to perfection.

As Carolina's strides brought her further into that sanctum of all that was fine and beautiful, she began to notice her reflection in the mirrored columns that supported the high, arched ceiling with its classic white filigree designs and dangling chandeliers. Everything held the light of precious metals, and it was all to reflect on her. Or girls like her. But she was now, most assuredly, a girl like *that*. One could see it, plainly, as the reflection passed from one gold-shot mirror into another, with the upturn of her nose and the careless cast of her pretty eyes.

She knew where they were going. The Holland girls had told Claire about it, and Claire had told her. They were going to one of the private rooms where special customers could sit in comfort and wait for things to be brought for them. She had even heard that there were sweets and champagne. Until that morning, she had never been sure whether she was even really wanted in any of the shopping emporiums. But now she felt completely taken up.

Just as they were about to pass into the elevator area, with its peacock-colored enamel-inlaid walls and large bronze arrows bouncing in arcs to show which floor the carriage was on, Carolina noticed something that made her lungs swell up with air and then crumple as though they had been rained on by shattering glass. "Oh," she whispered quietly, to herself, so that no one else could hear.

Over there, walking between tables of neckties as though he had just walked down the plank and onto the harbor of a foreign country, was Will. Beautiful Will, with his serious eyes and his hair a little overgrown looking around him in that meticulous way he had. His skin had somehow or other been darkened by the sun, and he looked as though he had seen some hard things. There was a sweet ache spreading all over, and she had to close her eyes so that the feeling wouldn't overwhelm her. In a moment she tried to open them, but found that she had to bring her hand up to cover her gaze again.

Maybe he really had read about her in the papers. Maybe he was there to fetch her. He hadn't seen her yet, however, and even in her brief glimpses of him, she knew that he hadn't made his fortune out west. He was wearing those same serge trousers, that same slightly too large black coat. There were no new comforts in his life, she could see that in a few seconds. But still she wanted him. The want had not faded after all.

"Miss Broad," she heard Tristan say.

She nodded, to him or to herself she wasn't sure. The elevator doors had opened, and other shoppers were passing them on their way to the registers. She moved her hand. It was somewhat easier to watch him when there were bodies passing between them. And though she felt so light as to have no control of her limbs, she found that a few more blinkless moments allowed her to see what she must do. The want was there, but she couldn't follow it. Will was so close to her, and she had come so far. He would understand how foolish he had been if he saw her, but then she would have to come down, and she couldn't stand that. She couldn't stand to fall even a little bit.

"Are you all right, Miss Broad?"

"Oh . . . yes," she said. She stepped away from Will and let go of the old wants. "Just a little headache that came and went."

As the operator brought down the iron grate, she told herself she'd made the right decision. Her new friend Penelope Hayes would not have stooped at the sight of some passing fancy from years ago. Her desires would already have been set on something far better. It would be so like Elizabeth to stumble on sentimentality, to give up everything for some old dream.

"Are you sure that you're all right?"

"Yes."

She wet her lips and forced air back into her lungs. She thought of Mr. Longhorn as a young man and how many young men she had met just two nights ago and of all the things she deserved. She thought of the difference between real kisses and imagined ones. She smiled, although it was a weak sort of smile. She could not help but think, as she was borne upward beside Tristan, who seemed like so many things and was never quite any of them, that it was unfortunate that she had ever known him. It was true that she might have been too shy or gaffe-prone ever to win Mr. Longhorn's patronage without him, but even so, he was becoming distasteful. He would have to be cut loose soon, too, she told herself, with that hardness that was taking form inside her heart. She would have to be nice to him for a while longer, but already she did not need him.

Her smile dimmed, but she kept looking at Tristan as she said, with a certain declarative panache: "In fact, I feel just perfect."

Forty One

There has been much talk about the deceased Elizabeth Holland as of late. Many have suggested that with the recent discovery of her engagement ring, she has likely perished at the hands of a band of thieves. If she is discovered, she should quickly be married upon her return, no matter what unimaginable things have occurred in her time away from society.

—FROM THE EDITORIAL PAGE OF *THE NEW YORK TIMES*, WEDNESDAY, DECEMBER 27, 1899

"IF ANYONE KNOWS ANY REASON WHY THIS MAN AND woman should not be wed, let them speak now or forever hold their peace. . . ."

There was a slight murmur of approval and amusement across the room, and then it became very evident that no one was going to object. The floor had been covered in white petals; the windows had been draped in lace. The lesser parlor, on the east side of the Holland town house, was still lacking in furniture, but it made a perfect place for a wedding. They had moved in a small settee on which sat Elizabeth's mother—much recovered from her illness, but still somewhat feverish and weak—and her aunt Edith, who had not stopped crying or smiling all morning. Behind them stood four of Snowden's men, in their worn leather waistcoats and thick, off-white collared shirts. Near the covered windows stood Snowden, holding a Bible and his duties seriously, and to Elizabeth's back were Diana and behind her Claire, both of them in white, both clutching the little bouquets of lilies of the valley and white roses that the three girls had put together that morning and tied with lavender ribbons.

In the center of all this was Elizabeth, wearing a new white dress of lined cotton eyelet that fit her perfectly despite not having been made just for her. There was lace tight against her skin at the neck and below the elbows, and it was cinched to show the little waist she used to be so proud of, but there was a certain bridal volume to the sleeves of the upper arms and to the skirt. The buttons at her wrists and the nape of her neck were covered in cream-colored silk, and very ladylike. Will had picked it out, since her mother had forbidden her from even so much as looking out the windows. Her hands were now extended, holding Will's. He could hardly meet her eyes and he was very still; she realized that he was nervous. She hadn't seen him nervous in a long time, and the realization made her heart swell up. He was wearing a new, dark brown suit with a waistcoat and white collar. She had had no idea what it would do to her, seeing him in a suit.

"Elizabeth Adora Holland, do you take William Thomas Keller to be your lawfully wedded husband, to have and to hold, in sickness and in health, until death do you part?"

"I do," she whispered. Her eyes were damp, and she couldn't stop looking at Will, with his broad shoulders and his big blue eyes rimmed in their dark lashes. It was an irony, she thought, that it was her engagement ring that had paid for flowers and a new dress and the suit, but she was glad that Will had been a part of selling it, and not just because he had bargained with the pawnbroker and gotten the best price. Years later, when Will had proven himself and they had watched each other change in time, they could tell their children that story. How an object that had once seemed like it might pull them apart had in fact bought the clothes they were wed in.

"Do you, William Thomas Keller, take this woman to be your lawfully wedded wife, to have and to hold, in sickness and in health, until death do you part?"

Now a smile began to creep onto his face. Once he said, "I do," the smile was there, and permanent. He had been holding their rings in his pocket, and he reached for them now. They were simple yellow gold bands that her mother had found amongst the family heirlooms, and they placed them on each other's fingers now without pomp.

"I now pronounce you man and wife. You may kiss the bride," Snowden said.

Elizabeth had thought of this moment with trepidation all through the morning. Her physical closeness to Will had been so long a secret, it seemed strange and a little frightening that she would have to kiss him in front of her mother and aunt. But in the moment there was nothing more natural. She wasn't even sure how he reached her, or how the kiss began.

But then their lips were together, soft and fervent, and she knew that for all the things she regretted leaving behind, there was a rich, bright future right ahead of her, full of everything she wanted and much that she hadn't even imagined yet.

When she heard clapping, she knew that the moment was over. She stepped back and Diana embraced her. Poor Diana—it seemed as though all the strength had gone out of her arms, even as she used them to hold on to her sister. Her shiny brown curls spilled all over Elizabeth's shoulder. Although Elizabeth had listened to several hours of tearful confession about Henry's betrayal, and though she had coaxed and reassured her and sworn that she was positive Penelope had played some trick or other, she could not help but be a little relieved that her sister would not be sneaking around with him anymore. She had told Diana, truthfully, that she believed Henry was in love with her. But she could not help but feel a little scandalized by what Diana had done with him, despite her years of slipping down to Will's carriage house bed, and she knew that she would sleep a little easier in California knowing that Diana was not always at risk of being found out.

Her mother had come, a little unsteadily, to her feet. Edith, still sitting on the mahogany and burgundy velvet settee, watched her to see that she could stand on her own. She could, and proceeded forward to kiss Elizabeth's cheek. Then she turned to Will.

"I have known you a long time and I have always liked you," she said simply. The skin above her upper lip was set and stern. All around them, in that sparse room with its sea green walls and carved wood ceiling, with its vases so recently filled with fresh flowers, the witnesses shifted and waited to see what Mrs. Holland would say. "And my late husband liked you more than I did. I would not have let this happen otherwise. I won't pretend that this was my first choice for how my child would marry, but I know that she'll be happy with you, and safe."

Will's face was at its most serious, and he nodded thankfully. This was the loudest endorsement he was likely to get from Elizabeth's mother, and he knew it. "Thank you, Mrs. Holland," he answered, and then extended his hand for her to shake.

Elizabeth watched as her mother gave him a curt smile and a faint nod. She knew that it was difficult for her mother to do even this much—it had been Edith's cajoling that had allowed as much ceremony and acknowledgment as this— and Elizabeth was very grateful for it. Later, on the train, she thought, she would tell Will how much they had Edith to thank, and they would plan some gesture of gratitude that they could extend toward her when their oil money really started coming in.

"Mr. Cairns, how lovely that was," her mother was now

saying. The obsequiousness of which she was sometimes capable had crept back into her voice. "How fortunate we have again been made by your presence. It seems you will surprise us with some new, secret ability on every new day of our acquaintance."

"I am honored to do it. But now you must excuse me—I have some small business to attend to, and I'm sure your family wants a few moments of privacy together." Snowden took Will's hand and shook it and then turned to Elizabeth, where his small eyes briefly lingered. She couldn't help but marvel at how lucky they were to have met Snowden, and at how naturally kind he was. She felt as warmly toward him at that moment as though he were part of the family. "My congratulations to both of you, Mr. and Mrs. Keller."

When he left the room, his men followed him, and then the Hollands were alone again, illuminated by the dappled light that was filtered by the lace curtains. Most of the original paintings were gone, but there were still a few grand depictions of roiled seas on the wall. The parlor retained the aura, which Elizabeth remembered it having when she was a little girl, of being the place where obscure, grown-up things occurred. Claire went to prepare tea and cake, and Elizabeth sat down beside her mother on the small settee.

"When Snowden returns to Boston, he will have the certificate drawn up and sent to you in California. It is less likely

to be noticed if he does it there. Oh, Elizabeth," she whispered, placing her hands on her older daughter's cheeks, "I will miss you, I will miss you. But you must go soon. The longer you stay, the more likely it is that you will be discovered. And you know it will be the end of this family if you are."

Elizabeth nodded and held her tears. She might have told her mother how much it meant to her that she had been married before the family, but in the end she decided it was unnecessary. There were a few days left of the year, and she would spend them in the company of those she loved most. They would eat meals together and get used to the idea that she was Mrs. Keller. Then, on New Year's Eve, which Snowden had advised would be a slow travel day and the time when they were least likely to be noticed, she and Will would collect all their things in two small suitcases and say good-bye to Gramercy a second time, and to New York forever.

The announcement this morning, in a one-line item in the *World*, that Miss Penelope Hayes is engaged to be married to Mr. Henry Schoonmaker is a lovely bit of news. Of course, given the report that the engagement ring young Schoonmaker gave to his previous fiancée, the late Elizabeth Holland, has resurfaced, we cannot help but wonder what will happen if the lady who used to wear that ring should resurface as well....

—FROM THE SOCIETY PAGE OF THE *NEW-YORK NEWS OF THE WORLD GAZETTE*, WEDNESDAY, DECEMBER 27, 1899

THE HALLS OF THE HAYES MANSION ECHOED AS Penelope ran through them, her small dog pressed to her chest. She was so close to everything she wanted, and yet she could sense all the insidious forces poised to take them away from her. Her long shadow fell across the black-and-white-tiled floor as she moved, under the impossibly high mirrored ceilings of the first floor of No. 670 Fifth Avenue, that red-brick-and-limestone colossus that few would feign call a home, and which was capable of spooking even a girl as self-possessed as Penelope on her rare vulnerable days. The rumors about Elizabeth's return had ruined her sleep, and the image of Henry and Diana together had destroyed what should have been per-fectly lovely waking hours. When she saw the English butler in the front vestibule, she paused and went breathlessly to him.

"Rathmill," she said. She was aware that veins had emerged on her white neck, but she couldn't help it. The beady black eyes of Robber, her Boston terrier, went all around the room in a kind of terror. "Where are my parents?"

"Mademoiselle Penelope, I believe they are in the drawing room having their tea. Would you like me to—"

"No, no," Penelope interrupted. She deposited the wiggling body of her dog into Rathmill's not-quite-ready arms. "*I'll* do it."

She walked away from him, toward that epic curve of marble stairs that would bring her to the second-story drawing room where her parents took their private tea. On the first step she paused and rested her hand on the cool balustrade. "You can tell my mother's social secretary that she will be needed very shortly, however."

No one had helped Penelope in achieving her not unreasonable desires, except perhaps Isabelle Schoonmaker, and so Penelope felt no compunction about directing her wrath in all directions. Rathmill, the butler, had been of especially no use. He had served several titled British families before he came to the Hayeses, and he knew, as the young lady of the house knew, that they were the kind of family that needed an English butler to teach them class. He was always giving them snide little looks, which her mother was too dense to notice, but Penelope saw them and understood.

Isabelle, for her part, could not have been more delighted with the announcement of the engagement, but every little gift she gave her future stepdaughter-in-law, every time she squealed in joy and winked with knowing excitement, seemed a mockery of Penelope. She had what she wanted, but she had bullied her way in, and didn't even have a ring yet to show for all her trouble. She had been so clever and so conniving for Henry's sake and for her own, and he couldn't even appreciate it. There had been no romantic gestures from Henry, no illicit glances. Penelope felt as lonely as she'd ever felt, and might have even wondered if there was any point to it anymore if it weren't for her pride.

But her pride was considerable. It was pride that kept her moving up the stairs, drawing back the gunmetal gray silk skirt that she wore with the black organza puff-sleeved blouse. She strode into the small, second-story parlor, which faced the avenue, like all the rooms they used frequently, without trying to disguise her distemper. Her parents were sitting by the fire, with its majolica-tiled mantel, and her brother stood not far off, by one of the two life-size cloisonné peacocks, smoking a cigarette. All three turned stupidly to look at her.

"Ahh!" she cried out in frustration.

The room, with its heavy purple and cold brocade, was a dark place, and this should have flattered Mrs. Hayes, but did not. That lady's corpulence was bedecked in green and white tarlatan, trimmed with black lace, and her dark hair was restrained with green ribbons. It was hardly seemly for someone her age, as the Hayes siblings might have amused themselves by noting in lighter times.

"What is it?" Evelyn Hayes said, setting down her tea-cup with a rattle. "Don't make that face—it will leave permanent lines."

"We thought you would be so happy now that you're engaged to the Schoonmaker boy." Richmond Hayes's voice was not without a touch of recrimination, and he switched the cross of his legs after he spoke. He couldn't be called tall, when you considered the height of his two children, and his features were framed by a dark beard and mustache, over which peered small eyes that never lost sight of their owner's self-interest.

Penelope fell back into the cream-colored sofa with the kilim pillows and slumped, her ears falling to her shoulders and her chin almost reaching her chest. Grayson turned slowly and rested his hand on a polished cherrywood screen before exhaling smoke.

"What does Penny want?" His words were heavy with sarcasm, and he looked at her the way he might have when they were children and Penelope was throwing one of her not infrequent tantrums.

"I don't want to live in this awful house anymore," Penelope spat out—cruelly, considering the money they all knew Mr. Hayes had sunk into the place. "I hate everybody."

"Why?" her brother asked, the same amused smile on his face. He took a last drag and flicked his cigarette into the fire. "When we all want the best for you."

"We are all so proud of you, Penelope, making such a brilliant engagement." Her mother winked at her daughter and tried to look encouraging. "Before your brother has even proposed once. We were all hoping he would come back lord of some manor or other, but this has not proved the case."

Grayson rolled his eyes and let his arm fall limp off the screen. He sighed audibly and moved, at a slow, urbane gait, to the sofa where Penelope slouched. He crossed his legs, dressed in pin-striped suit pants, and rested his elbow on his knee. His waistcoat had been made in London, and was of pearl gray silk. "Come now, dear sister," he implored in the same tone. "Tell us what will make you feel better."

Penelope looked at her brother, whose hair was pomaded and parted down the center so that it rose stiffly, back from his forehead on either side. She herself had not had the patience to let her maid treat her hair that morning, and so it was frizzier than usual. She paused to vainly brush it back from her face. Then she looked at her father, whose face had assumed that resigned expression it always did just before he wrote a very big check. Penelope felt calm all of sudden—or at least, calmer than she had all day.

"I want to have the wedding now."

"Now?" her mother sputtered.

Ever since Grayson had told her about seeing Elizabeth on the train, she had known that she had to do something, fast. It hardly mattered that Henry didn't love his previous fiancée—if she came back to New York, they would all wonder whether he should marry her still, and it wouldn't matter at all that Penelope was engaged to him now. Their wedding would be postponed indefinitely, and public opinion would turn against her. Penelope pushed herself up straight and placed her hands in a neat cross on her lap. She looked at each member of her immediate family, and tried to seem a little modest. All of the mad fury she had recently experienced had been replaced by a pure focus on making everyone awed and jealous of her. "Well, before the end of the year."

"Penelope," her father put in sternly, "we haven't a place reserved, or a minister. We haven't asked anyone to save the date."

"But you're Richmond Hayes! You can get a minister, and everyone will want to come to *my* wedding. And anyway, Mrs. Schoonmaker already said that we could use their place at Tuxedo to have a party to *really* celebrate the engagement. Why not just make it the wedding? We'll have the invitations handwritten tonight and sent out tomorrow! Oh, please, Daddy!"

Her parents appeared too stunned to deny or affirm her request. They looked at each other a little nervously across the gold tea service. It was Grayson who spoke first, and he now spoke in a reasonable tone devoid of irony. "Why not? It will be such a surprise, and that will create envy and excitement, and everyone will be falling all over themselves to make sure they are invited. It will remind all society what this family has become, and what sort of displays we're now capable of. I think old Schoonmaker will like the idea too. Did you see that bit on him in the paper today? Seems he passed out some bad turkeys at that parade of his, and a few slum girls have fallen ill." Grayson chuckled and lit another cigarette. "That's the kind of tragedy that begs for a distraction," he declared in his father's direction.

"But what will you wear?" Mrs. Hayes asked, her round face still open with confusion.

"I've always wanted to wear your dress," Penelope lied sweetly. "We can have it made over so that it fits me in a few days."

"Oh!" Mrs. Hayes smiled a little at this. "Well, why not? Don't you think, Mr. Hayes, that this might be the best thing?"

"If it's a surprise, and out of town," Penelope went on, assuming correctly that if she kept talking, her father would lose the conviction behind any of his objections and grow bored with the whole back-and-forth, "then there won't be all those unpleasant crowds and police barricades. There won't be endless newspaper articles for months before, about all the bridesmaids and what shade they're wearing. It will be much more elegant, don't you think?"

Her father examined his daughter for a moment and then shrugged. "If that's what you want, and you think the Schoonmakers will agree."

"Oh, yes. It's just perfect! And I *know* they'll agree." Penelope stood now and clasped her hands. The excitement had come into her mother's face now—she had several new jewels that she had not yet gotten to show off, as her daughter knew well enough. Grayson gave his sister a look of tickled admiration. "You'll go tonight, won't you? We all will, to tell the Schoonmakers the plan. And then tomorrow Henry and I, and his family, and all of you, can go up to Tuxedo and begin preparations. That way, we won't be bothered by all the hubbub!"

By *hubbub*, Penelope meant to imply the columnists who so exhaustively documented any wedding of remote social importance. Her parents were sensitive to how things were done, of course, and they could be persuaded to do anything that might avoid ridicule and social censure. But the hubbub Penelope was in fact thinking of was the kind caused by the Holland sisters. Once she got herself and her fiancé out of the city, then she would be able to sleep a little better. She would be that much closer to what was rightfully hers being hers—according to society and the public and, soon enough, God, too.

Dear Diana,

I once gave you a piece of jewelry

inscribed For My True Bride, and

I feel the same now as then, if not

more so. I know it must be difficult

for you to believe, but what I am

about to do is loathsome to me.

Trust me when I tell you she left

me with no other options . . .

ENRY DID NOT LOOK TO SEE THE CITY GO BY, and when the Schoonmakers' private railway car did emerge in the suburbs, he found little of interest in the rivers and icy landscapes that passed. He was not leaving willingly. He was leaving mechanically, which was the way he did everything these days. He had dressed by rote, in high white collar and black jacket, and he had combed and slicked his hair in the same habitual manner. This was the same manner he had used in writing notes to his friends, asking them to be his groomsmen, and to his usual salesman at Tiffany, who had arranged for the rings. The refrain in his mind was a kind of habit too. He told himself over and over that he was doing the good and heroic thing and that his actions would save Diana from certain ruin.

Now, as the train drew him closer to Tuxedo and a fate he found miserable while not yet being able to imagine, he tried to compose a letter that might explain what he had done. Diana must have heard by now. They would all be talking, and her mother would no doubt weigh against her daughter's former fiancé for getting engaged again so quickly, without any knowledge of how painful and humiliating the news would be to her other child. He couldn't stand the idea of Diana hearing from someone else. He would have liked to have held her and shown that it was all for her protection, but he doubted she would want that anymore. He'd never done anything heroic before, and he was unpleasantly surprised by how lousy it felt.

He'd written the letter a hundred ways in his head. He had explained that marrying Penelope was the only solution and the easiest one, that it would give Diana a second chance that circumstances made impossible for him. In one moment, he resolved to tell her that they would always be lovers, and in another that he would leave her alone so that she could have other, grander loves. He drew himself as a valiant savior and Penelope as girl made of pure evil, but he had ceased believing any of those things. There was no way to make sense with words of what had happened.

His bride-to-be was coming for him down the aisle of the train, resting her hands on the velvet seats to steady herself, but beaming with such confidence that she hardly seemed to need to lean on anything. She had been on the other end of the private car with the little girls who were going to distribute rose petals at the beginning of the ceremony, showing off her new diamond to them. She was wearing a white cashmere coat with a high collar, and her lips were painted the red of pomegranate seeds. Henry watched her coming toward him and crumpled the letter he had been writing to the girl he'd called his true bride. There was nothing more to say.

Forty Four

Police precincts all over the city have reported anonymous tips from people who claim to have seen Elizabeth Holland in all sorts of places: a Ludlow Street butcher's, on the Brooklyn Bridge, driving a hansom across the park in jodhpurs and top hat. This sheds even more doubt on the ludicrous rumors that she is still living.

——FROM THE FIRST PAGE OF THE *NEW YORK IMPERIAL*, SUNDAY, DECEMBER 31, 1899

*A*T GRAND CENTRAL THERE WAS AN AIR OF motion and confusion, and everywhere were men and women in their heavy winter clothes laden down with the impedimenta of travel. The waiting room of the station, with its rows of long, polished benches, were thronged and the sounds of delay announcements and cries for lost family members filled Will's and Elizabeth's ears. It was not, in fact, a slow day for travel, as Snowden had insisted it would be: Men who worked in the city were hurrying home to their families, and those who had come on benders and run out of money before the great New Year were heading away in shame. Meanwhile, revelers from the outlying boroughs were flooding the city. Good-byes had taken longer than they should have, and now they had to hurry. They had been warned by Mrs. Holland to be discreet, to do nothing that might call attention to them, but Will and Elizabeth Keller now found that in the rush of arrivals and departures they were all smiles and could not help grasping each other's hands.

It was almost a new year, and everything was in front of

them. They were going off to make their way, and this time with the assurance that everything was all right at home and with the blessing of the bride's relations. She was a bride, Elizabeth thought as Will's large hand gripped her small one, pulling her through the crowd toward the train shed with its arched ceiling of glass and iron. He looked back at her and smiled—for no particular reason, she supposed, or maybe because of everything—and she couldn't help but laugh. She tossed back her head with the laugh, and the hood of her cloak fell down. She reached up and touched her head, because she had placed her hat in its traveling case and her hair was only covered by a small amount of ornamental lace. She let go of Will's hand and stopped, so that she might put her hood back in order. That was when she heard her name—her old name, the way it used to be said—and turned.

"Miss Holland, Miss Holland!"

She looked, her face still smiling, her heart full of elation. Then she remembered that she was not supposed to be seen. The crowd was parting and there were several blue uniforms stepping toward her. She felt Will's hands on her from behind, one on her ribs and the other on her shoulder. She could smell his clean skin, with its faint whiff of Pear's soap, as his cheek touched hers.

"Run," he whispered. "You've got to run. Just run for the train. I'll be right behind you."

It was then that she realized that she should be afraid. Right afterward she was. She could feel the fear, cold in her throat and all down her spine. Then she turned again for the platform where the crowd was still thick, and she ran into it. There were bodies all around her, but she pushed through. Her feet and her panic carried her forward until she heard shouting, growing louder and fiercer with each word.

"Halt!" she heard.

"Stop!"

"Don't move!"

She kept running until she heard the shots. They were so loud that for a minute she thought they must have happened in her ears. They were horrible and repetitious and they lasted far too long. When they were over, she could barely breathe. Everyone around her had frozen. She turned again, slowly this time, and began to move back down the platform, where there was now shrieking. She was indifferent to her backward fallen hood, and she could not have gotten her hand off her open mouth for anything in the world.

She was moving faster now toward the place where she had last touched Will. It was with a wretched apprehension that she came on him again. He was on the ground now, and his shirt was all torn apart. Everywhere there was his gleaming, gushing blood. The blue uniforms were still there, this time behind a wall of raised guns. She could already smell the blood, even before she fell down next to him. Even before she began to choke on the odor and on her own tears.

"Will," she gasped.

His eyes had been closed, and then they opened, and she saw that they were pale blue and filled with fear. They searched for her and then he grabbed at her hand. She knew that he saw her, and she could see that the fear had gone out of his eyes.

"I love you," he said.

"I love you," she answered.

"I love you," he repeated with the same pained steadiness.

There was nothing for her to do but repeat it. "I love you," she repeated over and again. She would never know how many times she said it. There must have been only a few seconds she was by his side, though she would never be sure. She was so full of disbelief that they seemed impossible moments out of time. She remembered seeing his eyelids fall closed again, and that was when she felt hands on her. Her dress was all soaked in blood, and she felt too weak to say anything more. She was being carried away, by those rough male hands, through the crowd. She heard her name—the way it used to be—repeated over and over again by the massed people around her.

They were asking her if she was all right. They wanted to know what had been done to her. But her vision had started to fail, and she felt limp all over, and then everything went black.

Forty

Five

THE WILLIAM S. SCHOONMAKERS

REQUEST THE PLEASURE OF YOUR COMPANY

AT A VERY SPECIAL OCCASION

TUXEDO PARK

DECEMBER 31, 1899

SIX O'CLOCK IN THE EVENING

B Y SUNDAY PENELOPE'S BODY WAS SO RIGID WITH expectation that she could hardly smile. There had been so much preparation, and she hadn't slept more than an hour the night before. The dressmaker from New York was still adjusting the dress that morning—her mother's dress was now embellished with new pearls and old lace as it hadn't been before, and of course it fit better in the torso and trained more at the back. The bridesmaids' dresses were the ones from Isabelle's wedding, also hastily redone. It was a shame that she couldn't have a new design from Paris made especially for her to emphasize her finest features, and that the whole wedding party wasn't in the latest and best. But none of that mattered now. The wedding guests were assembled, and the tables were set, and the Hollands had most definitely not been invited for the greatest wedding of the year. "The last great wedding of the 1800s," to borrow a phrase that Buck had repeated to several newspaper reporters. In the New Year, Penelope thought with a flutter of her jet-black lashes, she would be Mrs. Schoonmaker, and Diana could call on her all she wanted.

Now she could feel the moment—right there, in front of her, down a straight and petal-strewn path—when it would all be done. The menu had been settled and the decorations done according to Buck's ruthless specifications. The invitations, which had gone out the twenty-eighth by special delivery promising a top-secret wedding of the best people, had proved a powerful lure to New York society. It had been a dull week, because of the holiday, and they were all just sitting around until the New Year passed so that they could travel to more exotic ports in Italy and Egypt. But this was an unanticipated thrill. Today they had traveled to one of their hideaway haunts to witness the union of two of their proudest names, and tomorrow they would be beset by all the uninvited for anecdotes of the Schoonmaker-Hayes nuptials.

The unlucky were at parties in Lakewood and Westchester, planning to celebrate the New Year as best they could and hoping for telegrams filling in what they had missed. The lucky invitees were out there in their rows, waiting. Penelope's face was done and her waist corseted and her legs hidden by tiers of ivory chiffon. Lace erupted from the V-neck of the dress, and her arms were decorated in tiers of lace bells. There were flowers on her wrists and in her dark hair, and pinned to her white bonnet were yards and yards of Valenciennes lace. Already the music was beginning. She looked at her bridesmaids—cousins of hers and Henry's, quickly assembled, as well as poor Prudie, looking quite uncomfortable in a pastel shade, and, as promised, Carolina Broad wearing a very proud expression indeed, and seeming somehow richer—but still could not bring herself to smile. When it was all over, then she would smile.

Buck was there in a dark suit, looking a little sleep deprived and moving, despite his girth, with characteristic grace. He had lined the girls up and was waiting to give them the cue to leave the ladies' dressing room and walk down the aisle. They were all—all but Prudie—giddy that they had been chosen and nervously anticipating their chance to go. Penelope didn't want to meet any of their eyes. She was just waiting for the moment when that last pale blue train had disappeared out of the door and it was her turn. Finally the eighth and last went and she was able to take a breath. She turned to Buck and paused as he checked her face to make sure it was perfect. He brought her veil down and fussed with it for a moment. Then the muscles of his face relaxed into a smile for the first time all day.

"They will stop calling brides beautiful after today—you have simply set the standard too high," he said.

Then she smiled too, a broad, triumphant smile that she knew she would somehow have to do away with before she walked down the aisle. She had not yet succeeded when she heard the first notes of the music that always introduced the bride. Buck told her to go, and she did.

All of the faces in the room turned to her. Penelope could see them through the scrim of lace, their mouths forming wide, appreciative circles, their hands clasped to their breasts. She had no idea whether she was walking slow or fast. She could scarcely hear the music. The distance to the altar was impossible, and yet she knew she would be there very soon. Henry was still and miserable looking in his shiny black tails, but he would see the genius of all her planning soon enough. He would remember how perfectly suited they were to each other, and see that Diana Holland had been nothing more than a passing distraction. When she reached the altar, she noticed that a few faces had turned away from her. Inexplicably, they were looking back in the direction from which she had come.

By the time the reverend began the ceremony there were murmurs across the ballroom of Tuxedo. She noticed that Henry's face turned several times to the place at the back of the room from which all the low voices were emanating. That was when Penelope reached for Henry's hands. The reverend hadn't arrived at that part yet, but it showed her impatience, and he responded by speeding up the service. Penelope's heartbeat was so wild in her chest that she scarcely noticed how unresponsive—how cautious—Henry's palms were.

Penelope had never paid much heed to premonitions, but she knew in a cold, settled way that what the assembled guests were talking about was Elizabeth Holland. She was back, and they were all wondering if Penelope wouldn't want to know before she promised to have and to hold her friend's former fiancé forever more. Penelope stiffened and waited for the rings to be exchanged. In her mind she dared all the busybodies in the audience to interrupt her wedding. They were cowards who lived by a code, as she knew well enough. Penelope bargained that if she stood still and left the rumblings unacknowledged, then the crowd would feel they had to as well.

As soon as she felt the precious metal slip over her left ring finger, she said, "I do," and then, without waiting for Henry to respond, she pulled back her veil and stepped toward him. He had said, "I do," she was pretty sure, although it hardly mattered. Nobody ever remembered the details of weddings, and anyway what was important was that she had moved in toward him and put her mouth to his. The touch of his lips was as light and unresponsive as his palms, and still it made her heart swoon a little to think that she was kissing Henry, and that Henry was her husband.

Then they both turned back to that room, done up in sprays of white flowers and pearl-colored bows. There was a long, awkward pause. Penelope saw her mother's social secretary standing nervously at the back of the room, her hands clutched together. The diamonds in the crowd twinkled and eyes blinked. Then she saw Buck step in front of the social secretary, as though to blot her out of everybody's mind. He began to clap.

Then all the faces of the crowd turned, slowly at first and then faster, toward the bride and groom. Some of them began to clap and some of them began to stand. It took only a few moments for conformity to sweep the assembled, and then they were all clapping. It was as though all the best people in New York had momentarily forgotten and had now been reminded that this was a beautiful and touching event. Tears followed for some of the older matrons. She had their attention and knew that right then she was the star of their stage.

The world was steady again, and she dared to take deep breaths. Everyone was clapping and saying how beautiful they were and what a perfect couple and how it just showed you that true love did exist. Her eyes had grown moist, and she looked out at all the guests, who were standing, and she felt full of gratitude that they had all been witnesses to her triumph.

Elizabeth Adora Holland has been discovered alive. It seems that she was kidnapped by a former coachman of the socialite's family. The young man evidently became obsessed with her when he worked for the Hollands and was planning on taking her to California with him. She had not, as was previously feared, been sold into white slavery. The young man was killed when he tried to abscond with the lady in what became a violent scene in the Grand Central Station. Miss Elizabeth Holland was returned to her family and was still in too great a shock to be interviewed today.

——FROM A SPECIAL EVENING EDITION OF THE *NEW YORK IMPERIAL*, SUNDAY, DECEMBER 31, 1899

*I*T WAS WELL PAST MIDNIGHT—THE NEW YEAR HAD come, and in the Hollands' home the wailing had stopped. The women sat at the great worn, wooden table in the kitchen, and all around them was a devastating silence. The kitchen was not a room any of them had ever spent much time in, but it seemed the most secretive place they could go. It was where they were least likely to be found. That night was the first time Diana had seen her mother prepare broth, which she did assuredly, before placing it in front of her elder daughter. She had insisted at several points throughout the night that Elizabeth drink it, and Elizabeth had a few times brought the bowl to her lips. But she did not give the appearance of drinking any, and the level of liquid in her bowl never went down. Diana watched her sister, who was slumped against the table. She had wept so hard it seemed impossible that she had not wrung out everything inside her.

It had been too much for Edith to take, and she had gone to her room so that her nieces wouldn't see her cry anymore.

Diana herself felt empty. She could not imagine an end to the emptiness. It seemed to her as though everything that was good and true had been blasted out of the world. All those things had been crushed, destroyed, made to disappear.

"Elizabeth, you must eat. You must try to sleep," her mother said. Diana couldn't remember the last time anyone had spoken. It could have been hours, or it might have been seconds. The cacophony of chimes and noisemakers, of revelers in the street leaving Midnight Mass or the Hungarian Peasant Ball at Madison Square Garden, had died down in the meantime.

When the policemen had brought Elizabeth home, proud and triumphant of what they had done, Diana had taken her upstairs and washed her in the bathtub. Elizabeth couldn't then do anything for herself, and there was little she could do now. Her hair had dried, and even though she was wrapped in a blanket, she shivered. She took a long time in responding and when she did she managed only a flat "I can't."

"Elizabeth," her mother went on slowly, "you might not be able to now, but you must soon. Everyone knows that you have returned, and they won't understand that you loved Will. They can't know it."

Elizabeth's brown eyes moved very slowly to meet her mother's. She blinked and her dry lips dropped open but she didn't say anything. Diana wished that she could make her mother stop talking. She knew, even now, that Mrs. Holland was incapable of not considering her social position.

"They think you were kidnapped, Elizabeth. That's what they'll believe, and we can't contradict them. This family has suffered, my dear. We have suffered too much. We will lose everything if they know what Will was to you . . . what you were to him. What you did. Do you understand me?"

Elizabeth looked blankly at her mother. Her eyes moved, slowly, until they met Diana's. The sisters stared at each other for a few moments, and Diana set her lips together at the thought of their mother's cold practicality. The younger girl's brows moved toward each other and she shook her head just slightly to let Elizabeth know how she felt about all that. "She understands," Diana said finally, speaking for the sister she knew could not speak for herself.

"Good. I don't want it to be this way, my dearest, but that is how it is." Mrs. Holland put her small, lined hands on the table and pushed herself upward. "We will shelter you for a while, but soon enough you will have to see people. You will have to seem happy that you are home. It is a lucky thing we are a polite society—no one will ask you what you have endured. But you must not give them reason to wonder."

Diana watched her sister, whose hair was undone and who seemed dead to every comment. How little everything that had ever happened to them mattered now, Diana thought.

Their mother smoothed her black dress with her hands and sighed.

"I will not force you to marry again, my dear Elizabeth," she went on. "In any event, Henry Schoonmaker is by this time already wed to your friend Penelope Hayes. It happened very quickly and quietly this same evening. What a strange, strange day it has been."

Diana heard the news of Henry's wedding with something like neutrality. Of course in a world of arbitrary and horrific murder Henry would choose a girl like Penelope. It would have shocked her beyond breath if someone had told her he was not now to marry Penelope, and it seemed almost a blessing that it should be over so quickly. She flinched, even so, and only hoped that Elizabeth hadn't noticed. She had enough worries already without thinking of Diana's heartbreak.

"I must sleep," their mother concluded suddenly. She pulled back her skirt and walked toward the door without meeting their eyes. "See your sister doesn't stare at the wall all night, Diana—you must get her into bed somehow," she added as she passed through the door.

They listened to the creak of the stairs above them as their mother retreated to her own room. Diana closed her eyes and exhaled. She was exhausted, but among the many things she could no longer imagine was sleep. She guessed Elizabeth couldn't, either. When she opened her eyes, she saw that her sister was looking right at her, and there was something new in her expression. Diana blinked and then, when she saw that the new intensity had not faded, she went to Elizabeth and sank down on the rough wood planks beside her and leaned against her lap. She threw her arms up around her sister's waist.

Elizabeth's face, which had still been touched by the sun when she arrived in New York, had now gone entirely white. She was so lacking in strength that it seemed a moderate gust could have blown her away. There was nothing to say, Diana knew, but she felt that if she clung to her, then that human warmth might bring her a kind of comfort. She closed her eyes and tightened her embrace.

They sat like that for a while, and then Elizabeth said, "Did you really love Henry?"

Diana was so surprised to hear her sister speak a full sentence that she did not at first realize what was being asked.

"Did you love him the way I loved Will?" she asked.

The younger Holland sister would not have guessed that these questions, at the slightest examination, made her heart flutter and yearn, or that the idea of Henry, once it was in her thoughts, made her not angry or despondent but instead full of an undeniable desire. This longing was the first emotion she had been able to feel since she had heard about the awful thing that had happened to Will. She knew if she could satisfy that feeling in any way, no matter what it did to her dignity, she would.

Diana closed her eyes and nodded, trying to keep from crying again. "Yes," she said at last.

Elizabeth brought her hand to Diana's hair and smoothed it with a slow steadiness. The younger girl had never felt so akin to her sister in all her life.

"Then we're going to get him back for you," Elizabeth whispered as she bent to fully return her younger sister's embrace.

Outside, the world was quiet and dark. There was a new snow on the ground, but everyone in Gramercy, and up Fifth Avenue, and downtown, where leisure and comfort were not such givens, was inside by now. The New Year had come, but nothing in it seemed even remotely real.

Acknowledgments

This book and I are lucky to have not one but two editors: Thank you to the gracious and brilliant Sara Shandler and the witty and lovely Farrin Jacobs, who both worked tirelessly to make the Luxe books bigger, better, and more logical. Thank you Josh Bank and Les Morgenstein, they of the magical powers. Thank you to Allison Heiny, Cristina Gilbert, Melissa Dittmar, Kristin Marang, and Jackie Greenberg for calling so much attention to this series. Thank you Andrea C. Uva, Alison Donalty, Barb Fitzsimmons, and Ray Shappell for bringing the pretty. I am also indebted to Nora Pelizzari and Lanie Davis, as well as everybody else at Alloy, and to Elise Howard, Susan Katz, Kate Jackson, and all the other wonderful people at HarperCollins. Thank you to the New-York Historical Society and all the fantastic librarians there. And thank you Ben Turner.

TURN THE PAGE FOR A PEEK AT

THE NEXT EXCITING BOOK
IN THE *Luxe* SERIES.

MR. LELAND BOUCHARD

REQUESTS THE PLEASURE OF YOUR COMPANY

AT A BALL TO BE GIVEN IN HONOR OF

THE MEMBERS OF

THE NEW YORK AUTOMOBILIST CLUB

ON THURSDAY EVENING

FEBRUARY 8, 1900, AT NINE O'CLOCK

18 EAST 63RD STREET

MRS. HENRY SCHOONMAKER, NÉE PENELOPE Hayes, had come far in her eighteen years. As she swept past Leland Bouchard's vestibule, where a gleaming black motorcar was displayed, she couldn't help but muse how she, like the horseless carriage, was a waxy emblem of the future. Ever since she was a little girl she had told herself that she wouldn't meet the other side of twenty without a deeply gaudy wedding band on her finger, and here she had beat her own goal by two years and in the process joined one of New York's most well-regarded families. There were those who still remembered how her maiden name had been hastily salvaged from the odious surname Hazmat several decades ago, but neither appeared on her card these days. Now, moving up the glistening curve of marble stairs toward the sound of a party already in full swing, she could not help but anticipate the joy of entering a room on the arm of her very handsome husband.

It was one of the great pleasures of her life, for Henry was tall and lean and possessed of a chieftain's cheekbones and a rakish

mien that made all eyes turn to him. As a debutante, Penelope had grown accustomed to being looked at, but the envious intensity of the stares she encountered upon entering the second-floor music room, which was full of old money and good connections on that Thursday evening, was superior even to what she was used to. She wore a haughty smile, her plush lips twisted up to the right no more than was necessary, and a dress of cardinal-colored silk that a thousand elegant darts brought in close to her lean frame. Her dark hair was collected in an elaborate bun, and a line of short bangs divided her high, proud forehead.

Penelope cast an appraising gaze at the paneled murals, done by one of the leading talents of Europe, and the polished mantel that had been transported in pieces from Florence. She knew this and much more about Leland Bouchard's home because she wanted Henry to build a town house for them and had collected newspaper clippings on this one and others like it. He had not yet given her any indication that he would do so, but, like everything Penelope wanted, it was only a matter of time and perhaps a little of her own rough brand of persuasion before it was hers.

Above the gentle din of decorous voices and clinking glasses, Penelope heard her name being pronounced with all its most recent and glorious trappings. "Mrs. Henry Schoonmaker!" went the beautiful sound, and Penelope turned. As she did, the fishtail of her skirt swept across the Versailles parquet. She immediately noted the approach of Adelaide Wetmore, who wore a dress of pewter faille. Her eyes were moist with self-regard, for her engagement to Reginald Newbold had only just been announced, and she was looking pleasantly weak with all the congratulations. She might have been pretty, Penelope reflected charitably, if not for her disproportionate mouth, and the way it garishly showcased her broad teeth.

"Why, Adelaide." Penelope extended her gloved hand so that the diamond bracelet she wore fell down her wrist and caught the light. "Congratulations."

"Thank you," the other girl gushed. She took Penelope's hand and made a dipping motion, almost as though she were going to curtsy. "We were all so inspired by your wedding," she added with painful sycophancy. "What a celebration of love it was."

Penelope communicated her gratitude with a few bats of her black eyelashes, and deduced from the way Adelaide was looking at the couple whose love she claimed to be inspired by that Henry's gaze had wandered, and that he was exerting exactly no energy in trying to seem interested in the matrimonial doings of their peers. Penelope smiled her goodbye, and then she and her husband—who she was now realizing smelled of musk but even more strongly of cognac—pushed farther into the room. That was when Henry stumbled almost imperceptibly, catching himself on her arm, and Penelope felt her self-assurance flag a little over the sudden fear that some-

one might notice Henry's drunkenness and begin to draw their own conclusions.

As she moved through the crowd, under the high polish of the vaulted ceiling, she tried to secure her grip on Henry. It wasn't easy—but then, of course, it never had been. She gave knowing little nods of her head in the direction of some of the younger Mrs. Vanderbilts, assembled near the vast central palm in the middle of the room, and didn't dare look in the direction of the man she was almost forcibly pulling along with her. She had believed him to be hers, time and again, but still she could not stay the feeling that he might at any moment slip through her fingers.

It had begun between them the previous summer, when her best friend, Elizabeth Holland, had been abroad, and she and Henry had started meeting amorously in the shadowy corners of their family homes. But then Elizabeth had returned in the fall and, with precious little reason, become Henry's fiancée. Of course, that had been according to the wishes of their parents, and Penelope had rescued both of them from an unhappy marriage by helping Elizabeth fake her death. As she felt Henry list just slightly, she considered how poorly her efforts had been repaid, for not long after Elizabeth's "death," Henry had taken up with her little sister, Diana. That turn of events had not been entirely bad, since the fact of the younger Holland's whoring about was the piece of information that Penelope had used to persuade Henry to marry her. All she had ever wanted was to be Mrs. Schoonmaker, and none of them wanted a messy scene.

Penelope possessed the mettle of a society lady ten years older, and there was forcefulness evident in her smallest movements. But even as Mrs. Schoonmaker, Penelope was unpleasantly surprised to discover that her ability to control Mr. Schoonmaker fell somewhat short. They glided amongst the guests, and when a waiter appeared carrying champagne flutes it was all she could do to keep Henry from lunging for one.

"Don't you feel drunk enough already?" she admonished. Her smile never wavered, and she brought her upper lip back just enough to reveal the perfect whiteness of her teeth.

"I've had a lot," he replied slowly, without particular venom, although the drink might possibly have been impairing his inflection. "But not enough to make me want to spend the evening with you, my dear."

Penelope briefly shut the lids of her large eyes and stifled any feelings his comment might have aroused. Then she batted her mascara-darkened lashes and let her lake blue irises roll right and left. No one had heard, she determined with a small release of her shoulders, except perhaps the waiter, who wouldn't have dreamed of looking her in the eye. When she spoke again, it was with effortless ease and a glass of champagne in her hand:

"When you put it that way, I suppose I should have one too."

Thus fortified, the most envied couple in top-drawer Manhattan moved onward through the throng. The members of the Automobilist Club were making grand pronouncements about upcoming races, and the ladies who wanted to be near them were smiling patient smiles and assuming the poses of eager listeners.

"Ah, the Schoonmakers!"

Penelope twisted the length of her white neck so that the full blaze of her smile could be fully appreciated by her host. "Mr. Bouchard," she purred, as he bent his long torso and placed his lips on her gray, full-length glove. The warmth in her voice was studied and convincing; it was a tone she reserved for men like Leland, who was heir to the Bouchard banking fortune and besides that universally liked. He was that rare high-born New Yorker who somehow or other had managed to make more friends than enemies, and was a particular friend of her brother, Grayson. As younger men they had lived in adjoining rooms at St. Paul's. Penelope, ever watchful, noted Grayson's presence by the window, where he was ensconced in conversation with her mother-in-law, the senior Mrs. Schoonmaker, whose dress of opalescent chiffon tiers did little to detract attention from her.

"I hope you're both enjoying yourself," Leland went on earnestly as he clasped Henry's hand. His light blue eyes were open wide beneath his broad forehead, as though their enjoyment really was a crucial issue for him, and for all Penelope knew, it was. "Did you see the motorcar downstairs?"

"Could not have mishedut," Henry answered enthusiastically, slurring the last two words.

Penelope elbowed him while maintaining her steady, bright gaze. "Such a beautiful object, Leland."

"Thank you." Leland's eyes drifted and his chest rose, and for a moment he was someplace else. "Speaking of beauties," he went on, his attention returning to Penelope, and this time with an added touch of sympathy, "how is your dear friend Elizabeth? It was terrible what happened, and not seeing her out has made us all worry."

Until that moment Penelope had maintained a strong, smiling posture, and had stayed uncowed by Henry's misbehavior or any askance glances from whichever young ladies in the room flattered themselves by imagining that they were the rival of the former Miss Hayes. But now her mouth constricted and she heard herself swallow hard. Leland went on looking at her with that same concerned expression. Henry's weight on her arm bobbed a moment and then grew heavier. She only hoped that her face did not betray the insecurity this inquiry brought on, for of course Elizabeth was her dear friend by reputation only. Penelope had barely seen her since her unexpected return from what was supposed to have been a long exile in a western state—for truly, what was there to say?

"She is very well." Penelope began to regain her composure, and even as she spoke reminded herself that she really would have to make a show of seeing Elizabeth, one that the papers took note of, and soon. "But it is still early for her to be going out. After her trauma. You understand, of course."

"Of course." Leland bowed his head, appearing almost embarrassed for having asked after a girl who had gone unaccounted for for over two months, and who might indeed have suffered any number of grave injustices. But before he could further anyone's discomfort, he succumbed to the calls of his fellow driving enthusiasts, and excused himself. "Please do enjoy," he said as he slipped into the crowd.

Penelope did not look after her host as he left. She stared straight ahead and reminded herself what a lucky thing it was that he was not a gossip and that he wouldn't be searching for signs that Mrs. Henry Schoonmaker's marriage or friendships were not what they seemed. For a moment she reflected on how to avoid such a mistake again, and then she turned toward Henry.

His dark eyes were focused in the direction of the huge windows and the night scene they held, and they looked less glassy than before. There was something almost like clarity in his face when he turned toward his wife, and when he spoke, it was deliberately.

"Promise me," he said, meeting her gaze, "that if someone brings up the Hollands again you'll take me home."

READ ON FOR AN EXCERPT FROM
ANNA GODBERSEN'S

BEFORE AND AFTER

By morning the city had fallen. We had not seen the sky in a long time; even the sky was made of fire. The State Street Bridge was impassable, they said. The Rush Street Bridge, too. The streets were littered with objects that had once seemed valuable enough to carry, but now lay abandoned. The explosions did not frighten us anymore, for they came too frequently—sounds rang out, like a battle being waged one block over, every time a building went down.

Some would never recover, while for others it was the beginning of everything. For the ruined and reborn alike, there was simply *before* and *after*. And the moment that divided these two eras—the moment that old barn turned to tinder—would become a source of wild speculation and grand mythology.

Despite all the talk, it had been just us three when the fire started, and we would remain, forever, the only ones who knew what really happened.

BEFORE

ONE

The pleasure of your company
is kindly requested
for a small luncheon to inaugurate the celebration
of the Carter-Tree wedding
at the Carter residence
Wednesday, October 4, 1871
Noon

The room was full of her name.

In the two years that Emmeline Carter had lived with her father in the limestone mansion on Dearborn, north of the river, the big front parlor had never been as full as this—full of people, and full of iced delicacies, and full of servants lifting golden trays laden with champagne flutes above the heads of the guests. Full of ruffled skirts cascading over extravagant bustles, full of the confident talk of men in tail-coats custom-cut just for them. But mostly it was full of the name *Emmeline*, whispered with envy and approval from every corner, so that the edges of her ears went pink and her eyes became bright. Her step was light and her laugh was easy and her dress, of blush crepe de chine, floated around her slender limbs like a summer cloud. She did not think she had ever been so happy. By week's end she would have everything she ever wanted.

"Miss Carter, my dear, come along," said Mrs. Garrison, whose name at birth had been Ada Arles Tree.

Emmeline, never overfond of being told what to do, chafed at this command. But come Sunday she would be calling Ada "sister," and now did not seem an advantageous time to contradict her wishes. So Emmeline banished her pout, clasped the hand of young Mrs. Palmer—to whom she had just been introduced—bowed her head, and made a low curtsy. "Thank you, truly, for coming to our little party," she said with a modest fluttering of eyelashes. "It is such a pleasure to meet you."

"No, no, contrary-wise, the pleasure is mine," said Mrs. Palmer, who was sitting on the divan with the silk sapphire upholstery. Although the piece was quite old—Father had recently become something of a collector—the wooden armrests were polished to a high shine. "I find you quite charming. Will you come for a tea at the house tomorrow?

I have a little afternoon every week, all the best girls. You must be one of us."

Although Emmeline wanted to clarify that by "house" Mrs. Palmer meant the massive hotel that bore her married name, she sensed that it would be gauche to do so. Rich people were always referring to mansions as cottages, to enormous carriages as buggies. And to be one of them, a girl had to adopt their funny way of talking.

As they continued through the throng, Ada clutched Emmeline by the elbow and said in a hushed, excited way, "I cannot tell you what a coveted invitation that is. She would never have you into her set if she weren't confident of your future success. *Nobody* is more discerning than Bertha."

Emmeline replied with a vague smile and a guileless tilt of the head, although she hardly needed any explication of Mrs. Palmer's importance. The name *Potter Palmer* was carved with gold leaf into the lintels of several big buildings in the shopping district—all the ladies knew him, because of his department store—and when he married Bertha Honoré a year ago it was all anyone had talked about. As a wedding present, he'd given her an actual *hotel*, the brand-new and very grand Palmer House, on State Street.

At this time last year, nobody had sent invitations to the Carters, a family of two who had installed themselves four seasons prior in the block-wide property between Huron and Superior, without having any social connection to the place. Emmeline had spent that fall greedy for every detail: of Bertha's trousseau; the names of those invited to her wedding, and what they ate; the pattern on the specially designed luggage for the round-the-world honeymoon via ocean liner. And she had vowed that by the time she was Bertha's age—twenty-one—she would have a wedding just as spectacular. But here she was, quite ahead of her goal—just eighteen and engaged to be married to Frederick Arles Tree, who was an even better groom than Potter Palmer: at twenty-four, he was two decades younger, and such a good dancer, and the son of a banker, besides. His uncle was a senator, and so might Freddy be one day.

Senator Frederick Tree, didn't that sound just perfect? She thought of him as Freddy, everybody did, although she would not say the nickname in his hearing. He preferred Frederick, and insisted on being called by his proper name.

Married! She could hardly believe it. He had only proposed three months prior; she knew the date exactly. It had been July third—moody weather, with big drops pelting the windowpanes—and he had come calling at the Carter residence, and said that he wanted to announce their engagement at the Ogdens' Independence Day picnic. The ring was a great cluster of diamonds that covered her finger from knuckle to joint, and she didn't hear half of what Freddy said, so distracted was she by its shimmery light.

She knew she'd never forget that day. It was the last she remembered rain.

A servant in burgundy livery—he must have been hired for the party, for Emmeline did not recognize him—passed then with a plate of strawberries, and Emmeline took one and put it in her mouth. "Who shall we introduce me to now?" she asked Ada, lifting an eyebrow in giddy anticipation. She had just met the most socially discerning woman in Chicago, and was aflutter wondering who would be next.

"Let us pause here a spell," Mrs. Garrison replied, drawing herself up and casting her keen gaze across the parlor. They had reached the doorway onto the foyer. The clatter and bustle of preparations for a lavish luncheon could be heard from the dining room on the foyer's far side.

Everything before her was new, except the objects that were expensively old. The herringbone floor gleamed, as did the gilt frames of the giant mirrors that hung on every wall. Emmeline caught herself in one of these, and admired the narrow waist and drooping sleeves of her gown, her full pink lips and sloe-eyed glance. Her brass-colored hair was parted at the middle and plaited at the crown, and it curled in little wisps along her forehead. Guests were still arriving, coming up the wide stone steps from the vast front lawn, and she felt annoyed with Ada, who could be so old and meddling and married sometimes. Emmeline had practiced

7

for several solitary years to be the center of attention, and now that she had arrived there, she was impatient to meet absolutely everybody.

"Goodness, what a showing." Emmeline overheard one of the new arrivals saying from just outside the parlor. "The whole world is here."

"How the curious do flock to the scene of the crime," replied another in an arid tone.

"My darling Miss Russell, don't be bitter," admonished the first speaker. "In time, it will ruin your face. Look around you. What a fabulous to-do!" She stepped into the doorway, revealing herself as a petite woman clothed in widow's black. "Mark my words, these nuptials will be the most talked about event in Chicago this year."

Ada leaned in toward Emmeline and whispered, "Mrs. Fletcher Fleming," in quiet reverence. "The most admired beauty of her day," she went on in a murmur. "In the drawing rooms of this city, her word is absolute."

Emmeline turned with naked curiosity to see the second speaker, who passed through the open pocket doors to join her interlocutor upon a sweep of vermillion skirt. She did not need to be told her name: it was Cora Russell, who had been escorted by Freddy at her coming out four years before, and who gossips said had waited too long for his proposal. In the spring, she had absented herself on a trip to

Paris in order that his heart grow fonder, which was when it found Emmeline instead.

"I don't care what you say," Cora said as she took Mrs. Fleming's arm. "What's all the fuss about? She's new, that's all. Freddy is always distracted by anything new."

"Pay no heed to that," Ada whispered as the two women were absorbed into the crowd. "She is jealous, of course."

But Emmeline was untroubled by Cora's words. They meant that she, Emmeline Carter, who two years ago had been a nameless nobody, was worth envying. There were so many eyes in that room, and they all seemed to search for her. The girls who had known Freddy since childhood and the men who frequented his club and the long-married women who entertained themselves by speculatively matchmaking the younger generation. On the far side of the room was Father, in a jacket of charcoal velvet, glancing at her now and then as though looking at his most prized possession. In another doorway Fiona hovered in her plain black pinafore, watchful to see if she were needed, her eyes shiny with excitement to match Emmeline's own. But mostly there was Freddy, in a cutaway jacket of dashing blue, his tall, lean body forging a path through the crowd as he strode in her direction.

Although Freddy had not called for the room's attention, he had it, just by walking. He was six feet tall and his blond hair grew long—he had to tuck it behind his ears to keep it away from his sable brown eyes. *Frederick*, she reminded herself, but that sounded so angular and self-serious, and Freddy wasn't like that at all. Freddy was wonderful. Whenever he came to see her he brought a dozen roses and afterward he'd take her out for rides in his fast little horse trap. People on the street stared, remarking, "There goes a handsome couple," for Freddy always dressed with care. He had his clothes made for him in Europe, a place they would go together, he said, once they were married.

Everybody turned toward him, ceasing their previous conversations. Upon reaching Emmeline's side he took her hand. As she gazed up at him, he put his free hand inside his jacket's lapel, and removed a leather-bound case—his every action smooth, as though for him the world contained no mysteries, and nothing he could not possess. With a flick of his thumb, the case popped open. Inside, resting on silk, was a golden diadem with a little ruby-dotted peak. Emmeline's feet suddenly seemed very far away; the jeweled crown was the stuff of little girls' dreams, almost too grand to believe. In the next moment, Freddy had placed it on her head.

"It belonged to my late grandmother," he said, adding, in an impressive tone: "to Genevieve Gage Arles."

The elegant guests were regarding her wide-eyed, as they had all afternoon, although perhaps more reverently. They very nearly gaped, as at a princess at her coronation.

She beamed at her fiancé, unable to disguise her sense of triumph.

"Oh, Freddy, thank you." She gasped. "It's perfect!"

He was staring down at her with a look she'd never seen before. His lips parted and his eyebrows went together, as though on the verge of a very serious thought. A fear arose, that he was angry at her for saying his nickname out loud. Then she saw it wasn't that at all. He wanted to kiss her; he actually might! He had never kissed her before—only on the hand and cheek, and that when no one was watching—although she had on occasion sensed that he wanted something more. But she had been careful, and always modestly demurred, the better to hold his interest, which had been Father's advice. *The trick is to have them always coming to you*, Father said.

Only once in her life had she been kissed for real.

For a moment, the memory of that kiss was more vivid than her surroundings, than any of the people watching her, more vivid than Freddy himself, and Emmeline was afraid that the girl she used to be was plain for all to see, and that they would know she was an impostor.

"A toast!" Emmeline heard her father's voice, booming from the far side of the room. "To the affianced couple, and the merging of our families."

Freddy was smiling like nothing had happened, and he took her hand chastely in his. A fleet of liveried servants appeared with fresh glasses and bottles of champagne. Emmeline was given a glass, and she tried to smile. From every corner people were shouting.

"To Frederick and Emmeline!"

"To happiness!"

"To love!"

Emmeline knew she ought to be joyful. But she could not shake a sudden feeling that something, somehow, was all wrong. She was surrounded by so many bodies, and the room was warm with their breath. The air was stale and heated by the sun on the big windows. Her skin prickled. She raised her glass, not quite to her lips, and tipped it.

"Oh!" she exclaimed, as though surprised. The champagne was cool down the front of her dress.

Freddy glanced at her, sidelong. "Are you all right?"

"A little overwhelmed, perhaps. How clumsy of me. Allow me just a few minutes to clean up."

A stark quiet came over the parlor as she hurried toward the doorway. Just as she reached it, she heard Cora Russell say, "Of course one *can* take the pigs off the farm. That is how ham is made."

There were many reasons that Emmeline was glad to have reached the door, the most pressing of which being that only a few people were positioned to see how Cora's comment inflamed her cheeks. But she did not yet regret spilling champagne on herself, did not regret making a scene. All she wanted was to be alone with Fiona, and to discuss the precise wording of the message that Fiona must deliver. The memory of that kiss had opened a window onto her previous life, and she knew that, however perfectly she had conducted herself since meeting Freddy, she had left unfinished some business of her old self, with its old desires. But, with Fiona's help, she could seal all that up and bury it for good.

And then her true life would finally begin.

Anna Godbersen returns to tell the story of an epic love triangle—one that will literally set the city ablaze.

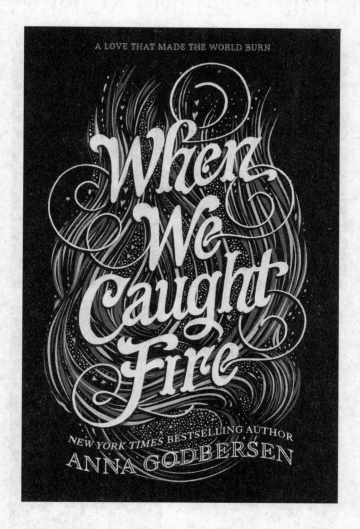

DON'T MISS A SINGLE PAGE OF THE DAZZLING ROMANCE!

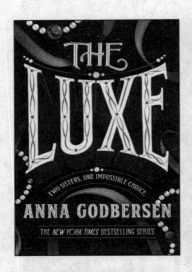

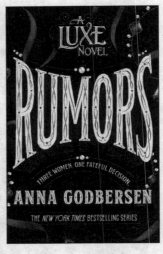

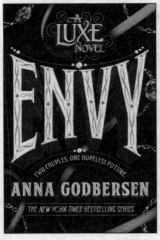

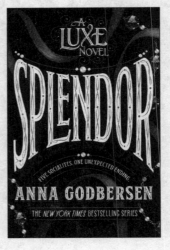